MAPLE NOTCH
BRIDES

MAPLE NOTCH BRIDES

THREE-IN-ONE COLLECTION

DARLENE FRANKLIN

BARBOUR
PUBLISHING

ISBN 978-1-61626-475-8

All scripture quotations are taken from the King James Version of the Bible.

This book is a work of fiction. Names, characters, places, and incidents are either products of the author's imagination or used fictitiously. Any similarity to actual people, organizations, and/or events is purely coincidental.

Cover design: Kirk DouPonce, DogEared Design

Published by Barbour Publishing, Inc., P.O. Box 719, Uhrichsville, Ohio 44683, www.barbourbooks.com

Our mission is to publish and distribute inspirational products offering exceptional value and biblical encouragement to the masses.

 Member of the
Evangelical Christian
Publishers Association

Printed in the United States of America.

Dear Readers,

Thank you for picking up *Maple Notch Brides*. It is my hope that these stories will give readers a taste of life in Vermont. When I thought about Vermont, it brought images of covered bridges to mind. In the first *Maple Notch Brides* story, the bridge has not yet been built, but an important tree that will be part of it is growing. The bridge is also an integral component of *Bridge to Love* and *Love's Raid*. I loved researching Vermont—it reminded me of my New England roots.

I hope that you can set aside the worries of life for a time and be entertained and inspired in your spiritual walk. I'd love to hear how my stories have touched your life or how I can pray for you. Please contact me through Barbour Publishing or at www.darlenefranklinwrites. blogspot.com

Blessings,
Darlene Franklin

THE PRODIGAL
PATRIOT

Dedication

To the granddaughters of my heart, Savannah and Shannon O'Hara.
You captured my heart the first time I met you;
I'm so glad God brought our lives together.

Chapter 1

Maple Notch, Vermont
May 1777

Today was a glorious day to be outside, Sally Reid decided as she went about her morning chores. Cool air flowed down from the mountains, scented with pine, the evergreen trees that gave the "Verts Monts," or the Green Mountains, their name. The sun overhead promised sunshine and warmth, and green shoots pushed up through the ground. She loved the rhythms of farm life, the cycles of sowing, growing, reaping, and resting. A song of praise burst from her lips.

"Good morning, Miss Reid! You sound cheerful this fine morning," a deep voice called out.

Sally stopped in mid-verse. Her singing called for no audience beyond the chickens who clucked along with her. Pa teased that she had the voice of a crow. Of all people, who should catch her in her morning serenade but Josiah Tuttle.

"Morning to you, Mr. Tuttle."

He smiled at her, the same grin that had infuriated her since childhood. It always put her in mind of the day he pulled the mobcap off her head after she'd had the measles. Clumps of her straight, oak-colored hair came off with the mobcap, and she had run home and refused to come out again. Remembering, she put a hand to the top of her head, making sure its covering was in place.

Josiah's hair was as black now as it had been then, the same red highlights created by the sun. But the years had transformed him from a skinny lad to a stalwart man, tall and well built. Not that she would ever make mention of the fact.

"Is Nathaniel about yet?" His voice had changed as well, into a marvelous baritone. He could sing far better than she could.

"I haven't seen him." Sally wondered if they required a chaperone for this conversation. Anyone could see them in the open dooryard. In fact, she saw a flicker in the opening in the cabin wall—probably her little sister, Nellie. Next thing Sally knew, Nellie would start announcing that Josiah was calling on her to everyone who stopped by.

The cabin door opened, and her brother Nathaniel came out. "Mornin', Josiah. Are you ready?"

Sally looked from one to the other. "What are the two of you planning?"

"Sorry I'm late." A younger version of Josiah ran into the clearing, his brother, Solomon. From a distance they looked much alike, both of a height, with dark hair and an easy gait. Up close, the resemblance was even more startling, the same high, broad foreheads and thin noses so like their father's.

"Where are all three of you going?" Solomon's arrival had piqued Sally's curiosity.

"Don't you remember what day it is?" Nathaniel seemed offended that she should ask.

"Of course I do. It's May 11."

"And two years ago today, Ethan Allen claimed Fort Ticonderoga 'in the name of the Great Jehovah and the Continental Congress.'"

"So you're off to celebrate the Revolution?" The word rolled off Sally's tongue. Her family supported independence—especially the Green Mountains' independence. With both New Hampshire and New York squabbling over who could lay claim to their land, Vermont had declared itself an independent country: the Republic of New Connecticut or the Republic of the Green Mountains. "Are you going off to win the war, then?" She doubted it. Pa would have alerted the family if the Green Mountain Boys were gathering.

"The war isn't a joke." Solomon used his most serious tone. He must have sensed her hesitation. Of the three young men, he took his responsibilities with the militia the most seriously. When Mr. Tuttle forbad his sons to take part in the glorious victory at Fort Ticonderoga, Solomon had almost gone in spite of his father's stricture against joining the Patriot cause.

Sally sobered. "Of course not."

"Some of us are gathering over by Whitson's farm to celebrate. Maybe drill a little." Nathaniel would gladly pitch his chores for an opportunity to do battle against the hated British. He liked drilling a lot more than farming.

"Does Pa know?" Sally didn't want to get into trouble if Nathaniel disappeared.

"I reminded him last night." Nathaniel grinned at her. "We'd best be going, or we'll miss the others." He and Solomon turned as one and raced toward the trees crowding the edge of the field.

Josiah stayed behind long enough to pull the front of his tricorne over his dark eyes. "I'll be seeing you, Miss Reid."

That man. How could he bother her so and leave her smiling at the same time?

Josiah whistled a happy song as he walked away from the Reid cabin, his face probably reflecting a silly expression. Women. He'd never understand them, Sally Reid in particular. When he saw her tug at her mobcap today, he knew she was thinking about that incident all those years ago. Would she ever forgive him for that boyish trick? Their little school had closed down, with so many out sick, and then the funerals started. They had buried his only sister during that awful time. His whistle faltered and stopped. Then he started up again. That was all a long time ago, and God had spared him and Sally, as well as many others.

He soon caught up to Solomon and Nathaniel. His brother took one look at Josiah and opened his mouth, a grin on his face.

Josiah glared at him, and Solomon shut his mouth. Wise man.

"What are your intentions toward my sister?" Nathaniel asked.

"If I have any intentions—and I repeat, *if*—I won't be telling you." Josiah wouldn't let Sally's brother rile him that easily.

A smirk formed on Nathaniel's face.

"Wipe that grin off your face. I'm still older and bigger than you."

"Yes, sir." Nathaniel straightened his lips with apparent difficulty and changed the subject. "What do you think we'll do today?"

Josiah didn't know. If this ran along the same lines as last month's celebration of the beginning of the Revolution at Lexington and Concord, young Whitson would bring corn whiskey. Add everyone's musket to the mix, and Josiah didn't care for the result. As his father said, whiskey and firepower didn't go well together. At least they both agreed about that one thing. If only Father could see the importance of fighting for the rights of the colonies and not see them as toys to be played with at King George's leisure.

Once again, he found himself lagging behind Nathaniel and Solomon. He spent too much time thinking about Sally. Given a choice of a morning teasing Sally or a morning listening to young men who should know better drinking whiskey and talking brave talk, he knew what he'd choose. He prayed he could be a voice of reason and override Whitson's wildness.

Whitson's farm lay at the far end of the valley between two mountains where Maple Notch nestled. By the time they neared it, the sun had risen high overhead. Loud laughter reached his ears, suggesting the keg had already made a couple of rounds. *Too late.*

He stopped in midstride. "Solomon."

His brother looked at him, annoyed. "Why are you stopping? We're almost there."

Josiah put a hand to his arm. "Promise me you'll keep your head."

11

Solomon shook him off. "I never go off at half cock, and you know it."

Because Father never lets it get that far. Once again, Josiah wondered if they had made a mistake in going. God help him, he wanted to be here as much as Solomon did.

A branch broke ahead of them, and Whitson stumbled into their path. "Welcome! We wondered if you would make it." He wasn't drunk, not really. Something other than whiskey had excited him. "We found ourselves a bit of fun to celebrate our independence."

Loud grunts like someone in pain reached Josiah's ears. Had a Redcoat found his way to Maple Notch? Was an army on the way? The distressed sound gave speed to Josiah's feet, and he sprinted to the clearing.

A man dressed in ordinary civilian clothes knelt on a waistcoat on the ground. His blood dripped from stripes across his back and stained the silk lining. The man's hair hung around his face, hiding his features. Ordinary breeches ended just below the knee. This man was no soldier. A spy?

A compass, telescope, quill, and paper lay strewn across the ground—the equipment of a surveyor.

"What are you doing?" The sound of his own voice startled Josiah. He hadn't meant to speak aloud.

"Please, sir, I beg of you, I am no lover of the British. I am here on behalf of the state of New York."

Josiah knew the man's origin as soon as he spoke. His broad accent marked him as a flatlander, not a Vermonter born and bred.

"I mean no harm." The man raised his head, and Josiah looked into clear blue eyes that pled for mercy but expected none. Josiah had little enough love for New York's attitude toward the Green Mountain region, but this was unconscionable.

"He's plotting *our* valley to give away to those New Yorkers." Young Linus held a rod between his hands.

"I say, let 'em try," said one of the men, drunker than the rest.

"We'll send this man back as our emissary." Whitson sounded like a schoolmaster instructing his students. "He can tell them what kind of reception to expect if they show up here."

Anger boiled inside Josiah. "Solomon? Nathaniel?"

The three of them formed a thin line between the surveyor and the celebrating militiamen.

"You've had your fun for the day. The Green Mountain Boys are better than this. You'd better hope Mr. Allen doesn't get word of what you did here." Josiah glanced at the man on the ground. "May I have the honor of your name, sir?"

"It's Van Dyke. Schyler Van Dyke."

"Mr. Van Dyke. Are you able to stand?"

In answer, he pushed up on one leg and lurched forward. Solomon draped one of the man's arms over his left shoulder, keeping his musket ready in his right, and helped him to his feet. With him standing, the extent of the man's injuries became more visible. One eye was already swelling shut; blood coated his nose, and his right arm hung limply by his side. He needed immediate care. Josiah knew he should leave without speaking further, but he couldn't stop himself.

"I'm sure you consider yourselves great Patriots, attacking an innocent civilian. An American, no less." He snorted. "Next time, save your bravery for when you see the Redcoats coming."

Nathaniel put an arm around Van Dyke's chest, avoiding the broken arm, and the three men walked toward the path home. Josiah lingered, walking backward, musket ready in his hands if someone interfered.

"At least my father's not a Tory." Whitson threw one last barb as the quartet approached the edge of the forest.

Behind Josiah, he felt Solomon stiffen at the insult.

"Peace," he whispered. "Now's not the time."

"My. . .supplies," Van Dyke managed to gasp. "All my maps. . ."

Solomon shook his head, but Josiah sensed how important they were to the man. "We'll get them later if we can. But I'm afraid they're lost to you. Be thankful you have your life."

Branches closed behind them as they entered the forest, and Josiah turned to avoid stumbling over unseen obstacles.

"Are you Tories, then?" Van Dyke panted through the words. "If you are, you keep strange company, showing up at a gathering of the local militia."

Josiah glanced at Solomon. Consternation twisted his face. With Patriotic fervor sweeping the colonies, the issue of Tory against Patriot divided more than mother country and colony. It sundered towns and even families. Josiah didn't answer.

Nathaniel jumped in when Josiah didn't reply. "These two aren't. They're good Vermont boys. But their father believes differently." He gave an apologetic shrug.

A sheen of sweat broke out on Van Dyke's brow. Josiah judged they had traveled far enough to afford a stop. "Let's tarry here a minute." He led the injured man to a large rock and handed him a skin of water.

The man's hands trembled as he lifted it to his lips, and some spilled to the ground before he managed to gulp down several mouthfuls. "It wouldn't matter to me if you were. I do my job and try to stay out of trouble." He grimaced and lost some of the water. "Most of the time I succeed, but not to-day." He handed the skin back to Josiah. "Where are you taking me? To gaol?"

A bubble of laughter escaped Josiah's lips at that. "The last I knew, sur-veying land wasn't a criminal offense. But you've raised a good question."

"We'll take him in." Nathaniel offered. "I'm sure Ma won't mind."

Josiah's heart quickened. "That sounds wise. Mrs. Reid has a healing hand." More than that, he would have an excuse to stop by and talk with Sally when he checked on Van Dyke. "But are you sure? I understand she's been feeling poorly."

"Ma would skin me alive if she found out I'd refused an opportunity to practice hospitality. She'd say Mr. Van Dyke here might be an angel unawares. She'll take care of anybody—even a Tory." Nathaniel flashed a grin so like his sister's that Josiah had to smile back.

"I don't want to bring trouble on anyone," Van Dyke protested. "If you could take me to the nearest inn, I'll be on my way."

"You couldn't make it there today." The man might not even manage the trip across the valley. "In the morning, we'll see."

The trip back took longer than the morning run, with frequent stops for Van Dyke's sake. During one of the rest periods, Nathaniel carved a strip from a willow tree. Josiah nodded his approval. Willow bark tea might help reduce any fever and pain.

The sun had passed the zenith by the time they reached the Reids' farm. Mr. Reid worked his way down a row, plucking small fish out of a bucket and dropping one on each mound as he went.

"Hallo!" Josiah called out in greeting.

Mr. Reid straightened his back, put a hand to his eyes to block the sun, and peered in their direction. "Nathaniel! Josiah, Solomon! I thought you had gone to celebrate the capture of Fort Ticonderoga. What happened?" He set down the bucket of fish and trotted through the field.

At least Mr. Reid knew why the local lads had gathered. Nathaniel needed no subterfuge.

"Whitson." Nathaniel spit out the *s* in the name.

"I'm a surveyor from New York," Van Dyke explained. "Some of the local boys took exception to my occupation."

"You need say no more." A scowl darkened Reid's face, whether because of New York's interference or the treatment the man had received at Whit-son's hands, Josiah couldn't guess. "Come ahead to the cabin. My wife will tend to you."

∽

Sally stirred the pot of beans another time, hoping Pa would come in for a bite of lunch soon. When would Nathaniel return, and would Josiah and Solomon come with him? *Stop thinking about Josiah.* Nellie would tell a tall tale for sure if she could read Sally's thoughts.

"I'll keep an eye on the beans," Ma told Sally. "Go remind your pa that lunch is waiting. He overdoes it when the weather is fine like it is today."

Sally smiled, checked her mobcap—why, she couldn't say, unless she hoped to see Josiah—and opened the door. Brilliant sunshine blinded her for a moment. In the field, she saw the figures of five men outlined in black against the sun. One of them was injured.

Josiah. Sally started running.

Chapter 2

Only a moment passed before Sally realized her error, but she lived a thousand lifetimes in that one second. Nathaniel and the others had returned with a stranger. She tucked a few stray hairs under her mobcap and went back inside.

"That was quickly done. Is your father on the way in?"

"He is. With an injured man."

"Nathaniel?" Ma's face blanched, and she put her hand over her dress where a new life grew within her. "An accident?"

Sally regretted causing her mother worry. "Not Nathaniel. A stranger. Perhaps someone was injured at the celebration today."

That suggestion did little to relieve Ma's worry. She sank into a chair. "A battle, do you think?" Even though a Patriot, Ma was like all mothers everywhere, Sally supposed. No one liked to see their sons go to war with the knowledge they might never return.

Ma's weakness alarmed Sally. "The others appear unharmed." Ma should eat soon, lest she faint, and not wait on the men. Unable to keep food down with the new babe on the way, she didn't eat much in the morning these days. And Pa had delayed longer than usual to come in for lunch. Sally dished up a bowl of beans and handed it to her. "Go ahead."

Ma started to protest before she accepted the wisdom of Sally's suggestion. One bite of corn bread and beans followed the next as she polished her bowl.

When they saw Ma eating, Nellie and Stephen rushed to the table. "You'll have to wait," Sally said. "We've got company coming."

"Who?" Nellie rushed to the door before Sally could answer.

"Nathaniel has returned with a stranger. And the Tuttles will be joining us, as well." Sally could sense heat creeping into her cheeks. Why did she feel embarrassed? It was the neighborly thing to do.

Before Nellie replied, the door opened, and Nathaniel came through, supporting a man who appeared almost unconscious. Sally strained to think of a time she had seen someone so badly beaten; even the last time Stephen had tackled Nathaniel in an all-out tussle, neither had been so bruised. Perhaps Ma's assessment of a battle had hit the mark. Blood and mud smeared

16

on the others' breeches and shirts. Behind her, she heard her mother's gasp.

"Don't worry, my dear." Mr. Reid came up behind the younger men and placed a gentle hand on her arm. "No one is hurt except this unfortunate soul. Nathaniel offered our care for him while he recovers."

"Of course." Color returned to Ma's face, and she stood. "Sally, I'll take over serving the meal while you prepare a bed for our guest."

"His name is Schyler Van Dyke, from New York," Josiah added. "We can make more formal introductions when he regains consciousness."

A passing regret at losing the opportunity to share a word with the young Mr. Tuttle bothered Sally, but she let it go. The need for a soft bed, and not hard ground, for Mr. Van Dyke's broken body took precedence over all else.

"I'll help." Nellie skipped up the ladder, with Sally following. When they reached the top, she whispered in Sally's ear. "That way, you can finish in time to sit with Josiah."

Sally peeked over the edge, but no one was paying attention. Nellie's whisper carried across a room, loud enough for anyone to hear if they wanted to.

In answer, Sally removed the bedding from the straw tick they slept on at night. They could sleep on loose straw until Van Dyke was better. After rolling the mattress into a large ball, Sally considered how to get it to the floor below. She couldn't throw it, not with four tall men crowding around the table. For covering. . .at least the weather had grown warm. They wouldn't miss the extra blanket. She wrapped a blanket over her arm and started down the ladder. "Hand the tick down to me when I reach the floor," she told Nellie.

The problem with that plan soon became apparent. Nellie could only dangle over the edge so far without risking a fall. Sally climbed one rung, then two, and stretched. If she could at least hold the bottom. . .

"Let me." Josiah's deep voice interrupted her thoughts. Taller than her by a good ten inches, he stood flat-footed and caught the tick as Nellie dropped it. "Where do you want me to place it?" His voice sounded odd, muffled behind the burden he carried.

The only possible spot was next to her parents' bed. As long as they had company, the space was crowded, but they still could manage. "Over there." She pointed.

Without further ado, Josiah carried the bundle to the corner and spread the tick on the floor. Sally knelt beside him and tucked a linen sheet over the corners and plumped up a feather pillow to create as soft a bed as possible. In spite of his injuries, the man appeared good-sized and well built. She hoped the hay would cushion his weight. What had caused the man's injuries?

~

"What happened?" Sally asked.

Josiah wondered how often he would retell the morning's events. "Some of the boys didn't like Mr. Van Dyke's line of work."

"Plotting land for people from New York?"

He nodded. If only explaining it to Father would come as easily. Father would demand further information until he had wrung every last detail from his sons—including the fact they had gathered to celebrate the conquest of Fort Ticonderoga. Only last week he had commented that Josiah was under his authority as long as he lived under his roof. He wouldn't countenance support of the rebellion in any son of his.

But for now, Josiah would enjoy these few stolen moment with Sally. She tucked a strand of hair, the color of wheat at harvesttime, under her mobcap. Did she realize how often she did that? Today, as always, she gave of herself to others first, forgoing lunch to serve her guests. He should send her back to his place at the table, but selfishly, he wanted her to stay.

All too soon, she finished smoothing out the bed. "It's ready." She rose, and he stepped closer. "Bring him over."

Nathaniel jumped up from the table. Van Dyke sat slumped against the wall where they had left him. Together, Josiah and Nathaniel lifted him to his feet. The surveyor awakened long enough to murmur, "What. . ." But his head fell back against the ticking as soon as they laid him down.

Nathaniel reached in his waistcoat pocket for a small packet. "I brought back some willow bark."

"Good." Sally nodded in approval. "That will be useful if he develops a fever."

"Josiah?" Solomon stood and wiped the sleeve of his shirt across his mouth. "We'd best be getting home."

Josiah grimaced. The time of reckoning had come.

"Wait a moment." Mr. Reid left the table and grabbed his tricorne. "I'll go with you to discuss the morning's happenings with your father. We can't allow the Maple Notch contingent of Green Mountain Boys to go unchecked."

"We'd welcome your company." The presence of a third party might delay the explosion that was sure to come. As divided as their opinions about the revolution were, the community united on the need for the local militia. Since Maple Notch had been settled after the close of the Treaty of 1763, the militia had protected them against Indian attacks and a renewal of the hostilities with the French. Only differences of opinion over the identity of the enemy separated the community now.

The path home sped as quickly as the trek from Whitson's farm had lagged. The short walk didn't allow Josiah enough time to fashion an explanation that might calm their father's anger. His steps slowed as they entered the clearing near the cabin.

"Does your father know where you were today?" Mr. Reid must have sensed Josiah's hesitation; he knew their father's stance on the revolution.

The brothers exchanged an uneasy glance. "He knows we were with the militia." Josiah didn't add any more.

"But not what you were doing, eh?" Mr. Reid shook his head. "I'm sure he knows the significance of this date."

Had he pretended ignorance for the sake of peace? Josiah hadn't considered that possibility.

"Tory or Patriot, it doesn't matter in this case." When Reid spoke, Josiah didn't know if he was reassuring himself or the younger men. "No responsible man will stomach the kind of show young Whitson put on today."

The field stood empty, heaping mounds of planted seed in straight rows crossing the ground between stumps. Father was cleaning his hoe when the three of them came near the barn.

"Decided to come home after all, did you?" In spite of the harsh words, Father's expression was calm.

Some of the uneasiness drained from Josiah. Their late arrival hadn't raised Father's ire. He had expected them home before nooning.

"Reid, what brings you here?" Father greeted their neighbor.

"There was an incident at the gathering this morning." Reid nodded at Josiah to pick up the tale.

Once again, Josiah repeated the story, hoping it was for the last time. He emphasized the discovery of the surveyor and left out the presence of corn whiskey that had fueled the beatings.

"Hmph." Father looked as though he wished he could lash at something. "These were militia boys, you say?"

Josiah hesitated. He didn't want everyone to get in trouble. "Brad Whitson was the ringleader."

"That one's always been trouble. Who else?"

Josiah didn't want to name names. Some of the boys present followed Whitson like proverbial sheep. Beside him, Solomon shuffled his feet.

"You didn't take part in it, did you?" Father's voice held a knife's edge.

"Of course not!" What did Father think of him, to ask such a question?

"From what I understand, Josiah and Solomon stepped in to stop the carnage. With my boy's help." Reid, for one, spoke of his son with pride.

"Come in, and we'll figure out what to do over a cup of tea."

Mother met them in the yard, drawing cool water from the depths of their well. After their day's exertions, even the elixir of life couldn't have tasted any better.

Bothersome black flies buzzed around Josiah's head, heedless of his attempts to brush them off. He splashed cold water over his face and joined the others in the cabin. He and Solomon remained standing while his parents and Mr. Reid took seats on the rough-hewn bench.

"Do you think we should tell the commander? Make it a matter of military discipline?" Reid suggested.

That's wise. Invite Father's opinion first. Josiah watched how the two old friends would iron out this situation.

"No need for that. We can handle this locally." Father's face reddened.

"Now, Mr. Tuttle." Mother poured out tea. "You remember what the doctor said after you had that apoplectic fit last year. Avoid upset, or it could happen again."

Father waved that aside. "Not even Whitson Senior would approve of beating up an unarmed man. We'll settle it at the next drill. Decide what punishment is appropriate." Father spoke with authority. Whatever the topic, he always had a strong opinion and wasn't afraid to voice it.

Even if no one else agreed with him.

∽

The next drill didn't take place for several weeks. Sally waited until Nathaniel and Pa had left before she took out the extra dried apple pies and rollie-polies she had made for today's picnic. Nellie had giggled so much all morning that Sally felt sure Nathaniel would guess their surprise. Once or twice, she had been tempted to giggle herself, but she restrained herself. A young woman of seventeen now, she practiced an adult demeanor—even when planning a party.

Van Dyke had planted the idea in the ladies' heads. The first day he felt well enough to sit at the table, Ma had baked pie. He ate every bite and even accepted the one leftover slice. "That was truly stupendous. My mother could make me do almost anything for a piece of her dried apple pie."

A light beamed from Ma's eyes, indicating his offhand comment had brought a plan to mind. Later Sally asked, "What're you thinking?"

"Why, how everybody enjoys a party. When there's good food, fellowship, and games, people feel too good to put up a fuss. I think it's time Maple Notch had a party."

Sally could guess the direction of Ma's thinking. "And the perfect time might be next Monday, when the militia gets together to drill?"

"And when the circuit preacher will be here for Rogation Day. It's the perfect time. I'll spread word among the town's womenfolk."

Rogation Day. Of course. Although usually planned for a Sunday, Maple Notch celebrated the day when the crops were blessed whenever their preacher was available. So the plan was born. Ma had fretted when Pa told her they intended to confront the miscreants at the next drill. The Whitsons, both father and son, were as likely to pull a knife or a musket when threatened as to listen to reason. Now, God willing, she might thwart the possibility before it arose.

All their preparations completed, the Reids made ready to depart. Sally paused long enough to speak with their guest. "Are you certain you don't mind staying alone?" Van Dyke had recovered enough to sit for short periods of time, but everyone agreed he'd best stay close to the farm. "We'll set aside a chunk of the pie just for you."

"I'm fine, Miss Reid. I'm sorry to have been the cause of such discord in your town."

"No one is blaming you for men's wicked ways, Mr. Van Dyke. I am sure you will be glad to leave us behind as soon as you are able." Sally tied her hair back with a pink ribbon before putting on her mobcap. *Vanity,* she thought. *Using Ma's best ribbon to show off your hair, because once Josiah mentioned how pretty you looked in pink.*

"Are we ready?" Ma had regained some of her vigor over the last few weeks, now that the difficult days of morning sickness had passed. According to her, these were the best months of pregnancy, before the ever-increasing weight of the baby sapped her of strength. She insisted she felt well enough to go to the picnic with them.

When Nellie appeared, a bit of flour smudged the elbow of her dress, but otherwise she was clean. Sally's little sister preferred outside play to working in the kitchen, and she was almost harder to keep clean than the menfolk.

The men drilled at the usual spot, on the town common. With Tory and Patriot alike coming together to address the problem of the surveyor, the area would be crowded. Ma tucked a couple of blankets under her arm, and Sally carried the heavy basket. They entrusted a small jar of buttermilk to Nellie.

A pale sun took the chill off the air and dried the dew from the grass under their feet. The grass had grown tall enough to brush the hems of their skirts. Sally thought about kicking off her shoes and running stocking-footed in the grass, but that would rip her newly mended hose and stain them beyond redemption.

Once they reached the river, she studied the water's flow. Not as high as it had been during spring runoffs. She decided to remove her shoes and hose long enough to cross. First Nellie skipped across, as surefooted as a deer on the mountains. Ma followed, placing her feet with care on each stone and handing the blanket ahead to Nellie. Last of all, Sally bent over at the river-bank, tugging at her shoes and hose.

"Sally." Ma's tone carried reprimand enough.

"No one's here to see." She placed her footwear on top of the basket, lifted her skirts with one hand, and waded in. Cool, delicious water caressed her skin, easing away dirt and soreness, even if she stubbed her toes on a rock or two. She squelched mud between her toes and then circled her ankles about to clean them of the day's dust.

Ma shook her head. "You're setting a bad example for Nellie. And what if someone came by while you had lifted your skirts? Anyone could have seen your ankles."

Sally looked around. "Where?" Seeing no one about, she pulled up her hose and laced her shoes. "There. All set to go."

"I'd like to do that on the trip back," Nellie whispered when Ma fell behind.

"Don't you dare. She'd tan me for sure." Sally smiled to let Nellie know she wasn't serious. Her sister hid her smile. Nellie could be a lot of fun.

They had forded the river close to town, and soon they approached the common. A ring of men surrounded Brad Whitson, his father, and a handful of other rough-and-ready farmers. The stern faces of watching men told Sally they hadn't arrived a moment too soon.

Josiah and Solomon stood with their backs to the women, two young saplings growing into tall trees. Mr. Tuttle continued to tower over them, although Josiah was fast coming up to the same size.

Approaching from the other direction, Sally spotted Martha Whitson, Brad's likeable sister, and her mother. They didn't want an argument any more than the Reids did. Other women of the town gathered. Josiah's head turned, as if the unexpected arrival of company distracted him. He said something in his father's ear that Sally couldn't hear.

"What's this?" Pa called out loud enough to be heard. Everyone in the circle looked in one direction, then another at the women carrying blankets and baskets.

"It's a surprise picnic, Mr. Reid." Ma moved more quickly than Sally expected for a woman in her condition. "To celebrate Rogation Day." Her voice held the same honey-coated knife's edge that kept her children in line most of the time.

A smile creased Josiah's face. "Gentlemen, I say, let's welcome the ladies."

Chapter 3

Josiah walked straight in Sally's direction, and she sucked in her breath. Solomon looked at their father, shrugged, and trotted over to stand beside Martha Whitson. Soon every man found a lady of his choosing, a welcome development of the picnic.

"Don't think we're through," Sally overheard Mr. Tuttle growl at the Whitsons. Their animosity ran deep, stemming from issues existing long before the surveyor had entered the picture. They'd fought over politics for years, since well before Independence.

But on this beautiful, sunshiny day, the women of Maple Notch had accomplished what they'd intended. Rogation Day, with the blessing of the crops and later the beating of the borders, would unite them in a celebration of the unique heritage that brought Maple Notch into being.

Josiah reached her side and took a blanket from her, spreading it across the grass. She sat down and kept her gaze on the ground. Was he seeking her out? Or perhaps he had joined the family group closest to him on the green. That was it, nothing more. She allowed herself a quick peek as she handed him a slice of cheese.

His gaze settled on her face, and she felt a blush creep above the collar of her dress. "Do I have a piece of cheese stuck to my teeth?"

He grinned at her. "No. Your teeth are fine. I'm sorry if I was rude."

She reached for a strand of hair that had strayed from the bow and tucked it behind her ear.

Ma stretched out a second blanket next to theirs, close enough to keep an eye on them but far enough away to give them some privacy. Sally saw Nellie whisper something in their mother's ear before giggling. Someone might as well post a sign above their heads stating "courting couple."

At least Josiah didn't notice, or if he did, he didn't seem to mind. Maybe he had wanted that to happen. The thought made the cheese turn dry in Sally's throat.

"How is Van Dyke?" Josiah managed a normal voice. He didn't seem aware of all the eyes following them.

"He's f—fine," she stammered, something she never did. "In fact, Pa thinks he'll be well enough to travel within a fortnight."

"You must be an accomplished herbalist, if he has already recovered from that beating." Josiah picked a dandelion from the grass and held it to his nose. "If you can make a tasty dish from dandelion greens, you must know other of nature's hidden treasures" He dug into the crock that held the referenced dish. " 'Tis one of springtime's pleasures."

"Every woman knows how to cook greens. Ma knows a lot more about medicinal plants than I do." Sally shied away from the praise. "And of course we've been praying for him, for his healing. . .and safety."

"It's best if Van Dyke leaves as soon as he's able." Josiah nodded toward Whitson. "He's embarrassed about what happened, and would as soon take it out on someone."

That's why we came today. To prevent an incident. But Sally didn't voice their concerns. No need to worry Josiah further. Men did what they felt they had to do, and many times women coped with the aftermath. Instead, she said, "And he may have family worried about him. We haven't been able to send word. Not with the British threatening to cut off Lake Champlain."

"Seems like New York would have enough to keep them busy with General Burgoyne breathing down their necks." Josiah dug into the greens again. "Why they'd bother sending out a surveyor to Vermont at a time like this. . . it doesn't make sense."

"Do you think he'll succeed?" Sally shivered. With Canada across the border and the approach of the British from Lake Champlain, Maple Notch was vulnerable to capture.

"I'm not the best person to ask. People don't tell me much." Josiah's brown eyes dulled to a dark gray as he looked at the gathered townsfolk. "Things look civilized at the moment, but as soon as the topic of the fight against the British comes up. . .might as well build a wall between us."

"How do you cope with your father?" Sally couldn't imagine the difficulties Josiah faced with their differences.

Josiah let out a low, bitter laugh. "We don't talk much, that's how—beyond discussing what crops to plant and which fields he wants worked. The Patriots won't talk to me because they're afraid I'll tell my father, and he won't talk to me for fear I'll tell the Patriots."

The loneliness evident on Josiah's face cut Sally to the quick. Perhaps she and Ma should visit Mrs. Tuttle. At least Josiah had Solomon, and so far Mr. Tuttle allowed them to drill with the militia. They got to see other people. But their mother might feel cut off. "Do your parents agree? About the British?"

Her ma and pa were of one mind about the Revolution. Ma didn't like fighting, but she believed in the Patriots' cause. Unless Britain listened to reason, armed conflict seemed the only option.

"I don't know. The one time I asked her, she said she planned to submit to his authority, in accordance with the Word of God."

Spoken like a true Tory.

"Enough about the war. We can find more pleasant topics to discuss." Josiah bit into the crust of the dried apple pie.

They sat in silence. Sally cast her mind about, looking for a topic, *any* topic, that had nothing to do with the war. Her mind remained as blank as a child's slate on the first day of school. *Oh, yes.* "There's an owl building a nest in the rafters of our barn." An owl would be as good as a cat in hunting down any mice that might threaten their grain.

"That's good. We used to have an owl nearby, but he's taken off." Josiah grinned. "Maybe the same one that's taken up residence in your barn."

Silence stretched between them again until Josiah spoke. "Planting is going well this year. The beans and corn are sprouting fast."

"That's what Pa says. He hopes we get a bumper crop."

They chatted about the weather, the proper amount of seed to use, the prospects of the growing season. Safe topics. Boring topics. Topics of interest to farmers, more immediate concerns than battles and independence.

The sun moved high overhead in the sky and would soon begin its journey westward. The circuit preacher, accompanied by Elder Cabot, called them together for Rogation festivities. Around them, people repacked baskets with whatever remained, folded blankets, and prepared to leave. After an afternoon in Josiah's presence, even if they had spoken of everyday, mundane things, Sally didn't want to return to the farm. But she mustn't dawdle any longer.

So far they had avoided the one topic closest to her heart. With her face averted so that Josiah wouldn't see her telltale blush and think her overly bold, she asked, "Do you think your father will let you go if the Green Mountain Boys are called upon to fight in this war for independence?"

"I. . .don't know. No, he won't agree. But I haven't decided how I will respond."

Sally sneaked a look at him, but like her, he had averted his face. Only the tension in his neck muscles, the way he jutted his chin, betrayed the turmoil he must have been feeling. Since Fort Ticonderoga fell without a fight, the Vermont militia hadn't done much to prove themselves. Sally had little doubt that they would be drawn into battle sooner or later.

"I'm praying for you. For all the families that have that choice to make. For our town."

"As are we all." Josiah stood and brushed down his breeches, scattering crumbs for gathering grouse. They joined the other townsfolk following the preacher as he walked around the village, asking God for a bountiful harvest. Then everyone headed home.

After the two families crossed the river, the rogation antics began. The four young men took turns bumping each other into the boundary stone and later the fence that separated the two farms. By now, all of them could probably walk the boundary between their property blindfolded.

The family groups walked away, giving Sally a moment of privacy with Josiah. "Thank you for a delicious meal," he said. "It was well thought." They stopped under the overhanging branches of a willow tree, where she turned her face up to his.

"Ma did most of the cooking."

"I'll speak with Father about Solomon and me accompanying Mr. Van Dyke back to New York. Neither my brother nor I want him encountering another party intent on harm."

Sally's heart fluttered at the thought. What dangers might await Josiah on the road? She kept her worries to herself. "I'll let Pa know. We'll send a message when our guest is able to travel."

∽

Josiah brushed at the mosquitoes that buzzed around any exposed patches of skin, far worse here than in Maple Notch. Transporting Van Dyke to his home via Lake Champlain had seemed like a good plan when Solomon had suggested it. Once on the water, Josiah wasn't so sure. Every insect in two states decided to feast on them en route. He also remembered rumors of General Burgoyne's progress in his plans to attack New York via the lake. So far, they'd had a peaceful journey and avoided any larger boats.

Today they expected to pass under the nose of Fort Ticonderoga and determine a portage to Lake George, from where Van Dyke promised the travel to his home was but a long day's hike through the woods. Once they reached the fort, Josiah felt he could relax. "There it is," Van Dyke called from the back of the canoe. "The path to the fort lies in that direction."

The sun glinted off the granite walls of the fort, making it hard for Josiah to see any details. He remembered tales from those who participated in the '75 campaign. Those brave souls had gone after a British fort before independence had been declared. Foolish, his father had said.

The fort, shaped like a misshapen star, derived its name from an Indian word meaning "where two waterways meet"—lakes Champlain and George. No wonder both sides valued the strategic location.

As one, Solomon and Josiah paddled toward the shore the fort guarded. As they approached, the reflected image of the buildings shimmered in the water. Red roofs peaked above high walls, red as blood, although thankfully none had been shed in the taking of the fort. It looked strong, stalwart—a symbol of America's strength and confidence. "Thou art our fortress."

"Do you think they'll take us in for the night?" Josiah asked Van Dyke, cocking his head toward the fort.

"They allowed me to stay on my way north." Van Dyke smiled at the memory before grimacing. "They won't be pleased with the reception I received. The lands along the border are essential to protection from invasion by the British from Canada."

"We can defend our own!" Solomon protested.

"The Continental Congress—and the state of New York—believes that the more of an American presence we establish along the northern frontiers, the more secure we are."

Josiah smarted inside. Did Van Dyke know Father supported the crown? That if the British invaded, he would be the first to join their ranks? More importantly, if that happened, what would Josiah do? How could he honor his father when he believed with all his heart that Father was wrong? Even the thought of his sons spending the night at an American fort would upset him.

Van Dyke guided them through milfoil and water chestnuts toward the bank, where trees grew so dense Josiah didn't see how even a fox could squeeze through. The canoe glided underneath the cool canopy, the lake only a slender line of blue through branches blurred by foliage. "There it is. The path I told you about." The only evidence was a few bent twigs.

"How can we carry the canoe?" Solomon looked at the growth in front of them. Even if they could maneuver the load through the forest, they would mark a path so wide that even a blind man could make his way to the fort.

The three men looked about them. "If we continue around the bend, will we find a better place to make the portage?" Josiah inquired of Van Dyke, since he had made the trip earlier.

"A little ways farther down the lake."

"Then we'll leave it here and come back for it tomorrow." Josiah decided. The three of them made quick work of hiding the canoe under branches and leaves. Where the birch bark shone through, it blended with the surrounding trees.

To give the man credit, Van Dyke hadn't slowed them down on their trip. He appeared to have made a complete recovery from the beating he had received. More strength resided in his arm muscles than Josiah had guessed upon first meeting him at Whitson's farm. Throughout the journey, the surveyor had proved helpful on several occasions. In fact, if Van Dyke hadn't come to Vermont on such a hated mission, Josiah would have warmed up to him sooner. But hadn't General Washington been a surveyor once upon a time? Josiah shouldn't hold Van Dyke's profession against him.

The men picked up their few belongings, a musket slung over each man's shoulders, and began the climb. They didn't speak, at first from caution, then because the path steepened. Even as work-toughened as Josiah was, he needed breath for each step. In the quiet stillness of the forest, he could scarce believe a fort filled with battle-ready soldiers lay ahead. The peace could fool him into thinking everything was right with God's world. A warbler sang out, and its mate returned the call. Chickadees darted in and out of the trees, as well as a dozen others he couldn't name. Every now and then, deer tracks crossed their own. The fort should be well supplied, provided they could gain access to these woods.

About midway up the incline, Josiah caught sight of a patch of red. Only the male cardinal sported that bright color. *God loves colors.* He could imagine Sally's voice. *See how He splashes it around creation.*

The same red flashed again, and this time he could see this was no bird. He stiffened. Behind him, Solomon stopped. He whistled, a low bobolink's call, the agreed-upon signal to get Van Dyke's attention. The man froze in his tracks before turning around with a questioning glance.

Solomon was already heading in the direction of the Redcoat. He could move almost as quietly as an Indian through the forest, certainly better than the field-trained soldier who now thrashed his way through the underbrush like a bull on a rampage.

Josiah wanted to call his brother back. Rash, impulsive, Solomon might be, but he should know better than to approach the man. Where there was one soldier, there might be more. But Josiah didn't dare call out, not when he might reveal their presence to the soldier. Perhaps he was a scout, sent ahead. General Burgoyne's drive through New York surfaced in his mind again.

Josiah inched forward. The man neared the trail, which, as faint as it was, might still attract his attention. He must be stopped.

Solomon was almost close enough to touch the soldier when a crow dropped from the sky, screeching, talons missing his face by inches. He cried out but once, but the soldier turned at the sound, bayonet poised for battle. Before Solomon could position his musket in his hands, the Redcoat brought him to the ground with his weapon.

All thoughts of caution fled Josiah's mind. With a single, fluid motion, he raised his musket and plunged through the few yards of forest remaining. He paused in midstep to aim and fired. The ball hit the Redcoat, and he collapsed.

Josiah ran past his crumpled body to reach Solomon's side. Already, his brother was gasping for breath.

"Must warn. . .the fort."

"You need a doctor."

"Leave me here." Solomon's eyelashes fluttered at him, his dark eyes clouding as he forced words through his throat. "It's too late for me."

Van Dyke joined them. "No one else has come. It appears no one heard the shot."

In his worry, Josiah had forgotten about the possibility of other soldiers in the vicinity.

"Go. Before. They. Come." Solomon forced each word through his throat with effort.

"I won't leave you." Josiah gripped Solomon's hand with his own.

"I'll go. But first, let's move farther into the trees. Away from. . ." Van Dyke gestured at the carnage around them. Josiah thought of the birds that would soon circle overhead and the evidence of the battle. But the bayonet had skewered Solomon's body to the ground. Removing it would hasten his death.

"No, you go on ahead. We'll—" Josiah's voice broke. "We'll catch up as soon as we can."

"I'll hide the Redcoat, then. When you're ready, the trail is right over there." Van Dyke placed a hand on Josiah's shoulder and then trotted away.

Solomon's every breath was a titanic struggle, but the sound pleased Josiah more than the sweetest bird's song he had ever heard. Each gasp meant his brother still lived. He knelt by Solomon's side and searched for words. He should pray, but what for? That time would go backward? That he could have taken the bayonet instead of Solomon? That they had never decided to go to the fort? That God would somehow, someway intervene and prevent the obvious from happening?

"Tell Father. . ."

"No last words." *I refuse to listen*.

"I'm sorry." In the depths of Solomon's eyes, he looked older than the elders of Maple Notch and held all the mysteries of life in his hand. "Say. . .a psalm," Solomon begged.

The words of Psalm 23 sprang to Josiah's mouth: "The Lord is my shepherd; I shall not want. He maketh me to lie down in green pastures. . . ." David could have been speaking of the glade where they waited, green with the new growth of spring. Josiah stumbled, willing himself not to cry.

A smile replaced the pain on Solomon's face, and his grasp on Josiah's hand relaxed. As Josiah recited the final words of the psalm—"And I will dwell in the house of the Lord for ever"—Solomon slipped away into that eternal rest.

Chapter 4

The British are approaching Fort Ticonderoga." Nathaniel preceded his father into their cabin with the news.

Sally stopped chopping the carrot in front of her. "They're *here*—in Vermont?"

"Near here."

Sally's eyes drifted to Ma, who looked at Pa with a resigned expression. "When will you be leaving?"

"Our militia will meet at sundown. We'll leave by sunrise, if not before. We'll travel light." He looked at Nathaniel, who straightened his shoulders and looked very grown-up, in spite of his scant sixteen years. "Your Ma would like you to stay home."

Sally held her breath. Surely Nathaniel wouldn't go; he was hardly more than a child. . .a year younger than herself. The same age as Solomon Tuttle, who had left home on an important mission.

Ma placed a hand on her abdomen, where the coming child was becoming obvious, and sat down without speaking.

"I practice with the militia."

When had Nathaniel's voice deepened so that he sounded so much like Pa that it hurt?

"What good is drilling if I don't fight?" Nathaniel's face set in determined lines.

A moan escaped Ma's lips.

Pa put his hand on Nathaniel's shoulder. "It is your decision, son. All I ask is that you talk it over with God before you make up your mind." He patted him awkwardly on the back. "I will finish the chores for the day while you think about what to do."

Nathaniel looked at Ma, then at Sally. "I'll do as he says. I'll go down by the creek and pray. But I already know the answer." His shoulders filled the doorway as he walked outside.

Sally put her arms around Ma. "Whatever shall we do, Ma?"

She spread her fingers far apart as if to measure the distance between them. "Why, we'll trust God and do our patriotic duty. I knew this day was coming as soon as we heard about Lexington and Concord."

Sally wanted to storm outside and scream. Tears formed in her eyes.

"None of that." Ma spoke in gentle tones. "I wish I hadn't been so weak just now. We need to be strong for the men. For the children."

Sally wondered if Nellie would worry. Young Stephen would wish he were old enough to go with them. She was grateful they were fishing by the river today and had a few more hours of peace until they heard the news. Would they see Nathaniel? Would he tell them what had happened?

True to her word, Ma roused herself from the table and gathered a few simple foodstuffs the men could carry easily. What did they consider basic supplies? Would they want a covering if the nights grew cold? Flint for fire, a skein for water, a pan to cook in, perhaps? A change of clothes? Definitely a powder horn and bullet mold. Sally could think of a hundred things they could use and only a handful of things that were truly necessary. She showed Ma what she had assembled.

"You've shown good sense." Ma examined the supplies Sally had laid out while she had whipped together a batch of corn pone. "I won't let them leave without eating something. Who knows when they'll have their next hot meal?" She rubbed her nose but stopped short of a sniffle.

Pa came in early from the fields, followed by Nellie and Stephen. Nellie looked sad enough to cry, Stephen so excited that he would burst if he couldn't talk. Pa must have warned them to keep quiet, because they went to a corner in the room and talked between themselves.

Nathaniel followed not half a minute later. "I'm going." He didn't expound.

Pa's eyes sought out his wife. "Mary." The look that passed between Sally's parents was the same one she longed to see from her husband's face some day. Understanding, love, support—regret. Pa led Ma by the hand to their bed and hung a blanket from a rope for privacy. The murmur of their voices told Sally her parents were exchanging words of farewell, of love and longing—intimacies they didn't care to exchange in front of the children. Sally chased Stephen and Nellie outside.

The pone had finished baking by the time Ma and Pa pulled the blanket down and called the family to the table. Stephen and Nellie were bickering, but Ma didn't seem to have the heart to interrupt. Pa spoke in a voice low enough for only Sally to hear.

"Sally. I'm depending on you to keep things going around here. Stephen may need help with the fields. I'm sure you'll know what to do." He sighed.

Sally nodded while her mind raced. Danger could assail them without Pa or Nathaniel to protect them. She remembered Ma's words. *Be strong.* "God will be with us." She said it with more confidence than she felt. The words of Holy Scripture would become more than words spoken by rote before this was over, she feared.

"And Sally?" Pa made her look at him.

"Yes, Pa?" She blinked to keep tears from falling.

"Josiah Tuttle's a good man. When he returns, ask him for help if you need it." Pa kissed the top of her head, and Sally felt she had received his blessing.

All too soon, Pa and Nathaniel took their leave. Sally looked at her brother, at his fierce expression, and flung her arms around him. He stiffened, then relented and returned the embrace. The touch expressed everything Sally dared not put into words. She joined Ma and the younger children at the door, watching as Pa and Nathaniel crossed the yard, the fields. . .until they were little more than a speck against the encroaching forest. Nellie hiccuped a sob and ran inside.

Sally's thoughts strayed to Josiah and Solomon, thankful they were absent from Maple Notch, and not facing the terrible dilemma of their father's opposition.

∽

Josiah could have stayed by Solomon's side all night. He could have run screaming into the forest, hoping to awake and discover it was all a nightmare. But he didn't have the luxury for the first choice or the imagination for the second.

Not relishing the task, Josiah pulled the bayonet from Solomon's still body. In life, his brother had been nigh on to Josiah's own height, and only a few pounds lighter. The additional weight would double the path's difficulty, but Josiah would not, could not leave his brother behind. What had Van Dyke done with the Redcoat? He thought he caught sight of a patch of red beneath an uprooted tree, underneath pines and dead leaves. No one would notice it if he wasn't searching for it.

The color in the sky, drained by the trees, had grown even darker while Josiah finished his tasks. He hurried to reach the fort before night fell, even if it was only days past midsummer's eve. More and more branches hit his legs and arms and face when he could no longer make out the path. In the distance, he saw flames burning atop Mount Independence, suggestive of the battle the single soldier represented.

The conflagration provided light enough for Josiah to make out the gate to the fort straight ahead. The sight gave strength to his tired legs, and he ran as though a fiery wind blew him to safety. Panting, he arrived at the door. An eye appeared in a peephole. "Halt! Who goes there!"

"A Patriot," Josiah managed to stammer. "Of Maple Notch."

The eye disappeared, and the door swung open to reveal a young soldier in a makeshift uniform, much the same age as himself. "Van Dyke said to expect you. That you escorted him here from the north." Then he took note of the burden Josiah carried. "What happened?"

"My brother." Josiah's voice caught in his throat. "We came upon a Redcoat on the path. Solomon charged him and caught his bayonet." Josiah told the few, sad facts as he scanned the inside of the compound. In light of the British threat, he'd expected the place to teem with soldiers. Even with his limited knowledge of battle strategy, the fort seemed poorly garrisoned. Perhaps twice their number could defend the fort.

"Major General St. Clair will want to speak with you."

"My brother—" Josiah recognized the need to inform St. Clair. He must be in command, although he wondered what had happened to Gates. But the burial of his brother took priority.

The sentry's face softened. "I will arrange for him to be placed in the infirmary. We cannot leave the fort to bury him until dawn, if then." He paused. "If the commander permits, you may go there after you speak with him and make whatever preparations you wish."

Since Josiah was at the soldier's mercy, he agreed and headed in the direction of the major general's headquarters. A soldier blocked his entry until Van Dyke called out a greeting.

"Here's our man." Van Dyke sounded relieved.

Josiah wondered what sort of grilling the commander had subjected him to and what he himself now faced.

"Tuttle, is it? One of Ethan Allen's Green Mountain Boys?"

"Yes, sir."

St. Clair studied him. "Are the militia on the move? From Maple Notch, or elsewhere?"

"Not when we left, sir."

The man paced the small room. Maps studded the walls, splashed with red flags Josiah guessed represented the British. St. Clair's pacing had a frantic quality to it, as if he could find the path to victory in battle if he moved fast enough. The major general collected himself and stopped long enough to face Josiah directly. "I understand your brother was mortally wounded tonight by a British soldier. And that you responded bravely. I thank you for your service."

The look St. Clair directed at him focused all the rage and anguish roiling inside of Josiah. Without thought, he blurted, "I wish to stay here and fight, sir."

A thin smile played around the commander's lips. "Very well, Tuttle. I will consider your offer. We will have need of all the good men we can muster in the next few days, and Allen's militia has earned a good reputation."

Dismissed, Josiah checked on Solomon's remains. He wished he had a change of clothes to put on his body. After closing his brother's eyes and crossing his arms across his chest, Josiah did what he could to prepare him for burial. A lump formed in his throat. He had no way to alert the family to his death, to let news of the impending ceremony spread throughout the community so they could gather for a funeral dinner. What would he say to Father to explain what had happened? Guilt rained down on him like a thunderstorm in its intensity. He could think of only one person who might understand, who would at least listen without censure. *Sally.*

Josiah tarried by Solomon's side long enough to say a prayer for him, for himself, for all those who faced battle on the morrow. Then he approached the sentry who stood guard at the door.

"Do you have any scrip and quill that I can use?"

The man looked as though he would make a humorous remark but refrained when he glanced at the dead body. "I'm sure I can find something. Come, let me show you where you will spend the night.

A few men sat across the floor of the room where the guard conducted him. Soft snores suggested a few slumbered, while others read or wrote by candlelight. Josiah found a space near a wall sconce and propped his back against the wall.

He needed rest, but he doubted any would come. Instead, he took the time to consider what he would say to his father. As soon as he had paper and ink, he wrote the words that had formed in his mind. *Dear Sally. . . .* His heart poured out as the gloom of the night deepened.

Who knew if the letters would ever reach their intended recipients?

∽

Loud knocking rattled the door to the Reids' cabin, the sound a harbinger of anything but good news.

"Go into the loft," Sally told Nellie and Stephen. "Hurry! Now!"

The knocking repeated, and this time a loud voice called out, "Open the door in the name of the King!"

"What king?" Sally muttered to herself. Tories come to torment them while Pa was away fighting at Fort Ticonderoga. But she dared not ignore the demand.

Ma's face was whiter than the flour she was using to make bread. But she moved to the door, Sally following close behind. *Lord, protect us. Be our rock and fortress, as Your Word promises.*

A group of men circled the door, every one a Tory. Ben Tuttle was not among them, which surprised Sally.

"How may I help you?"

How did Ma keep her voice so calm? Sally's voice would sound like a schoolgirl if she spoke.

Marshall Hawkins, the brawniest of the Tory men, moved forward until he stood less than a foot from Ma. "You can 'help' us by getting off this farm. We claim your land in the name of King George."

"As you know, Mr. Hawkins, we do not recognize the right of the sovereign of England to dictate what we will or will not do." Ma spoke with nary a quiver to her voice, her chin high and steady in the air.

Indignation replaced Sally's earlier fear

Hawkins moved closer still, face-to-face with Ma. "Do you think you can stand up against us?"

Sally had heard enough. She pulled Ma behind her and placed her hands on the stays of her dress. "You're as bad a bully as your son was in school, Mr. Hawkins. If you wanted to help King George, you would have joined General Burgoyne. You wouldn't be coming around here, trying to frighten a bunch of women and children." Determination to do her Pa's bidding and protect the family filled her. "We won't be pushed off our land by the likes of you."

Hawkins looked around the farmyard—at the chickens clucking in their pen, the cows angling their heads over the fence rail, the corn shooting up in the field. "This is a lot for young Stephen to keep up by himself. It would be a shame if something happened to him."

The threat was plain.

Stephen. Fear shot through Sally.

"I must insist that you leave. Now." Ma's voice remained as steady as ever. Only Sally could feel the trembling of her arm where she put it around Sally's shoulders.

"Think about what I said." Hawkins gestured to the men surrounding him. "We *will* be back."

Sally and Ma stood in the doorway while Hawkins climbed on his horse's back and the gathering galloped away, straight through the cornfield, trampling several rows of new growth. She gritted her teeth.

The younger children must have watched them leave, because they scrambled down the ladder. Nellie flung her arms around her mother, sobbing. Stephen stood tall, looking so much like Pa that Sally wanted to cry. Her little brother was a boy trying to do a man's job. At thirteen, he was too young for such responsibility.

"What shall we do?" Ma's petticoats muffled Nellie's voice.

"We'll stay and raise our crops. Right, Ma?" Stephen asked for affirmation.

"We can't let those Tories stop us."

After the men left, some of the starch seeped from Ma's frame, and Sally led her to a chair. Pa expected Sally to take charge. If Pa were here, he'd fight them. But Pa wasn't here, and that was the problem. The Tories' threat endangered all the Patriot families whose men of fighting age were gone.

"Perhaps. . ." Ma swallowed the little tea left in her cup. The small drink seemed to revive her spirits, and she straightened in her chair. "I don't believe these men will hurt us. They are our neighbors, our friends." She placed a tender hand on Stephen's cheek. "If you wish to farm the fields, then of course we will stay. But it would be prudent for two of us to stay together at all times. Whether in the barn or plowing or here in the house. I know how to use a musket, if needed. Your father taught me when Indian attacks were a possibility."

Pride swelled in Sally's heart. Stephen was too young to remember the French and Indian War, and Nellie hadn't even been born then. Sally recalled several fearful nights when they had huddled under their beds and their parents had kept guard at the windows. Ma had shown plenty of courage then, and Sally could emulate her example now. She would fight General Burgoyne himself if he showed up to threaten her family.

"I'll go milk the cows." Stephen spoke as if nothing out of the ordinary had happened.

"Remember," Ma warned.

"I'll go with him. We'll finish more quickly that way." Sally seized the opportunity.

Nellie's face crumpled as she realized she would have to stay inside.

"You can help me finish the bread," Ma said. She was so good at soothing rumpled feelings. "But we left the dough to rise too long. We may have to start over with biscuits." Nellie shrugged and covered her hands with flour.

When Sally and Stephen were heading back to the cabin after milking, a lone figure appeared on foot at the edge of the field. Ben Tuttle. *Josiah's father.* Fear rushed into Sally's heart, whether for herself or for Josiah, she couldn't say. She pointed him out to Stephen, and they hurried inside.

"Mr. Tuttle's coming," Stephen announced.

"Alone," Sally hastened to add.

"Ben Tuttle has been our neighbor for my entire married life. He means us no harm."

Ben Tuttle the neighbor might mean them no harm, but Sally wasn't so sure about Ben Tuttle the Tory. Did he come with ill tidings about Josiah—or another friendly warning?

Nellie placed the biscuits in the oven as Tuttle arrived at the door. His gentle knock let them know they had a visitor. Ma cleaned her hands on her apron, straightened her skirts, and opened the door.

"Mrs. Reid." Josiah's father doffed his hat and inclined his head. "May I come in?" His shoulders sagged, as if his sons' absence weighed on him, but his usual belligerence was absent. Sally relaxed a fraction.

"Please enter. We were about to have a bite of supper, if you would care to join us." Ma offered the same invitation she had hundreds of times before.

Tuttle smiled, a sad smile that echoed Josiah's expression but without his warmth and good humor. "I don't think that would be appropriate in the circumstances."

Fear crept back up Sally's back. "Have you news from—about Mr. Van Dyke? Has he returned to safety?"

Tuttle shook his head. "It's too soon for news. No, I came because I'm aware of Mr. Hawkins' actions this day." His chest heaved with a great sigh. "I don't agree with this declaration of independence from Britain. You know that." He twisted his hat in his hands. "I also don't agree with threats of violence against women and children, but others do. They feel any means are—acceptable—in the battle we face." He looked straight at Ma, but his gaze encompassed Sally and the children. "I would not be a good neighbor if I didn't warn you. Other Patriot families have moved into town. For your own safety, I urge the same on you."

Sally wanted to respect this man, Josiah's father, but she couldn't remain quiet. "You are little better than they are. You say you don't sanction violence, but you're after the same end. No different. You want us off our land."

"Only until this—thing—is resolved. For your safety," Tuttle pleaded.

Stephen took a step forward, but Ma restrained him. "For the sake of our long friendship, Ben, I won't speak against you. But we will not give in to threats. My husband left me in charge of this land, this farm, and we will work it to the best of our ability."

Nellie crept next to Sally and glared at Mr. Tuttle.

"Thank you for your concern, Ben. But I think you'd best leave." Any hesitation Ma had shown earlier had fled.

Tuttle looked as though he would speak, then placed his hat on his head and turned to leave. He stopped long enough for one final comment before he opened the door. "Don't say I didn't warn you."

The door closed behind him with a whisper of wind.

The scent of freshly baked biscuits rose from the oven, and beans bubbled on the stove. Everyday, familiar events. Sally wondered how long they would continue.

After she served the meal, Ma led in prayer. When at last they said *Amen*, she looked at each child in turn. "We need not be afraid. *God* will protect us."

But Pa isn't here. Not even Nathaniel. Sally didn't know how her mother could express such certainty.

Her own heart harbored tremendous doubts.

Chapter 5

S t. Clair said *what?*" Josiah couldn't believe the command relayed to him by the guard who had greeted him upon his arrival at the fort.

"He gave the command to retreat. Both from here and from Mount Independence." The guard looked uncomfortable. "We're undermanned here. No one expected the British to drag cannon up Mount Defiance."

Perhaps, but give up the fort without a fight? Josiah couldn't imagine Ethan Allen doing such a thing. But the Green Mountain Boys weren't here, and his job under Major General St. Clair's command was to obey orders.

"I wanted to thank you again." Van Dyke, fully returned to health, found Josiah in the chaos surrounding their withdrawal from the fort. He now wore the makeshift uniform of the other soldiers. "You reminded me that there are some things worth fighting for." He glanced over his shoulder at an officer assembling his men. "Please convey my deepest sympathy to your family."

"God be with you." Josiah couldn't manage a warmer farewell. He rued the day he had ever set eyes on the New Yorker. Not that he blamed Van Dyke for the British attack on the fort, but apart from him, Solomon would never have left Maple Notch. God was sovereign, and Solomon would have given his life for his country ten times over. Nevertheless, his death seemed so pointless to Josiah. "I may join you later, but first I must break the news to my father."

Van Dyke gestured at the gathering troops. "It looks like they'll have need of all who are willing. God go with you, friend." He slapped Josiah on the back before marching away with determined steps.

As instructed, Josiah departed with the soldiers. A crazy part of him wanted to stay at the fort, to descend on the incoming British with a shout and die a heroic but needless death. When he thought of his father and his own role in Solomon's death, he knew he wouldn't, even if it were possible. When he thought of Sally, her sweet smile and winsome ways, he didn't want to. Not that he deserved her, or any woman, not after what he had let happen to his brother. So he passed through the gates. Only instead of heading to Lake George, he turned northeast into the woods. He wouldn't attempt the lake route again. Too many unfriendly eyes might see him from the shores; now that he traveled alone, he'd stand a better chance of avoiding encounters in the woods.

The following morning after he had breakfasted on hardtack and some newly ripened strawberries, he took his bearings and headed in the direction of Maple Notch. Before long, rustling in the bushes stopped his progress. He froze and then sought cover in the crook of a tree. Last night, he could have sworn that British troops had passed by. He had slept in fits and starts, certain he would be discovered at any moment. Had reinforcements arrived?

A bobolink's distinctive call sounded—the signal for the Maple Notch militia. Someone answered. Relief flooded through Josiah. *Friends*. He pushed through the foliage in the direction of their call. When he determined they were but a few yards away, he whistled.

"Who goes there?" David Frisk's familiar voice called out.

"Josiah Tuttle. I am coming in from the southwest." He didn't want some anxious militiaman to take aim.

"Approach."

No one had ever looked so welcome as the dirt-encrusted, weary men from Maple Notch—even the face of Brad Whitson.

"Josiah, what news do you have of the battle?" Mr. Reid came near and looked around him. "I thought Solomon was with you."

The welcome feeling that had enveloped Josiah a moment before fled. "Solomon's dead." The words forced themselves past his teeth.

A harsh murmur spread through the group.

"In battle?" Reid asked.

"What battle?" Josiah asked. "A handful of shots were exchanged, and then St. Clair ordered the troops to withdraw." He made no attempt to hide his bitterness. "We stumbled upon a British scout on our way to the fort. Solomon received a bayonet wound before I could fire."

Around Josiah, the faces of the men hardened. One of their own had died. "How do we reach the troops?" Reid wanted to know.

"We can't. The British lie in between. I considered staying, but someone has to tell my father what happened."

"Don't worry, lad. We'll find a way. We can avoid the fort easily enough."

That much was true. The walls gleamed in the sunshine, much easier to spot than the handful of men who blended in with the trees.

Josiah debated the reversal of his steps as he followed with the militia. With their arrival, he couldn't turn his back. He had written letters home, and someone would see they were delivered. The men wound their way around the bottom of Mount Independence, the site where Josiah had seen the fire burning. Was it only two nights ago? *Could the British still be there?*

A shot rang out. Battle had found Josiah after all.

∾

The Sunday after the militia's departure, Sally and her family attended church in Maple Notch. Even though their itinerant preacher wasn't in town, the Patriot families had decided to gather to pray for the militia as a community. Never had the promise "where two or three are gathered together in my name" meant so much.

But what about the Tories? The thought troubled Sally as she climbed down from the wagon with Stephen's assistance. How could they feel welcome at a church gathering such as this? They probably hadn't been invited. How did Christians with different political views worship together? Both sides believing in the same God, both praying for victory. . .her head swam in confusion. She could almost hear Nathaniel's teasing voice—*Leave the cogitation to the menfolk.* On the other hand, Josiah might listen because of his painful experience within his own family.

When they arrived at the white clapboard church, Sally saw none of the Tory families in attendance. Nearly all the Patriot families had gathered, and Sally remembered Mr. Tuttle's comment that others had moved to town. Was it true?

As soon as they stepped inside the church, Mercy Bailey scuttled in their direction. A warm-hearted soul even if given to a plenteous diet reflected by her girth, she greeted them warmly. "Mistress Reid. I am *so* glad you could make it with your family." She reached into her reticule and pulled out a slim sheet of paper. "Your husband left this with me for you. If you hadn't come today, I would have brought it to the farm."

"Thank you, Mistress Bailey." Ma tucked the letter, unopened, into her pocket and gestured for the children to find their usual bench.

First sight of the letter sent shivers up Sally's spine. Had something happened to Pa? To Nathaniel? Of course not. Pa had written only hours after the last time she had seen him. They hadn't even left town yet. Curiosity plagued her, and she wished she could read the letter for herself.

Elder Cabot walked to the front of the building with the aid of a cane. He moved well for a man missing half a leg. In spite of his three score years and ten, he had a warrior's heart like the psalmist David, and he would have gone with the militia if he could march with the others. Sally was selfishly glad he'd come to speak words of comfort and peace to the families left behind. His daughter came up beside him to move the heavy pulpit Bible in front of him, but he waved her away.

"I am speaking today from Psalm 66, verses 10 and 11: 'For thou, O God, hast proved us: thou hast tried us, as silver is tried. Thou broughtest us into the net; thou laidst affliction upon our loins.'"

The unexpected words sucked the breath out of Sally's body. Where were the verses promising victory from the God of battle and glory who strengthened their arms for war?

Elder Cabot removed his spectacles and rubbed at his watery eyes before continuing. "Our boys have not fought a battle for many a year. God has spared us. But elsewhere in the Good Book, in Judges, chapter 3, God says, 'Now these are the nations which the Lord left, to prove Israel by them, even as many of Israel as had not known all the wars of Canaan.' He left some nations unsubdued, so that every generation would learn the art of war." Cabot curled all but his index finger toward his hand and pointed at the congregation. "God always tests His people. Sometimes He tests us in illness and hardship as we go about our business. But at this time, He is testing us in war—both the men who are fighting, and those of us left behind." He came out from behind the pulpit and walked down the center aisle, every thump of his wooden leg seeming to count off one member of the militia.

"We have gathered here to pray for the safety of those we hold dear. I challenge you, let us pray rather that when we are tested, we will come forth as pure silver. Even if that means we go through the fire of affliction."

In spite of the July heat and the talk of fire, a chill ran through Sally, as cold as if she had plunged into the river in midwinter. She thought of the letter in Ma's possession and prayed it didn't portend bad news.

Somewhere behind them, soft sobbing broke out. Hannah Frisk, Sally guessed. She had lost her first husband in the French and Indian War and, of all the people gathered in the church, had the most to dread in this extension of military duty to her second husband.

Satisfied that he had done his duty, Elder Cabot returned to the pulpit and put his spectacles back on. His demeanor returned to that of a harmless schoolmaster. In a less commanding voice, he announced, "I will now read the names of our men who have gone to fight. I will pause after each name, to give us a moment to pray silently." He waved a sheet of paper. "I have written them down in alphabetical order. I don't remember things as well as I once did." A few giggles broke out across the room.

Orderly in this as in all things, Cabot didn't reach Pa or Nathaniel's names until near the end. He skipped right over Josiah and Solomon's names because they had left before the men heard of the battle. Still, Sally said a quiet prayer for their safe return. For Van Dyke, as well. The forest held other dangers than that of the marauding British.

The prayers lasted the better portion of an hour, but not even the youngest children fidgeted in their seats. At length, Cabot read the last names—William and Brad Whitson—and said, "*Amen.*" He closed in prayer, focusing on those left behind.

The chill that had pervaded Sally's soul vanished when they threw open the doors and summer sunshine streamed in. On such a beautiful day, she had a hard time believing any harm could befall the militia, and the balmy weather cheered her soul.

Later, after Stephen and Nellie had retired to bed, Sally dared to ask Ma about the letter from Pa. "What did he say?"

Ma took it out. The thin sheet already showed wear and tear from unfolding and refolding. She flattened it and handed it to Sally. " 'Tis nothing private. I'm certain he wants you to see it."

Pa mentioned the rumor that Tories would pressure the families of the Green Mountain Boys who were leaving for Ticonderoga. "But do not fear, beloved. Remember that the psalmist promises that God has given a commandment to save us in our just cause."

Apparently Pa and Elder Cabot disagreed on that point. Sally wanted to believe her father.

The letter continued. "If the pressure mounts, remember the strong habitation that God has provided for us. If you go there, you need not fear any evil."

"He's referring to Psalm 71, of course. It's one of his favorites." Ma tapped the words with her fingers.

Be thou my strong habitation, whereunto I may continually resort: thou hast given commandment to save me; for thou art my rock and my fortress. Sally recited the words to herself.

"And of course we must have faith in God while your father is absent from us." Ma's mouth twisted. "But I sense he is referring to something more." She brushed a weary hand over her forehead. "With this baby and in this heat, my mind doesn't seem to work as well as it used to."

Sally held back a gasp. Ma had birthed two dead infants in addition to her four living children; did she fear what was to come? Surely Pa would return before her time came.

"Does it suggest anything to you?" Ma asked.

Sally yanked her thoughts back from the fearful track they had headed. "A strong habitation. He's built the cabin well and strong, but he can't mean that. We're already here."

"We must pray God will make it clear to us. Now we'd best get to bed, or else we won't get any work done in the morning. Away to the loft with you." Ma settled into bed while Sally climbed the ladder.

When Sally blew out her candle, she saw the light of Ma's candle still burning below. Sally prayed that she could help ease the heavy load.

The men of Maple Notch took a different route home than Josiah had taken to the fort, sparing him the reminders of each stop and sight he and Solomon had shared on the trip south. Days and nights blended together, but at last they reached the turnoff for the Reid and Tuttle farms. They had marched since before dawn, and the sun had risen far enough that he could see the river's flow, low enough for him to cross without having to go north to the bridge that spanned the water.

He considered traveling the extra miles with the group to the bridge, in any case. He didn't relish the task that lay before him. But that was the coward's way out, and he was no coward. He turned to Nathaniel. "Shall we go, then?"

Nathaniel followed him blindly, moving in a daze. He went where directed, without apparent thought, ready to jump into a dry creek bed if told to do so. Josiah's sigh offered a prayer to God for strength, and he clasped his hand on his friend's shoulder. "Come, we're nearly home."

They splashed through the water—Josiah straightening Nathaniel when he stumbled over a rock midstream—and climbed out on the other side. The trees thinned, marking the way to the cleared land. The Reids' farmhouse lay no farther than a mile and a half distant. Josiah would rather it were ten miles, a hundred.

"Your mother will have breakfast ready by now. Warm vittles will be welcome." He forced cheer into his voice.

Nathaniel nodded as though it were expected of him but not understanding what had been said.

Josiah feared that he might run into Stephen at work already, but he didn't see the young man in the fields. Well and good. They neared the barn, and Stephen spotted them from where he was putting his tools away. Shouting, he raced to the cabin. Although Josiah couldn't make out the words, the boy's actions betrayed his excitement. Studying the neat, even rows provided a short distraction. Stalks of corn pushed into the air. They should have a good harvest. How had his father's farm fared?

"Ma." Nathaniel spoke for the first time since breakfast. He pointed across the field.

Mrs. Reid had left the cabin and ran toward them. When she saw who was coming, she stopped long enough for her children to join her. Nathaniel picked up speed at the point Josiah would have slowed. Resolute, he shouldered his musket and fell in behind.

"Nathaniel?" Mrs. Reid ran forward and pulled her son into her embrace. "Oh, thank God, thank God." She looked over her shoulder at Nellie, hovering near them. "Don't stand there gawking. Go get your brother some fresh water. He must be thirsty."

Without releasing her son, she turned her blue-green eyes so like Sally's on Josiah. "I fear you don't bring good news."

With God's strength, Josiah stilled the trembling that threatened his limbs. "The fort fell to the British." He started with the less devastating news.

Sally looked at him then, her face flushed with the summer's heat, her mobcap on sideways, and strands of oak-colored hair tumbling out. Even her worry was alluring. He wanted to erase the tiny lines that formed around her mouth. She stared into the forest, as if willing more men to appear. In no more time than it took to grab eggs from an unsuspecting chicken, she assessed the situation and turned her attention back to Josiah. "Where is Pa? And Solomon?"

Josiah felt Mrs. Reid's unspoken words. *Don't say it out loud. Don't make it true.*

"Pa's dead." Nathaniel pushed back from Ma. "Everyone else from Maple Notch got away, but they killed Pa." With the spoken words, the malaise that had affected young Reid disappeared for the moment, and he straightened to his full height.

Mrs. Reid wailed, and Nellie spilled water from the well at the sound. Josiah didn't know if he could bear it.

Chapter 6

S ally's eyes filled with tears at the news, but she sensed Josiah carried a heavier burden. "And Solomon?" She asked in a voice low enough for only him to hear.

"Dead."

Trial by fire. Elder Cabot's warning scorched through her. If this was what it took to become silver—she'd rather remain dross. She didn't bother holding her tears back but let them fall. Ma had her arms around Nathaniel and the younger children. Josiah stood alone with his grief. She reached out to touch him, wishing to comfort him as Ma comforted the others, but she held back. "Oh, Josiah. Thank you for letting us know." She couldn't manage any more.

Although Nathaniel draped a protective arm around the family, he had once again buried his head on Ma's shoulder.

"What—did anything happen to my brother?" Sally worried.

Josiah shook his head. "Shock. It hits some men harder than others."

Although only a year her senior, the weeks away had transformed Josiah into a man full grown. He had shouldered not only his brother's death but also the task of informing her family about Pa. A man she could depend on to do the right thing, at whatever the cost. Sally wished she could lean on him, but his expression told her he had set his face to return to his father and make that one, final act of contrition. She wanted to tell him she knew how hard that would be, that she would pray for him, but she didn't know how.

They stood in awkward silence for another moment before Josiah cleared his throat. "I must go home before someone else takes the news to Father." He heaved a sigh and seemed to lose six inches of his height.

"My prayers go with you." Sally paused. "Were there any other casualties among our men?"

Josiah shook his head.

Why my father? His brother? But Sally didn't voice her questions aloud.

"I will be back to help in any way I can, as soon as possible."

Oh Lord, help him. Only God could see them both through the hard days ahead.

∽

Josiah wanted to find a route to the farm that didn't retrace steps he had taken a hundred times with Solomon. But whichever way he turned, he found something that reminded him of his brother. That glade was where Solomon had gotten lost as a young boy, crying when at last Josiah had found him and brought him home. Over yonder was a rock where they had skinned Solomon's first deer. That tree marked the end of their races, which Josiah almost always won.

All too soon, he reached the edge of the clearing. Father faced away, checking the progress of the plants on the opposite side of the field. When had he grown old and frail? Or was it Josiah who had aged in the short fortnight of the trip south? A surge of love, of fierce protectiveness, washed over him. He would do whatever it took to care for his parent, even if it meant not fighting for the Patriot cause.

With renewed determination, he took a step forward, then another. Soon he was trotting. Less than half the field remained when Father turned. A wide smile spread across his face, then slowly turned to a thin line, neither smile nor frown.

"Welcome home, son." The embrace Father offered held none of the reservation of his smile. "Did you return Van Dyke safely to his home?"

"In a manner of speaking." Van Dyke had joined St. Clair's troops at the fort before he made it home. "He was well when last I saw him."

Father looked up at Josiah. When had that happened? When had he grown taller than his father? Or had Father shrunk, as sometimes happened in latter years? "Come to the cabin, and tell your mother and me about it at once."

Father didn't say another word and didn't even ask the obvious question—*where is Solomon?* Josiah didn't know if he should be relieved or worried.

"Mother! Our son has come home!" Father bellowed in the farmyard.

Almost at once, the door flung open, and his mother burst through. She ran and flung her arms around Josiah. Then she looked around his girth, to the right and the left, peering across the field. "Where is Solomon?" The panic he had expected from Father came through full force from Mother.

"Let's go inside." He didn't want to talk about Solomon's death in the barnyard as casually as if he were announcing a stranger come to town. He held the door for his parents and followed behind.

"Has Solomon joined up with those rebels, then?" Father sounded resigned. "I feared as much when the militia took off last week." A tired smile welcomed Josiah again. "Although I'm a little surprised that you came back, in that case."

"That's not what happened." Josiah quaked. "Solomon is. . .dead." He brought the word out with difficulty.

Mother's hand shot to her mouth, and she shook her head. "No, no, no!"

Bit by bit, Father pulled every last detail from Josiah. How Solomon had engaged the British sentry, how Josiah had killed the sentry. How he had spent the night at the fort and fought with the Green Mountain Boys, and how Mr. Reid had also died.

"These Patriots and their illusions of independence. It's evil, that's what it is." Father slammed his fist onto the table hard enough to send a splinter into his hand. "And now we're the ones suffering for it. At least you had the good sense to come home." He leaned toward his remaining son. "I tell you this much. I know you have a soft spot for the Reid girl. But don't you dare think of helping them out. Or any of those traitors to the king. I had urged moderation in the treatment of those wretched Patriots, but not anymore."

Confusion must have shown on Josiah's face, because Father continued, shouting now. "I won't be satisfied until we chase every one of them off their land and get it back for King George. Including those Reids. And if you set one foot in an enemy's house—don't bother coming home."

After Solomon's death, Josiah would do almost anything his father asked. Except neglect Sally Reid.

∽

How different this was from the homecoming Sally had expected. She thought when the men returned home she would fall asleep as soon as she lay down, at ease now that someone else could carry the burden.

Instead, she lay on her bed, twitching and turning at every sound, every hoot of an owl, every passage of a cloud over the moon. Rather than ease her mind, the return of the militia had multiplied the weight on her shoulders. Pa would never return. And Nathaniel. . .something about her brother had changed. He had taken his bedroll out to the barn, distancing himself physically as he already had mentally.

Without Pa, without Nathaniel, she and Ma were still in charge as much as before. With every passing day, the babe in Ma increased, and her physical exertions grew more limited.

Sally gave up trying to sleep. Instead, she prayed. As always, she started with praising God. The tremendous needs pressing on her fought to gain expression, but Sally wanted to focus first on God. *Almighty Father.* The familiar words stuck in her throat. Almighty? Then why had He allowed Pa and Solomon to die? Father? Then why had He taken her earthly father?

Lord and Savior. Jesus her Savior loved her, and nothing could separate her from that love. Clinging to that hope, she recounted the myriad ways God had shown His care for them that day. From the eggs the chickens laid for breakfast and the milk the cows gave, to a well that didn't grow dry, and even Nathaniel and Josiah's safe return. . . The fact that Pa now waited for them in heaven. At the thought, she buried her face in her pillow to stifle her sobs. As long as Nellie had taken to fall asleep, Sally didn't want her unrest to awaken her sister.

She slipped out of bed and stood by a small hole in the wall, the soft night breeze wafting through her hair. "What shall we do, Father? What if the Tories do come to force us out of our home?" She threw the question up at the sky. A fierce sense of protectiveness surged through her. She wouldn't let that happen. This land meant everything to Pa, after God and Ma, of course. The land was the reason his grandfather had left England and come to the new world. She wouldn't give it up, not without a fight.

The words of Pa's letter came back to her. *Remember the strong habitation that God has provided for us.* Looking at the night sky stirred a childhood memory. *So that's what Pa was talking about.* In the morning, she would discuss it with Ma.

∽

When Sally woke in the morning, having fallen asleep after her midnight prayer vigil, sun streamed through the rafters. Ma was calling up the ladder. "Sally! Come down!"

Sally slipped on her dress and skipped a rung or two on the way down the ladder. A pang of guilt hit her. She had stayed awake so long worrying about Ma that she had overslept and not helped when morning came. But something more than breakfast troubled Ma; Sally could hear it in her voice.

"Nathaniel has gone." Ma kept her tone even, but her knuckles where she kneaded her apron were pale white.

"He spent the night in the barn." Sally started for the door.

"No. Stephen has already gone out to check." Ma gestured for Sally to sit down and dished out porridge.

Stomach awash with new worries, Sally wasn't hungry, but she did as Ma requested.

Stephen came back in, a few pieces of hay stuck to his clothing, his hair askew. "He's cleared out. But he left this in the saddle bag." He handed over a small square of paper crammed with tiny script. Sally grabbed it from his hands and squinted at the faint letters.

"What does it say?" Ma held aloft the spoon she had used to dip the porridge, oats ready to drop on the floor. Absentmindedly she put it back in the pot and stirred the mixture.

Sally scanned the document twice. "He says. . ." She didn't want to say the words aloud, as if speaking them would confirm their reality. "He says he can't stay home and pretend nothing has changed. He wants Pa's death to count for something, and he's gone off to join St. Clair and the troops." She bit her lip to keep from crying. "He's joined the regular army, Ma."

Ma's face crumpled, and she let Stephen lead her to the table. "What will we do now?"

Stephen looked out the open door, as if calculating how he would finish growing the crops by himself. "I figure it's only a matter of time before all the Green Mountain Boys join in the battle. If I was old enough, I'd go, too."

Sally's throat constricted. Every boy old enough to play with toy soldiers dreamed of the day when he could fight in a real battle. But please, not Stephen, too.

"If that happens, the Tories will come back." Ma sounded less certain of herself than before Pa's death had left her in sole charge.

Sally thought of her middle-of-the-night conversation with God. "I think it's time we take Pa's advice. Last night I think I figured out why he mentioned that verse in Psalm 71. Remember that cave near the edge of our property? Over by the river?"

Ma gasped. "The cave. Of course."

"Sure I do. Nathaniel and I stayed there a few times." Stephen dipped a ladle into the water bucket and took a drink.

Sally stared at the man-boy before her. "If the Tories threaten us again, can the family live there?"

Stephen shrugged. "It's not home, but there is space enough for bedrolls and a fire pit. We could bring a few things from here and still be handy to the fields."

"What a wonderful idea!" The prospect of living in dismal, primitive conditions didn't bother Ma. She smiled. "That's it. Of course. Your father and I spent a few nights there after our wedding."

Sally conjured up an image of a wedding night spent in a cave and repressed a shudder.

"The cave will make a fine home. The Tories would have to work hard to catch us there, and we can continue to work the farm." Some of Ma's earlier enthusiasm had returned. The smell of scorched porridge steamed from the pot hanging over the fire, and Ma removed it. "Unless you think we should move into town with the other families." Her voice trailed off.

"Pa would want us to work the land." Sally wondered why she was lecturing her mother on her father's wishes. But Pa *had* asked her to watch out for Ma. "If they threaten us, we can leave the fields that day. But there's nothing to stop us from returning, not as long as we're close by."

"I think she's right, Ma." The challenge had excited Stephen.

"Can you handle the work by yourself, Stephen?"

"I'll help," Sally said.

"Me, too!" Nellie added.

"Very well, then." Determination straightened Ma's spine. "Let's get ready for the cave. Move things a few at a time, so as not to arouse any suspicion." She looked around her kitchen, and Sally saw it with her eyes. The shelf Pa had built to hold a candle and the family Bible. The flour and sugar tins bought from a traveling peddler. The well-crafted oven built into the side of the fireplace. Everything a well-provided cabin could offer. And Sally was asking Ma to give it up to cook over an open fire in a hole in the ground.

Elder Cabot's words came back to her. All of them would have to sacrifice to bring the new republic to life, a birth by fire.

After promising to come back at lunch to carry a few things to the cave, Stephen took Nellie to the barn to choose which tools to move. Sally sat down with Ma and surveyed the kitchen.

"How shall we manage to move it all?" Sally looked at the jars and crocks along the wall.

"We won't. We don't need much. A pan or two. A few staples. We'll live simply." Ma patted Sally's hand. "Thank you for speaking up. You're right: it's what your father would have wanted."

With the decision made, Sally pondered the implications. If they lived in the cave, would anyone know they were there? Should anyone? What if they were still there when the time came for Ma to have her baby?

"I want to tell Josiah." The words popped out of Sally's mouth.

"Josiah Tuttle?" Ma raised her eyebrows. "That we're going to the cave?"

Sally hadn't intended to voice the thought, but it felt right. She nodded.

"I don't think that's wise, dear. Josiah has been a stalwart friend, but he has problems of his own now."

An ache pounded in Sally's heart. She wanted to speak with Josiah to ease his pain as she shared her own. Of all the people she wouldn't see once they moved, she would miss Josiah most of all. The tears she had held at bay ever since hearing about Pa spilled down her cheeks.

"Oh my dear girl." Ma dabbed at her cheeks with the corner of her apron. "I know, I know. But Ben's been given an awful burden to bear, and he won't look kindly on us, I fear."

That's not right, Sally fumed. *It's not our fault Solomon died.*

But the heart didn't always listen to reason. Even Sally knew that. She drew in a deep breath.

"If he comes looking for us?" Sally voiced her hope aloud.

"Then we'll see."

Sally helped Ma sort through her kitchen things, putting together a small crate with essentials. As she placed a crock of molasses, a tin of flour. . . with each item she packed, she said a prayer.

Oh Lord, let it be. Let it be.

Chapter 7

A familiar bobolink call drew Josiah's attention as he walked through the fields. The militia wanted his attention. But Father worked only two rows over. He couldn't slip away undetected.

The dinner bell sounded, solving the problem. Josiah called to Father, "I'll be right there. I think I see a rabbit at the end of the clearing. Perhaps we can have some stew this evening."

Lord, is that a sin? Josiah decided it wasn't. He had seen movement that could be a rabbit, even though he didn't think so. He strolled to the edge of the cultivated area, but as soon as Father went into the house, he sprinted toward the woods.

To his surprise, David Frisk, not Nathaniel Reid, waited for him.

"The Green Mountain Boys are gathering?" Josiah asked.

David nodded. "Allen has called us together. It's time for us to fight the British with the rest of the colonies."

Josiah shifted his feet. A month, even two weeks ago, he wouldn't have hesitated, no matter what Father said. But now, with Solomon's death, everything had changed.

"When?" was all he asked.

"On the morrow. We're joining with groups from Stowe and St. Albans and going to meet Allen." When Josiah didn't reply, David made as if to move. "We'll see you, then, on the green at daybreak. I have others I need to alert."

"Wait a moment." Tomorrow didn't give Josiah much time to decide. Not that he needed any. No amount of waiting would change the circumstances. "I can't come with you." The words pulled from the depths of Josiah's soul like coal being dragged from the fire in his belly through his throat. "Not with Father so opposed. Not after Solomon's death."

"You're not turning into a Loyalist, are you?" Frisk frowned. "Of course not. You're in a difficult position. We all recognize that. I can't say I'm surprised. Sorry to lose you, though. You're a good man."

A good man. That was a laugh. A man who had let his own brother die. "What about Nathaniel Reid? I expected him to bring the news."

"Young Reid? I thought you knew since you're so close. He's already

54

gone." Frisk waved farewell and melted back into the forest.

Josiah's heart followed Frisk's footsteps before he headed back for the cabin. A rabbit did cross his path, and Josiah made a halfhearted effort to catch it before it hid in the tall grass.

So Nathaniel had already joined the battle.

No matter what Father said, Josiah had to visit the Reids.

∽

"Now there. This isn't so bad." Ma placed her hands on her hips and relaxed a fraction. They had finished moving the last of their things into the cave.

Sally didn't agree. The cave had seemed spacious enough upon first sight, only a little smaller than their cabin. The problem was that they had twice as much to put in the same amount of space. Without a loft, all four of them would have to sleep in close quarters.

"At least it's summer. We won't need a fire as much," Sally observed, although she pulled her arms close against the cold.

Ma shook her head. "It won't get much warmer in here. It stays pretty much the same temperature year round. Caves tend to be that way, Don told me." She pointed to the fire pit, a small indentation between the bedrolls. "And I already have a place to cook."

Sally rubbed her elbows. It might work, although the adjustment from midsummer heat to the dank coolness of the cave might bring on a cold. Of course they wouldn't work in the crucible of the daytime. They hoped when the Tories found the abandoned cabin with letters from Ma's family in far-away Dover, they would think they had left. Perhaps they would relax when they discovered the Reids weren't at home or in town.

All four of them had spent the last couple of days moving things to the cave, scurrying two at a time, in the predawn hours and again in twilight's fading light. They had brought three of their laying hens with them. Their livestock had given them the greatest concern. If they had truly moved, they would have brought the animals with them. But as things stood, they couldn't sell them or tend to them on a regular basis without alerting the town to their real plans. They let the horses and bulls go to forage in the fields; during the summer, the animals should have plenty. The milk cow required daily attention. They put her in a fenced area near the field.

They considered working during the nights. On evenings when the moon and stars provided sufficient light, they did. But most times they couldn't see with the available nighttime light and didn't want to run the risk of artificial illumination visible from miles away—from the Tuttles' farm, specifically. The best times to work proved to be predawn and twilight.

They made a quick supper of leftover beans and headed for the field, neglected too long in their haste to move.

"Do we have to?" Nellie covered a yawn with her hand. Poor Nellie. The first night she had chattered nonstop, talking so much that Sally was afraid her very voice would give them away. Last night, she had drooped a little, and tonight, when they needed her in the fields, she could hardly move.

"I don't wish to leave you here alone." Ma hugged her youngest to her. "But bring your coat with you. If you get too tired, you can use it to cushion your head and take a nap."

Stephen scowled a bit at that announcement—probably wondering why he had to work when Nellie didn't—but Ma's compassionate wisdom impressed Sally as always. She grabbed the hoes waiting by the entrance and stooped to exit the cave.

A couple of hours later, Sally wished she could join Nellie where she lay on the ground. The hoe proved useless, so she dropped it and pulled at the weeds with her hands. *Stop slashing so hard, or you'll pull up the plants by the roots.* She felt so lonely, so cut off from people. Without Pa—Nathaniel—Josiah—and only Ma and her younger brother and sister for company, she could predict how each day would go, how each person would act and what they would say. She missed Josiah more than she thought possible. Until their contact had been cut off, she hadn't realized how much she *counted* on seeing him.

Ever since she was a little girl, Nathaniel would head over to the Tuttle farm to play, or Josiah and Solomon came their way. How she missed those days. Her heart swelled with longing for all of them. Josiah. Nathaniel. Solomon. *Pa.* Maybe she focused on Josiah's absence because she didn't want to think about Pa's death. She blinked back tears. If Ma, who had loved Pa enough to marry him and was still carrying his child, could keep on working, so could she.

She glanced one row over, where Nellie lay curled up on the ground, shawl tucked around her shoulders. Ma bent over and took the spade from her hands. When she straightened, she put her hand to the small of her back to support her increasing bulk. She saw Sally watching her and smiled wearily.

"Not much more to do tonight."

Sally looked at her half-finished row. *Move faster,* she scolded herself. She didn't want to hold the family up, to need their help to finish her task so they could all retire for the night.

"It's a mite bit dry." Stephen ran dirt through his fingers. "It would be good if we could water it."

"We can bring water from the river in the morning." Sally glanced at Ma.

"Since we only have two yokes, Stephen and I will go. Why don't you stay home with Nellie?"

Home. What a strange word to apply to a cave. By this hour of the night, she was ready to go to their new home, whatever it might be. Sweeping down the rest of her row, she tugged out a handful of weeds and announced, "There. I'm done." She bent over Nellie and shook her awake. She wished one of them could carry her sister, but the fact of the matter was, not even Stephen was big enough to carry his half-grown sister.

The four of them trudged under the canopy of trees, following a trail that became more defined each day. Perhaps they should change the path they took. If someone came looking for them, they would spot their tracks easily enough. The thought hopped into Sally's mind like a rabbit and then out again. Nellie entered the cave first and lay near the far wall. As the least likely to roll and get hurt, Sally went next, by the fire, with Ma on the opposite side. Musket ready to hand, Stephen slept nearest the entrance. Flames flickered across Ma's tired face, and Sally lifted her up in prayer. She recited her ABCs—*The Lord is almighty. He is blessed. He is compassionate*—before she succumbed to sleep. Predawn hours came early during summer.

When Sally woke the next morning, Ma and Nellie still slept soundly. *And may they stay that way*. Ma needed the rest. Sally scooted around the fire and Ma's sleeping form to join Stephen at the entrance to the cave.

"Good, you're ready," Stephen whispered as he handed her a yoke with two canvas satchels attached. "We need extra time since we're going to the river first." Instead of climbing the slope, he headed down the bank and dipped his first satchel into the water. This summer, he seemed to grow by the day, his legs ever lengthening, making it harder and harder for her to keep pace. But he was right. They needed to get started as soon as possible. If only they could check on their cabin. The militia had only been gone a few days, but had one of the Tory families already taken up habitation in their home? Surely not, for they would have seen the crops growing. She shook her suspicions off and sped her steps.

The river felt cool to the touch, but a sniff of the air promised another heat-laden day. If God didn't send rain soon, they might lose most of the crop regardless of their efforts. All the discomfort and worry of hiding out from the Tories would count for nothing. Stephen finished filling his sacks first and slung the yoke over his shoulders before he helped her balance her yoke. They were fortunate, she knew, to have two yokes for hauling supplies, even if neither was fitted to their size. Pa and Nathaniel had originally used them.

Due to the added weight and the care needed to walk through the forest, they arrived at the clearing later than usual. She hated to think of a return trip if they spilled the precious water. Stephen was starting on his second row by the time she arrived at the edge of the clearing. The corn had grown tall, but not yet tall enough to hide any of them except for Nellie. When she bent low enough to trail some water along the roots, the growing crop hid her form. Darkness was turning to deep lavender in the east. The possibility of discovery always frightened her.

Sally had worked halfway down her first row when Stephen came up beside her. He slid onto the ground and pulled her with him.

"I thought," he panted out in a whisper, "I saw someone at the edge of the field."

"Who?" Sally's worst fears bubbled up in her throat.

"Not sure. Might have been my imagination."

When Sally attempted to get to her knees, Stephen stopped her. "Wait." The whisper sounded as loud as musket fire to her sensitive ears.

Using her arms and legs like a baby, Sally crawled through the dirt to the edge of the field. Long morning shadows should keep her presence hidden. She wiggled to a spot where she could see most of the farmyard, dawn's light revealing the familiar outlines of barn and cabin.

She also saw one familiar outline that had no business being there. One revealed by the brush of light. Tall, dark-haired, broad-shouldered.

Josiah Tuttle.

∽

Josiah had chosen the early morning hours to visit the Reids' farm in the hopes of deflecting his father's interest in his activities. A promise of a fresh catch of fish gave Josiah the opportunity he needed, and he would go to the river—eventually. First of all, he wanted to check on the Reids. If he were honest with himself, he wanted to check on one Reid in particular. *Sally.*

A cursory glance around the cabin confirmed that the Reids were no longer in residence. A thin layer of dust coated their table, and the family Bible had disappeared. No fire burned on the hearth.

They weren't in town, either. Quite pleased with himself, Father had come back from his most recent trip with tales of all the traitors who had fled to town. But no stories about the Reids. "They've gone to New Hampshire, or so I've heard."

Josiah spotted a letter addressed to Mrs. Reid from a Sarah Huckaby of Dover that confirmed the rumor, but he couldn't bring himself to believe they had left Maple Notch for New Hampshire. Not Mrs. Reid. Not Sally. Vermonters through and through, they would see out the war, no matter what happened—although losing a loved one could change a person, as he knew from personal experience. Look at what had happened to his father. He changed overnight from a compassionate man, even if they disagreed about politics, to a man set on revenge. Perhaps Mr. Reid's death had set Mrs. Reid scurrying for the closest protection she could find.

Josiah swept through the cabin again, seeking some evidence of where they might have gone. Not only clothes were gone, but also foodstuffs and other necessities. In searching the barn, he found no sign of the expected implements. Did they take their hoes and axes with them to town?

In the yard, he saw numerous signs of absence. Weeds had grown over the kitchen garden, and a plank covered the well, to prevent accidents. He spotted broken blades of tall grass at the border of the clearing and walked through. A few feet ahead, he saw the one thing he didn't expect—a field of standing corn, beans, and squash, with every evidence of tender nurture.

The stalks of corn parted, and two figures emerged from between the rows—Stephen and Sally Reid.

Not in New Hampshire. The thought comforted Josiah at the same time it terrified him. *Here, on the farm.*

When he stared at the beauty with hair the color of oak before him, a lump the size of Rhode Island formed in his throat. He didn't know what to say, if he could say anything. "Sally." Her name squeaked in his effort to get it out of his mouth. "You didn't go." In spite of the mud coating her clothing, she had never looked so beautiful to him. Perhaps he was drawn to the spirit shining from her eyes. This woman never gave up, no matter what. One thing was for certain: the Reids had continued to work their farm.

"Josiah." A sad look splashed across her face. "You didn't go with the Green Mountain Boys."

The disappointment in her voice burned Josiah to the core. *Sally, it's me. Josiah.* He wanted to reassure her, but he didn't. He knew the heavy burden her family carried, and another thought occurred to him. "Daniel Frisk told me Nathaniel went."

"Of course." Stephen was less patient with Josiah than his sister. "Not like *some* people who change their minds when the going gets tough."

"Stephen!" Sally's green eyes flashed with annoyance.

Josiah relaxed a tiny bit. Not everything was lost if she still defended him to her brother.

Stephen harrumphed but quieted. Sally glanced around them. "Did you come alone?"

"Yes, I'm alone." Josiah had endured enough of their doubts. "I came, hoping to find you. You left without a word. You weren't in town. We've been neighbors too long"—*You've been in my heart too deep and too long*—"to leave without saying good-bye."

Sally looked at the ground. When she faced him again, determination gleamed dark green in her eyes. "That might have been true. Before the war came and changed everything."

"Nothing has changed between us." He shook his head, as much to clear his mind of what Father would say if he learned of this conversation, as in denial of Sally's words.

"How can you say that? *Everything's* changed. Your brother's dead. My father's dead. Things will never be the same again."

And my father is one of the people driving you off your land. But Josiah didn't voice that thought. "That's why we need to help each other. We've both experienced a great loss."

"Are you saying you want to help us?" Stephen had heard enough. "Come, Sally. Leave him be. You can't trust him or his father."

Josiah considered ways to convince them of his sincere desire to help. Actions might work where words failed. Without asking permission, he grabbed a canvas satchel of water and walked down the row, tipping a little onto each plant as he passed.

∽

Stephen glared at Josiah and then at his sister. She knew her brother wanted her to reprimand Josiah, to tell him to leave. But pain had filled his voice.

Sally spoke. "We can't go home yet. Not while he's here. If he's truly a danger to us"—her words earned a scowl from Stephen—"he'd follow us to the cave. Is that what you want?"

"Of course not."

Josiah finished the row and headed back across the clearing in the direction of the cabin—and his home.

"What are you doing?" Panic surged through Sally. Was Josiah going back to his farm, satchel in hand as evidence of the Reids' continued presence on the land? She wavered, fighting her instinct to bolt, unwilling to assume the worst.

Josiah stiffened. He set down the satchel and strode down the row until he faced them again. "I'm helping. That's what I'm doing. We haven't seen much rain." He gestured with the satchel. "If you help me, we might finish before the sun comes up."

Without waiting for Stephen's reaction, Sally picked up her other satchel and started down the next row. Stephen hesitated for another moment, then joined in. They didn't speak again until they finished watering the field.

Josiah broke the silence. "Tomorrow morning, I must catch some fish, or Father will begin to question the use of my time. But the day after that. . ." He glanced at Stephen before focusing his warm, brown eyes on Sally. "I'll be back to help as much as I can." He tipped his tricorne and left.

Josiah had said he was coming back.

Sally wasn't sure if the news made her glad—or scared.

Chapter 8

D id you catch any fish?"

Josiah cringed at Father's harsh voice. The sun had already risen by the time of his return. Father had completed all the chores, a job that made him grumpy. "A man expects his son to help around the farm."

Josiah shook his head. "You knew I wouldn't be here this morning."

Father grunted. "And now I suppose you'll be wanting breakfast. Your mother has it waiting for us. Time was that if a man didn't catch food, he didn't eat."

Another one of Father's favorite topics—how much harder life *used* to be for farmers. The colonists had wrested food from the untamed land and the land from the unfriendly Indians and made life, if not easy, more bearable for their sons. They should thank the English kings for making the opportunity possible.

Why couldn't Father see that times had changed? No matter what opportunities the king had provided his subjects in the past, he had pushed the American colonies beyond the breaking point through unfair taxation. Taxation without representation went against law and common sense. All that the Patriots wanted, at least at the beginning, was the same consideration their fellow citizens in Britain enjoyed. But Father and those like him considered the Patriots a bunch of traitorous ingrates.

Josiah knew better than to voice any of those thoughts. Instead, he sniffed the air to draw attention away from his morning's outing. "I do appreciate Mother's cooking. It smells like she's frying bacon."

Father smiled. "And hasty pudding browned in the grease. Come on, lad. Fill up. We have a full day ahead of us."

The men didn't speak much as they ate their breakfast. Afterward, Father took the Bible down and read from Romans 13, with its pointed directive to submit to government. "These Patriots aren't just rebelling against the king; they're rebelling against God's order." Father looked at him, but Josiah kept his gaze straight down, refusing to meet his father's eyes. He didn't want to get into an argument.

"I'm talking to you, son!" Father thundered. Mother made a fluttery motion with her hands that caught the corner of Josiah's eye. Lest he cause her more distress, he looked up at last.

"It says right here, 'If thou do that which is evil, be afraid; for he beareth not the sword in vain.' I'm thinking I've been too soft toward these Patriots. Perhaps the others are right. We should insist they turn over their farms to us in trust for the king."

Josiah bit the inside of his cheek to keep from saying something he might regret.

"They've done evil! They've attacked the king, and they killed *my son*!"

Josiah was certain that Father wouldn't want a reminder that Solomon had died at the hands of a *British* soldier.

"I want to do my part. Tell me, son, what did you see when you passed the Reids' cabin today?"

Panic flooded through Josiah. If Father inspected the neighboring farm, he would guess the Reids hadn't left the area. The simple fact that the crops were thriving would advertise the fact to a casual observer. Father mustn't go to the farm. A possible solution to his dilemma took shape.

"They're not living there." Josiah spoke the literal truth while he scrambled to see if his idea would work. No objections came to mind. "But they had already planted the crop, and young Stephen tended it well before they moved, from what I've seen." He bit into a crisp slice of bacon and chewed on it. God didn't stay his spirit. "It seems a shame to let the planting go to waste. I'd be willing to work their fields." *Alongside of them, for their benefit,* of course, but he didn't voice those words.

Father stared at him. "You would work the Reids' farm? For me?"

"And for myself." He may not have gone with the Green Mountain Boys to fight, but he could help those who were left behind. He would work harder than he ever had in his life, not for his father's sake, but to help a fellow Patriot—to help *Sally*.

"I don't know." Father frowned, and Josiah held his breath.

Please, don't let him object.

"I need your help here around our farm." He blinked once. "With Solomon gone. . ."

"I think Josiah's plan is a good one, provided he continues to work with you in our fields." Mother placed fresh hasty pudding on the table. "You mustn't overwork yourself, Mr. Tuttle. The doctor warned you after your illness last year." Dear Mother. She might guess the real reason for Josiah's interest in the Reids' farm, but she hadn't mentioned it. "I'll do whatever I can around the farmyard."

"Very well. As long as you keep up with your work here, I won't keep my son from earning the right to land of his own."

"I promise. I'll go early or late, but I'll work with you in the fields every day."

Josiah ate with a better appetite. He no longer needed an excuse to travel to the Reids' farm.

∽

"Do you think we'll see him tonight?" The prospect of Josiah's presence had brightened Nellie's day, and she had started for the field eager to begin work.

At least one person in Sally's family shared her happiness at the prospect of seeing Josiah again.

"I hope not," Stephen said.

"Whyever not?" Nellie asked.

"Because his father is a Tory." Stephen made the word sound like the unpardonable sin. "And he didn't go with the Green Mountain Boys."

"But his brother just died," Sally reminded him.

"So did Pa, but that didn't keep Nathaniel at home, did it?" Stephen had raised his voice beyond the whisper they employed on their way to the fields.

"Stop it! All of you!" Ma's voice came at whisper level but with all the intensity of a preacher's oration. "We already laid this to rest. Stephen, we'll welcome his help. On the farm. But we won't let him know where we are living."

She turned her burning eyes, too bright for her wan face, at Sally. "*And we will take different routes back and forth to the field.*" A branch reached out and struck Ma in the face before she had a chance to brush it away. Tonight was the first time they had taken this particular route, one that lay through a thicker stand of trees. "Now hush so that we don't give away our presence."

Sally appreciated, welcomed, *wanted* Josiah's help. The past two days had sped by in anticipation of seeing him tonight. But would their friendship alienate Stephen? Why did the war have to come between neighbors? Between family members?

What would Pa have wanted her to do? *Josiah Tuttle's a good man.* His words echoed in her mind. How she wished she could talk things over with Ma. But with everything that had happened—Pa's death, Nathaniel's absence, the coming baby—Sally didn't want to add to her distress more than necessary.

Besides, war was no time to think about love and family.

Sally broke her stride. *Was* that how she thought about Josiah? *Don't be a ninny.* How had she construed his offer to help them with the farm into an offer of courtship? Pulling her attention away from thoughts of Josiah, Sally started moving again.

Nellie fell back and gestured for Sally to bend over. "I like Josiah," she whispered in Sally's ear.

Sally squeezed Nellie's hand in answer but didn't give voice to the words echoing in her own heart.

I like him, too.

Stephen reached the field first, Ma next, while Sally and Nellie brought up the rear. Another time, they might go in two groups. Going through the forest all together as they did, they must sound like a pair of bucks in battle. Sally parted the trees at the edge of the clearing, and her breath caught in her throat.

The early dawn revealed the muscular back of a man already at work on the rows. *Josiah.* He looked so stalwart, so steady—all the things that Stephen longed to be but hadn't yet attained. Why couldn't *he* see the good in his brother's friend? And why did Ma seem so—ambivalent? *Cautious.* That was the better word, and the course Sally had to agree was wise.

Upon their approach, Josiah turned, and Sally thought she caught a smile on his face, although the dark made it hard to tell.

"So you came." Stephen approached the taller man with all the swagger the role thrust upon him demanded.

"I did." Josiah's voice matched the smile spreading across his face.

"Your father?" Ma made it a question.

"Father won't be a problem. I told him I plan on working your farm as my own."

Sally's mouth fell open. Unwilling to give Josiah the satisfaction of seeing her discomfort, she clamped it shut. Did Josiah see helping them as a means to gain their land as his own?

"So he thinks I'm here every day, working the land for the King. . . ."

Are you?

"And he's fine with that, as long as I go back and help him with our farm, as well."

Ma nodded, as if she had expected this development. Fury raced through Sally. The first thing Josiah did after discovering their secret was tell his father he would work at their farm every day. What would happen if Mr. Tuttle decided to pay a visit? What then?

If Josiah has already betrayed the working farm to his father, what else might he betray? She couldn't shake the thought. From here on out, she vowed to be careful.

∽

A week later, Sally still hadn't decided whether she could trust Josiah. She jammed her hoe into the dirt with her foot. Instead of pulling out the weed, she bent the delicate corn stalk in half, and the hoe broke away from the handle from the pressure. Her hand slid down the wood, and a splinter dug into her finger. She lifted it to her mouth and sucked on the blood that trickled out.

Josiah noticed her distress and sprinted through the field to her side. "What happened?"

"I'm not a child. It's only a splinter."

He lifted an eyebrow at the broken implement and fallen plant. But he didn't mention them and instead took her hand in his. "I'll have you know I'm an expert at splinters. Solomon got them all the time."

How could he say Solomon's name so easily? Her family rarely mentioned Pa. The pain was too great.

"This is a pretty big one. Hold your breath. It may hurt as I take it out."

Doing as Josiah suggested didn't ward off the pain, and Sally bit her lower lip to keep from yelping. It left a small, ragged hole, and she sucked on her finger to stop the bleeding. She didn't want to distract the others. She needed to return to work, but how could she without a hoe?

Replacing the hoe would be a problem. They had—used to have—four hoes exactly, one for each of them. An abundance, one for Pa and each of the two boys with a spare. Since everyone had started working the fields, all four had seen constant use.

What could Sally do? The tools to make a new handle had been left in the barn. They couldn't go to town and buy one. Without a hoe, Sally would be about as useful as a dry spring on a hot day.

Pieces in his hands, Josiah looked at her as if reading her mind. A smile flickered across his face. He pressed the broken ends together before grimacing. "Can't be mended."

She already knew that.

Stephen noticed they had stopped working and came over to check. "What happened?" He scowled at the broken hoe in Josiah's hands.

Upset as Sally was, she couldn't let her brother blame Josiah. "I used it too hard, and it broke apart."

"Gave her a big splinter." Josiah flicked the offending piece on the ground. "She'll need to keep watch that her finger doesn't become infected."

Why was he telling Stephen, as if she couldn't take care of herself?

"We brought a froe with us, but we'll have a hard time finding a suitable log in the dark." Stephen's shoulders slumped. "I guess you could use Nellie's hoe until we make another one. She doesn't get a lot done." He glanced to the spot where his sister poked at weeds between yawns.

All Sally could think about was the hurt Nellie would feel if she took her job away from her. "Or I could use Ma's hoe so she could rest."

"Don't worry about it. I'll get you another one." Josiah flashed a big smile at them. "Tomorrow. The night is full dark. Our time for work is over for the day." He turned his back so he wouldn't see the direction they took to their hiding place.

How could Josiah get them another hoe without giving away their secret to his father? Sally pondered the question of Josiah's loyalty all the way back to the cave, wondering if he watched their every move.

～

Josiah waited until the Reids left the field before he began the journey home. Every day they played the same game. The Reids tarried, not wanting him to see the direction of their abode. In turn, he waited, thinking that his presence in the field would explain any disturbance created by their work. As a consequence, they often worked past the point of safety. He would speak with Sally about that.

No, not Sally. Mrs. Reid or Stephen. Although Sally might listen more readily.

When no further sounds reached Josiah's ears, he allowed himself to scan the forest for any telltale signs of their movements. As usual, he saw none, not so much as a bent stalk. He breathed a sigh of relief and headed toward home.

With any luck, he would catch a few hours of sleep before arising for another day's work. He rubbed his eyes and picked up his pace along the path worn between the two farms over their years as neighbors.

Neighbors. And who is my neighbor? The parable of the Good Samaritan had come to life. Nothing had separated the two families—not until the Continental Congress and the Declaration of Independence. Now Father would no more countenance Josiah helping the Reids, classified as "the enemy," than the Levite had stopped to help the wounded Samaritan. He would pass Josiah, wounded and dying at the side of a mountain road, if he were dressed in a Patriot uniform.

Oh, Lord, heal our families. Our hearts.

To distract himself from those dismal thoughts, Josiah turned his mind to Sally, to the way she had held back her tears when he pulled the splinter out of her hand, the smile that played across her face while she hummed to herself and plied the hoe.

The hoe. He couldn't return home with his own implement and pretend it had broken overnight. Even worse to bring back two hoes. Wearily, he retraced his steps back to the Reids' barn and left his own hoe there. Father wouldn't be pleased about his carelessness, but he shouldn't guess that Sally was the one who had broken it, especially not in the dim light of the barn.

Half an hour later, Josiah fell asleep on the hay in his barn, not even bothering to go into the house. He didn't awaken until the rooster announced the dawn on the following morning. *Too late, too late.* Already he heard Father opening the door and pulling a milking stool up to their cow.

Groaning, Josiah wondered what to do. Father thought him gone at this time of day. Should he announce his presence or not?

Father gave a sharp cry. "What's this doing here?" Enough light came through the cracked door to reveal the thin slab of wood in his hands.

The hoe. The thought roused Josiah to action. He made noises suggesting he had only then awakened. "Father! Are you up early?"

"So that's where you are." Father threw the hoe away from the cow and continued working her udders. "I'm not early. You're late. You know that the early bird—"

"Gets the worm. I know."

"Repair that hoe, or you'll be no use to me today." Father crinkled his nose. "And take a few minutes at the pump, for your mother's sake."

At least Father hadn't probed any farther into the matter of the broken hoe, Josiah mused.

"What's this?"

Josiah had given thanks too soon. Father was turning the broken end in his hands. "Looks like blond hair. Not yours." He pulled a strand from the site where the blade met the wood.

Josiah held his breath. Would Father make the connection with the light-haired Reids?

Father pulled his lips together, as if to recall a memory.

Pretending to study the offending hair, Josiah flicked it onto the straw, where it disappeared. "It's silver, Father. We can't see very well in this light. Probably came from your own head."

"Humph." Father finished with the cow. "Take this milk to your mother. I'll see to the chickens."

Josiah sighed. Another threat averted.

Tomorrow he *had* to get up on time. No matter how late the night.

Chapter 9

*W*here is he? Sally's gaze shifted to the far side of the field for the tenth time in as many minutes. The sky had turned from dark blue to pale lavender, with sunrise just over the horizon. Still Josiah hadn't come.

She shook her body to get rid of the mosquitoes that buzzed around her. If only she could get rid of her worries that Josiah might have gone to his father with news about their activities as easily. Her mind drifted along unhealthy paths.

Ma spoke to Nellie for a moment and then joined Sally. "He's probably seeing to the hoe." Ma kept her voice low so Stephen couldn't hear her words.

That was what Sally feared—that Josiah was showing the broken hoe to his father and—

"Remember the verse your pa gave to us: 'Be thou my strong habitation, whereunto I may continually resort.' I hate to see you fret yourself. Keep resorting to the Lord. He'll keep you safe."

"The same way He kept Pa safe?" Sally wanted to throw the hoe to the ground, but she restrained herself. She didn't want to destroy another one.

"Oh Sally." Ma took her into her arms as if she were a child, even younger than Nellie. "It's all right to cry."

Ma was saying that? Ma, who had added a grave marker out in the field, even though Pa's body had been left back near the fort? Who had prayed at the memorial site, wiped away her tears, and organized their move to the cave as if she had lost a puppy and not her life's mate?

When Ma sobbed, Sally's own tears fell. Their cries twined together, dissolving the hard shell that had formed over Sally's heart. The hoe fell to her feet, a different instrument needed for the softening taking place in her heart. God willing, they would reap these plants, watered with tears of grief and loneliness and fear, with joy, like the psalmist promised.

"What's the matter?"

Stephen spoke, but Nellie was the one tugging at Sally's sleeve. "Are you all right, Ma?"

Ma brushed her hand over her eyes, tears glistening on the dark circles that marked her face these days, and smiled. "We're blessed. Aren't we, Sally?"

For the first time in many weeks, Sally could whole-heartedly agree.

The extra sleep must have done Josiah good. He sped through the day's tasks, so much so that they finished the fieldwork well before supper, and he had time to work on a new handle for the hoe. He wanted it smooth enough so that Sally needn't worry about any more splinters.

Josiah hadn't finished sanding down the handle when Father came out to milk the cow. "Still at it, son? You're whittling it down to nothing. This isn't a fancy walking cane. Come on, now, your mother has supper ready."

No, not a fancy walking cane. But a hoe for someone who deserves wood as smooth as her skin. Many things were beyond Josiah's reach at the moment, but he could at least make Sally a good tool. It was little enough to do, in light of all the things he wanted to make possible for her someday.

Dared he hope? Could he speak of his feelings to her? With the death of her father, and Nathaniel's absence, whom should he ask for permission to court her? Perhaps, as in the break of the colonies from the tradition of English rule, he could break another tradition. When there was no father or elder brother, could he speak with Mrs. Reid? Or even Sally, directly?

As Josiah pounded the handle into place, his chest collapsed in a deep sigh. With Father so dead set against the Patriots, he couldn't ask Sally for anything. His job for now was to honor his father as the Bible commanded— even if his heart broke.

He could at least prove the sincerity of his devotion to Sally. The smooth texture of the hoe handle pleased him as he ran his hands along the length. Good, sturdy wood, well seasoned, should prove less likely to break under hard usage. He set it aside and dipped his hands into the bucket of well water before heading in to supper.

The sun was casting long shadows when they finished their meal. Day by day, the hours of daylight shortened.

"I suppose you'll be heading over to the Reids' tonight." Father shook his head.

"Since I missed this morning. I have double the work to do." He also needed to explain his absence to the Reids.

Father stretched and drank from his mug. "Since we finished early today, perhaps I'll come along. I'd like to lend a hand and see your progress." He beamed as if he had offered his son a finely wrought silver cup.

Josiah's heart twisted. Father was offering a peace branch, but he must refuse it. Danger of discovery lay down that road. "That's not necessary. I over-spoke the amount of work." His mind scrambled for alternatives should Father insist on accompanying him. His eyes rested on a partially assembled chair, a project they had abandoned since Solomon was no longer a presence at the table.

"Mother has been asking your help with fixing things around the cabin, like the chair." Josiah nodded in that direction. "And the step by the front door. We keep avoiding the broken tread, but one of these days we might forget and stumble."

Father looked at the empty place at the table, at the space where Solomon always sat, never remembering to remove his tricorne until reminded, the spot that Mother attempted to fill with fresh flowers and their open Bible.

"It's time." Mother spoke from the counter, where she cleaned off the dishes. "We never know when we might have company."

Father grunted and picked up the chair legs in his hands. "I'll do that, son. But ask if ever you need help. I'll see you get it."

"I'll keep your promise in mind." *But I have all the help I'll ever need—from four determined Patriots.*

~

Nellie darted back to the cave, delaying their departure another few minutes. Stephen and Ma had already left. Sally suppressed a sigh. She wanted to get to the field, to start work. . .to see if Josiah had come tonight. If her fears of the morning had been for naught.

"Do you think Josiah will be there tonight?" Nellie demanded as they set off through the trees.

"Shh." Sally automatically reproved her sister. "Quiet, remember?"

Nellie looked around them as if to say, *Do you see anybody here to hear us?* "Well, do you?" She lowered her voice to a whisper, but intense enough to startle a partridge perched on the ground into a short flight. Something skittered through the brush underfoot. Sally reminded herself that they didn't want to run into her any more than she wanted to run into them, and she didn't worry about it.

"We won't know until we get there," Sally whispered in a way that modeled how Nellie could lower her voice. Poor Nellie. For an eight-year-old, she had been remarkably patient. Sally remembered her own eight-year-old summer, when she had spent long hours in the sunshine, working with Ma in the kitchen garden and playing hoop ball with Nathaniel and Stephen. They laughed and cried and got brown and healthy, not the pasty sallow color Nellie sported after a month spent in the cave by day, her only hours in fresh air under the moonlight.

Sally searched her mind for something she could do to make this time special for her sister. "Tomorrow I'll make you a new doll. Would you like that?"

"That's *wonderful!*"

Sally's announcement lifted Nellie's spirits, and her voice rose accordingly. Nearby an owl flapped its wings but stayed on its branch. Most of the wildlife seemed to accept the Reids' presence as part of the natural order.

They arrived at the edge of the clearing. Sally paused before entering the open space, searching for the signal the family had arranged to indicate it was safe. The scrap of red wool—from a real Redcoat, back in the days when Pa had fought in the French and Indian War—dangled from the limb of a tree. Sometimes darkness and full foliage made seeing difficult, but tonight she could make it out clearly. She stepped into the clearing.

Josiah must have seen her at the same moment she noticed him, because a smile crossed his face, and he ran in her direction. Sally's heart took flight as the partridge had earlier, and all her pretense of not caring vanished. Her face must have given away her feelings, but she hoped the darkness near the trees would mask it.

"Sally and Josiah. . ." Nellie started a teasing rhyme but had the sense to keep her voice low enough for only her sister to hear. She stuck her tongue out before she raced to where Ma stooped over a plant, pulling weeds around the base.

"I brought your hoe." Josiah offered the repaired item as if it were a prize pair of oxen.

Looking at it closely, Sally marveled at the workmanship. The wood gleamed as if oiled, and she ran her hands along the grain. Even the blade, the portion retained from the old hoe, shone clean, not worn from use. She hefted it in her hand and dipped it to the ground—the right height. Pa had designed the older hoe for a taller person, and at times she had found its use awkward. "It's perfect."

He grinned. "I'm glad you like it."

She slipped the handle back and forth between her hands, admiring the smooth finish. "Is this what kept you this morning?"

As beautiful as the hoe was, Sally would rather have had his company. Anything was preferable to the uncertainty that went through her every time he disappeared in the direction of his family's farm.

"No." Josiah sounded embarrassed. "I fear I overslept. I needed additional time to mend your hoe, and I didn't want to arouse Father's suspicions."

So his absence had been for the sake of their safety, not against it. She should know by now that she could trust him.

He bent his head over hers, his dark hair blocking out what little light the moon provided, and Sally grew faint. In a low voice, he asked, "Fixing the hoe for you has been my pleasure. Is there anything else you need?"

A dozen things crowded Sally's mind. They needed Pa. They prayed Nathaniel would come home safe and sound of mind and body. She longed for her home in the cabin and had determined to get back there before Ma's time came.

She didn't say any of those things, but only shook her head. "No. Nothing you can help us with. You're already doing so much. Too much. I fear you put yourself at risk on our behalf." Her voice trailed off. She expected Josiah to move away, to return to working, but he paused another moment.

"Next week, weather permitting on Monday evening, I would like to spend a few minutes with you by the trees. If we can share a bite to eat, just you and I."

Sally felt her eyes widen. Their last picnic, on the day the militia had gathered on the green, seemed like a hundred years ago. How innocent their concerns about the Whitsons and the surveyor seemed after all that had passed since.

"You would?" Moonlight picnics? The prospect seemed absolutely frivolous, yet exciting at the same time.

"I asked your mother, and she agreed. What say you?"

"I say...I would like that."

Josiah squeezed the tips of her fingers, where she held the hoe, then skipped away to his spot on the row next to Stephen.

Sally flexed her fingers, marveling at the scorching sensation the touch of his hand had given her. With a lighter heart than she had felt in many a day, she dropped the hoe to the dirt and dug at the ever-present weeds.

Ma did more than agree to the picnic. She insisted Sally wash in the river. They hadn't bathed, any of them, in longer than she could remember.

Sally scrubbed at the dirt caked onto her face and arms and in her hair until the water looked almost as muddy as during spring runoff. Now that the dirt had been washed away, her hair was restored to a golden glow. She wished she had a clean dress to wear, but she satisfied herself with brushing down her second gown. Ma laced the stays, tighter than she had needed when they first moved into the cave. Muscles had formed on her arms after the long hours working in the fields. Thin and muscular, not feminine nor pretty—Sally didn't feel good enough for Josiah.

Then she remembered the hoe, the beautiful, smooth hoe, that Josiah had made specially for her. A thing of beauty, yet fit for the task. Maybe he saw her the same way.

Nellie fiddled with tying a bow at Sally's back. She finished and stared at Sally, her face a mask of concentration with her tongue stuck in her cheek.

Glancing over her shoulder, Sally could make out the tail ends of the bow Nellie had tied. She couldn't see much more over the mass of cloth below her waist. "Thanks, Nellie."

Nellie took out the corncob doll she hadn't let out of her sight since they had fashioned it together. She danced around the cave, singing. "Josiah's courting Sally."

"That's enough!" Ma scolded Nellie and gestured for Sally to sit on a stool beside the fire pit, then combed through her long hair.

"Ouch!"

"Your hair is full of briars and such." Ma tugged gently and Sally bit her lip. "This is no kind of life for a young woman."

"You said you loved it," Sally reminded Ma. She wiggled her toes in their freedom from shoes, which she would put on as soon as her socks dried by the fire.

"I loved your pa and didn't care where we lived." Ma looped Sally's hair to hang from a knot at the back of her neck. She settled her mobcap over her head, tucking a stray strand of hair under the cloth. "One more thing." She reached into her pocket and pulled out a snow-white handkerchief, with the initial *R* embroidered between an *M* and a *D*.

Sally hardly dared touch the fabric, which she recognized as part of Ma's hope chest when she had left New Hampshire behind to go with Pa into the Vermont woods. "I can't take this. It'll be dirty before I even reach the clearing."

Ma curled her fingers over Sally's, pressing the square into her hand. "I have precious little to give you, my daughter. But when I started out on a new life, I had this, and now I want you to have it. To remind you of what can be, what may be, that things will not always be as they are now."

When Sally took the precious cloth, she didn't know what to do with it. Ma must have sensed her confusion because she took it out of Sally's hand, folded it into a small square, and tucked it inside her bodice. "Next to your heart."

All the attentions made Sally feel as transformed as Cinderella on her way to the ball. She only hoped they weren't misreading Josiah's intent. She looked at the floor and spoke her fear. " 'Tis only Josiah. I shouldn't be making such a fuss."

Ma straightened the mobcap on Sally's head, put her hands on either side of her face, and looked her in the eye. "When a young man plans a moonlight picnic with the daughter of his father's sworn enemies, he's serious. Mind you don't play with his affections. If you don't care for him, you must tell him so."

Care for Josiah? As for. . .a husband? "Ma, how do I know?" She felt heat rising in her cheeks, but she had to ask.

"Oh, you'll know. Like I did with your pa." Ma wrapped Sally in a tight embrace. "I think you already do."

∽

That night, Father dallied over every detail. Josiah wanted to wash and dress for the picnic, but he didn't dare. Such behavior would alert Father that something was afoot. Instead Josiah settled for scrubbing his arms and hands and face more thoroughly than usual before supper. He felt too nervous to eat and worried how to explain his lack of appetite.

His hunger returned full force when he saw the meal Mother had set out. She had outdone herself, with crisp, brown corn bread, savory beans, and milk kept cold in their spring.

He stared at his plate, wishing he could share the bounty with the Reids. Mother noticed his hesitation.

"What's wrong, son? You're not feeling poorly, are you?"

Father looked up. "You've been working hard these past few weeks. Perhaps you shouldn't go tonight."

"I'm fine." Josiah didn't want to give either one of them any reason to suspect anything amiss, so he dug into the beans.

"Are you sure?" Mother asked.

"Leave the boy alone." Father made a dismissive motion with his hand. "He's a grown man. Doesn't need you to tell him when to eat."

Josiah scoured the edge of the plate with his corn bread, but neither parent paid any further attention to how much he ate or didn't. At long last, the meal ended, and Josiah took leave of the table. Mother started to crumble the corn bread into the pig slops. Josiah interrupted her. "Can I have that? For the chickens instead?" He smiled beguilingly.

"I don't see why not." Mother handed it to him. "Here you go."

Josiah broke off some crumbs in the chicken pen, in case Father came looking, but carried the bulk of corn bread tucked underneath his shirt. Ever since the thought of the picnic had occurred to him, he had saved bits of bread and meat and stowed them in the deep well to keep cool. That, plus fresh cream and blueberries, should sweeten Sally's taste buds after days of beans and corn.

In spite of his worries that the meal had delayed him, Josiah arrived at the clearing before the Reids. After checking the perimeter, he dug the red cloth out from underneath the bush where they hid it and hung it on the usual oak. Seeing the rough bark on the tree struck his whimsy, and he dug a spud from his tools. On the back side of the tree, where no one would see unless searching for it, he stripped a small square clear of bark. Exchanging his knife for the spud, he dug the tip into the living wood with slow, laborious strokes. He was putting away his knife when he heard Stephen arrive.

Sally's brother looked Josiah up and down. The young lad had grown after his hard work of the summer. If the war continued, he would want to go the way of his father and brother and join up with the Green Mountain Boys. Josiah's heart ached at the thought of what that additional loss would mean to the Reids.

"You asked to sit with Sally tonight." The statement carried a challenge with it. Josiah reminded himself that he didn't answer to the young man.

"Yes, I plan on a light repast under the stars tonight. I spoke of it with your mother and with Sally last week."

"Treat my sister well. This year has already had its share of burdens." Stephen's smooth chin, still devoid of facial hair, jutted forward, leading his body in an awkward protective stance. Josiah wavered between laughter and liking of the boy so determined to act as his sister's champion.

"I will, Stephen. Speaking of Sally—where is she?"

Stephen let out a snort, half laughter, half disgust. "She's spent the day preening, with Ma and Nellie's help." He drew his lips together. "She wouldn't like me telling you that."

So Sally had spent the daytime hours preparing for this evening, had she? Josiah ran his fingers through his hair before pulling it behind his head. A black ribbon almost the same color as his dark locks kept it in place. Maybe the darkness of the night would hide its filth.

Muffled laughter announced the arrival of the others. *Please, God.* Josiah's heart pounded hard in his chest, wondering, hoping what the night would bring.

Mrs. Reid came first and waved a greeting. Nellie followed, bowing as if a lady-in-waiting to a queen. At last, Sally stepped through the trees. The first star of the night chose that moment to make its appearance, and it directed its light upon Sally's golden head.

She looked as beautiful as an angel sent from heaven descending Jacob's ladder, and Josiah was struck as dumb as all mortals in the presence of the angelic host.

Chapter 10

Sally hesitated at the edge of the clearing. First Josiah's face lit up with pleasure, then froze, a silly expression contorting his features. She expected something else, something more. . .welcoming?

Ma must have sensed the awkwardness between the two young people. She crossed the clearing to where Josiah waited with Stephen. "Good evening to you. God has given us a clear night, like you asked for." Smiling, she handed him a blanket she had carried from the cave. As they had everything else, they had beaten the blanket with brushes, shaking out the worst of the dirt and other debris accumulated over the months.

"Nellie? Why don't we start among the potato patch tonight?" Her voice dropped as the two of them walked away, but she turned a blazing look on Stephen.

He tightened his hold on his hoe. "I'll be working among the turnips, myself."

At last Sally was relatively alone with Josiah. He looked different tonight—he had taken time with his hair. A black ribbon held it in place, away from his face, showing his strong chin to good advantage. Dark stubble darkened his cheeks, but Sally decided she liked it. He looked stalwart, dependable—a formidable foe if challenged in battle.

If he ever moved, that was. He hadn't moved or spoken a word from the moment he had spotted her.

"Shall I put the blanket down here?" Why did he ask her to a picnic, if he didn't intend to speak with her?

Josiah blinked his eyes at her question and came to life. "Yes, this is the perfect spot." He flung the blanket out with a twist of his hand, and it settled on the grass. "I brought a few things. Fresh cream and eggs and butter and some other things I managed to sneak away." He spread out his offerings and blushed, as if ashamed. " 'Tisn't much, but I didn't want to raise Father's suspicions."

Sally thought back again to that picnic on the green when no one cared who brought what food or who shared it. So much had changed. And what about the man sitting across from her? He had changed as well, as had they all—but for the better or worse?

Looking into his dark eyes, she could only believe she liked the changed Josiah better. He was constant in his support of her family. He was here, now, helping them and. . .*courting* her. The thought sent goose bumps up her arms, and she wrapped her arms around her chest.

Josiah spread the food on the blanket, even a few small chunks of corn bread he had carried next to his skin. He offered her the largest piece. "I couldn't think how else to carry it without Father seeing," he apologized.

Sally struggled to keep from laughing and took a bite. "It's delicious. Your mother has always had a light hand with baking."

Before eating, Josiah lifted a hand. "I'll return thanks, shall I?"

Sally nodded.

"Dear Lord and Father of mankind, we thank Thee for the bounty Thou hast provided for us. We thank Thee that we can share it together, at Thy table. And Lord, may there be many more such occasions, when this present conflict is over."

Many more such occasions? Heat warmed her cheeks, and she held up her hands to ward off the thoughts flooding her mind.

Between them, they had more than enough to eat, but Sally wasn't hungry. Josiah's prayer had set her heart all aflutter, and she scarcely tasted the food, even when he dipped a blueberry in fresh cream and handed it to her. She took it between her lips, his fingers brushing her mouth. Closing her eyes, she focused on the flavor of the berry, letting the juice trickle down her throat. When she opened them again, she saw Josiah's laughter-lined face a few inches distance away from hers. He looked so tender, so sweet. . .the berry lodged in her throat. When he offered her another, she shook her head.

Instead, she spread butter and mashed blueberries across a biscuit Ma had baked before offering it to him. "Almost as good as preserves," she said.

He took it from her hands, her fingertips tingling where they touched.

Between them, they finished everything, even the crumbs of corn bread. Josiah laced his hands behind his head and settled back against the tree, his gaze focused on the sky. "It's been too long since I took time to enjoy the sky. 'What is man that thou art mindful of him?' We're so insignificant in light of all of God's creation. Someday the war for independence will be over. America will be a free nation. . .and we'll have to make amends and come together. Patriot and Tory."

"Stephen wouldn't like to hear you say that. He thinks if Tories want a king so badly, they should return to England or at least make haste to Canada."

Josiah's laugh wasn't pleasant. "He's not the only one who feels that way.

Some Tories have done that already, and Father has decided to send Mother across the border. Since we're so close here in Maple Notch, he hopes he can join her there later, when things have settled down." He straightened his back and hugged his knees to his chest. "My point is, this can't last forever." He jumped to his feet and pulled her up alongside of him. "Here. Let me show you something."

He walked into the trees, and Sally wondered why. Did he mean to search for their hiding place? No, she didn't believe that of him. Did he want to get her alone, out of sight of the others? Her heart sped up. Without Pa's protection, she felt vulnerable, uncertain.

Before she could decide, he stopped under the canopy of leaves at the far side of the tree where they hung the red cloth to indicate safe passage. "It's in here."

What could he want to show her in a tree? Curious, Sally stepped forward. She could make out little beyond shades of dark. "What is it?"

"It's on the tree." His voice sounded disappointed. "Can you see anything at all?"

Sally squinted. At first, everything appeared in varying shades of gray, until her sight adjusted and she could see what he was pointing to. Bark had been stripped away from a small square, perhaps five inches across. Pale wood gleamed against the darker trunk.

"Come closer."

As Sally stepped closer to the tree, she could see he had carved something into the wood. He took her hand and placed it on the pale spot. Underneath her fingertips, she felt gouges in the wood.

"Can you tell what I carved?" His breath warmed her neck.

Sally shook her head. "No."

"It's *J*—" He dipped their hands down and then made a small loop at the bottom. He lifted her hand to the next shape: a straight line across, intersecting with a vertical line.

"*T*," she said.

"For Josiah Tuttle." She imagined his mouth curving in a smile.

Two lines crossed in a simple addition sign.

"*Esss. . .*" He drew the sound out as he slid their fingers around the curves of the letter. "Last of all, *R*."

JT + SR? Josiah Tuttle and Sally Reid. He had carved his heart, his dreams, into the living flesh of the tree. Into an organism that would still be alive in ten years, a hundred years—until after the end of the war. He dreamed of a future—with her. Her heart hammered, making breathing difficult.

"Dare I hope, Sally? That you will consider a future with me?"

"Oh Josiah." Tears clogged her voice. "How can it ever happen?"

∽

Slowly Sally's answer registered in Josiah's consciousness. She hadn't said yes—but she hadn't said no, either.

He wanted to continue standing under the tree, Sally's arm entwined with his while he traced the letters he had carved into the tree. He wanted to kiss that arm, bury his face in her soft flaxen hair, so clean and smelling so sweet, but her answer didn't give him that liberty.

Instead he drew in a deep breath and stepped back and pulled her into the moonlight of the clearing. He satisfied himself with kissing the tips of her fingers. "May I hope for a different answer at a later time?"

Sally hesitated. "Ma said to be honest with you." She smiled, a hint of sadness in her voice. "I can't give you an answer, given the present circumstances. Your father. . ."

Father. Resentment flared in Josiah, hot and fierce. He didn't want to have to wait until war's end to court the woman he loved. "I will honor Father in every way I can, as best I can. But I believe God will change his heart in His time. He must. Otherwise. . ."

"You take a great risk, helping us here."

Josiah hated to see the concern cross Sally's sweet features. "Only God knows how He will work it out. But as long as He is our fortress, we don't have to be afraid."

Josiah spoke the words but felt like a fraud. He had said much the same thing to Solomon before their encounter with the Redcoat. The only shelter God had provided that night had been his brother's body coming between Josiah and the musket ball. That was why he wanted to make a difference. *He* should have died, not Solomon.

"I confess I don't understand God's workings." Sally's soft voice barely penetrated Josiah's hearing. "But Ma says I don't have to understand. I can trust His goodness and His love."

Sally's words reminded him yet again that the Tuttles were not the only family to suffer loss. Solomon's death paled when he remembered that the Reids' husband and provider hadn't returned, either. Not only that, but Nathaniel had reported for battle as well, and they were hiding in some inhospitable place in order to work their farm—a situation his own father had helped create.

Did God feel torn when the twelve tribes quarreled among themselves? How did Jesus feel when his handpicked disciples argued about who would sit at His right hand? It would take the wisdom of a Solomon to sort this one out. *And Solomon isn't here.* Josiah ran the back of his hand over Sally's soft cheek. "Trust you to remind me about God. You're right. He loved us enough to send His Son to take care of our worst problems. I guess we can both trust Him with our circumstances."

Overhead the moon had risen in the eastern sky, casting a pale light that outlined the figures at work in the field. Sally saw the direction of his gaze and turned away.

"We'd best be getting home before the moon gets any brighter." She flicked a few crumbs off her skirt. "And I didn't do any work this night."

"You did the work of your heart. That's important." Josiah forced a smile. "In the morning, I'll try to get here earlier than usual and put in some extra time."

When Mrs. Reid approached, Josiah folded the blanket and gave it to her.

She accepted it with a smile. "Did all go well?"

Sally colored, but Josiah didn't speak. He hadn't received the answer he had hoped for on this evening.

"Ma, I told him that. . .I wasn't ready." Sally looked ashamed.

"Say no more." The older woman's face sagged, and Josiah sensed her disappointment. "The Teacher himself says there is a time to love and a time to hate. Your time will come." She reached up and brought Josiah's head close to hers so she could speak in his ears. "I know Mr. Reid would approve."

Her kind words touched Josiah, and he rushed to respond. "If there's anything more I can do for you, please let me know."

Mrs. Reid's gaze swept across the well-kept field. "You are doing plenty. God is taking good care of us. And now, we must be leaving."

Josiah watched them, mother and daughter, walking together to the edge of the field. He loved to watch their skirts sway as they walked, to see Sally hold on to her mother, easing her over small clumps of soil. He willed himself to look away, to keep his promise not to seek their place of refuge, not to follow their progress into the woods. His deceitful heart followed them into the trees. He could find their hiding place if the need arose. For now, the less he knew, the safer they would be. If he located their exact abode, he might draw his father and anyone else looking straight to their place of safety.

The moon was fast approaching its zenith. His mind filled with thoughts of Sally—he had tarried longer than he should. Now he must hie home. He checked the ground where they had supped, making sure no evidence remained. He came upon a corncob doll, dirt smeared and worn down. *Nellie's doll.* He frowned at it. What should he do with it? If he left it in the field, anyone who found it would guess it belonged to the girl. But he couldn't take it home nor return it until the morrow. He decided to leave it.

No one had checked the fields yet; he would risk one more day.

Josiah's heart sang a love song all the way home, and he fell asleep easily in the hayloft. The next few days fell into an easy rhythm. He awoke early, in the expectation of spending extra time with his lovely Sally. They had much opportunity to talk. The crop was thriving and needed less and less attention. Mrs. Reid shooed them away for a few minutes each day, and even Stephen granted them grudging privacy.

～

A few weeks later, all of the Reids left early, while Sally stayed behind for a few stolen minutes with Josiah. She could find her way back to the cave blindfolded, if need be, and she treasured this short time with Josiah each evening.

"So why do you think Asher didn't have a captain in David's army?" Sally continued the debate she and Josiah had been having. Why were some of the twelve tribes of Israel mentioned, but other times left out? "Even the Levites had a commander. But not Asher. Did they have something against David?"

Josiah laughed. "I don't know. You'd think Benjamin might hold a grudge, since Saul was their king, but Asher? I don't know." He grew serious. "Maybe they were like the colonies. Each one wanting to do their own thing. Even Vermont has refused to join with the other colonies."

"The Republic of New Connecticut. I know." Sally sighed. "I, for one, think we'll all need to work together if we're going to survive apart from England."

As if punctuating Sally's comment, thunder cracked through the atmosphere. She jumped. A drop of water settled on her nose, then her fingers.

"Rain!" They both yelled as the clouds overhead opened. Had so much time passed, or had the storm come up that quickly?

"I'll see you tomorrow." Sally picked up her hoe.

"Wait." Rain plastered hair to Josiah's face. "You mustn't go under the trees, not while it's storming."

"We're not any safer in the middle of the field. We're the tallest things out here." The corn had grown but still didn't reach beyond Sally's shoulder. "I suppose we could sit among the plants." She looked at her skirt; she would return home covered in mud, but it couldn't be helped.

Josiah didn't speak but took her by the hand into the corn and sat down with her, pulling his jacket over their heads.

Conversation was impossible while thunder crashed in the sky overhead. It followed so close after lightning scorched the sky that Sally felt the heat. She hoped her family had made it back to the cave before the storm started. She never thought she'd long for the cave, but in this weather, she would gladly have taken shelter in it.

Thoughts of her family, the cave, and the warm fire that would dry her when she reached its sanctuary kept her mind away from Josiah. She didn't want to think about him while they huddled under his jacket, so close that their shoulders touched, so near that she inhaled his strong masculine scent with every breath. If she let herself, she would dream of his hand holding hers, his lips seeking hers. . . .

Feeling her cheeks grow warm, she was grateful for the darkness that covered her face. Next to her, Josiah adjusted his position. Did his thoughts run along the same lines?

While she considered that line of questioning, thunder rumbled into the distance, and rain stopped pelting Josiah's jacket, which had grown sodden during the storm. Water ran in rivulets between the rows of corn, but no new rain fell. Josiah stood first and helped her to her feet.

"Be careful at the river." Josiah's mouth twisted, and she guessed he had seen the wariness of her face. "If you cross the river. I only know it lies in that direction." He nodded at the trees where they disappeared every night. "Hasten home to rest. Dawn will be here quickly."

Sally walked to the edge of the field before she turned back to wave good-bye. The hours until morning, when she would see him again, stretched before her as long as a midwinter's night.

～

Josiah was thankful the storm had ended when it did. Sitting so near to Sally under the blanket, in the dark, had burned through him in ways no Christian man should consider. Those feelings spurred him to action, to fly across the muddy fields. Even so, the time approached the midnight hour before he made it home. He needed a fire to dry his clothes and warm his bones. The night air held a nip, a hint of the approaching fall.

Dare he seek the fire in the cabin? Best not to chance it—he doubted he could enter without awakening Father. Instead he removed his outer garments and draped them over the walls of the stall, where the horse's warm flesh might remove some of the dampness. Burrowing into the hay, he fell into an exhausted sleep and awoke somewhat refreshed in a few hours' time.

His shirt had dried reasonably well, but he still could have wrung enough water from his breeches to irrigate a small garden. He risked lantern light to look for the extra pair they kept in the barn for the dirtiest of jobs. His nose wrinkled at the stench, but at least they were warm and dry. His father's clothes hung a little too large on him, so he belted them tight around his waist.

A shaft of light alerted Josiah to the opening of the barn door. He climbed down the ladder from the loft. Father was examining the still-wet leggings.

"You stayed out in the storm last night?" Father's voice held a hint of disbelief.

"It caught me unaware." He had been too focused on Sally to think about the gathering clouds.

"You should have at least sought shelter in one of the outbuildings. No need to get drenched. I don't want you getting sick at harvesttime."

When the rain had come, all Josiah thought about was the need to protect Sally from the elements and the chance to spend a few more minutes with her. "There wasn't time. I hunkered down in the field for safety's sake. The lightning was fierce."

"Humph." Father grabbed the offending clothing. "I'll have your mother work on these today. The rain will be good for the crops. We haven't had enough moisture this summer."

Josiah thought back to the morning he had discovered Sally and Stephen watering their crops and suppressed a smile. He missed part of what Father said.

"I'll see you later, then. Get on with you."

Chapter 11

Once out of Josiah's sight, Sally hastened toward home. The slick grass underfoot slowed her passage, and wet leaves slapped her in the face. When she neared the cave, she heard a sound that sped her steps. *Screams, like someone in pain.*

When she neared the cave, Stephen, face as pale as the moon overhead, stumbled through the opening. He motioned for her to hurry. "It's Ma."

But Ma had said the baby wasn't due for another month. Sally rushed into the cave. Ma lay on the floor, strain pulling the skin of her face taut. An anxious Nellie hovered at her side.

"Do you want a wet cloth, Ma? A stick?" Sally asked. *A knife underneath to cut the pain?* In view of Ma's obvious distress, the old wives' tale didn't seem so foolish, even if all it did was calm her spirits.

Sally knelt by Ma's side and took her hand. Ma exhaled deeply and relaxed a fraction. She kneaded Sally's fingers and reached out to touch her hair. "You were caught in the storm."

"Don't worry about that, Ma. I'm fine. But what happened?" Something must be wrong. Sally had been about the same age as Nellie was now when her sister was born. Joy at having a sister filled her memories of that occasion and not much else. But she had assisted at her mother's last birthing, when the babe was stillborn. *Please God, don't let that happen again.*

"The babe is impatient. Like his brother Nathaniel. The pains started when we returned to the cave." Ma gasped, and the smile fled from her face. She squeezed Sally's fingers and then let go.

"A girl, please God." Sally wanted to distract Ma. "I would like another sister."

Ma shook her head. "I've asked God for a boy. One just like his pa." This time, she didn't hide the grief those words brought. "You don't know how often I have thanked God for this child since your father died."

Tears stung Sally's eyes. "A brother would be fine."

They waited out the next pain. Ma collapsed against the floor, and Nellie looked at them both anxiously. "How long does it take?" she asked.

Sally looked at Ma. "It will be over sometime today."

"Before we go to the fields?"

Did Nellie think Ma would jump up from giving birth and go out to work?

Ma opened her mouth to reply, but Sally spoke first. "I'll take care of it, Ma. You just worry about getting that baby here." She had asked God to let them be home before the baby's birth. Why hadn't He answered? How would they manage? "We'll not be going to the fields today, Nellie. But later, you can fix us breakfast. Do you think you can do that?"

Nellie nodded her head. "But can't Stephen 'n' I work?" Ma's situation must have made her anxious to get away.

"Stephen will go for the midwife." Sally made the decision as she spoke. After the trouble Ma had had with the last birth, Pa had promised she would have a midwife this time. Sally intended to honor that promise, especially in light of the problems Ma was experiencing.

Ma shook her head. "Don't be foolish, Sally." She panted, clenching her daughter's hands tight.

Sally waited until her mother relaxed again. "Pa promised."

"But he's not here, and I am." Ma showed some spirit, and that made Sally glad. "And I don't want to lose everything we've been working for, living in this—hole—by running for help the first time things get tough. I'm fine."

After her refusal to seek help, Ma gained strength. She asked Nellie for some water and called Stephen to hang a blanket. "Go on to the fields as usual. It's better if you're not here. And take Nellie with you."

Sally helped him arrange the blanket and then motioned for him to go outside the cave entrance with her. "I know what Ma said, but I'm asking you to stay close by," she whispered. "If things get worse, I'll send you for the midwife in town. Goodwife Hitchcock. She lives on the green. You know her house?"

He nodded. "But do you think it will come to that?" He sounded like a frightened little boy.

Muffled cries came from the cave. "I don't know. But I recollect things should be farther along than they are."

He dropped into a huddle by the door and drew his arms around his knees. She hated to ask more of him, but she had no one else. "And I need you to do something more for me."

Stephen glanced in the direction of the partition.

"Nothing to do with the birthing. But if you can distract Nellie, that would help tremendously. Read with her, or take her outside, nearby. Best of all if you can help her go back to sleep. You know how easily she gets upset."

Stephen stretched out his right leg. "I can do that." His gaze swept the cave, face twisted in perplexity before he nodded to himself. "Hey, Nellie!"

he called out, his voice deepened now and never rising to the telltale squeak that bothered boys turning into men. "I need your help over here." He stood.

Sally passed Nellie at the partition and gave her a hug. "All will be well. Stephen needs your help."

"But Ma—" Nellie's scrunched-up face said it all, her worries, fears, sense of helplessness. They heard Ma's groan from her side of the partition, and Nellie shuddered.

"You can help Ma most by going with Stephen." *And pray for us,* but Sally didn't say that out loud. Nellie already knew to do that, and the admonition rang hollow and might only deepen her fears. They had prayed for Pa and the other Green Mountain Boys, hadn't they, and things hadn't turned out well. Sally forced back the doubt. No need to think bad thoughts while waiting on Ma.

"If you have a chance, get some rest. 'Twill be a long day otherwise. Now, go." She guided her sister toward Stephen before going behind the partition.

The fire lay close to Ma, the low flames dancing on the roof overhead. "Thanks. You've been such a blessing to me." Ma spoke between pains. "I don't know what I would do without you."

"Oh, Ma. I wish there was more I could do." Sally knelt next to her mother and offered her water. There must be some way to make Ma more comfortable. She thought of a book, *Treatise on Midwifery* by a Benjamin Pugh, that Goodwife Hitchcock had lent her. After reading bits of it, she had decided against asking the midwife for permission to accompany her. Now she wished she had paid closer attention.

"I believe I read that midwives sometimes recommend their patients get up and move around."

"Stand up? It takes all my strength just to. . .get through the pains."

Ma looked like she was losing strength while lying there. "Let's try it, Ma. I'll help you." Sally reached down as she would to a fractious child and put Ma's arm over her shoulders, then lifted her to her feet. The roof hung close to their heads, but they could stand upright.

They walked in a tiny circle, cramped by the size of the cave. One lap, two.

"I can't go farther," Ma panted.

"You're doing well. Color is already returning to your face." Sally encouraged her mother to keep going.

"Ah!" Ma bent over double, almost pulling them both to the floor. She clasped her hands about her middle. Once the pain passed, she leaned against the cave wall and blinked at Sally.

"I believe that was easier." She managed a weary smile. When she spoke again, she lowered her voice. "But something isn't right with the baby. I fear a breech delivery."

"But that's. . ." Sally's voice trailed off. She knew little about birthing. From what she had seen of animal births, mothers had the easiest time when the baby slipped out headfirst. "I don't know what to do." For the first time, panic as ponderous as the thunderstorm last night gripped her heart.

"God will see us through, but I might need your help to pull the baby out. When it's time." Ma bent over again as another pain hit.

From the other side of the partition, Sally heard the gentle sound of Stephen's singing and Nellie's soft snore. He had done well to get her to sleep. Should she send for the midwife?

"You can do this." Ma spoke as if she had read her thoughts.

For now, Sally would wait.

⤴

Josiah trotted to the Reids' field. All the plants had welcomed the night's rain, their leaves stretching for the sun. Things seemed to have shot up by inches since the previous evening. Could the rain have the same effect on him? He felt taller and stronger than he had yesterday, ever since the minutes he had spent with Sally beneath his jacket.

The thought of his beloved sped his progress. He couldn't wait to see her again this morning. Every day his sweet, sweet Sally grew more precious than the day before.

As usual, he arrived at the fields first. He spread out the mud at the spot where he had huddled with Sally, packing it around the corn plants that had shot into the air. A few stalks had fallen on the ground, blown by the wind. Josiah pulled the husk off an ear of corn and checked the kernels. They were already ripe, ready to harvest. As soon as the fields dried, they could work with a will. The rains had encouraged the growth of weeds as well, even more so than the corn. He began pulling them out by the roots, which refused to disappear completely.

His work with the weeds made him think about Jesus' parable about the wheat and the tares. He prayed he wasn't making any mistakes. Which Reid would arrive first today? Would it be Nellie, full of giggles and a happy good morning? Mrs. Reid, more tired and worn-out each day, but with a warm smile and welcome? Stephen, who continued to scowl at him even as he occasionally asked his advice on a farming matter? Or might it be Sally, her shy smile saying all that needed to be expressed between them until they had a chance for words?

Thinking of the Reids, he realized the time had passed for them to arrive. The sun already glimmered behind the mountains with the brilliance of a day after rain. He had expected them to arrive early, eager to work this morning, maybe because of his own excitement singing through his veins.

He finished a second row and heard their old rooster holler, announcing the morning. Josiah frowned, concerned at the Reids' continued absence. But he had promised he wouldn't seek their hiding place, and he wouldn't break his word. Not unless he had proof they were in danger.

After three rows, his earlier excitement had drained away, replaced by worry. Had the storm caused them problems? Perhaps the river had flooded their camp. Were they even now struggling to salvage what they could of their belongings? *Should I go?*

Josiah straightened and stared in the direction of the trees where the family disappeared every night. He could find their hiding place if he wanted to—he was sure of it. What harm could it do? If he started now, he might find them and still get home in time for breakfast. He grabbed his hoe and walked in the direction of the forest.

"It's looking good!"

Josiah stopped still in his tracks.

Father.

~

Ma's pains came close together. The last stillbirth had been nothing like this from what Sally remembered. This was going on long, too long. Each spasm left Ma weaker. If the babe didn't make its entrance soon, Sally feared for Ma's life as well as the baby's. *Oh, Lord, please no. Haven't we been through enough already?*

Ma lay back against the floor, panting after the last battle. Sally eased past the partition and blinked against the dawn light beaming through the entrance. Nellie lay curled in a corner, sound asleep. Stephen sat by the entrance, his eyes closed. They fluttered open at her approach. She motioned for him to go outside.

"Ma?" he asked.

Sally nodded. "Go for the midwife. I've written a letter explaining the situation." She had scrawled a few lines in between times of helping Ma to her feet and getting her around.

"Should I go to the farm, for the horse?"

Sally chewed on her lip, debating. "No. But perhaps you can borrow one in town." After today, they would not be able to keep their presence on the farm a secret. After all their months of work. . .

"And here. Take this." She handed him a piece of johnny-cake, the last bit of food left from supper. "Godspeed."

Ma cried out, loudly enough so that Nellie stirred under her covers.

"Go! Quickly!"

As Stephen turned to go, they both heard an unexpected noise at the same time—the snap of a twig in the trees beyond the cave entrance. He stared wildly at her and then slipped back into the cave.

Sally stood her ground, straining to distinguish the sounds. The hum of a familiar voice reached her ears, and she relaxed. *Josiah.* She wanted, welcomed, *needed* his help in this emergency.

Stephen reappeared at the entrance, musket in hand. He motioned for her to join him. Ignoring him, she walked toward the noise.

"It's coming from this direction!" someone called.

"Josiah!" The word burst from Sally's lips before she identified the speaker. *Not* Josiah.

Chapter 12

Sally. Relief washed through Josiah at the sound of her voice. The cries of distress didn't come from her.

Just as quickly, panic replaced relief. Any hope he had of keeping the Reids' secret had vanished with that single word.

Surprise and anger played on his father's face. Before he could react further, Josiah plunged through the forest in the direction of Sally's voice. He ran straight and true, following the light trail their feet had made. The sound of his father's footsteps only seconds behind him spurred him on. He burst through the trees at the edge of the river, stopping himself before he plunged into the water.

A few feet away, Sally appeared. He ran to her like a bee to honey, and she collapsed in his arms.

"It's Ma." Sally sobbed the words into Josiah's shirt.

They had no more time before Father found them.

Amazed comprehension grew on Father's face as he took in Sally in Josiah's arms. "Sally Reid?" Disbelief and anger resonated in every syllable of her name.

"You stay away from my sister." Stephen appeared from the darkness near the riverbed. The musket on his shoulder aimed straight at Father. Josiah suspected the only reason he wasn't the target was that Stephen couldn't hit him without endangering Sally.

"Stephen!" Sally slipped out of Josiah's embrace. Immediately, the boy swung the musket in his direction.

"Stephen Reid? Is that you?" Father scowled. "So where's Nathaniel then? Or perhaps Mr. Reid has returned from the dead?"

Sally's face blanched at the unkind statement. "Nathaniel has gone with the Green Mountain Boys, as you well know."

"I don't know anything. You're supposed to be long gone to New Hampshire, according to this. . .man here."

Another cry emanated from the darkness behind Stephen, and comprehension dawned on Josiah. *Mrs. Reid*. Panic put color back into Sally's face. The distressed sound, however, didn't stop the force of his father's building fury.

"So this is what you've been doing all summer while you've been pretending to work the Reids' farm?"

Josiah willed himself to stand firm. "I have worked the farm. I just didn't tell you everything."

Father's face grew even redder. "You've been working with these traitors? You're no son of mine." He spat on the ground in front of Josiah and Sally.

"I said stay away." Stephen ground out the words through closed teeth.

Another cry came, louder this time.

"Father." Josiah interposed himself between the weapon and his father. "Mrs. Reid's time has come. I am going to do what I can to help her. Later, you may do what you will with me."

Father released the grip on his hoe. An expression, somewhere betwixt kindness and anger, passed over his features. "Very well, then. I will not bother you on this day." He pointed at Stephen, who hadn't lowered his musket. "But be warned. I have marked this place well in my mind. I will come back tomorrow with others, and I won't guarantee your safety if we find you here." He turned on his heel and headed back into the trees. He paused when he realized Josiah wasn't following him.

"Josiah." His voice held a command.

Josiah didn't budge. He wouldn't. He couldn't. Sally and her family needed him now more than ever.

"Very well. You have made your choice. You know that parable about other people enjoying the fruit of your labor? That's going to happen to you. I'm going to gather the other men of the town, and we're going to reap the corn that is ready for harvest and use it for the good of God and king." He turned about without another word and marched into the dense foliage.

After all his months of hoping, praying, working, and wooing, Josiah was left with this.

No home, no crop, not even a place to lay his head.

∽

As soon as Mr. Tuttle disappeared, Sally called to Stephen. "Go! Get the midwife!"

"Wait."

Stephen halted at Josiah's request.

"Go!" Sally repeated. Stephen looked at both of them before speeding into the trees.

Sally glared at Josiah. "Why did you ask him to wait? It may already be too late. I fear for Ma." She stopped her words. Tears would solve nothing at this point in time. She headed for the cave and gathered Nellie in her arms.

Josiah shuffled his feet. "I only wanted to say that this. . .discovery. . .may stir up the Tories. The Patriot families in town should be warned."

"Sally!" Ma's desperate voice called out. Sally bent low at the entrance and whipped around the partition. A small trickle of blood seeped through Ma's bedclothes.

"What's happened?" The sight alarmed Sally. If Ma had started bleeding. . .

Ma's gaze locked with hers, something akin to panic in her eyes, and she grabbed Sally's hand so hard that the feeling went out of her fingers. Another spasm of pain passed through mother to daughter, the tips of Ma's fingernails biting into Sally's flesh. When it passed, the glaze lifted from Ma's eyes, and she became herself again.

"I sent Stephen for the midwife," Sally told her. "It was past time. And I have prepared rags, such as we have, and there is hot water available. And a knife. We are ready for the baby when he arrives."

Ma shook her head. "Don't have much time. I need you to turn the baby."

Turn the baby? Sally envisioned what Ma meant. Did she. . .could she?

Another spasm hit, and Ma's limbs stretched with the effort. Her eyes pleaded with Sally for help. She couldn't say no. She brushed the hair back from Ma's face. "I'll do what I can. Rest when you can. It will be over with soon."

Lord, You created the way we come into this world. I trust You to guide my hands. Her mind steadied, and a plan began to form. She peeked around the blanket.

Josiah sat on the other side, reading the Bible to Nellie and looking so at home that he might have spent the last months living with them.

"I need your help."

Confusion passed over Josiah's features. Asking for a man's assistance, especially someone who wasn't even a family member, was highly unusual. But she had no choice.

"I want you to hold Ma's head and shoulders. You don't have to. . .see anything. But I need you to hold her fast while I work."

Josiah looked at her, his dark eyebrows drawing together in a worried furrow, before he nodded his acceptance of her request.

"I'll help you." Dear Nellie. Sally couldn't accept her sister's offer. The girl grew faint at a splinter; she couldn't witness a birth.

"That's all right. You can help Josiah."

Another pain came, and Sally sped up her arrangements while Ma writhed on the floor. When it ended, Sally lifted the edge of the blanket and tugged Ma's head and shoulders to the other side. "Ma, Josiah came." She'd tell her the rest later—if there was a later. There *had* to be a later.

She refused to believe otherwise. "He's going to help us. Grab a hold of his hands, because this may hurt."

Sally looked at her dirt-encrusted hands. The book on midwifery hadn't said anything about clean hands that she could recall, but she didn't like to think about touching the baby after all the places her hands had been that day. So she poured hot water into a pan and scrubbed her hands and arms with soap. The next spasm passed, and she called across the partition. "Are you ready?"

"Yes."

Sally didn't waste any further time. She settled her hands in place, said a brief prayer, and started to work. In between pains she moved the baby's body into the right position. When at last she had finished, Ma screamed one overwhelming cry, and the baby slid out.

Relief flooded through Sally, leaving her weak at the knees. *Thank You, Lord.* But her work wasn't done. She cut and tied the cord and rubbed a warm, wet cloth over the tiny squalling infant.

"What is it?" Ma's voice called through the blanket.

"A boy."

"What did you say?" Nellie's voice penetrated the blanket.

"We have a brother!" Joy sang through Sally's heart. "Mr. Donald Allen Reid Jr. Isn't that right, Ma?"

"I want to see my Donny boy."

Sally took a moment to examine the baby. Ten fingers and toes, hair as pale as the silk on an ear of corn, toenails so tiny several of them would fit on a ha'penny—perfect. She wrapped him in a clean cloth and clutched him close before poking her head around the blanket and handing him to her mother. "He's beautiful."

A beatific smile lit Ma's face as she took the baby in her arms. Sweat beaded her brow, the exhaustion of a job well done. No worry bothered her. She kissed the top of Donny's head. "Welcome to the world." She raised her eyes, now at peace, to her daughter. "I couldn't have done it without you."

"I only did what needed doing." Sally didn't want any praise. Anything she had accomplished had been by the grace of God.

"Let me see him." Nellie reached out her arms. Sally showed her how to support his head and handed him over.

Josiah stared at the infant with an amazed expression on his face. "It's a miracle, that's what it is." He reached for the baby's fists, then withdrew his hands.

"Go ahead."

Josiah lay a single finger on the baby's arm, so long that it covered it from elbow to fist. "I haven't seen a newborn. He's so tiny. A gift from God."

He smiled at Ma. "And well named. Your husband must be rejoicing up in heaven, although I know you must wish he were here."

Sally looked at the baby in Ma's arms. One last, final gift, a reminder of Pa's love and faithfulness. How natural Josiah looked with the baby. What a good father he would make one day.

Maybe someday. She caught Josiah looking at her, and she knew the same thoughts ran through his head. Heat flooded her neck, and she turned away.

Josiah tore his eyes away from Sally's. Temptation lay down that path. God willing, the day would come. He looked again at the infant, so precious, so perfect. He marveled again at God's miraculous gifts.

"Let me finish up so we can move this curtain and Ma can get some rest." Sally handed the baby back to Ma and ducked behind the blanket again. Josiah shook himself out of his trance. He had tarried because Sally and Mrs. Reid needed him, but now he must get moving.

"I can't stay." He removed his finger from Donny's arm, and the boy squirmed in Mrs. Reid's arms.

"What's that?" Sally poked her head back out, disappointment flaring in her eyes.

Although he hated to be the cause, he had to act now. He had already delayed longer than he should. "Father wasn't joking when he said he would inform the other Tories about your crops. I have stayed on the fence with him long enough. It is time I take my stand." His jaw clenched as he said the words, but he had determined to see things through this time. "Stephen must be on his way back with the midwife by now. I will meet him and learn if he has warned the families in town. Then I'll decide what to do."

The joy went out of Sally's eyes, joy that the baby's birth had brought only minutes before. "We have to move." Her voice dulled, full of dread. "But Ma..."

"I will do whatever it takes to keep this family safe." As Josiah said the words, he wondered how he could fulfill his promise. He didn't even have his musket with him. "I hope to encourage some of the Patriots to come protect your fields—and your home."

Who, he didn't know. All the men of fighting age had gone with the Green Mountain Boys. But those left behind must see that if they could win the battle for the Reids' farm, all of them could return home.

"Go, and Godspeed." Mrs. Reid held the baby on her shoulder. "We will do what must be done here."

Sally looked so lost that Josiah lost restraint. He kissed her cheek.

Sally clung to him before pushing him away. She spoke softly. "If you see Stephen with the midwife—please ask her to come ahead. Ma had a hard time of it."

Josiah nodded his agreement and left before resolve and common sense departed from him altogether.

∽

"He's a good man." Ma said the words that were pounding through Sally's heart.

"He is." Josiah was good, capable, and strong. She couldn't have done what Ma needed without his steadfast presence, the assurance that come good or ill, he was with her. But now he had left, charging into the face of danger, and she had much to do. What would they do? If they decided to move, how could she get ready in time?

For now, Ma needed rest.

"Let's get you and the baby comfortable." Sally watched baby Donny sleeping, hands curled up against Ma, so peaceful and trusting. If only she trusted God like that. . .

Trust me, child. The Holy Ghost spoke words of peace to her soul. She had made her needs known to the Father, and He would take care of her. She must hold that thought close.

Since both men had left, Sally considered pulling down the curtain partition. She decided to clean first. The mess might disturb Nellie. Their resources were limited, but Sally came up with an idea. "Why don't you put on my nightdress, Ma? Then I can wash yours."

Ma nodded and sat up long enough to remove one and slip on the other. Sally gathered the dirty linens into a bundle. As soon as she could leave the cave, she would rinse them in the river. At last, she took down the blanket and laid it on the ground for Ma.

"Thank you, dear daughter." Ma managed a weary smile. "I believe I will rest for a little while."

Nellie held baby Donnie while Ma settled on the blanket. "He's so *small.*" He yawned and closed his eyes, and Nellie laughed. "I love you, baby brother."

Sally expected Ma to fall asleep as soon as she laid down, but she didn't. "Sally?"

"What is it, Ma? Can I get you something?" She offered her some water.

"Not me." Ma smiled and took some of the water. "Although this tastes refreshing. No, I'm concerned about you. You've taken the weight of this whole turn of events on your shoulders."

"Oh, Ma." The baby let out a mewling cry, and Nellie handed him to his mother. "God reminded me I'm no more able to take care of my own needs than little Donny here. I have to trust Him."

"I'm so glad you see that. 'Thou hast given commandment to save me.'"

" 'For thou art my rock and my fortress,'" Sally finished quoting the verse with Ma. "I'm asking God to show us where we need to move tonight."

"If we move. I have a feeling we're supposed to stay right here." Ma tucked Donny next to her, and the two of them fell asleep as if things were that simple.

Sally looked about the cave, taking stock of their resources. Was there any hope of staying here? If they did, would they be trapped like a raccoon up a tree?

Had Josiah gone for help as promised?

Sally shook away her doubts. She would trust him. She had to.

All their lives depended on it.

Chapter 13

Josiah felt like he possessed the hind's feet of scripture as he leapt from stone to stone across the river and climbed the embankment. Trotting, he took the most direct route to town, trusting Stephen had as well. He hoped to run into him escorting the midwife to the cave. Josiah would have sprinted if the distance were not so far. People spoke of Paul Revere's ride on the night before the battles of Lexington and Concord, warning the minutemen of the British approach. But Revere had the advantage of a horse and roads; all Josiah had were his own two feet and the faintest trace of a path.

He swung left and intersected the trodden track that led from the Tuttle and Reid farms into town. Once on the clear path, he gathered speed, no longer worrying about tripping over tree roots or brushing branches out of his face. He took a drink from his skein of water and continued running. He had reached the farthest clearings that constituted the town proper when he spotted Stephen headed in his direction, Goodwife Hutchins following. As well as . . .

Nathaniel! The sight of his old friend gave impetus to Josiah's tiring legs, and he raced harder. He knew the instant they spotted him. A wide smile broke out on Nathaniel's face, and he pointed in Josiah's direction. The two men embraced for but a second before Nathaniel pulled away. "Ma?"

"You have another brother."

Goodwife Hutchins stopped in her tracks. "She's had the baby, then?" She sounded like she had misgivings about following them into the woods.

"Yes, but Sally—Miss Reid—asked that you come ahead. Mrs. Reid had a difficult time, and we would all appreciate your assistance."

She fiddled with her bag as if that would hold the answers she needed. "Very well. I'll come. If I've said it once, I've said it a dozen times. Babies take no mind of their parents' politics, and they come when they've a mind to. Lead the way. But none of this telling me how to find it on my own. I'm a midwife, not a woodsman."

Nathaniel and Stephen exchanged a look. "I'll meet you at the farm," Stephen said. "After I take the goodwife to Ma." He headed for the cave.

"Have you warned the townspeople?" Josiah wanted to know.

"That the Tories are stirring?" Nathaniel nodded. "They're meeting on the green."

"Have the Green Mountain Boys returned?" Josiah held some slight hope. If they joined in the fight, Sally and her family would be secure.

Nathaniel shook his head. "I realized I had left home precipitously. They allowed me to return home with messages for their families and to make sure Ma was settled." He grimaced. "I'm here for two days, maybe three. They expect me back within the week."

"You arrived in the nick of time." Josiah considered the situation. The green was generally considered neutral ground, but the Tories might see this as an opportunity to nip opposition in the bud—if they knew about it. Then again, they might be meeting at a place of their own, like his father's farm, to decide what action to take against the Reids. "You know the defenses we have here."

"The willing but less than able." Nathaniel nodded. "Elder Cabot, missing his leg from the French and Indian War. . ."

"Mr. Bailey, who can't see past the end of his nose without his spectacles. . ."

"Young boys like Stephen who can't wait to get involved."

The two men looked at each other. Their help lay in men who had stayed behind either because their time to fight had not yet come or because it had long since passed. But no one doubted their courage. They headed for the green.

Perhaps a score of the willing had gathered. They ranged in age from ten-year-old Willie Smith to Elder Cabot. Even a woman stood in their ranks.

Meg Turner saw their surprise. "I can shoot a musket as well as the rest of you. It's time we take a stand for ourselves."

"Tuttle, what are you doing here?" Cabot might be missing a limb, but he hadn't lost any of his peppery spirit.

"I've come to warn you of danger." Josiah spoke forcefully. "I don't know how much young Stephen told you."

"Why should we believe you? Any true Patriot would have gone with the Green Mountain Boys," Cabot said.

A murmur told Josiah others agreed with him.

Nathaniel stepped out from behind Josiah. "I'm here, and I'm a Patriot. I stand with him. You all know the losses our families have suffered. Now listen up. We don't have time to argue among ourselves."

Nathaniel spoke with the confidence of a born leader. Quarreling died down. "Josiah knows what has been happening here better than I do. Pay attention."

Josiah outlined everything that had happened since his return from Fort Ticonderoga, starting with his work on the Reids' farm. "Now that my father has discovered what I've been doing all these months, he has threatened harm against not only the Reids, but all the Patriots of Maple Notch."

When he determined he had their attention, he struck another blow.

"Mary Reid, left with only her daughter and two young children, found a way to do what all of you wanted to do. She continued working her farm. She was determined not to let the Tories win everything she and Mr. Reid had worked so hard to obtain."

He looked at each of them. "If more of us had done that, perhaps the Tories wouldn't have had such an easy time in Maple Notch. If we had stood our ground. . ." He paused. "Yes, I'm saying *we*. If *I* had taken a stand against my father, perhaps even now you would be gathering food and preparing for your sons and fathers to return home instead of staying in town and wondering how you will feed your families next year."

No one dared look at him, keeping their eyes fixed on the ground. Only Elder Cabot lifted his musket above his shoulder with a shout. "I say we fight them!"

The reaction Josiah hoped for. Needed.

Hiram Bailey, about the same age as Stephen, raised his weapon as well and started chanting. "Fight! Fight! Fight!"

Nathaniel took up the chant, raising his arm with every repetition of the word, gesturing with his musket. Soon every man standing was stomping his foot and calling for battle.

"Then come with me! To my family's farm! We have a chance to round up these Tory troublemakers." Leadership of the group had slipped to Nathaniel, but Josiah gladly gave it over.

As the men ran for the forest, Josiah tapped Nathaniel on the shoulder. "I'm going back to the cave. There's a chance Father will come to force them out. I promised Sally I would protect them." He hated to burden Nathaniel with the possible move his family faced, but he needed to know.

Nathaniel brushed him aside. "We must be on our way. Tell me what happened as we head down the path, since we travel in the same direction." He trotted after the others without another word.

Josiah ran beside him and explained the situation at the cave. "If the midwife says your mother shouldn't be moved, I'm not certain what can be done. It's urgent I remain with them. If any harm comes to your family. . ."

Nathaniel's step hesitated a moment; then he continued his forward motion. "I trust you to do what needs to be done. I think the farm is a greater risk. . .more valuable to the British." He took note of Josiah's lack of weapon. "But you're unarmed! Take my musket."

Josiah wanted to protest. Nathaniel would be foolish to approach a confrontation or attempt to lead men without a firearm.

"I have another." Nathaniel must have sensed his hesitation.

They had reached the point where the paths to the field and the cave diverged. Josiah accepted the musket and sprinted in the direction of Sally and all she held dear. As he ran, he sent up a prayer to the Lord Almighty for His protection on everyone involved in today's confrontations, even the Tories, his father included.

When he arrived at the cave, young Stephen paced outside the entrance, musket in hand, cold determination stamping his young face. When he heard Josiah's movement in the trees, he stiffened and then relaxed when he saw who it was. Surprise replaced the worry on his face.

"Josiah. I expected you to go with the men to the farm."

Josiah shook his head. "I promised Sally I would protect your family. If my father returns. . ."

Stephen's dark expression returned. "Since you showed him the way to our hiding place, you mean?"

Before the argument could escalate to needless anger on both sides, Sally came to the cave entrance. "Josiah! I thought I heard your voice." She ran to him.

Although her mobcap sat askew, her hair fell in tangled ringlets about her head, and exhaustion showed in her face, Josiah didn't care. She had never looked more beautiful to him. He took her in his arms and let her collapse against his chest. For the moment, the nightmarish quality of the preceding twenty-four hours melted away. All that mattered was the woman in his arms and the desire he felt to cherish her and protect her from all harm.

Then reality intruded. The sounds of a baby's cries came from the cave, reminding him of all that was at stake this day.

∽

Josiah had returned. Sally didn't want to move from his arms. When he held her, sheltering her, she felt as if she was in God's strong habitation, protected and safe. Reluctantly, she stepped back and straightened the cap on her head as best she could.

"How is the babe? And your mother? What says Goodwife Hutchins?" Josiah's soft voice comforted her as much as his arms had done.

"I can tell ye that for meself." The plump matron looked worn-out. "Things would have gone poorly if Miss Reid here hadn't done what she did. Mother and child are fine, but in need of rest. You can't be moving them, sir, no matter what that rascal father of yours says."

Sally saw Josiah stiffen and hastened to reassure him. "We don't hold you accountable for your father, Josiah."

Goodwife Hutchins snorted. "Never thought I'd live to see the day a man would ask a woman to move when she's lying in. No matter which side of the war they land on. I won't speak for her health if you make her move."

With the midwife's every word, Stephen's scowl deepened, and Josiah drew back into himself. Sally had to intervene before they came to blows or did something else they'd regret.

"We thank you for your services, Goodwife." She opened her money purse.

The midwife waved away the offer. "You did all the work before I ever arrived. I'll not be taking your money."

"Then you'll be on your way?" Sally asked.

Goodwife Hutchins looked aghast. "With the men of the town wandering about like knights looking for battle? I think not. Besides, I want to keep an eye on your mother for a time yet." She tilted her head forward under the low roof and bustled back into the cave, muttering to herself, "They're all daft."

A pained smile had replaced the frown on Josiah's face. "She's an ornery creature; that's what my mother always said. But she's served Maple Notch well ever since people settled here."

"But what about what she said? What are we going to do? If we can't move Ma. . ." Stephen sounded as uncertain as any lad his age would be.

"First, I suggest we go inside the cave. No need to continue our discussion in the open air where everyone can see and hear." Josiah gestured for Sally to go ahead of them. "It offers some shelter."

Sally thought of Ma's need for peace and rest and wished they could remain outside. But Josiah was right; they needed the relative safety of the cave. She reentered the darkness and let her eyes adjust.

Ma was sleeping with baby Donny tucked by her side. She looked so peaceful that Sally almost envied her. Behind her, Stephen knocked over a piece of firewood, which clattered as it hit the ground. The baby's arms flung outward at the sound, and he whimpered softly. Ma stirred, opened her eyes, and she struggled to a sitting position. Sally frowned and then shrugged. Perhaps it was just as well.

Josiah knelt down next to Ma. "May I?" he asked, reaching for the baby.

"Certainly." Ma handed the baby to him.

Some of the weariness that had filled Josiah's features fled, replaced by joy and wonder. "Of all of God's creation, a newborn is the finest." He shifted the baby in his arms, and Donny let out a loud squall. Josiah laughed. "He's a brawny, brave lad. I believe he's saying he wants his mother." As he said the words, he looked at Sally, wonder and questions in his eyes. *Will this day ever come for us?* Then the light disappeared from his eyes, and he turned serious. "Mrs. Reid. I'm glad you're awake. It's best if you're involved in the decision making, since it affects you most of all." He handed the infant back to his mother.

As Josiah explained the situation, different emotions played over Ma's face, emotions that echoed in Sally's own heart: fear, uncertainty, exhaustion, hope. They listened to all the options without speaking.

"We should—"

Ma lifted a finger, and Stephen fell silent. "Since your father's death, I have asked a man's job of you, and you have done well. But I am the head of this family, and I will make this decision." She softened her statement with her next words. "Although I value your opinion—all of you. But right now, let me think."

They could have heard grass grow in the silence that settled in the cave, broken by an occasional mewling sound from the baby. Even Nellie didn't move from her spot beside the fire.

"You say the Patriots hope to not only protect our farm but also round up the Tories who have been plaguing their families?"

Josiah hesitated. "They have built up their anger and want to take action. They're tired of being pushed around."

"And the Tories want to make an example of my family and farm to show the Patriots they mean what they say?"

Josiah paused longer this time. He hung his head. "That's what my father threatened to do."

"Your *father*." Ma emphasized the word. "You owe him more than a date with death. My son, your father, and every other man young or old left in Maple Notch are gathering in our fields to fight. People will die this evening if someone doesn't do something to stop them."

Hearing it stated like that, Sally felt even worse about the upcoming confrontation. She looked at Josiah, at the deep, dark hurt in his eyes.

"Dear Josiah. I've known you since you were the size of little Donny here." Ma held the baby against her chest. "I love you as if you were my own. You can't let this happen."

"But what can I do?" The anguish in Josiah's voice was painful to hear.

"Go to your father." Ma looked surprised he had to ask. "Sally, I think it best if you go with him. Remind him of the long years of friendship that lie between our families."

Startled, Sally looked from Ma to Josiah and back again.

"Mrs. Reid, no." Josiah stood.

Donny let out a cry, and Ma shushed Josiah's protest. "Your father will hesitate to commit violence in the presence of a woman. He will gain some time to react with reason and not from anger." She smiled confidently. "I trust you with her safety."

"But who will protect you, Ma?" Sally asked.

" 'The Lord is my rock and my fortress.' And Stephen will be with us."

Stephen bit his lip. He probably wished he could go fight, take his place among the men. Ma reached out a hand and touched his shoulder. "Stephen, you'll have the most important job of all. . .protecting me and the baby."

He straightened his shoulders and puffed out his chest, grown broad over the summer's work.

Sally scrambled for alternatives and found none. Ma was right, and they had no time to waste. "Josiah, let's get going if we're going to stop your father before a quarrel breaks out."

Josiah grabbed his musket and headed for the cave entrance. "If it's not already too late."

Sally looked around the cave for something she could use as a weapon. The only possibility was the hoe Josiah had so lovingly crafted. *Don't be a dunce.* How could she convince Mr. Tuttle she came in peace if she arrived bearing arms? *I'll be wearing the armor of God,* she reminded herself. She had the best protection of all: the breastplate of righteousness, the shield of faith, and feet shod with the gospel of peace. Saying a prayer for the Lord's help, she followed Josiah into the thicket of trees.

"We'll pass close to your farm on the way to my family's cabin," Josiah remarked. "Pray we don't hear gunfire." His lips twisted in what was supposed to pass for a smile. "We'll move slowly and surely. There is no need to run like wild things and announce our presence."

A squirrel jumped from a tree branch, and it swung through the air with a snapping sound. Sally jumped. *The gospel of peace,* she continued praying. The American colonies wouldn't win freedom without bloodshed. *Including Pa's.* But not today, not between neighbors and friends and family. Not on account of her family, and not while she could do something to stop it.

The sound of the squirrel also caught Josiah unaware, and he put his finger into the air for a warning signal and stopped. After a pause, he started walking again. He spoke in a low voice. "The folks from town took the main road, but I don't know which way the Tories are coming. They might shoot before thinking. Follow my lead."

Sally nodded, fear screaming down her legs that she should run, fast. The noise of her heavy skirts as they dragged through the trees made her doubt their plan of action. Without her along, Josiah could move quickly and quietly. *But Mr. Tuttle might listen to me when he won't listen to his son,* she reminded herself. She lifted the edges of her skirt and walked as softly as she could manage.

Josiah detoured on a route that bypassed the Reids' field. Sally wondered why until she determined he was heading straight for his farm. Perhaps they would avoid both militia and king's men and accomplish their task. She hoped God would speed their steps so they could arrive before the gathering and speak sense to Mr. Tuttle.

Josiah stopped so abruptly that Sally put out her hand to prevent herself from running into his back. He examined the leaves and branches around them without speaking.

"What is it?" Sally whispered.

He whirled around, his attitude making the act more threat than comfort. "Someone's already been this way, heading to the farm. I don't know what we'll find there." Without warning, he set off again, leaving Sally to catch up. Given his state of mind, she wasn't sure if he was ready to listen to reason any more than his father was. She prayed for all of them as she followed Josiah's footsteps.

As they progressed, she could see signs of the passage of a number of men, although they had not yet seen or heard them. At last she heard a faint groaning from beyond the next copse of trees. The sound of an animal in pain, or someone injured. . .dying. *We're too late.*

Chapter 14

Josiah looked into Sally's eyes, questioning pools of pale blue-green, and suspected she saw the same question in his own eyes. Who, or what, had they heard? If human, there could only be one man; more would make a greater amount of noise. Unless the Tories were aware of their approach and someone had faked an injury, hoping to lure them to a surprise attack. He gripped his musket and signaled for Sally to wait while he took a few cautious steps forward.

When he saw the man sprawled on the ground, he sprinted forward.

"Father!" His voice rang out like a bird's call, loud and clear. Heedless of the danger, he plunged through the growth, dropped to his knees, and set the musket down. Father lay on the ground unmoving, eyes staring straight ahead without blinking. Josiah's heart jumped into his throat, cutting off his breath. The doctor had warned his father about controlling his anger and his too-rich diet. Had the confrontation between father and son on the previous day brought this on? Josiah felt more guilty and torn than ever.

Behind him, he heard Sally gasp. "Is he...dead?" Her voice sounded faint and far away, or perhaps his sense of hearing had dulled.

Josiah took Father's wrist in his hand and felt for a pulse. For a long, tense moment, he couldn't find it. Then he felt it, a slow, almost imperceptible beat, a rhythm that made his heart sing more than any hymn of praise.

"He's alive." Tears coated his voice, but Josiah didn't care. "Praise the Lord. He's alive." The last words came through a choked throat.

"Amen." Sally's heartfelt agreement rang in his heart. She knelt next to Josiah. "Praise God from whom all blessings flow." The words lifted from her lips like an offering to the Almighty, and Josiah joined her in singing. "Praise Him, all creatures here below." Birds swooped in front of them, adding their cries and calls to the song of thanksgiving.

Josiah broke from the reverie, remembering where they were and why they were there. "If anyone was looking for us..." He attempted to swallow a bitter laugh without success. "We've just given them directions."

Beads of sweat dotted his father's brow, as if he had been working in the fields during the height of summer instead of walking through the forest on a cool autumn day. It looked like several people had come this way. If so, why had they left him behind? With the doxology, Josiah and Sally had announced their presence. The others could return at any second.

"We need to get out of here." What had he heard the doctor say about apoplexy? Was there a certain way they should position the body? He couldn't worry about that. He slung his father's body over his left shoulder and lurched to his feet. The weight made him stumble. *Lord, give me strength.*

Two strides later, he paused. "Where should we go?"

"Our cabin is closest." Sally took off in that direction without waiting for his reply.

"But. . ." The protest died on his lips. Here or there, it didn't matter as long as they got moving. He shifted his father's weight and lumbered down the path behind her.

&

Mr. Tuttle was ill, perhaps to death. Sally couldn't believe it. Whatever animosity she had felt toward Josiah's father for his opposition to her family and the other Patriots fled in the face of the apoplectic fit. She didn't want him to die.

She swerved from her course to intersect the path between the two farms. Speed mattered more than staying hidden. As she raced down the trail, she saw signs of recent passage—many feet. Her heart palpitated, but she kept pushing onward. No one they encountered would harm a woman and a sick man, not their neighbors, people she had known all her life.

Then why have we been living in a cave these past few months? Why have we been farming by dark? Because everything had changed. Freedom would come at a high price. In her heart of hearts, did she believe it was worth the cost?

Josiah panted behind her. His father must outweigh him by several pounds. How he managed to carry him at all amazed her. When she glanced back to see if she could help in any way, she noticed he wasn't carrying the musket.

Fear flared in Sally's heart. She lifted her skirts and prepared to race even faster for the cabin; then she halted. The cabin offered little protection and no weapons, not even the hoe she had disdained in the cave. No protection but the armor of God, she reminded herself. That would be enough. It would have to be.

"What's wrong?" Josiah pulled even with her.

"The musket." Fear must have shown in her eyes. "You left it back in the thicket."

His mouth opened and closed, not finding any words sufficient for the situation they found themselves in. This close, she could hear the thready sound of Mr. Tuttle's breathing. He needed a bed and quiet, as soon as possible. Only one possibility came to mind.

"You go ahead to the cabin." She took a deep breath. "I'll go back for the musket." She didn't wait for the protest she was sure would come, but lifted her skirts well above her ankles and raced—their lives depended on it.

∽

Josiah wanted to toss his father on the ground and run after Sally. Of all the foolish, idiotic things he had ever done. . .and Sally's rash decision to rush into danger. But he had no choice in the matter. He had to render care to his father, and the cabin was only a short distance away. He said a quick prayer as he started in the direction of the Reids' property.

It's your own fault, he reminded himself. If he hadn't left the weapon behind. . .

He called himself every name in the book and made up a few more. The name-calling couldn't keep his mind off the danger to which Sally raced. *Will the Tories find her? If they do, what will they do to her?* He tore his mind away from the images that flooded his mind and went back to inventive self-flagellation. *You're more selfish than the Levite that passed by the Samaritan, you oaf.*

He reached the edge of the clearing and stopped before walking into the open. Anyone nearby would have heard his approach, but he didn't need to walk into an ambush. He gave the bobolink call in case Nathaniel and the others had come to the farm. No response. No sounds intruded on the silence. He moved forward, the weight of his father pressing upon his back and threatening to slip off if his balance shifted by so much as a penny-weight. At the door, he used its surface to prop up Father's body while he turned the knob. It sprang open, and Josiah caught his father just in time before he fell onto the floor.

The soft tick bed beckoned from the corner, and Josiah laid down his father's body. How much harm had the run through the forest caused? Panic set in when he had to press his fingers hard for a pulse. Finding it at last, he sagged over his father's body.

What had the doctor said after Father's last attack? Did he need to be warmer or cooler? Would a blistering plaster help or harm? Not that he could find the ingredients for a plaster in the kitchen—the Reids had emptied it out when they moved—or that he would know how to make it. Such knowledge usually resided with the women of the family, but they were in Canada. The doctor's instructions were at his family's cabin. Maybe he should have taken Father there, after all. He did remember the doctor had said to call him to bleed the patient.

But Josiah was here, in the deserted home of the Reids, while the doctor, a Patriot, was away fighting with the Green Mountain Boys, without any herbal remedies available. What else could have the doctor suggested? *Raise Father's head*. He could do that much. Loosen his clothes and keep him cool—now he remembered—so no blanket.

Sally should be here by now. After he had done what he could without more supplies or the doctor, Josiah paced the cabin and wondered when she would arrive. Why, oh why, had he forgotten the musket? Why had he allowed her to go back after it? Why had God allowed his father's apoplexy and the threat to all their lives to happen at the same time?

No answer came. He knew it was foolish to think about it; wondering why wouldn't change a thing. Perhaps now that Father was settled, Josiah could chance going back to escort Sally to the cabin.

"Tuttle, we know you're in there."

Josiah recognized Hawkins, one of the Tory leaders.

"We have something you want."

Dread seized Josiah, and he flung the door open.

Hawkins held Sally close, his arm hugging her neck, knife to her throat.

～

"Josiah." Sally couldn't keep the quiver from her voice, in spite of her best efforts. Because of her failure to retrieve the musket in time, they were in more danger than ever.

"Josiah, is it?" Hawkins imitated her voice, making her sound like a helpless maiden without a knight to come to her rescue. He pressed the knife tip into her skin, and she flinched.

Josiah took a step forward.

"Stop there, Tuttle. Come any closer and. . ."

Sally felt the knife cross her throat, a whisker's breadth from her skin.

Josiah stopped moving.

A foul stench invaded Sally's nostrils when next Hawkins spoke. "It seems like you and 'Miss Reid' have become good friends, very good friends indeed. To think that all this time you've been pretending to be such a good son to your father."

Had her single, involuntary cry of Josiah's name put them in even greater danger? She pled for forgiveness with her eyes. She dared not speak again.

"Hawkins." Josiah held his position and extended his arms in front of him, showing them all he had no weapon.

My fault, all my fault. Sally moaned, and Hawkins put his hard hand over her mouth. "No noise making."

"You're not thinking clearly," Josiah said, not moving from his spot.

"What? Because I believe God's command to honor the king?"

109

Sally didn't believe even the hated King George would approve of Hawkins's actions on this day.

"Because the Hawkins I know wouldn't harm innocent people. Women, children—sick men like my father."

"Your father is the reason we're here. Some in the group said how we ought to go back and check on him—it wasn't right to leave him there. And that's when we found Miss Reid here, retrieving the musket." He brandished it with his left hand.

Coming from Hawkins's mouth, *Miss Reid* sounded like a curse. Sally forced herself not to shiver.

"If you believed in the king's cause, you'd have joined General Burgoyne in his campaign." Josiah seemed to be sneering at Hawkins. "Real men fight real battles. They don't pick on women and children." His eyes focused on Sally, willing her to some action that she couldn't determine.

"Why, you—"

"Afraid to fight like a man?" No doubt about it, Josiah was taunting the Tory.

"I'm not afraid of you." Hawkins dragged Sally forward a few inches, thrusting his knife in Josiah's direction.

"Not willing to fight on equal terms, no weapons, hand to hand, one on one?"

Hawkins moved forward until Josiah was only inches away. "I'm ready whenever you are."

Josiah cocked his fists but spoke to the gathering. "Promise me you won't let your men run like wild things if things go poorly for you?"

Josiah glanced at Sally and then at the woods. Sally thought back to Josiah's warning as they walked through the forest. *Does he mean. . . ?*

"Or will they run away like scared rabbits?" When he looked at her this time, she was certain she understood his meaning.

"Don't know why I should promise anything to a rebel like you." Hawkins shoved Sally aside.

She lifted her skirts and fled in the direction of the forest, where she knew every tree and leaf and hollow. If she could get away, she could go to Nathaniel and the other Patriots for help. *Lord, please, please protect Josiah.* Brambles tore her skirt and left scratches on her ankles as she headed into the woods. As soon as she judged it was safe, she circled back to the fields.

A shape loomed in front of her, gripping her shoulders, and clapped a hand over her mouth before her scream could escape. She saw it was Nathaniel and relaxed.

"Why are you running through the woods like a deer escaping a hunter?" he asked.

"They have Josiah." She paused, taking a deep gulp of air. "At our cabin."

Nathaniel gestured, and for the first time, Sally noticed the others gathered around him. "They took the battle to the cabin instead of to the fields," he said. "Let's go."

They fled into the trees before Sally caught her breath and could move again. Elder Cabot hobbled up to her, making surprising speed with his wooden leg. "Would you keep an old man company and see what we can do to help?"

"Of course." She took the man's arm, his other hand holding on to a cane, and they followed behind. Now that she was no longer running, the scratches on her legs began to burn. She focused on listening for gunfire.

A single shot rang out, and both of them picked up speed. They arrived at the clearing only a couple of minutes behind Nathaniel and the others, but the sight that greeted them brought tears to Sally's eyes. Each Patriot had a Tory at gunpoint. Smoke curled from the end of Meg Turner's musket. She must have fired a warning shot.

Only Josiah and Hawkins continued to fight, hand to hand, as promised. They looked like death alone would stop the combat.

Chapter 15

Josiah had heard Nathaniel's call, the warning shot, the thud of weapons dropping on the ground. But he didn't let any of the action distract his attention from Hawkins.

Hawkins, however, looked at the commotion. Only for a moment, but that was long enough for Josiah to land a solid punch on his jaw that sent him staggering back. "That one's for Sally. For threatening her." He said it so low that he doubted anyone heard it in the general melee.

Hawkins's eyes narrowed, and he tried a counterpunch that Josiah easily dodged. "Your help has arrived." He sneered.

Josiah darted in long enough to land a couple of blows on Hawkins's exposed abdomen. "And *that's* for calling me a coward."

Hawkins doubled over, but Josiah didn't slow down. He rained blows on his head. "And that's for leaving my father to die in the woods."

Hawkins moaned.

"Josiah! Stop!" Sally's gentle voice penetrated the angry fog created by the months of grief and alienation that had swarmed around him. The red haze cleared from his vision, and he looked at Hawkins with amazement. The man lay prone on the ground. Sally didn't pay attention to his injuries, however. She dipped a rag in a bucket of water from the well and held it up to Josiah's face. It came away smeared with mud and blood.

The touch stung, but he wouldn't have stopped Sally's ministrations for anything.

"You're hurt."

"Time will heal me. But—"

"I'm so sorry. If I hadn't let them catch me. . ."

"I'm the fool for leaving the musket behind."

"Shh." She wrung out the rag and ran it over his face one more time. "Your father? Is he. . . ?"

Father! How could Josiah have forgotten him in the midst of the fight? "He was still breathing when Hawkins and the others arrived." He wiped his hands—covered with Hawkins's blood—on the rag and walked for the door. Sally followed.

Father was breathing heavily, noisily. Never had his labored breathing sounded so sweet, since only an hour earlier the breath of life fluttered silently within him, almost nonexistent. Josiah flung himself by his father's side.

"You're alive!"

Father's eyelids fluttered open, and dark eyes glared at Josiah. "I should hope so." He lifted his head a quarter of an inch, dropped it back against the pillow, and grunted. "Where am I?"

"You're in our cabin, Mr. Tuttle." Sally knelt by his other side. "Praise God you've awakened. You gave us a fright."

"Get me"—Father made an effort in earnest to sit up before he sank back against the tick—"out of here."

"You're not going anywhere." Josiah could bark as well as his father.

Sally threw a reproachful look his way before she put a soothing hand on the old man's brow. "We found you in the forest and brought you here since it was closest."

"I'd rather—"

Sally rode over his protest. "Now rest. All this fuss can do you no good."

"Josiah." Nathaniel had entered the cabin.

Sally lifted a finger to her mouth and gestured for the two men to go outside. Josiah spared a glance at his father, debating whether the man would give Sally a hard time, and decided no, he wouldn't. Besides, Father had already closed his eyes again. Josiah stepped outside with Nathaniel.

"We got fourteen of 'em. Fifteen, if we count your father." Nathaniel spoke with all the excitement of a newly minted commander.

The Tory men stood in a circle, rope tied betwixt and around them. Josiah was relieved to see Hawkins on his feet. "So I see. What are you going to do with them?"

"String 'em up!" That cry came from one of the young boys, hotheaded and eager for battle. "For being traitors to their country."

Hawkins straightened his shoulders and glared at Josiah from underneath swelling eyelids. "It's you who are the traitors. You can kill us if you like, but your time will come."

Josiah had to admire Hawkins's courage. He started to speak but stopped himself. Because of his father, any pleas he made on the Tories' behalf might do more harm than good. Instead he looked at his friend. "What does Nathaniel think?"

"I have no use for the lot of them or their cause." Nathaniel paced around the circle of captured men. "But they're our neighbors. We used to call them our friends. We've worshipped together."

"Too scared to kill us?" Hawkins taunted.

Be quiet, fool. Hawkins's outburst frustrated and frightened Josiah.

Nathaniel drew a deep breath. "I say we lock them up until we can hand them over to Major General St. Clair. Let them face military justice. We can set up shifts guarding the gaol until then."

"Confiscate their property!" one of the young bucks called.

"No, son." Cabot hobbled to the front. "The Good Book says to do to others as we want them to do to us. Not like they treat us. We are the better men and should leave their families in peace. Let St. Clair deal with them and make the decisions."

A murmur of agreement spread through the crowd at Cabot's words of wisdom, and Josiah relaxed. The meeting broke up as the men decided how to get the prisoners into town.

"For a moment there"—Josiah looked at Nathaniel—"I was afraid you'd have a mutiny on your hands."

"Me, too." Nathaniel shook his head. "I've had enough fighting without engaging people I've known my whole life. Now tell me about your father."

Josiah explained about the apoplexy and the doctor's warnings after his father's illness last year. "There's not much more we can do now, since the doctor went off with the Green Mountain Boys. Sally offered your cabin."

"Of course. Leastwise until we get Ma back. I'm going over there to check on her now." He glanced at the sky to gauge the time of day. "Looks like we've still got some daylight left. I'll go tell Ma she can come back home when she feels like moving." He put a hand on Josiah's shoulder. "Thanks for everything you've done for my family. But right now, you need to pay attention to your father and"—he offered a slow grin—"my sister, if I'm not mistaken." He pushed Josiah in the direction of the cabin. "Go, take care of business, friend."

Josiah strode to the cabin with the lightest heart he'd had in months.

☙

A shaft of light told Sally someone had opened the door to the cabin. She felt Josiah's welcome presence before she saw him, and smiled as she turned around to greet him. "He's resting comfortably."

"They're taking Hawkins and the others to gaol as prisoners of war. They'll turn them over to the army as soon as they can figure out how to get them there."

Sally shivered. "Good. Hawkins at least meant serious harm."

"So did my father." Josiah sat next to her and reached for her hand. "How can you be so kind to him, after what he did to you and your family?"

Sally looked at the sleeping figure on the bed. Josiah resembled him so strongly that it was like looking at a portrait of him from the future. "He's your father. How can I do any less?"

"Oh, Sally." Josiah lifted her hand to his lips and kissed her fingertips. "I don't deserve you."

A pleasant shiver ran through Sally's body, a portend of better times ahead. Ma had given birth to a healthy baby boy, the confrontation between the Patriots and Tories had ended without bloodshed, and their harvest was safe. So far, Mr. Tuttle had survived. "God is so good. He has been a strong habitation on this day."

"Amen." Josiah smiled. "The doctor left some medicines for Father with us."

"Go get them." Sally didn't hesitate. "He is resting now, but I don't know what to expect when he awakens."

Josiah kissed her fingers again and left. The door closed behind him.

"Hah!" Mr. Tuttle opened his eyes at the noise. "Josiah?" The words came out faint.

"He's gone for your medicine. He'll be back as soon as he can."

"Sally Reid." Mr. Tuttle said each syllable slowly, painfully, before slipping back into unconsciousness.

Sally didn't know whether he said her name as a question or a curse. It didn't matter. He was Josiah's father, and she would love him and care for him as if he were her own dear pa come back to life.

～

Peace at last. Sally valued these quiet hours when the men went to the fields to harvest the crops. Most days they allowed Nellie to tag along. After the close quarters in the cave, the cabin seemed spacious indeed. Even so, the family made a fair amount of noise before they headed out to the fields before daybreak.

Ma left the beans simmering in the kettle and sat down next to the bed where Mr. Tuttle slept. Donny rustled in his cradle, whimpered, and she snuggled him close. "There, there. Ma's got you, and you're safe. Keep quiet so Mr. Tuttle can sleep."

Sally didn't know how Ma did it. Within days of giving birth, she had organized the family's move back to the cabin. She shared housekeeping duties with Sally so that she could sit with Mr. Tuttle. The only thing that kept Ma from going to the fields was the rest of the family's insistence that she take things easy.

"Do you think he's getting better?" Sally asked. She knew so little about apoplexy; she was following the doctor's written directions from last year, praying, and answering when Mr. Tuttle spoke. The most physically demanding part of his care was changing the bedding when the laxative of sweet butter and salt the doctor had recommended did its work. Feeding him his meals of broth, tea, and toast was no trouble at all.

"He still lives. God has shown His great mercy. Josiah has suffered enough." Ma pursed her lips. "More than that, Mr. Tuttle would do well to get out of bed. Perhaps between us, we can help him to his feet the next time he awakens."

Sally hated to ask Ma for help. The baby awakened her at all hours of the day and night. But she couldn't support Mr. Tuttle's weight on her own. "We'll try."

As if he heard them, Mr. Tuttle stirred, squinting at the sunshine coming through the window. "What day is it?"

That was new. He had been asking where he was upon awakening. Perhaps he was regaining his memory. "It's Friday, Mr. Tuttle."

He raised himself on his elbows and looked around the cabin, sparse since they hadn't yet returned all of their possessions from the cave. "How long. . . ?" The question tailed off.

"It's been four days since you had an apoplectic fit. Josiah is out with our family, bringing in our harvest and yours, too. He'll be here in the evening."

"That son of mine." The tone hovered between rancor and admiration.

Ma burped Donny and set him back in the cradle. She nodded at Sally, who squared her shoulders.

"Mr. Tuttle, we're going to help you get to your feet."

"Don't need your help." He swung his legs over the side of the bed, panting from the exertion.

"You've been very ill and need to get your strength back. Lean on us, and you can rise." Sally bent over and slipped his arm around her shoulders. Ma did the same thing on his other side and helped him up. He swayed on his feet, his teeth gritted in grim determination.

"Can you walk as far as that chair?" Ma nodded at the seat she had just vacated.

He grunted assent, and they kept pace with him. One step, two brought him to the chair. He sank down in relief.

"It's *so* good to see you up!" Sally wanted to laugh with happiness. Josiah's father was on the mend. "Let me fix you some broth." She dished soup from the kettle where they kept it warm and brought it to him.

When she turned around, he was staring at the baby. "Boy or girl?" he asked.

"A boy. Donald Reid Jr.," Ma said.

"I am sorry for your loss." For the first time since the tragedy at Fort Ticonderoga, he offered condolences.

"As we are for yours. No one can replace a son."

"Nor a spouse. I miss my Martha, away in Canada, but I hope to see her again." He looked sad, and Sally hastened to cheer him.

"Come now and eat. You need to build up your strength." By the time he finished eating, he had tired, and they helped him back into bed.

"Keep up the good work, and soon you'll be able to greet Josiah at the door when he comes back at night." Sally checked his coverings.

"I'd like that."

∽

Every one of Josiah's muscles ached after a stretch of sixteen-hour days. They only rested on the Lord's Day, when work ceased and they worshipped in the cabin. With Nathaniel and Stephen's help, they had brought in all the crops from both farms. God had blessed them with enough to see them through the winter and to share with the Patriot families not as fortunate as they had been in raising crops during these troubled times.

Stephen and Nellie lugged a bucket of corncobs between them for an evening feast. Chewing and swallowing still caused Father problems, but he could eat the kernels if they cut them from the cob. Or Sally might make mush with the fresh grain. Father must be tired of soups and broths. Josiah wanted him to enjoy the plenty with the rest of them.

When they returned to the clearing, Nathaniel headed for the barn to milk the cows while Josiah and Stephen went to the cabin. A smile spread across his face at the thought of seeing Sally. Through the long days of Father's illness, she had been so sweet and hardworking and kind.

The door opened, and instead of Sally, he saw. . .

"Father!"

Clinging to a cane, his father stood straight and proud.

Josiah rushed forward and embraced him. "It's good to see you on your feet and walking, sir!"

Sally had assured Josiah that his father was making progress, but he'd had little opportunity to observe with the long hours of work. Once or twice, Father had been sitting in a chair, finishing his meal, when they returned. An unspoken truce existed between them, and they had exchanged little beyond pleasantries.

"I've received excellent care." Father gestured at Sally and Mrs. Reid as if they were friends and allies. Never had his father's words sounded so sweet to Josiah's ears.

Father wobbled, and Sally took his arm. "Don't press too close. And now"—she smiled up at Father—"you promised to sit back down."

"I did, didn't I?" He turned around good-humoredly and accepted Sally's assistance to sit in his usual chair. "There. I've done as I promised. Now let me have a few minutes alone with my son."

She smiled indulgently at him. "We'll leave you two alone for a few moments while we shuck the corn. Don't take too long."

Mrs. Reid had already joined the others outside. Both Father and Josiah stared after Sally's departing back. When she closed the door, Father cleared his throat.

"Son, I have some things I need to talk with you about. Last year, the doctor warned me not to get too riled up or something even worse might happen. He was right, and I'm not only talking about this." He gestured to his body.

"Father, you're still recovering. This may not be a good time to talk." Josiah didn't know if he wanted to delay this conversation more for his sake or for his father's.

"This won't take long." Father paused to take a deep breath. "I've been every kind of fool. I still believe the Bible commands us to honor the king, but I've had no right to treat you as I have. To blame you for Solomon's death. The Lord gives and the Lord takes away. Not me, not the king, not the Patriots—not you. Can you ever forgive me?"

Even more convincing than Father's words were the tears in his eyes. The hard, cold, hurt place that had resided in Josiah's breast since Solomon's death broke apart. "Can you forgive me for taking him with me into danger?"

"There is nothing to forgive." Father reached up his arms, rather like a child asking for his mother, and Josiah embraced him. When he felt the older man tremble, he released him.

"Let me get—"

"Wait a moment. I have one more thing I need to say." Father's voice was sharp. "You'll be ten times the fool I've been if you let a woman like Sally get away. You two belong together. Mr. Reid knew it, and I knew it until I let pride and anger get in the way."

Josiah felt tears in his own eyes. "So we have your blessing?"

"You have my blessing."

Josiah shouted so loud that the entire Reid family barged in.

Epilogue

M
a says you'd best hurry up. If you stay in that water much longer, you'll be all wrinkled for your wedding." Nellie peeked around the curtain. "Are you almost done?"

"I'm coming." Sally sighed and reached for the towel Ma had set aside for her use. She felt clean, inside and out, and couldn't wait for the morrow, when she would wed Josiah Tuttle.

To think that only a few weeks ago she had thought this day would never come. After Mr. Tuttle gave his blessing to the couple, Josiah had once again asked her to marry him. This time she'd said yes.

Since Nathaniel and Stephen had been banished to the barn while the ladies prepared for Sally's big day, she slipped on a robe and sat before the fire. Ma took out her beautiful, mother-of-pearl comb she saved for special occasions and worked on Sally's hair.

"I know I gave my blessing for you to marry Josiah, but I didn't expect such short notice." Ma sounded aggrieved and then softened her tone. "You're my firstborn, and it's hard to let go."

"We couldn't know a circuit rider would come into town before Josiah had to leave. He and Nathaniel are itching to join the Green Mountain Boys."

"And you may not see him again for months. I remember what it's like to be young and in love." Ma's hands tugged at a knot in Sally's hair. She made a small sound, and baby Donny responded with a whimper. They both looked at the infant.

Ma spoke again. "Of course you want that time together, and maybe even, with God's blessing, a living reminder of your union." She hugged her daughter. "I pray he comes back to you safe and sound."

Sally's heart tensed. Josiah faced a difficult road. First he would escort his father to Canada, where he could wait with his wife and others loyal to the king until the war ended. If he remained in Maple Notch after he recovered from his illness, Mr. Tuttle faced the same prison sentence the other Tories had received. After that, Josiah would join the Green Mountain Boys and fight for freedom.

Between now and then, they would have one blessed day and night.

Sally planned to enjoy every minute of their time together.

The following morning, Josiah woke earlier than usual. How good God was. The necessity of leaving Maple Notch before he could wed Sally had pained Josiah, yet his father's safety and the call of the militia had to come first. But then the circuit rider had appeared in town on Sunday and agreed to wed them. They would have a day and night together before his departure, time they would spend in the cave that had sheltered the Reid family over the summer.

"I've got your razor ready for you." Father had set out essentials for grooming. "And something else." He shook out a velvet jacket in the old style, a trifle worn but elegant and well made. "I wore this when I married your mother. You haven't had time to get new clothes made, nor even to wash the ones you have. I'd consider it an honor if you would wear this. We're much of a size. It should fit."

Josiah had considered himself fortunate that his best breeches were clean. Now he had a gentleman's coat to wear with his cleanest shirt. "I only hope Sally will be as fortunate."

Father chuckled. "If I know Mary Reid, she has something up her sleeve for the girl." He held up the coat for Josiah to put it on. "Besides, you wouldn't care if she wore her milking dress. Come, let's get going."

Everyone left in town gathered under the sugar maples, elms, and oaks that sheltered the green, their bright autumn colors carpeting the ground underfoot. Cold snapped in the air, a hint of the coming winter days. Sally's thoughts strayed to the layers of petticoats that served to keep her warm.

The preacher stood in the center of the green, but she scarcely noticed him. Josiah waited, resplendent in a soft blue coat and white shirt, dark hair pulled back with a plain black ribbon. She gripped the basket of asters Nellie had gathered and walked toward the altar.

Toward the future.

Toward freedom.

Together.

BRIDGE TO LOVE

Dedication

*To my mother, who taught me how to keep on going even when it
seems impossible, and now cheers me on from the sidelines in heaven.*

Author's Note

I n April 1815 a volcano erupted east of Java, far removed from Western civilization. Slowly winds carried volcanic dust around the world, disrupting weather patterns as they went. In 1816 temperatures dropped significantly across the northeastern United States and Northern Europe. Frost and/or summer snow killed crops every month during the short growing season. Famine and starvation dogged the rugged New Englanders, so much so that many people emigrated to warmer climes. The year 1816 became known as "The Poverty Year," "The Year of No Summer," and even as "Eighteen Hundred and Froze to Death."

Calvin Tuttle used the same method to grow a successful crop as did real Vermonter Nathaniel Foster. Both of them also rejected offers for their seed corn of five dollars a bushel from the bank and instead sold it for one dollar to their neighbors. Foster's town became known as "Egypt," after the biblical story of Joseph and the famine.

Chapter 1

T hey're all dead!"

Beatrice Bailey shivered in her cotton dress outside her house on one side of the town square in Maple Notch, Vermont. She wanted to stomp her foot in frustration, but that was childish, as well as downright dangerous with the slippery snow under foot. "Oh, there you are." She found a sprig of purple lilacs to bring inside the house.

"What are you doing outside in this weather?"

Mama.

She continued fussing at Beatrice. "You don't even have a coat on. You'll catch your death of cold."

At Mama's reminder, Beatrice felt icy water seeping through the thin soles of her shoes. "I didn't expect it to be so chilly. The sun was shining yesterday."

Her mother shook her finger. "You're acting like you've never seen snow in May. It *does* happen."

Beatrice followed her mother into the kitchen, where Papa waited at the table.

Mama continued her tirade. "Mr. Bailey, what are we going to do with this girl? She went outside dressed like. . .this!"

Papa lifted his eyes from the newspaper—no doubt reading about the price of potash and other trade goods—and looked at his daughter over his spectacles. He took them off and looked again, frowning. "Where *is* your coat, Beatrice? I won't have my daughter wandering around outside like a pauper's child."

"Oh, Papa." She gestured toward him with the flowers. "I only wanted to get some lilacs for the table. I know you like them, too." She frowned. "But the sprigs are all falling off our lovely bushes. All the white lilacs are gone, and most of the purple ones, too."

"Oh? Is that all? Well, they'll grow again next year."

"It's not only the lilacs. Last night's snow will have killed the baneberries and harebells as well. Not to mention the kitchen garden."

"Hmm." Papa had returned his attention to the paper.

"Papa!"

With a sigh, he set the paper down again. "Yes?"

"Can you pick up some more seeds for me the next time you go to Burlington?"

"Of course." He smiled at her, and she kissed him on the cheek. "Now may I read the paper in peace?" He buried his nose back in the page.

Beatrice stared out the window at the snow weighing down tree branches budding with the new year's growth. Last night's frost and snow would affect more than her flowers. Why, people said the maple sap hadn't been running true to form, and the freeze might stop the apple trees and cranberry bushes from bearing fruit.

Don't be a ninny. Snow did fall in Maple Notch in May from time to time.

The animals wouldn't like the cold weather either. Beatrice looked underneath the Franklin stove, one of the few in northern Vermont, her mother's pride and joy. Patches, their calico cat, had taken to sleeping there during cold snaps. After all, it was the warmest spot in the house, as Mama bragged. No black-and-brown tail slapped the floor, betraying her presence.

"Here, kitty, kitty. I've got some bacon for you." Beatrice dangled her hand near the floor, but the cat didn't appear. "Has anybody seen Patches?"

Papa snorted from behind the paper. "Not this morning. I'm sure she's fine."

"I do hope she's someplace warm." Patches ran out the door whenever it opened and might be caught in the snow.

"As soon as I'm finished, I'm going outside to look for her." Beatrice rushed through her plate of johnnycakes, eggs, and bacon. Mama would scold her if she left something uneaten. Five minutes after finishing her meal, Beatrice buttoned on her coat, taking the time to pull on her gloves and boots. Anything less, and both parents might make her stay inside. As soon as she opened the door, Patches darted inside and headed straight for the stove.

Papa drained his coffee cup. "Care to walk with me across the green?"

"Of course, Papa. I always do." No amount of snow could keep a born-and-bred Yankee inside very long.

"Your bonnet?" Mama asked, handing her a wide-brimmed hat that would protect her hair from falling snow. A part of Beatrice wished she could run across the common and catch the snow with her tongue as she had when she was a young girl. But no young woman of nineteen would behave in such a hoydenish way.

Still, Beatrice enjoyed the morning strolls. She suspected Papa liked her to accompany him to impress the people of Maple Notch with her fine wardrobe—the best New York had to offer, often the latest fashions all the way from Paris. But Beatrice treasured their few quiet minutes together. Not often did she claim his entire attention.

"Have you given any further thought to my proposal?" Papa asked.

Beatrice dipped her head, glad for the bonnet that hid her expression. Papa wanted her to stay with her grandmother in New York for a time—this summer and fall, perhaps. He wished her to marry some well-to-do young man who could succeed him at the bank.

Beatrice had traveled to New York several times, but the city stifled her. Her home and gardens gave her ample pleasure, but she'd never been able to make her father understand. She sighed. "I'm happy right here. I don't want to go to a city among so many people. I'll lose myself."

Papa chuckled. "You don't have to worry. You'll be a lovely rose wherever you're planted, and you deserve to experience more of life than this." His arm swept around the view of the common.

The sight he dismissed so easily brought great joy to her own heart. She thought of her grandfather when she passed the statue commemorating the Green Mountain Boys who had fought with Ethan Allen. The meeting-house where she had come to know the Lord had seen fifty years of weddings and funerals. The maple trees provided sweet sap in the spring and brilliant colors in the fall.

"Everything I want is here," she repeated.

"Only this morning I heard you complaining about the cold and snow." Father sneaked a sidewise glance at her. He was teasing her.

She giggled. "I confess I will be happy when summer comes."

∽

In spite of his boots and winter coat, Calvin Tuttle shivered—perhaps because he didn't have his mittens on. He couldn't examine the tender young plants with his hands covered. "Any luck yet?" He paused at the end of the row to ask his friend and partner, Tobias Heath.

"Nope. I'm hoping to find something here under the shelter of the trees where the snow didn't get so high. Maybe some of the seedlings survived." Tobias blew on his fingers.

"Maybe." Calvin joined him at the rim of the clearing and dug through the finger-numbing snow, still deep in spite of the protection of the trees. The tender shoots were frozen clear through, with that almost-translucent color of ice. When he touched one, the bud where the ear of corn would eventually grow broke off in his hands.

Tobias brushed the snow aside to the bare ground, where they had planted potatoes for the eyes to sprout. One came up in his hand, blackened, shriveled roots dangling from the spud. The squash vines hadn't fared any better. "Maybe you can feed some of this to your animals." His voice sounded uncertain. "They must be getting as tired of this winter as we are."

"That reminds me. Keep an eye out for bear sign. If the storms are killing the wild plants, too, they're going to be searching for anything to eat, anything at all."

The two men continued working in silence. Calvin walked among the last of the plants with little hope, and found nothing to change his mind.

"Do you get these late storms a lot?" Tobias asked.

Calvin shrugged. "You ought to know. You're from Vermont, too."

"In town, though. I never was a farmer." Tobias slapped his hands together and thought about it. "Snow is as common on Easter as not. But I don't remember too many storms in May."

"It happens. We'll plant another crop and trust the good Lord to provide come harvest time."

"Not what you were hoping for, is it?" Tobias looked at him sideways as they walked in the direction of the cabin. "You told me that with the two of us working the land, we could make up for lost time. And now this." He gestured at the snow-covered fields.

Behind him in the forest, Calvin heard a tree branch cracking under the weight of the heavy spring snow, and he shook his head. "No use arguing with the Almighty."

"Yeah. We both know who would win that argument." Tobias grinned.

Beneath the teasing banter, Calvin heard the painful questions that plagued his friend. When they'd volunteered to serve in the army in the recent war with Britain, they'd known they'd see people die in battle. But they hadn't expected to see more people die of disease than from musket balls. Tobias had lost his sweetheart and come to Maple Notch to mend his broken heart.

No use thinking about that now. Calvin looked across the clearing where he sought to establish a farm of his own. This year's crop required extra care. He'd have to put off clearing more land and rooting out the tree stumps for another season.

"There's always next year," Tobias said.

"What, are you reading my mind now?"

"You always stop at that same spot and look over the fields. It's not hard to guess what you're thinking."

Calvin began moving again. "The problem is I cleared this land back before the war. Then I joined the army, and the forest grew back over some of what I cleared. I've only had one full growing season."

"And you've got that bank payment on your mind. I know. But God will provide."

God had to. Or else Calvin might lose it all. He held no illusions.

The banker, Hiram Bailey, would demand every penny of the payment. He'd say he owed it to his investors. Little things like bad weather and poor crops didn't enter his calculations. Bailey had called a meeting of the farmers later in the day, and Calvin wondered what he would have to say.

The destruction wrought by the night's frost couldn't be undone. Calvin would have to replant, that was all, and work all the harder. Maybe he could speak with Pa about borrowing old Abe, the ox, so he could work faster. Turn the ruined plants under for mulch at least, to get some good out of it. Once he'd done that, hopefully the ground would be warm enough to replant.

Should he consider changing up his crops? Study on what yielded the highest profit? No, it wasn't prudent to try unproven crops in a year when everything seemed to be going wrong. Stick with what he knew worked in his fields. Corn, beans, and squash, as well as potatoes.

He stared to his right, at the smoke curling from his brother's chimney. To his left lay Uncle Stephen's cabin. No use wishing for an ox. They shared an ox between them. Most of the time it worked out fine, but the men with families to feed would need Abe first.

"Let's go get the plow and start to work." Calvin headed for the barn, with Tobias following. Midway to the door, he heard someone calling to him.

"Calvin! Mr. Heath! Wait up!"

Calvin turned around with a smile. Peggy Reid, his cousin, waved to him from the fence line.

"Ma said for you to come over today during the nooning. She told your brother Solomon earlier but wanted to be sure you knew about it."

Nice of Aunt Hilda to send them a personal invitation. Folks had been going back and forth between the Reid and Tuttle farms since the first settlers came to Maple Notch.

"Great. We'll be right there as soon as we clean up."

Peggy hesitated as if expecting him to say something more. When he didn't, she waved good-bye and headed in the direction of the Reids' cabin. He waited until she had gone a few yards before he called his greeting after her.

"Happy birthday!"

She grinned and waved.

Peggy was all of nineteen today. He wouldn't have many more celebrations with his cousin before some man came along and claimed her. He glanced at Tobias and wondered. His friend deserved some happiness after losing his sweetheart.

"Let's get going," he told Tobias. "We can grab her gift later."

After the celebration, he would bring up the problems with the crops with the family. Maybe together they could come up with a solution.

∾

The morning had turned out ever so nice, so much better than Beatrice had feared when she walked to the bank with her father early in the day. Today was her best friend's birthday, and she had never missed a single celebration with Peggy Reid, not once since they started school together all those years ago. A few inches of snow on the ground wouldn't keep her at home.

"Mama, I need to head over to the Reid farm today."

"In this weather? Don't be foolish."

Predictable. "It's Peggy's birthday today. And look, the sun has come out, and it's turned out to be a lovely day. I'll ride Princess, so I won't get all dirty."

"Very well. Just be sure that you're home well before dark and presentable before supper." Mama smiled. "You know how your father gets when you go out visiting the farms."

"Why, the road goes straight through the woods. It's not dark and dangerous like it was when he was a boy. Besides, I've been there hundreds of times." Papa would prefer she not have any friends with "that sort." The problem was, then she'd have no friends at all.

"He only wants the best for you, young missy." Mama's smile was gentle, taking the sting out of her words. "He's eager for you to go to New York and take your rightful place in polite society." Beatrice could hear the echoes of her father's voice in her mother's words. It was an old argument, and one that wasn't going away any time soon.

"I promise I'll be home in plenty of time." Beatrice avoided responding to Mama's statement. "Thank you! For everything." Her mother wouldn't speak of Beatrice's outing to her father unless she must, so she would do everything possible to honor that trust.

Beatrice took Princess through the back gate. If she rode across the town green, either Papa would see her riding or someone would comment on it. Perhaps Mrs. Dixon, the storekeeper's wife. She had clear ideas about what constituted proper behavior for young ladies. Beatrice's flower garden qualified. Her trips into the meadows and forests in search of unusual plantings did not. Why, when one complemented the other and both reflected the hands of the Creator, Beatrice had never figured out.

As soon as she had reached the spot where the road headed through the woods to the bridge crossing Bumblebee River, she let Princess have her head, and they galloped at a brisk pace. Half an hour there, half an hour back. . .that left her an hour to spend with her dear friend. Their friendship had been simpler in the days when they both went to school and needed no excuse to see each other on a daily basis. Of course, Papa had been gentler in those days, too, before he made all his money that had half the town jealous of him and the other half suspicious of where he had come up with all that cash. They accused him of profiteering, when good men were dying in defense of their country.

Beatrice shook off her worries. The Reids had always welcomed her, and today would be no exception. She might even see Peggy's Tuttle cousins. Perhaps she could exchange more than a simple *hello* with Calvin, the best man in the family in her opinion. When she reached the river bank, she reined Princess in to check the bridge. Were the dark splotches simply from melted snow, or were the planks slick with ice? She dismounted. A couple of tentative steps confirmed the bridge's firm footing. Leading Princess behind her, she walked forward a few steps at a time, avoiding the wet spots where possible.

Something flashed past Beatrice's shoulder and splashed in the water. A female mallard landed and began paddling in the swift-flowing water. A second bird followed, passing within a few feet of Princess's head. The horse snorted and backed up. Her movement threw Beatrice off balance. Her foot found an icy patch, and she fell backward, landing on her rump.

For a stunned moment, Beatrice sat on the bridge, unmoving. Princess bent over and nudged her with her nose. Beatrice moved her right arm, then her left, and wiggled both legs. Everything appeared to be in working order. Around her, the bridge felt slick, and she didn't dare try to stand. Rising to her knees, she crawled forward inches at a time, seeking a safe place to stand. Her lovely coat would be filthy. Perhaps she should turn around straightaway and return home. But Mama would be furious whether she returned early or late, and she still hadn't seen Peggy. She would go ahead to the house.

"Did you lose something on the bridge?"

Beatrice looked up from her unladylike position on the bridge. Calvin Tuttle, Peggy's cousin. Of all the people to find her in this situation. . . Princess whinnied a greeting.

The wood beneath her felt dry, and Beatrice stood with the help of Princess's bridle. "I. . .took a little tumble." She knew her nose was as high in the air as Papa's ever was, but a girl had her pride.

"Oh, Bea."

Bea. Only Calvin Tuttle had ever called her that. Once, back in her first years of school, he had sent her a Valentine's card that read, "Will you bea mine?" That had started it, all those years ago. He'd teased her unmercifully, at least until the day she'd wished he'd notice her. By then, he saw her only as his younger cousin's friend and, as such, too young for his attention.

"Let me help you." Calvin closed the distance between them. He looked her over from head to toe. Probably checking to make sure she wasn't injured, but she felt her cheeks glow warm against the breeze that blew across the water. "You're not hurt?"

"Only my pride." She returned his gaze. Since he had returned from fighting in the recent war, their paths had not often crossed. They saw each other at church and at the occasional young people's frolic, but most days, he buried himself away at his farm. Papa had talked about it, how those Reids and Tuttles were building another farm west of the river, and whether or not it was a good idea. For herself, she thought it was industrious of Calvin.

"That bridge is slick. Let me help you over those last few steps." He walked onto the planks, the cleats of his boots sounding as sure as ice picks. When he reached her, he tucked her arm beneath his elbow.

She looked up into bright brown eyes. Oh my, Calvin had turned into a fine man. Always handsome, the last few years had only improved his appearance. His shoulders looked broader underneath his winter coat. His dark-brown hair settled, a little long, over the collar to his jacket, and the smile in his eyes warmed her to her toes.

"Thank you very kindly." Her voice sounded breathy.

As she walked the last few steps across the bridge and onto the road on the far side of the river, the horse following behind her, her insides quivered like jelly.

No matter what Mama or Papa might say about today, she was mighty glad she had come.

Chapter 2

Not many women of Calvin's acquaintance could manage to look ladylike and demure when crawling on their hands and knees. But somehow Beatrice Bailey managed it. She looked up at him with her doe-brown eyes, and he went all weak in the knees. The way she accepted his arm when he offered it made him feel like he was the Prince Regent of England escorting a fine lady to a ball, not a humble farmer helping a woman he'd known since she was a girl in pigtails. Back then, he'd called her "Bea" because of the way she buzzed around the classroom, curious about everything, butting her head in everywhere it didn't belong.

But now Beatrice was a grown woman, a *beautiful* woman, and the old teasing words stuck in his throat. He couldn't believe he had let the old nickname slip from his lips moments before. The creature standing before him was "Miss Bailey," and he'd better remember it.

Her mare cozied up to Bea and nuzzled her. "I'm fine, Princess." She reached into her pocket and held out a carrot with her gloved hands. *Princess.* So the Baileys treated even their horses like royalty. The mare was a beauty, no doubt about it, and of a sweet disposition like her mistress.

Bea took hold of the saddle and glanced over her shoulder at Calvin. "Would you mind turning your back?" Her voice held a hint of both imperious demand and nervous embarrassment.

"No need." He could have kicked himself for not thinking of her predicament sooner. "Let me assist you." He put his hands on her waist and lifted her into the saddle. The glimpse he caught of white petticoats, ruffles, and woolen stockings brought a blush to his cheeks. Why, he wasn't sure. He had assisted many ladies, not all family, onto the back of a horse, but none of them affected him the way Bea Bailey had.

Overhead, sparrows sang as if in celebration of the event. Apparently, even the birds of the forest agreed that Bea was pretty enough to inspire a song. His hands lingered on her waist a moment longer than necessary.

"Thank you."

Bea's voice broke his concentration, and he stepped away, his mind scrambling for something to say. "Are you headed for the Reids?"

She nodded. "For Peggy's birthday. I wouldn't miss it for all the world."

She looked at her bedraggled dress. "Although I'm ashamed to show up like this. But I must dry out, and Peggy will see the humor of my adventure. Mama would keep me home for a week and call me irresponsible."

"Perhaps she should." *If you were in my care, I would do anything in my power to keep you safe.*

She looked at him as if he had said something offensive. "Why, Calvin Tuttle, would you keep me in a cage?"

A picture of her in a cage, wings fluttering against the bars, struck his imagination. *No, you should join your song to that of the birds in the sky. Fly alone, solo, to the heights of the heavens.* But no man would speak such sweet words to a woman unless. . . He shook his head. "I'm sorry. I spoke out of turn. I thought only of your safety."

She laughed, her pretty, even teeth flashing at him. "You're forgiven." She lifted the reins and urged Princess forward. "You are going to the celebration as well, of course?"

He nodded and walked alongside the horse. "We'd best make haste, or else the cake will be all gone before we get there." He stroked Princess's side. "But don't slow down on my account. Go on ahead and let them know I'm on my way."

Bea looked down at Calvin, her face unreadable. "I would rather walk with you." She shrugged her shoulders. "But if I want to avoid any ill effects from my fall, I'd best get warm and dry as soon as possible." Bending down, she spoke in a low voice. "Promise me we'll talk again later?"

"When we have opportunity."

Beatrice pressed her legs into the mare's sides, and she increased her pace. Calvin watched horse and rider heading down the road ahead of him, his throat dry in spite of the moisture permeating the air and ground around him.

∿

Beatrice resisted the urge to glance over her shoulder at Calvin. She hadn't seen much of the farmer in recent weeks. She had spotted him at church, where her parents kept her ensconced between them and away from any glances the young men of Maple Notch might send her way. She knew they did; no woman remained unaware of masculine attention, but so far none had dared come before her father. Perhaps they all knew Papa had determined only someone from New York, say a banker or a lawyer, would be worthy of his daughter. Someone ready to take over his business. Certainly not the son of a farmer.

So today's encounter felt almost God-ordained, one unplanned by either party. She had known she might see Calvin at Peggy's birthday celebration.

But not like this, the two of them alone together.

A breeze stirred her clothes, and she shivered. Ahead she could see smoke spiraling from a chimney, announcing the proximity of the Reids' home. She urged Princess to a trot and entered the clearing.

Half a dozen horses were hitched to the railing in front of the cabin. Too many for the family; besides, they would walk, not ride the short distance between their farms. Princess whinnied and sped to reach the others. One of the horses neighed in response and turned his head.

A white star blazed down the forehead of a bay gelding. She recognized the markings. *Duke.* Before she had opportunity to process the implications, the door swung open.

"Beatrice Alice Bailey, what you are doing here?"

Papa.

She gulped. "I came to celebrate Peggy's birthday." Would Papa notice the state of her dress?

"That explains it." He accepted her unexpected presence with surprising ease.

"Welcome, Beatrice! Peggy will be so glad you came." Mrs. Reid came to her rescue. "Adam, come, help Miss Bailey down from her horse."

Beatrice hopped down onto a relatively dry patch of grass by the door. Her muddy cloak swept across Adam's legs, and he hesitated. Heat rushed into her cheeks, and she sped into the house, hoping Papa wouldn't notice.

He followed her in, and she held her breath. But he focused on the group gathered in the main room. In addition to family members, several other farmers from Maple Notch had gathered.

Before Beatrice could figure out what was going on, Peggy beckoned to join her in a partitioned-off area at the back of the cabin. Beatrice sped to join her, hoping her friend had a way to repair the damage to her clothing.

"Dear friend." Peggy hugged Beatrice. "I didn't think you could make it after last night's snowfall!" She glanced at Papa. "Especially when Mr. Bailey didn't mention you were coming."

"I didn't decide to come until after he had left for work." Beatrice checked to make sure no one could hear and lowered her voice. "And there's worse. I fell on the bridge and—"

"Did you hurt yourself?" Peggy's hand flew to her mouth.

"No." True, tomorrow black-and-blue places might appear, but no serious damage had been done. "But my clothes are a different matter." She took off her cloak and for the first time examined the damage. Mud and splinters spattered along a dark stain down the back. The hem drooped from a small rip. She turned the cloak over to check the inside. Only one small spot had soaked through. She ran her hand down the length of her gown and found a tiny spot, no bigger than a two-bit piece. Relief flooded through her. "Oh, that's not so bad."

Peggy had left the room and returned with a cup of tea. She studied the cloak. "You won't want your father to know what happened." The two girls shared a conspiratorial look and giggled. "We can brush out the worst of it, and I've got needle and thread to fix the hem." Her voice sounded uncertain. "My pa wouldn't notice, but will yours?"

"It depends." Beatrice chewed her lip. "Do you know what's going on?" She giggled. "Unless all the families in Maple Notch have gathered to celebrate your nineteenth birthday. What's the name of the young man Calvin brought home?"

"Tobias Heath."

"Tobias. That must be it. He's of marriageable age, and he came."

"Stop that!" Peggy colored. "Everyone knows he's heart-broken over his sweetheart, who died during the war." She brought her hand to her mouth as if to hide a giggle. "Unless you fancy him yourself."

"The thought never entered my mind." Besides, dark curls and bright brown eyes came to Beatrice's mind when she thought of suitors. Not Tobias's pale looks.

"Of course not. Mr. Bailey won't let one of those gentlemen so much as look at you as long as he's present."

Beatrice heard the compassion beneath her friend's words. The thought made her sad, and she missed getting the thread in the needle.

"You do fancy someone. I knew it. Who?" Peggy's voice rose playfully.

"Shh." Beatrice felt heat rush into her cheeks, but blamed it on Papa's close presence. She dropped her voice to a whisper. "Not when *he's* here. You never answered my question." Perhaps she could distract Peggy's attention. "Why is everyone here?"

"Mr. Bailey came by this morning and asked if local farmers could meet today. Just my luck that it happened on my birthday." She shrugged.

They heard the rattle of the cabin door, and Beatrice peeked to see who had arrived. Calvin. Her heart sped up, and she realized she had held her breath. She took a sip of tea to cover her nervousness. Emptying the cup, she stood up.

"Let me get you another cup." Peggy stood to her feet.

"I can do it while you work on my cloak. Your stitches are better than mine. Thanks." She flashed a smile at Peggy and went to the spot where the teapot sat on the table.

Mr. Reid had greeted Calvin and led him to a seat by the window, facing away from the fireplace. The walk had reddened his cheeks, and the curls on his head sprang up like wildflowers. He exchanged a few words with his brother Solomon. The low murmurs of conversation seemed a bit tense. She poured the tea and carried her cup back into the bedroom.

"Girls?" Mrs. Reid came into the room, and Peggy folded over the offending cloak. "Are you ready to help me serve refreshments to our guests?"

"Of course." Beatrice was eager to hear what the meeting was about. "We already have tea steeping."

"That's good. Peggy dear, I'm afraid all I have to offer them is the cake we intended for your birthday."

"Of course we should share it. We're fortunate that we have it available." Peggy winked. "I'll cut a small piece for myself as well." She smoothed down her dress, and the two girls followed Mrs. Reid into the main room.

About twenty men had gathered in the cramped cabin. What would Mrs. Reid do for cups? Mama, known for setting the finest table in Maple Notch, only had place settings for fifteen, no more.

Peggy knew where to look. She reached onto a shelf over the work table and into cabinets, pulling out tankards and mugs and cups of every description. Mrs. Reid dug out a stack of platters. Of course, they served groups almost as large as this whenever their families gathered together.

Beatrice saw the cake, plum with a rich rum sauce, and her stomach rumbled. Breakfast seemed a long time ago. She spotted a wheel of cheese and decided to ask for a piece after they had served the guests. The *other* guests.

Peggy brought the first cup of tea to Papa, and Beatrice mouthed "thank you" to her friend. She moved silently among the others, tapping Calvin on the back and handing him tea. He tipped the cup to her in appreciation, and she smiled in return.

At that moment, Papa looked up and frowned in her direction but returned his attention to the gathering. "You must be wondering why I have called this meeting today."

Beatrice poured boiling water over fresh tea leaves to brew a second pot for the men.

∾

Yes, I do wonder why you asked us here. What with rescuing Beatrice from her tumble on the bridge, Calvin had forgotten about the meeting Hiram Bailey had called for the farmers.

"I am grateful you all made it here safely, with the bad weather we've been having." Bailey spoke with every appearance of sincerity. "But I thought the weather provided an opportunity for us to meet, since you won't be out in your fields working."

A low grumble greeted that remark. Last night's storm had struck a blow to more people than Calvin. He caught sight of Beatrice giving Tobias a mug of tea. She looked so natural, so gracious, as if this were her home and she the mistress. Had she known her father was coming? He doubted it. Bailey didn't seem the sort to appreciate his daughter interfering in his business affairs.

"This winter that is hanging on for an unseasonably long time is the reason for this meeting. I know that after last night's frost, many of you will need to replant. My daughter reminded me of that this morning, when she asked for more seed." He nodded in Beatrice's direction, and she looked up, a startled expression in her eyes.

Seed? What kind of seed did Beatrice need? She wasn't a farmer, but maybe they kept a kitchen garden or even flowers. She always brought unusual flowers and plants to school.

"And so you see. . ." Mr. Bailey had said something. *What?* How foolish of him to let his attention wander. Thinking about Beatrice, of all things, even if she did have a sweet smile and kind nature. He lifted his eyes to the banker and gave him his full attention.

"I know this is a difficult time for all of us here in Maple Notch."

How did the prolonged winter make business difficult for the banker? He didn't have to worry about whether another frost would kill his crops or if he would have a harvest come fall.

"I thought we could meet, neighbor to neighbor, to discuss our options."

Calvin thought he heard a snort. Beside him, Tobias hid his face in his mug.

"I don't see there's a problem, Hiram," Frisk, another Maple Notch old-timer who had seen more winters come and go than most of them, said. "We'll plant a new crop, soon's the ground's thawed out a bit. It's nothing we ain't seen before." He fidgeted on his seat. "Iffen that's all you got to say, I got farm work that needs doin'." Others nodded their heads in agreement.

"How are you set for seed?" The banker glanced again at Beatrice. "As I said, my daughter's question brought it to mind."

"Why? You got some for sale down at your bank?" That question came from Whitson, known for his quick wit and even quicker temper.

"Now, Seth," Micah Dixon, the storekeeper, said. "He's asked a valid question. I've laid in a store of extra seed at the emporium, if anyone needs to buy."

What you'd expect the storekeeper to say. If the farmers needed extra seed or money to purchase it, Dixon and Bailey would profit.

Beatrice circled by again and refilled Calvin's cup. She smiled at him.

How could her features, which resembled her father's, be so appealing, and his, so prideful?

"I wanted to let you know that I'm here to help." Bailey spoke in a voice that sounded too loud for the cramped room. "Anything I can do. If you need something to help tide you over a rough patch, come on down to the bank."

"In exchange for a chunk of the crop, I expect." Uncle Stephen clapped Bailey on the shoulder. He shrugged and offered a gentle smile.

"We can't give away money; you know that, Mr. Reid. But I guarantee I'd give you fair terms. Can't say any better than that."

"I'm sure you will, Mr. Bailey. But Lord willing, I hope not to take advantage of your generous offer."

Calvin knew his uncle well enough to hear the tongue-in-cheek tone behind his comment. As for Calvin, he already owed money to the bank. He *had* to find a way to make this crop grow.

One way or another.

∽

Papa had said some interesting things today. He was fond of saying money didn't grow on trees and other such nonsense, as if she didn't know that. So he hoped to lend money to farmers in need because of the hardship caused by weather conditions. She didn't know how that made her feel.

Well, they had to get money from somewhere, didn't they? Since banks were needed, why not Papa? Even though his true intentions were kind, he sounded a bit like King Midas, who wanted to make gold from everything he touched. After his speech, he conversed with Mr. Whitson. Her eyes scanned the room, checking for Calvin. Of course he would stay for Peggy's birthday celebration.

She looked at the pan that had held the birthday cake, all gone but for crumbs. She resisted the urge to dip her fingers in the pan and gather a few for herself. Behind her, someone giggled, and she turned.

Peggy had a tiny piece on a plate. "You should have kept a piece for yourself. No one would have minded. That's what I did." She took a delicate bite in her mouth and pretended to swoon with pleasure at the flavor.

"Of course. It's *your* birthday." Beatrice smiled at her friend.

"Are you staying for the party?" Calvin appeared at her elbow.

She looked up, all the way up, into those eyes the color of the rich earth when it had been turned for planting, deep and dark and brown.

"What party?" Peggy had finished her cake and brushed the crumbs into the dustpan. "The cake's gone."

"You haven't opened your presents yet." Calvin reached into his coat and pulled out a package wrapped in plain brown paper. Peggy reached for it, and he twisted away, bumping into Beatrice in the narrow confines of the kitchen.

"My apologies." But his grin gave lie to his words. He lowered his voice. "Were you able to make repairs to your cloak?"

She wiggled her hand in a manner indicating yes and no. "Can I see the present?" She held out her hands for the package, and he handed it to her.

"Hmm. Nothing obvious, like a book." She held it up to her ear and shook it. A slight clinking reached her ears, but not from a bell or a chain. "I can't tell. You'll have to open it to see." She gave it to Peggy instead of back to Calvin.

"Not fair!" He protested.

"Beatrice." Papa's voice interrupted the good-natured teasing. Momentarily, she had forgotten that the piper would call his tune and expect her attendance at any minute.

"It's time to go, daughter." His voice, although pleasant enough, brooked no alternative.

"I brought a gift for Peggy's birthday. May I stay?"

"I'll be happy to see her safely home, sir," Calvin said.

"That won't be necessary." Papa used his King Midas voice again. "Go get the gift, and then we'll be on our way."

"Yes, Papa." Beatrice walked into the bedroom. Behind his back, Peggy pouted, then grinned, letting her know she harbored no hard feelings. Shaking out the cloak, Beatrice decided one wouldn't notice the dirt unless one looked closely. She extracted her present, a bottle of scented Florida water she knew Peggy liked, and returned to the living room with dragging steps.

Beatrice handed the package to her friend and hugged her. "I'm sorry I can't stay."

"Another time," Peggy promised.

Without volition, Beatrice's eyes sought out Calvin. Another time, *he* wouldn't be there.

She didn't know why that thought made her sad.

Chapter 3

Calvin shivered inside his cabin. By the summer solstice, he expected the advanced season to make a hearth fire unnecessary overnight. But as his feet slammed onto the cold planks of his floor and he pulled his shirt tight around his chest, he regretted the lack of warmth.

By the time he shrugged into his work shirt and breeches, Tobias had already started a small fire. "Thought you said it wouldn't get cold last night."

"It shouldn't have." Calvin's voice was low enough to register as a mumble. He wasn't sure if Tobias could hear, or if he even wanted him to hear the discouragement in his voice.

"Maybe not."

So Tobias had heard.

"But take a look outside." Tobias jutted his chin in the direction of the window.

Calvin approached it slowly. As he feared, a world of white covered the ground yet again. Snow enchanted and delighted in October, signaling winter's stark beauty and a season of rest ahead. In March and April, heavy snowfall had signaled winter's last hurrah before the land sprang to life again. It promised adequate snowmelt to water crops during the summer months. By May, snow was unwelcome, and in June, unheard of. Would it even snow at the height of summer, in July?

Calvin blew against the window as if by that action he could disprove the evidence of his feet and his eyes, and that instead of unseasonable cold, summer reigned with its temperate climate. But the place where his mouth had touched the pane formed a circle of droplets. He shook his head. Yet another crop dead in the fields. Good thing he had held some seed back in May, in fear snow would fall again.

He dug his woolen socks out of the darning basket and pulled his boots from underneath his bed. A storage box held his winter things since he'd expected nothing worse than muddy fields over the next few months.

"Hey, have a biscuit and some coffee before you head out in that cold." Tobias plunked down a couple of plates on the table. "I'm not going out there until I get something warm in my stomach."

"City boy." Calvin accompanied this grumble with a smile and joined

141

Tobias at the table. They wolfed down the grub in a matter of minutes and headed for the fields. On the way, Calvin glanced at the barn, where he had placed the yoke in hopes of borrowing Solomon's ox. If the fair weather had continued, he'd intended to clear more of his field. Not now. He pulled on mittens and a hat and headed for the clearing.

He walked up one row and down another until he reached the stump of an oak tree that looked as though it had been there since before the first white man had arrived in the New World. He had made a wide berth around the tree when he scattered seeds. Anything planted in the neighborhood of the tree roots got suffocated in their extensive, underground system.

But when he looked by the old stump, he had a thought. Could he make the tree's root system work for him? He had to find some answers. When May ended without more snowfall, he had breathed a sigh of relief. Who would have expected it on the twenty-first of June? Had Bea planted new seed as she planned, hoping it would grow? If so, she faced disappointment as well.

Rubbing his chin, he pondered the stumps of oak, maple, and elm trees scattered across his field. The thought process diverted his attention while he walked up and down the rows, confirming that once again, frost and snow had killed the seedlings. Would the stand of trees crowding the edge of the fields provide cover if he planted close by? Could they shield the plants from more snowfall or insulate them? He shook his head. Anything he planted there would compete with all the bounty of God's creation for the earth's nutrients, or provide food for wild creatures. He might harvest a small amount, but not enough to hold off the bank's foreclosure.

He began the painful process of turning under the plants, churning ideas as he did so. An answer eluded him, but he would find it eventually.

∽

Beatrice looked at the cotton dress with a pattern of lilac sprigs she had planned to wear in celebration of the first day of summer. Sighing, she hung it in her armoire and settled for her dark-green linsey-woolsey dress. The garment was serviceable, even pretty. But she tired of wearing it after the unrelenting coolness of the year.

Early this morning, Papa had left the house, his face set in stern lines. Had he called another meeting of the farmers at the Reids'? She considered running after him, asking about his plans, and begging to go along to visit with Peggy if that happened. But she didn't. He would only refuse.

Beatrice brightened. At least the snow would delay her departure for New York, where her parents hoped to spend Independence Day. Did she dare hope they would cancel the trip altogether? If she didn't go this year, perhaps Papa would let go of this foolish notion of her marrying some city fellow, when she could imagine nothing better than to settle down with one of the men of Maple Notch.

Calvin Tuttle's face swam into her mind, and she felt heat rush to her cheeks, thankful no one could see. She took a seat by the small fire Bessie Angus, Cook's helper and Beatrice's maid, had started earlier. Her Bible opened to the pressed lilacs she had rescued during last month's snowfall. Today's Bible reading took Beatrice to the Song of Solomon. Some of the things Solomon said made her blush, and she wouldn't ask for an explanation, not even of Mama. But other things, like the beautiful description of springtime, made her spirit sing. Even this year when summer never seemed to come, she listened to the chatter of birds outside her window and hoped with them for a break in the weather. Her cat, Patches, enjoyed it, too, watching them and striking at the pane with her paws from time to time.

But this morning, the birds remained quiet, at least too quiet to hear through the heavy glass. Over the town green, geese flew in lazy circles. Did they feel as trapped as she did? With another day indoors, Mama would insist she spend the hours stitching on the napkins, tablecloths, and other linens for her hope chest. In a word, *boring*. She already had enough, given to her by Great-grandmother Bailey, for a family of twelve. She, who didn't even have a husband yet, nor the prospect of one. The thought made her giggle. Who was the special someone God had in mind for her?

"Beatrice." Mama's voice floated up the stairs.

Beatrice flexed her fingers and sighed. "Yes, Mama?"

"When are you coming down, dear? The sun's been up for hours. As Ben Franklin said, 'No morning sun lasts a whole day.'"

"I'm ready now." Beatrice closed her Bible and set it on the table by the window. She looked across the green and caught sight of a group of men making their way to the church. Maybe Papa *had* called a meeting today, at the meetinghouse.

One of the men looked up, and she caught a clear view of the dark hair framing his sun-kissed face and brown eyes. Calvin. He lifted his hand to his eyebrow as if to salute. Then he turned his head and laughed at something one of the others had said.

Beatrice decided to attend the men's meeting.

~

Calvin thought he had glimpsed Beatrice in the second-floor window of her parents' house. It sat on the edge of the town green, proclaiming itself the finest in Maple Notch and even better than most of what Burlington had to offer.

"Sounds like Hiram Bailey wants to make a second fortune." Solomon shook his head. "Whatever the man needs all that money for is beyond me."

"Ma says Mrs. Bailey goes to Burlington to shop," Adam said. "Dixon's Emporium isn't good enough for her."

We're as bad as a bunch of old biddies. Calvin thought of Bea's face and bit back a smile. *If I had someone as fine as Bea to buy for, why, I'd give her everything in my power.* He looked again at the window, but she was gone. Maybe he'd seen a pine branch waving its snow-laden limbs in front of the window.

"That's enough," Uncle Stephen said. "He's doing honest business."

"Which is more than we can say for his conduct during the war." Solomon huffed.

"None of which was proven," their uncle reminded them. "We're almost there. And we've all agreed to hear the man out." He nudged Solomon in the ribs. "Besides, some would say the Tuttles have no call to talk against him, since your grandfather was a Tory sympathizer."

Solomon bristled, as Uncle Stephen surely had known he would. Did he do it on purpose? To divert attention from gossiping about Mr. Bailey?

"He who is without sin can cast the first stone—is that what you're suggesting?" Calvin asked.

"I'm saying, listen without judging him ahead of time. Let the past stay in the past."

"Amen," Tobias murmured.

Was he thinking about his painful past and the losses he had sustained? His smile removed Calvin's doubts. He suspected they were both thinking of the plan they had concocted when they toured the field that morning. What would the other farmers think of it?

Much the same group gathered at the meetinghouse as had come to Uncle Stephen's home last month. The men sat on benches across the front of the church, where daylight streamed through the windows, providing natural light. The sun shone so brightly it was hard to believe it had snowed only last night, or that the air was crisp and cool and free of the insects that usually plagued Vermont by this time of year. In spite of the four walls and the fire burning in a small wood stove, the air remained a cold reminder of the night's disaster.

The Reid and Tuttle men, with Tobias, took up one entire bench. When everyone had settled, Pastor Cabot walked to the pulpit. "Good morning, gentlemen. As always, I am glad to see you in the Lord's house, but I regret the circumstances." He spoke in his solemn voice, the same one he used whether describing the Lord's glory or the death of a saint. The tone said, "Listen up. This is important."

Calvin settled down. The parson's sermons could take awhile. He focused his gaze on a picture of Christ praying in the garden that hung behind the preacher at the front of the church. Times like this, he felt a bit like Peter, James, and John, who couldn't stay awake to pray with Jesus for an hour. Everyone agreed that prayer and the preaching of the Word were important, but sometimes Calvin's mind tended to wander. All it took was a sound like the creaking of the church door. He twisted his head to see who was coming in before he thought about it. Silhouetted against the cold sunshine pouring in with the rush of cold air stood a feminine form, with sunshine gleaming on her golden hair.

Bea Bailey. With her entrance, the air in the church warmed by about twenty degrees. Calvin forced himself to look forward, where Pastor Cabot had paused in mid-sentence but didn't comment on Bea's arrival.

"And so, brethren, it appears God has decided to visit us with a season of snow. A year without a summer, in fact."

The Year of No Summer. The *Farmer's Almanac* hadn't seen this one coming.

"It's only June," Whitson quipped, and nervous laughter broke out across the congregation.

Cabot managed a thin smile in recognition of the witticism. "Brother Bailey suggested we gather together to beseech the Lord's favor for seasonable weather through the remaining summer months and, if it be His will, to even delay fall's arrival until we have a full harvest. This church is a house of prayer, and I am always glad to open our doors for that purpose."

So Calvin's earlier rambling thoughts about the disciples in the Garden of Gethsemane had hit close to the mark. This *was* a prayer meeting. He stole a glance around at the men gathered. Some shuffled their feet; others stared at the floor. Old man Frisk had his hands tucked under his armpits as if to keep them warm. Tobias stared straight ahead, focused on the planks lining the back wall of the meetinghouse. Perhaps he was counting the boards or the knotholes. Calvin had done that many times as a child.

"That's all fine and good, Parson, but I for one would like to know what people plan on doing about the blight on the year. Does anyone have any ideas?" Frisk had dropped his hands to his sides and stood up.

Frisk voiced Calvin's thoughts. He suspected most of the men present were asking themselves the same question.

"I've already asked my wife to use our food sparingly. But no one expected this in time to set aside from last year's harvest."

"Men." Bailey stood to his feet. "I appreciate your concerns. But you have my assurance that no one in Maple Notch will go hungry because of the weather."

No, we'll just all be in debt to you. Calvin didn't voice the thought.

"But perhaps as Parson Cabot says, if we repent and seek the Lord's face, He will turn this disaster away from us."

At that, Whitson jumped to his feet. His face as red as a maple leaf in autumn, he said, "If anyone needs to repent, it's *you*, Mr. Bailey. Profiting from the sale of potash across the border during the war. The *illegal* sale."

Tobias's head jerked up at that. Calvin mouthed *later*. The banker wasn't the only Vermonter to make good money from the thriving potash trade during the embargo of trade with Britain. What had turned the folks of Maple Notch against him was the way he continued to smuggle the wood ashes—useful for everything from making soap to tanning hides—into Canada during the war. They saw it as helping the enemy.

"Mr. Whitson, there is no need to insult me. I only seek to face a common problem together."

"The way you faced the British?" Frisk spoke now. "We didn't trust you then, and we don't see any reason to trust you now."

Calvin heard feet tapping the floor behind him. Bea. What must she be thinking, feeling, as the men of the town attacked her father? Without further thought, he jumped to his feet.

"I have something to say."

His entrance into the fray surprised the others into silence.

"Yes, Mr. Tuttle?" The preacher invited him to speak.

Calvin turned in a circle, looking at the people gathered in the room. Tobias winked at him and nodded. Bea looked at him, her eyes seas of frothy water. At least Whitson had settled back on the bench.

"Speak up, man." Bailey sounded relieved someone had interrupted the fracas. "I'm sure we're all anxious to hear any insights you have into this situation."

Calvin reviewed the proposal that he and Tobias had formed yesterday. It seemed so simple, he wondered why others hadn't tried it.

"I have an idea for a way to keep the ground warm when. . .if. . .another cold spell hits. I had planned on pulling out the tree stumps left in my field this summer, but this inclement weather has thrown all my plans off." He brushed his hand across his forehead, pushing his hair back. "So yesterday I was thinking about how the tree roots tangle up my plants and wondered, why not make that work *for* me? Instead of yanking them out with a pair of oxen, I'll burn them out."

"We all know how to do that. That's nothing new." Frisk voiced what others probably were thinking.

"I know. It's a slow, smoky process. That's why most of the time we do something else. But I thought, if the roots are burning, it will help keep the soil warm. Warm enough to withstand a day or two of snowfall, at least."

Blank looks answered his idea. At last Solomon cleared his throat. "That's an interesting idea, for sure, but it seems to me more likely that snow would put out the fire."

"Even if your idea works, it won't help those of us with older farms where we've already cleared out those tree stumps." At least Frisk put his disapproval in kind words.

No one else spoke. Maybe Calvin's great idea wouldn't work after all. Before he sat down, he noticed Bea smiling at him, a thoughtful expression on her face. She nodded in his direction.

Why did her approval warm his heart? What did *she* know about farming?

Chapter 4

Beatrice couldn't believe the other farmers had dismissed Calvin's brilliant idea with hardly a word. Could she adapt it to her own garden? She was considering leaving before her father commented on her presence, when Parson Cabot stood up again. "We will coordinate distributions for those in need here at the church. Anyone wishing to donate or anyone in need, please contact me privately."

Beatrice decided to stay and talk with him after the conclusion of the meeting; Papa would approve of her desire to help those less well off than they were.

The preacher closed in prayer, and the men prepared to leave.

"Heating the ground from the roots up. That's an entertaining notion." Mr. Reid clapped Calvin on the back. A dull red crept into his cheeks.

"I don't know." Frisk joined in the bantering. "It's better than waiting for snow to kill the next planting."

"Anything's better than that." Whitson chuckled. "Unless it's a keg and a chair by the fire to keep me warm." He glanced in Beatrice's direction. "Not that you folks know anything about that."

"Maybe you're just jealous." Beatrice's heart warmed when Solomon spoke on his brother's behalf. "You don't have any stumps left to burn." He gestured to the door. "Let's be on our way."

Beatrice stood when they passed her bench, wanting to speak a word of encouragement to Calvin, but not daring to be so forward. She didn't have to worry. He paused while the others went on.

"I'm glad you're here today." The red had left his cheeks. "Peggy loves the fragrance you gave her for her birthday. When I go to their cabin, I feel like I've walked into a Paris salon."

"Tell her I'm glad she's enjoying it. Mama recommended it." She lowered her voice. "I think your idea is brilliant. I'm going to see if I can adapt it for our kitchen garden."

He worked his lips. Perhaps she shouldn't have spoken. Like her father, he might think women shouldn't worry about such things. After a moment's pause, he said, "Thanks for the encouragement, Miss Bailey." He dipped his head and took his leave.

"Godspeed, Mr. Tuttle," she whispered after him. Then she shook herself. She didn't want Papa to catch her staring after Calvin Tuttle. Instead, she walked to the front of the sanctuary where Mr. Dixon and Papa were speaking with the preacher.

"Beatrice." Papa's voice held a note of caution. "Are you waiting for me to bring you home?"

"No, Papa. I wanted to offer my assistance in gathering goods to help people through this hard time." She smiled.

He opened his mouth, closed it. Before he could speak, Parson Cabot said, "I'm sure you will do an admirable job. Mrs. Cabot has already started making plans, but I'm certain she'll be glad of your assistance. She's scheduling a planning session for tomorrow afternoon, if you care to join the effort."

"She'll be there with Mrs. Bailey." Papa didn't give her a chance to answer for herself, but at least he agreed to her participation. "We will take our leave of you then, Parson. Good day." He took Beatrice's arm and walked with her out the door.

"You don't need to walk home with me. 'Tis only around the corner of the green." Beatrice enjoyed the brisk air on her face, warmer now than in the early morning. Already the snow patches on the green were shrinking.

"It's my pleasure, Beatrice." To her surprise, Papa steered her in the opposite direction from the house. "This gives us a few quiet moments to talk."

In spite of the promised conversation, Papa didn't say anything for a short time, as he helped her avoid puddles forming in the street.

"Beware of becoming overly involved with the charity project." When he spoke at last, his words surprised her.

"Why? Aren't you always encouraging us to help others?"

"That's not it." They reached the bank and passed it in silence. "You will be leaving for New York once the roads are clear. I have made arrangements for you to stay with my mother for a time."

"But, Papa." *I don't want to go.*

"You will obey me in this. I am not comfortable with you mingling with the farmers and their families. We have higher hopes for you."

Doesn't what I want matter? Ultimately, no, it didn't. Beatrice swallowed her disappointment. "Yes, Papa. But. . .until then. . .I can plan on going to the parsonage tomorrow?"

Papa nodded his head. "Yes." He brought her to the door of their house and waited for her to enter before heading to the bank.

∽

Calvin lagged behind, not wanting to endure his family's good-natured teasing. His ploy didn't work. Solomon trudged on ahead, anxious to get back to his home, but Uncle Stephen stayed behind with him and Tobias.

"Are you really planning to burn out the root systems?"

Calvin shrugged. "At the least, it will rid my fields of the stumps."

Uncle Stephen turned to Tobias. "What do you think of this idea?"

"It's not my farm, but I want to do it."

Good ol' Tobias, standing up for him.

They stopped by the fence, and his uncle jumped up on the crossed poles after clearing off the snow. The trees looked odd, snow coating the few green leaves that still hung on to the branches. Uncle Stephen hit the wood with the flat of his hand and surveyed the trees around him. "We always stopped by this very spot on Rogation Day, back when I was a boy. We no longer do that. It's a pity."

"Rogation Day. What's that?" Tobias asked.

"I suppose a town boy wouldn't know about that," Calvin said in a teasing voice. "Back before Maple Notch had a church, the circuit preacher came around to bless the new crops. Dad says there was a lot of good-natured bumping and pushing around the boundary markers, so they'd know where their parcel began and ended."

"That's right." Uncle Stephen nodded. "As I said, we always came this way. I knew every rock and tree. When I was a boy, there were a lot more trees here. We had cold winters, I suppose. I don't rightly remember. I had fun playing in the snow and helping Pa fix up the farm. Leastwise, until he died. After we won our independence and my brother chose to move away. . .well, it seemed like nothing could separate me from this land." He brushed the rest of the snow off the fence and jumped down. "But now, I wonder."

Was his uncle considering moving away? He had heard rumors among the other farmers, but not in his family.

"Come on. Let's go." Uncle Stephen joined him, and they continued walking down the trail.

A few yards ahead, they reached the spot where their paths separated. "I'm praying for you, Calvin. One of the things I learned during the War for Independence was that God will make a way when it seems impossible. He did for us."

"Calvin's told me some of the stories." Tobias flashed a grin. "That his mother lived in a cave near their fields with her family when the Tories wanted to take over the Patriot land. How his father helped her, against the wishes of his grandfather."

"That's right." Uncle Stephen's mouth formed a thin smile that remembered a faraway time. "Don't be afraid to ask for help, Calvin. You've got family here."

Calvin strove to loosen his clenched teeth. How could he hope to ever make a home for himself. . .for a wife and a family. . .if he ran home when hard times came? But he knew the love behind the offer and refused to take offense. "Thanks."

∾

The following morning, Calvin and Tobias headed to the fields early. They spent the better part of the morning turning the ruined crop over and preparing the ground for yet another planting. At noon, they dug out the sandwiches they had made that morning.

Tobias sat down on the stump of a maple tree and propped his knee on the weathered wood. "So how do we go about setting the roots to burning?"

"You're as bad as a little kid." Calvin responded with good humor. "I have to tell you everything."

"But you have to admit that I'm a fast learner. Good thing I'm humble, too. Good looking to boot." Tobias took a bite and chewed before adding with a sly grin, "Not that Miss Bailey would ever notice. She only has eyes for you."

Calvin's shoulders jerked in reaction to Tobias's unexpected comment. "Miss Bailey's father has noticed *both* of us, and we don't pass muster. Now let's get to work."

In spite of the warm air, Calvin built a fire. He would lay the auger in the center, to bring the end to a red-hot point before he would insert it into a tree stump. "Let's go back to the cabin. I'll return the hoes and get the auger. You go into the cabin and fill up the kettle with water and bring it on out. I'll grab the salt."

Tobias crooked an eyebrow at Calvin as though wondering about his sanity.

"You'll see." The snow had melted away since the storm, and once again, birds sang in the trees. Too bad he couldn't relax and enjoy it, search out the goslings that had left the nest not long before.

"Too bad you don't have two of those things." Tobias pointed to the auger as they returned to the field. "Not that I know much about it, but I could learn."

"We'll see what progress we make today. If I don't finish today, we'll ask Solomon if we can borrow his tomorrow. Today, you can watch and learn." He didn't mention that he needed practice himself since he hadn't burned tree stumps since he was a little boy.

After the water was heating over the fire and the auger prepared, Calvin touched its point to the center of the stump. The wood smoked as the auger hit it and charred through the surface. Calvin twisted the tool, making the hole wider and deeper. Once the opening was about half an inch across, he lifted the tool and checked the end. Still hot enough for a second hole.

He turned to where Tobias stood watching. "Now it's your turn. Pour salt into each hole as I make it."

Working as a team, the men repeated the process, pausing to reheat the auger once, creating a series of holes in a diagonal line crisscrossing the stump. "That's enough. Next we pour hot water into the holes. I brought the dipper."

Tobias stopped by the boiling kettle. "Why water? How can you burn something with water in it?"

"It decays faster." Calvin started on the next stump while Tobias filled the holes with water.

"I'm done," Tobias announced. He brought the salt to the stump where Calvin worked.

"Wait a minute." Calvin set down the auger, glad for a break. "Now we start the fire." He piled kindling and small branches on top of the stump Tobias had treated and lit them. "I still need to come up with something to make a chimney for the fire. Burns better that way."

Tobias looked across the field. "And we have to do this for every stump in your field?"

Calvin nodded. "We'll relight the fire every day. Normally we'd clean out the ash it leaves so it would burn faster, but I want to keep the ground warm as long as possible. Time enough to clean out the mess when we're sure the weather's going to stay warm."

Tobias whistled. "That's going to take us awhile. Let's get busy."

∽

" 'Tis hard to believe that we had snowfall here only two nights ago. Already the ground has dried," Mama said as she walked with Beatrice to the parsonage.

"Someone built a snowman on the green." Beatrice cocked her head to study the lopsided figure now melted to a lump not much taller than a child. "Must have been the parson's children." Here and there among the muddy morass of the town common, the ever-hopeful grass poked short shoots into the air. The trees were in worse shape. She stopped to check the buds on her favorite oak that dominated the side by their house. She found a few fledgling leaves clinging to its branches, branches that by this time of year should be invisible under the foliage. But by and large, she couldn't even find any green emerging from the buds, promising the new year's growth had started.

"That snowman will be gone tomorrow if the weather continues warm as it is." Mama patted Beatrice's hand. "Since we're so far north, I'm sure the weather to the south has been more pleasant. We will have you in New York in time for Independence Day—have no fear." She slowed her steps as they approached the meetinghouse. "I was your age when I met your father. You are of an age when your thoughts naturally turn to marriage and motherhood."

Beatrice's cheeks pinked. Mama rarely spoke of such personal things.

"He came to New York on a business trip, and even then I saw the man he would become. You might not guess it now, but he was handsome and strong. I knew then he would be successful at whatever he turned his hand to."

"Did Grandfather Purcell object to you marrying someone from the north country?"

"Not for long. He could see Mr. Bailey's sterling qualities. And my mother helped persuade him." Mama looked quite pleased with herself. "And soon some young lad as fine as your father will be occupying your mind and heart."

Beatrice's thoughts strayed to Calvin, but she suppressed the image. Papa wouldn't entrust her future to someone who hoped an experimental stump burnout would save his crops—his livelihood.

Somehow, Papa had convinced Grandfather Purcell that he was worthy of her mother's hand in marriage. What would a local boy have to do to convince Papa of the same?

Mama patted Beatrice on the arm. "We'll leave on the next stagecoach that comes through Maple Notch." The look in her eye told Beatrice Mama couldn't wait to get to New York.

Beatrice looked at the shrinking snow patch and almost wished snow would fall another time, even after the advent of summer. Clear roads meant travel became possible.

"Ah! Here we are, at the parsonage."

Mrs. Cabot came to the door. "Come in! Lovely weather today, isn't it?" She took their coats and hats and gestured for them to find a seat. A handful of ladies had gathered. Peggy gave a tiny wave in Beatrice's direction, and her heart lifted.

Mama took her place in a cushioned rocking chair, the most comfortable seat in the room, as if it was hers by right. Mrs. Cabot hesitated before taking a chair by the kitchen. "This is a good seat. I can go in and out easily from here."

Her statement made Beatrice wonder if the parson's wife had been sitting in the chair Mama had claimed. She herself took a chair by Peggy.

"I believe we're all here now." Mrs. Cabot's smile welcomed all, from little Nellie Warner, too young to help in any meaningful way, to Mama, sitting in her chair like the queen of Maple Notch. "This year has been difficult for all of us, but especially for those who are farmers in our midst. So far every crop has failed, and if there is another freeze, there is little chance for harvest."

Beatrice's thoughts skittered to Calvin's plans to warm his fields. Would he succeed? She jerked her mind back to Mrs. Cabot's words.

"Mr. Cabot suggested we make preparations for the worst as a community. The church always sets some things aside for the needy, but our cupboards are almost bare. I fear things will get worse before they get better. I hoped that together we could suggest some means to meet the needs arising among us."

"I don't know about that." Mrs. Whitson, as quarrelsome as her husband was contentious, spoke. "Times like this tax all our resources. I don't have nothing left over to give away."

Beatrice harrumphed to herself. The Whitsons had one of the most successful farms in the valley. Papa had talked about the good business they brought the bank's way.

Murmurs of agreement spread across the room. "We want to help," Peggy said. "But we're not sure how to do it."

Beatrice waited for her mother to say something. They had resources, and their livelihood didn't depend directly on the whims of weather. But if the fields didn't produce, no amount of money could buy enough.

Beatrice thought back to the Bible stories she had read so often and spoke. "Perhaps we can learn a lesson from Joseph. Of course, God didn't send any of us warning that we'd have this bad year, but couldn't we set aside some of what's left from last harvest? Collect it in a central place?"

"Like a tax?" Mrs. Whitson asked. "We already pay enough to the government."

"Think of it as an investment. In our community. A protection against next year."

"And who'd be in charge of it? You? Your father?"

Uneasy laughter rippled across the room.

"Of course not." Mama frowned at her.

Beatrice felt the need to defend her idea. "We could reassess the need next year. God willing, the farmers will have bumper crops next season. I thought knowing something was available if this year's crops fail might bring peace of mind."

Furrows appeared between Peggy's eyebrows, as if she were turning Beatrice's idea over in her mind. Her friend seemed uncertain of her plan, and that troubled her.

Mrs. Reid, Peggy's mother, spoke. "Beatrice, I'm sure your heart means well, but you're not a farmer. We plan for special circumstances such as this.

Our families have been through troublesome harvests before, and will again. We'll weather the storm, you'll see, even if we have to make do without some things."

The women in the group murmured their agreement, and Beatrice knew they wouldn't heed her ideas. She struggled with her disappointment. Was she imagining problems where none existed? Was she only thinking of things as a banker might, in terms of profit and loss, not in terms of personal hopes and dreams?

A few minutes later, the meeting broke up with little progress beyond a verbal agreement to gather food if a need was expressed. Beatrice wished she could shake the unease that plagued her. Not everyone had families. And some without families wouldn't want to ask when others had more mouths to feed.

Someone like. . .Calvin.

Beatrice hoped it wouldn't come to that.

Chapter 5

Before the church ladies could meet a second time, Mama announced a change of plans for Beatrice. One morning, Mama came into the room to look over the gowns that hung in the armoire. She pulled out a buttercup gown that had been fashioned for Beatrice last summer. "This will have to do."

Beatrice had worn the gown to Sunday meetings and a few other special festivities. Never during the middle of the week. "What's happening?"

"Your father has invited us to go with him to Burlington tomorrow. He asked that we dress in our best. I think that while we are in town, I shall buy fabric for some new gowns."

"But if we go to Burlington, we'll miss the church women's meeting."

Mama clucked. "They can manage without us this once, I fancy. Your father rarely takes us on his business trips."

Beatrice's heart went out to Mama. In truth, her few trips out of Maple Notch were always occasions for rejoicing, opportunities to visit with her sisters who remained in the larger town. Inside her portmanteau, Mama had packed only one gown. A dark-blue morning dress lay on the coverlet for her traveling costume. Beatrice breathed a sigh of relief. Without more dressy garments, they couldn't be planning to ship her to New York.

"Mr. Bailey thought you might enjoy shopping for seeds. Decide for yourself what you might want to plant in the garden."

Beatrice's heart sped up at the prospect. "Perhaps I can learn how others are combating the frosts the farmers are battling this year."

"No need to trouble your mind about that, dear." Mama stepped close, and for a long moment, Beatrice feared she would pinch her cheeks to make them appear pink. But she didn't move her hands, and the look on her face reminded Beatrice of the day she saw a robin pushing her babies out of the nest. Was this, in fact, not a trip to Burlington but New York? She glanced again at the scant items in her traveling bag. *No*, she decided.

Mama bent over the bag and rearranged the contents, tucking in Beatrice's Bible. "Perhaps we can make time to visit the booksellers while we are there. My sister Rose has mentioned a new book, *Waverley*, that you might enjoy."

Beatrice blinked at that. Mama rarely encouraged her to visit the bookshop and never to read such frivolous-sounding titles. "I'd like that." She kept her reservations to herself, lest Mama change her mind. "When are we leaving?"

"Later this morning. The roads are clear today, and Mr. Bailey wants to get as far as the ordinary at Milton by nightfall."

"But Mrs. Cabot—"

"I've already sent her a note. She'll understand."

A trip of a couple of days, with the promise of a new gown and more books. Beatrice warmed to the idea. What harm could she come to in such a short amount of time? In case they were delayed, she decided to write short notes to both Calvin and Peggy. "We shan't be gone long," she penned, then stuck the tip of the feather between her teeth, wondering what to say. She sent a prayer up to heaven. "I'll pray for good weather to hasten the growth of this year's crop and so we won't be stranded in Burlington. I long to return to Maple Notch before Independence Day."

❧

Calvin looked up to see Tobias leaning on his hoe, staring down the lane for the third time in an hour. "She won't get here any more quickly if you stare all day. Haven't you ever heard that a watched pot never boils?"

Tobias didn't pretend not to know what Calvin was talking about. He had been looking down the road to town for the ladies returning from church for the last hour. A single question to Calvin—*"Is anyone calling on your cousin Peggy?"*—was all it had taken to diagnose Tobias's interest. Glad as Calvin was to see his friend coming out of the grief-filled daze that had dulled his mind since his betrothed's death, he didn't think twice about the unfortunate inclinations of his own heart. Hiram Bailey would *never* consider a farmer good enough for his daughter.

Calvin decided to take mercy on his friend. "But it is past noon, and we've not yet eaten. Let's take our midday break. And pray the ladies come along while we're resting."

Tobias laughed and stretched his arms, causing the muscles to ripple across his back. Perhaps they should continue working. Peggy might take more notice of Tobias's honest labor and growing farm skills than of two men at their leisure. But if they did that, Calvin couldn't hide his own growing agitation about what news of Bea Peggy might bring.

He drank from the water dipper and allowed himself another ladle to sprinkle over his head to cool it down. Looking across the sun-kissed field, he wouldn't believe snow had covered the ground only a couple of days ago unless he had seen it himself. Of course warmth from the smoking tree stumps added to the rays beating on their backs. He reached for their shirts and tossed one to Tobias. "We'd best get presentable."

The two of them stuffed their arms into sleeves and pulled the tops on. With the water he had dribbled over his head, Calvin felt as fresh as if he had just stepped out of the river. Tobias poured water over his hands and ran the hands through his hair, giving himself a similar look. Would the ladies think they had whiled the morning away?

"They'll know how hard we've been working when they see the corn mounds. . .if they can see through the smoke, that is."

Once again, Tobias appeared to have read Calvin's mind. He shook his head. Some of the smoke had darkened his shirt, so it did look a little work worn and not fresh from the laundry. The golden highlights the sun teased from Tobias's hair glittered with the water. "You'll set Peggy's heart aflutter, that's for certain." Calvin cut the cheese wedge in half and was handing it to his friend when they heard soft laughter beyond the copse of trees on the edge of the clearing. One thing about Calvin's land: it lay straight on the route from town to the Reid and Tuttle farms.

Peggy noticed them first and waved. Calvin expected her to have eyes only for Tobias, but instead she called, "Cousin! I have a letter for you."

"Beatrice." Tobias mouthed her name, his eyes dancing with mischief.

Calvin's heart leaped at the sight of the fine linen paper, such as someone like Bea might use. He repressed the desire to break the seal and instead tucked it inside his shirt. "Did you have a good meeting today?" A great deal of restraint kept him from asking about Bea by name.

"Not as many came today. I believe people hope the good weather of the last week will hold." Aunt Hilda gestured across the field where Tobias and Calvin had been working. "You have made good progress, I see. I continue to pray the Lord will reward your efforts come harvest time."

"What think you?" Tobias asked. "I might not be a farmer, but I've seen what hunger and cold can do to people. It seems wise to make plans in case the need arises."

"Beatrice suggested a plan at the last meeting. Something about gathering a portion of everybody's present stock and keeping it in a central place for emergencies. Kind of like what Joseph did in the Bible," Peggy said.

"Oh? Did she forward that plan again today?" Calvin hoped his ears didn't look as red as they felt.

Peggy and Aunt Hilda exchanged glances. "The Baileys didn't come to today's meeting."

"Too good for us," Aunt Hilda said.

"Ma," Peggy spoke reproachfully. She looked at her mother over her shoulder. "Mrs. Cabot said Mrs. Bailey sent her apologies, but unexpected business took them out of town."

"Out of town?" Calvin dredged the words out of his throat.

"I heard them say. . .New York," Peggy whispered.

Calvin's heart froze in place as hard as the earth after the last snowstorm. Once Bea arrived in New York, he might never see her again. Only the letter warming the space above his heart gave him any hope.

∞

"Mama. We have been to the dressmaker's shop three times already, and we have yet another fitting scheduled. I already have far more than I need for our stay in Burlington." Beatrice looked at the storm clouds gathering to the north. *Please, heavenly Father, don't let a storm keep us from returning home as promised.* "And we've yet to go to the storekeeper in search of seeds."

"I thought Rose had given you some from her garden," her mother said.

"She keeps promising, but not yet. Besides, I want to see what varieties are available. I know what Aunt Rose has in her garden. The storekeeper may carry different stock."

Mama's harrumph told Beatrice she didn't believe it. "Tomorrow, dear, I promise we will do our best to go to the storekeeper. But today we must go to the milliner's to get hats to match your new garments."

Beatrice again looked at the gathering clouds. She suspected that come morning, Mama would use the excuse of the summer downpour to keep them from going out.

The time at the milliner's went more quickly than Beatrice had expected. She did enjoy a pretty frock, and seldom had opportunity to acquire fashionable head coverings such as the lace and muslin *coiffure à l'indisposition* that Mrs. Finch suggested, in a color to match her new outfit. Even more seldom did she have occasion to wear such finery, since she chose not to dress like a peacock when her friends' clothing resembled the equally beautiful but less colorful ducks and geese.

"I'll have the bonnets ready for you next Monday," Mrs. Finch said. Her own cabriolet bonnet, with the brim flaring away from her face, testified to her skill as a milliner and didn't look in the least out of place on her graying hair. Beatrice tried to envision the same hat on Mama's head and couldn't. She wore clothes of the best quality, but no amount of the dressmaker's art could make her stylish.

"You seemed to enjoy your time in Mrs. Finch's shop," Mama said.

"Oh yes, she had a lovely assortment of hats. And illustrations of the latest fashions from Paris." Although when Beatrice would wear such things in Maple Notch remained open to question. "Will Papa bring them home?"

"Why, we'll pick them up ourselves. And you shall put on your favorite as soon as you step foot in the shop."

"But, Mama. . ." Beatrice hesitated before continuing. "We were supposed to stop in Burlington for no more than a week. It's been that and more already."

"Maple Notch will not disappear while we are gone" was Mama's only reply.

Beatrice looked at the storm clouds overhead and tugged her pelisse about her against the wind. Back at the house, she excused herself and went up to her chamber. Between Mama's less-than-forthcoming response and the gathering clouds that looked heavy with rain or even possibly snow yet again, Beatrice feared she might not make it back to Maple Notch any time soon. In fact, the new wardrobe, hairdresser, cobbler, and linens they had searched for all added up to one thing: New York. If snow fell, as she feared it might, Mama would seize on that as an excuse for not returning north.

Beatrice thought of the sums of money they had spent on clothing. The same amount of money could buy food and seed for the needy in Maple Notch. Why spend all that money on a summer frock that she might not wear this year if the weather remained cold, when others needed essentials?

She took out her reticule and counted up the money left from the sum Papa had given her to buy whatever "fripperies" interested her. The coins stung her hand, like money snatched from the mouths of children. She would spend no more. Papa had said she could spend it however she chose, and she knew exactly what she wanted to do. She had to get a letter back to Maple Notch.

She looked at the writing table waiting by the window. The cousin who used this room before her marriage was given to flights of poetry. She must have a supply of paper and ink nearby if it hadn't been removed since her wedding. Beatrice opened the drawer and found the supplies. Looking for a way to fix the dull pen nib, she dug in the corners of the drawer and found a knife to sharpen it. After a few exploratory scratches on the blotter pad, she began writing. She wanted to get her letters mailed before the weather closed in.

Beatrice addressed the first letter to Mrs. Cabot, explaining her desire to help with whatever plans the church ladies developed for aiding the poor, and enclosed her offering. She sprinkled sand to dry the ink while considering what to say in the second letter. Although Peggy would be interested in new styles, Beatrice didn't want to brag about her new clothes. She settled for saying, *Mama has kept me busy dawn to night outfitting me with a new wardrobe. I fear she and Papa plan to take me direct to New York from here, without ever returning to Maple Notch. If their plan succeeds, I don't know when I shall return home again. Whether I shall come home again. You know their desire to see me married to a city man.*" The ink from that last word spilled a little because of her shaking hands.

"Beatrice?" Mama said from the other side of the door. "You've shut yourself up quite long enough. Your cousin has come to see you."

"I'll be there momentarily." Beatrice added another sentence to the letter before losing the will to do so. "*Storm clouds gather to the west even as I am writing. Please tell the farmers, and Calvin, that I am praying for the weather to remain warm. I am curious as to whether Calvin's experiment works out.*" She scratched her name, addressed and sealed her missive, and tucked it into her bag as the door swung open.

"Beatrice! How lovely to see you again!" Her cousin Esther entered, face beaming with newlywed bliss.

Beatrice closed the flap of her satchel and settled down to enjoy her cousin's visit.

～

An unnatural silence greeted Calvin when he awoke. The ordinary clucking of the hens and the lowing of the cows, usually audible in the cabin, sounded muffled. He knew even before he opened his eyes that snow had fallen during the night. Again. His stomach clenched. Today would be the true test of his radical idea.

Tobias scampered down the ladder from the loft. "Snowed again. Weirdest thing I've ever seen. It's as if we've moved to the northern provinces of Canada."

"Or that we're celebrating Christmas in July." Calvin forced himself out of bed to check on the damage. A brief glance out the window showed that snow dappled the new grass. "Could be worse."

Tobias leveled a look at him. "Could be better is what you mean."

Calvin shrugged and opened the door. The cold air that greeted him made him grateful he had kept his long johns on even in the height of summer. He took one look at his hearth and shook his head. Instead, he slipped on his outer clothes, coat, and boots and headed for the door.

"Hey! What about breakfast?" Tobias had started coffee.

"I'll be back." Calvin broke into a trot for the clearing.

Never had the sight of charcoal ash warmed his heart so. A few of the fires had gone out, but smoke still seeped from the majority of stumps. Best of all, no snow covered the growing corn mounds. The short green shoots stood untroubled by the night's storm.

"Hallelujah!" He jumped high enough to clear the pasture fence.

An echoing whoop sounded behind him. Tobias had shrugged on his coat and boots and followed him. The two friends threw their arms around each other and screamed, "We did it!" Calvin wanted to howl at the early morning sun. Instead, he ran up and down the rows of corn, checking to make sure he hadn't misjudged the state of the crop.

Tobias followed at a slower pace. "I'm no expert on farming matters, but these look about the same as they did yesterday. And that's good, right?"

"That's very good, my friend."

∽

"Will you look at that." Uncle Stephen stood with his hands on his hips. "Your crops are growing right along as if this year has a summer after all."

"Warm the ground, keep the crops growing. Your cockamamie idea worked." Solomon crossed his arms over his chest. "You'll have half of Maple Notch by to see this marvel."

"Maple Notch? We'll have folks coming here from Burlington and beyond once they hear about it."

Burlington. One person who had prayed for his success wasn't here to enjoy it with him. Bea. Mr. Bailey had returned to Maple Notch in time to go to Sunday meeting last week, but the Bailey women remained absent. Peggy had ascertained they had indeed gone on to New York. Not even the missive he received from Bea could undo the worry settling around his heart.

"I fear it's too late in the growing season to start over again. Even if we could figure out how to duplicate trees roots since we've already cleared the stumps from our fields." Solomon bent down next to the nearest stump and cocked his head to one side, studying the rocks that held the chimney above the wood to vent it. "Looks almost like a smoke shack."

"Same principle. Slow and steady burn." Calvin allowed himself a moment of pride at succeeding where his older brother had failed. "I plan to share my crop with the family, of course."

Uncle Stephen clapped him on the back, but Solomon only grunted.

Tobias snapped his suspenders. "I keep telling him I'm his good luck charm, but he won't believe me for some reason."

"It's looking good." A new voice joined the congratulations. They all turned to study the newcomer. Hiram Bailey sat astride his horse. "I thought I would come see things for myself. And I must say it looks impressive, very impressive indeed."

Calvin could almost see dollar signs in the banker's eyes. For the first time, Calvin held the possibility of financial wealth and success in his hands—two things that might make him worthy of Hiram's daughter in the man's eyes.

So why did the calculating look in Bailey's eyes make his heart colder than the water flowing in the nearby stream?

Chapter 6

Ice pellets smaller than chicken feed rattled the windows outside the bedroom where Beatrice was staying with her grandmother in New York City. Today she would not enjoy any of the diversions the city had to offer. No carriage rides, no paying calls, no afternoon salons. Not that it mattered. None of it mattered. The weather only reflected what she had felt inside since coming to the city where her parents had determined she should make her match.

Beatrice touched the window pane and traced a tree in the thin mist. She glanced around, fearful she might be caught in the act. Mama would scold her for creating more work for the servants, leaving fingerprints. Never mind; she would clean the glass later. She turned her head sideways and allowed her fancy to take flight. She drew some grass under the tree and beyond that, a simple rail fence. Something was missing. Her fingers moved without conscious thought to fill the void and created a row of mounds. A field, of corn and beans, the kind she had seen every summer in Maple Notch.

What nonsense. She wiped away the picture with her handkerchief and went for cleaning supplies.

Did the sleet here in New York mean snow fell, yet again, in Maple Notch? Beatrice prayed for the farmers, for the families whose lives depended on the yearly cycle of seedtime and harvest. This wasn't a famine as she had ever imagined it, yet the cold would create a shortage of food as surely as any drought.

She considered the half-eaten breakfast tray she had set outside her door with a guilty conscience. No one would suspect the scarcity of flour in Maple Notch if they spied the variety of pastries piled on her plate to tempt her appetite. As it was, she had lost so much weight Mama scolded her that they needed a dressmaker to alter her gowns. "You're getting too thin and pale. You must make an effort, dear."

She means well. New York, once the capital of the country, offered much to celebrate over the anniversary of American independence. The fireworks had surprised her, beautiful and terrifying at the same time. She had clapped her hands over her ears like a babe in arms. A number of young people laughed at her, behind their hands, of course. All except for one. Matthew Hubbard was presentable, a graduate of Harvard College, skilled with figures, from a well-to-do family—in a word, everything Papa wanted in a son-in-law. He also possessed everything most girls would want in a husband: charm, good looks, generosity—a man who loved God first and people second.

Only. . .he lived in the city. And even such a grand place as Grandma's house felt like a prison without the sight of the crops and smell of hay drying in the fields. She missed Maple Notch more than she thought possible. She wanted to know how the farmers were faring and if the ladies had succeeded in setting up a system for distribution to the needy; if Calvin's plan to keep his corn growing even during frost had succeeded.

Why not admit it? She missed Calvin. She took the cloth she had used to clean the window pane and dabbed at her damp eyes. Splashing cool water from the basin on her face, she gave in to the sobs that wouldn't leave her heart.

"Beatrice?" Grandmother Purcell's normally soft voice had an insistent tone.

Beatrice whirled around. "Grandmamma, I didn't hear you come in." She stood rooted to the spot, waiting for the scolding she was sure to come.

Instead, the agitated look on her grandmother's face disappeared, and she opened her arms. Beatrice took one step and then stopped.

"Come here." Grandmamma nodded her head, and Beatrice flew to her side.

Grandmamma led her to the bed, and they sat there together, Beatrice quietly sobbing while Grandmamma remained silent. When the muscles in Beatrice's back complained of their awkward posture, she realized how much time had passed. She lifted her head.

"There. We are quite alone." Grandmamma patted her hand. "Tell me what is troubling you."

Beatrice dabbed at her eyes with the still damp handkerchief. "I must look dreadful. What you must think of me, acting like a silly girl."

"Nonsense." That single word, spoken in her grandmother's sternest voice, brought a trembling smile to Beatrice's lips. "I have been looking forward to your visit for weeks, but you haven't been happy since you arrived."

"I didn't know it was so obvious." Beatrice blinked, her heart racing with renewed agitation. "I have done my best to please Mama and Papa."

"No one could ask for a better daughter. And you know your parents only want the best for you." Grandmamma stood and poured a glass of water before handing it to her. "But it seems God gave grandmothers extra eyes and ears. You aren't happy here in New York."

Beatrice feared tears would come into her eyes again, but she remained dry-eyed. She stood up and walked to the window, looking out at the sleet hitting the trees that swayed in the wind. "I wonder if it's snowing today back home."

"Surely not. Winter lingered extra long this year, 'tis true, but surely it won't snow in July, not even in Vermont."

"But it has. Every month this year. And the farmers are afraid they won't have a harvest this year if it snows again." She hugged her arms tight around her, as if to shut out the cold railing against the window panes. "And that is what troubles me. My friends and neighbors are facing a hard time, while I am in New York buying clothes and going to parties."

"Your father wishes to protect you from the harshness of life."

When Beatrice whipped around, Grandmamma raised a hand. "But he doesn't see that you are strong—strong enough for whatever challenges life might bring." She slipped a frail arm around her granddaughter's waist. "Remember this. No one's life is completely easy, whether they are in a palace or a log cabin. But I have faith you will persevere." She gestured to the tea tray sitting on the table. "Now will you eat a little to make your mother happy?"

Beatrice straightened her skirt and settled in the chair. The fragrance of hot tea teased her nostrils, and she discovered she was hungry. She poured herself a cup and noticed the bowl of strawberries, dewy and red as if they had just come from the fields. She groaned. "Strawberries. I love these, and ours hadn't come in." Her voice trailed off.

Grandmamma took a seat opposite her and leaned in close. "I will speak with your mother. Perhaps between us, we can convince her to let you return home." She straightened and folded a napkin in her lap. "But until then, please at least pretend you enjoy seeing your old grandmother."

Grandmamma's rigid exterior had returned, but the twinkle in her eyes gave her away. Beatrice relaxed in the knowledge she had found an ally at last.

∾

Calvin checked the fire on the last stump. The saltwater holes had long since burned away, but he decided not to create new ones. He didn't want to risk burning through the roots too quickly. He shook his head, wondering at himself. Ordinarily farmers begrudged the time needed to rid a field of a tree's root system, to free up more arable land. This year, Calvin wanted to slow down the process, keep the ground warm and pliable every day until winter set in again with full force.

"What's so funny?" Tobias asked. His face had by now taken on a healthy tan, and his shoulders had filled out. With what he had learned working with Calvin, he would make a good farmer if he decided to stay. He'd have his pick of the girls of Maple Notch—if he was looking. So far the only one he'd expressed any interest in was Peggy. Calvin grinned at that. Keep Tobias in the family. He liked the idea.

"I repeat. Why are you smiling?"

Calvin straightened the lines of his lips. He wouldn't tease Tobias about Peggy, not today, not ever. "I was thinking what a strange year this has turned out to be. Snow every month. Not even my grandparents have ever mentioned a year so severe, when they carry on about how bad things were in the old days, getting settled in the Notch."

"Then your smoking trees. Never heard of the likes of that before." Tobias leaned on his hoe. "It's peaceful here. I see why you like it. Sometimes it's quiet enough that you can hear a leaf fall in the forest."

Calvin shook his head. "That's another strange thing. Usually I hear birds singing, at least in the mornings when I come out. This year it's been mostly quiet. I suspect the birds winged their way back south."

"The weather to blame for that, too?"

Calvin nodded. "A few succeeded in hatching a clutch. I'll show you a family of goslings I discovered the next time we go into town."

"Sunday morning. I can't wait."

He couldn't wait to see Peggy, but Calvin wouldn't mention that. He had his own reasons for wanting to see his cousin.

She had received word from Bea Bailey.

∽

"Beatrice says she hopes to make it home by the end of August. Before, if she can convince her mother."

That was indeed good news after the string of descriptions of city life Peggy had relayed from Bea's letter as they walked to church Sunday morning. Tobias carried her basket while she relayed bits of news from the letter. Calvin strove to keep his face expressionless.

"There's no need to look as if you swallowed a lemon." Not enough to fool his cousin, apparently. "She *wants* to come back. That's a good thing, isn't it?" The three young people hung behind the others, talking together in low tones.

Calvin hesitated, but Tobias didn't. "Of course it is." He slapped Calvin on the back. "She'll be here in time to see how splendidly your crop is doing." His smile broke into a frown at Peggy's dour look. "I'm sorry. I know others aren't as fortunate."

"We'll get by. That's what Ma keeps saying. Pa says we might have to tighten our belts for a short time. Meanwhile when I go out to milk the cows, they look at me expecting their summer ration of grass in the meadow."

Tobias stuck his hands in his pockets, scowling, and Peggy seemed to realize she might have upset him. She glanced up at the sun and smiled. "But today is a lovely day and not a time to worry about tomorrow. This is the day the Lord has made. I will rejoice and be glad in it." She hummed a few bars of "Sometimes a Light Surprises."

Calvin put a finger to his lips. "Sh!"

"My singing isn't that bad, cousin." She grinned saucily and started singing again.

"Be still and listen for once."

Ears straining, they all waited. Calvin wondered if he had imagined it when there it came again. A soft *peep, peep.* "I told you we'd see them today!" He pointed in the direction of the river, across the brownish ground ordinarily high with green grass at this time of year. A line of fluffy yellow goslings waddled in a row behind their parents, whose brown feathers almost blended in with the background. "At least one family survived." *And so will we.*

The good weather and the sight of the goslings buoyed everyone's spirits. Even Parson Cabot seemed happy when he began his sermon. He preached from the eighth chapter of Genesis, when Noah and his family came out of the ark after the flood. "Last Sunday many of us struggled to make it to services because of yet another unseasonable freeze. This year has brought weather never before seen. I have heard some speculate that perhaps we are seeing the end of days, and the Lord must be coming soon. I am ready, but I do not expect it until I hear the trumpet call in the sky."

A few people in the congregation chuckled at that.

"But no matter how this year's weather has treated us, I want us to remember another time when the seasons were turned upside down. It rained for forty days and nights, so much water that all dry land was covered, even our beloved Green Mountains. After the flood, God gave Noah a promise. Does anyone remember the sign God gave Noah?"

A little girl with shiny black pigtails and wearing a blue pinafore answered, "The rainbow."

"That's right." The parson came out from behind the pulpit and bent over the little girl. "And tell me, what does the rainbow mean?"

"That there'll never be another flood." She scrunched up her face. "But it doesn't say anything about snow."

Laughter rippled among the adults, and the child's face turned bright pink.

"No, it doesn't." The preacher returned to the pulpit. "But I'll tell you what it does say. God promised that 'While the earth remaineth, seedtime and harvest, and cold and heat, and summer and winter, and day and night shall not cease.'"

As the words sank in, a hush fell over the congregation. Cabot waited before continuing. "I wanted to remind us of that. Seedtime and harvest will never cease. We may have a temporary aberration. But they will not cease. Harvest will come again. With a spirit of thanksgiving, let us raise our voices in the hymn 'The Sower.'"

The hymn was a favorite among the farmers, much as Jesus' parable delighted those who first heard it. From the first verse, "Ye sons of earth prepare the plough," to the last, "Father of mercies, we have need," the congregation sang with full voice, raising a joint prayer to the Lord, thanking Him for future harvests and trusting Him for the present.

After the service, no one hurried home. Instead, the ladies of the town had decided to enjoy a picnic under the sunny skies. Various colored quilts appeared on the ground. Even Peggy had packed one in the gigantic satchel Tobias had carried for her.

"Someone should have told us. We may be bachelors, but we could have brought something."

"Nonsense," Aunt Hilda said. "I'm sure the two of you will have your pick of dinners to share." She smiled at Tobias and Peggy, her cheeks dimpling in a rare show of good humor. "Including ours."

"Mr. Tuttle?"

Calvin allowed his gaze to wander while the speaker addressed his brother—*the* Mr. Tuttle in Maple Notch. No matter how many times he checked the gathering, he couldn't make the Baileys appear when they hadn't come to the service. Had Hiram indeed returned to New York? To fetch home his wife and daughter? He felt a smile creep to his face.

"Calvin, Miss Rusk is speaking to you," Aunt Hilda said.

"Mr. Tuttle—oh. I'm far too young to be Mr. Tuttle." The words stumbled out of Calvin's mouth before he could recall them. A look of chagrin passed over the face of the pale young woman standing before him, her arms holding a basket from which the savory smells of baked chicken arose.

"My mother said we could invite you to join us. As you see, we have plenty."

Calvin looked about for Tobias, but his friend had already taken a chicken leg from Peggy's basket. When another glance revealed no escape, Calvin gave in with good grace and walked with Frieda Rusk to the spot where her family was seated.

"Thank you for accepting our invitation." Mrs. Rusk's smile echoed and enlarged Frieda's shy look. "Frieda and I fixed enough food yesterday to feed half of Maple Notch. It's been too long since we had an excuse to celebrate summer."

Calvin nodded and bit into the stewed chicken. Taste melted into his mouth—far better than anything he or Tobias cooked up. He forced himself to chew and savor each mouthful.

Even after he slowed his pace, Frieda only managed one bite for every two or three of his. Her good cooking and generous spirit made up for her rather plain looks. She would make some farmer a good wife someday. *But not me.* He hoped she didn't interpret his presence on her family's picnic blanket the wrong way.

Frieda kept quiet, except to ask if he wanted a second helping of chicken or another corn cake. Her parents didn't bring much to the conversation either. The silence was broken only by occasional requests for more apple butter or squash. Across the green, Calvin saw Tobias and Peggy engaged in animated conversation and wished he were with them. He held back a sigh and tried to think of something, anything, to ask Frieda. His mind remained blank. After a second helping of everything, he demurred. "I can't eat any more and walk home. I'm so full, I'd slip on a stone and bust open. But it's delicious. Thank you."

She blushed. " 'Twasn't nothing."

Silence again descended while the others continued eating. When Mr. Rusk at last finished, he wiped his hand across his mouth. "I hear your crop is doing well. Your tree stump theory appears to have some merit."

"God has been good." Calvin hesitated to take credit. "We only lost a handful of plants with this last frost."

"Snow in July." The farmer shook his head. "Wouldn't have believed it if I hadn't seen it for myself."

"And your crop?" Calvin hated to ask but felt compelled.

"Gone." Rusk stood and gestured for Calvin to walk with him. When they had moved a few yards away, he said, "I don't like to say much in front of my wife, but our supply of seed corn is running low. If you have any extra next year, keep me in mind."

Seed corn. A thought danced around the edges of Calvin's consciousness but didn't take root. The success of his own crop remained in doubt, with the late planting. He didn't know if he would have seed corn available; and if he did, his family's needs would come first. But. . .

"I will keep that in mind, Mr. Rusk. But I still am not certain I will have more success than the rest of us."

Rusk's genial face turned serious. "I pray you do, Calvin. God help us if no one grows seed corn this year."

On the road home, Tobias and Peggy continued their lively conversation, while Calvin walked ahead of them, wrapped in silence. Was God giving him the opportunity to play Joseph to his Egypt, the people of Maple Notch? To provide food in a time of famine? *Right. If you're not careful, Calvin Tuttle, the next thing you know you'll imagine yourself the George Washington of Vermont. Or at least the Ethan Allen of the nineteenth century.* Try as he might to screen the possibility out, he couldn't stop thinking of options. If he had extra seed corn and sold it for a reasonable price…he could pay off the debt he owed the bank. He could make improvements to the property. *I could make a home ready for a wife.* Bea Bailey's face swam into his consciousness, but Calvin shook it off. *It will take more than the profit from one year's crop to satisfy her father.*

When he came to the wooden bridge that crossed the river to their farms, he paused. The others had lagged behind, and he was alone at the riverbank. Below him, water rushed by, still high from the constant runoff of snow this year. He wouldn't want to plunge into its icy depths. He took two tentative steps on its planks when a warning *snap* ripped through the air. Spreading from the center of the bridge in both directions, a crack appeared in two of the planks.

Behind him, he heard lighthearted laughter.

"Stay where you are!" Calvin called. He backed off the bridge with measured steps, almost running into Tobias.

"What did you say?" Tobias reached the bridge first.

Calvin flung his arm around his friend, pulling him back.

The other members of Calvin's family gathered around them. "What's the matter?" Solomon asked. "The wife is tired, and we're ready to get home."

Calvin nodded at the bridge. "Big crack. I fear it won't support any weight."

Uncle Stephen nodded and turned north. "Come, let's check out the larger bridge farther up the river." When Calvin didn't fall in with the family, he asked, "Are you coming?"

Calvin shook himself out of his trance. Weather, crops, Bea's letter, the bridge—it was too much to take in. Perhaps he should be glad circumstances disallowed him time to think about everything. He caught up with the others as they headed for the next closest river crossing.

Only a fool would cross the bridge with the danger so high.

Chapter 7

The cold drizzle couldn't dampen Beatrice's high spirits. Not when every *clip-clop* took her away from New York and closer to Maple Notch. Today they would reach the shores of Lake George. From there, they would travel by boat most of the way home. Along the way, they would pass Fort Ticonderoga, on Lake Champlain, which had played such a major role in the War for Independence.

Ticonderoga. As a child she had thrilled at the schoolmaster's description of the Green Mountain Boys' capture of the fort without a life lost. Unfortunately, when it fell during the second battle in 1777, two men of Maple Notch died: Solomon Tuttle and Donald Reid—Calvin's uncle and grandfather. Surprising that the same fort hadn't been a factor in the recent war with Britain.

Her grandfather had fought with the Green Mountain Boys, an experience they never discussed. But none of the men had died. What was it like for Calvin? Had his family told and retold their part in the struggle for America's independence? Is that what had inspired him to go off and fight when war broke out in 1812?

She shook her head to clear the thoughts of him in uniform—she had seen him once, with the tall shako felt hat and bright scarlet epaulettes—in the midst of a smoke-filled battlefield. She replaced that image with the way she had seen him last, sharing his idea for keeping the ground warm enough to grow a crop by smoking out the tree stumps. Thoughtful, committed, hardworking—these characteristics of the men that brought the republic into being lived on in their sons.

Overhead she heard a purple martin, the rich, gurgling call that awoke her on so many spring mornings. At least she thought it was a martin. She brought her hand to her forehead, blocking out the sunlight while she scanned the sky. Her thoughts went to the family of geese that had taken up residence on the town green after the goslings had hatched. The same geese returned summer after summer. Sometimes two or three pairs took care of as many as fifteen to twenty youngsters. This year, only one pair had remained on the green, with only four young. The cold weather had exacted payment from the local wildlife as well as the human population. Again she thought of Calvin and hoped his plan had worked.

She would see for herself soon enough; the road to Maple Notch took them past his farm. Her heart sped up, warming her skin as well as her heart, to the point she hardly noticed the cold air. How could she, when thoughts of the handsome young man who captured her heart's attention more than anyone else she had ever met filled her mind?

∽

"I know, it's cold and you want to get home." Calvin patted the neck of his gelding. "But I need to check on the bridge." With the horse's strong legs underneath him, he felt safe to go into the river. As he'd expected, the wooden planks showed signs of the year's bizarre weather patterns. Water had seeped into the wood, expanding in the damp, contracting when it heated and dried, increasing the crack. In a home, one patched spots if the damage grew too severe. But in a structure such as a bridge, a single crack could break a plank in half. Could they repair the damage, or would they need to rebuild?

The crack had extended to within inches of the trestle. With his pocket knife, Calvin dug into the wood around the crack. Soft. Diseased. The crack might seal when the wood dried, or it might simply break apart. He'd discuss solutions with the family later.

He kneed his horse into movement, glad to leave the freezing water. The sky, sunny when he had arisen that morning, had clouded over and the air held a chill. *More snow?* He prayed it would be no worse than a cool rain and not another freeze. Could they have at least thirty days without a freeze before the next winter season snowed them in again? Would they experience summer at all, however fleeting?

With August fast approaching, he doubted it. Autumn began its inexorable descent into winter by the beginning of September. Summer's window of opportunity had almost passed them by. Only God's grace would allow him to grow any grain at all.

Horses whinnied and he looked up to see Uncle Stephen and his family on the road, accompanied by Tobias.

"We thought we'd come and take a look. Tobias told us where you were." Peggy glanced at him as she said it, a pretty pink blush staining her cheeks.

"What do you think?" Uncle Stephen asked.

"It's going to give way sometime soon, is my guess."

Aunt Hilda clicked her tongue. "That would be downright dangerous, with the river still so high."

And cold. But Calvin didn't say that. The womenfolk didn't need to know he had gone into the water. They would only rail at him for being so foolhardy. "I'm planning to block both ends of the bridge today, so people will know not to cross."

Uncle Stephen shook his head, a passing shaft of sunlight highlighting the gray streaks in his hair. "It will be a nuisance, to have to go north every time we go into town. Tomorrow I'll come back and make repairs. Easiest all around. Too much traffic passes this way to keep it closed for long."

Calvin hesitated but a moment. "I've been thinking of the traffic and the need for a safe crossing. We face this same problem every winter." He blew out his cheeks. "I'd like to build a covered bridge. And charge a toll to those who cross over it."

"A *toll* bridge? Why would we want to charge our neighbors?" Aunt Hilda sounded scandalized.

"A covered bridge?" Uncle Stephen puzzled.

"Someone in Pennsylvania came up with the idea a few years ago." Calvin looked at the bridge, envisioning the newer, stronger span that would replace it. "I crossed one when I was away to the war."

Tobias nodded his head. "I know the one you mean. Like a big old barn sitting atop a river. It felt rather spooky in there. An owl flew down from the rafters and hooted, and I near jumped out of my skin."

"Why would we want to do that? I helped build this bridge, remember. We've only needed to make minor repairs, at least until now. Leave well enough alone. We have other things that would do us more good, like a mill wheel." He added half under his breath, "If we get corn and wheat to grind."

Calvin bit back the protest on his tongue. So Uncle Stephen didn't want to invest Reid family money in a bridge. And Calvin had precious little of his own. Not that it would take much. . .but he was already in debt to the bank, with repayment uncertain. Once again he sent his prayers heavenward for a healthy harvest.

"A covered bridge." Uncle Stephen shook his head. "Using tree roots to warm the ground and covering rivers with barns. What will you think of next, nephew?"

A lot of things. If only Calvin had the money to try them all.

∽

Beatrice's heart urged the coach horses to plod faster, to eat up the miles remaining from the moment they had left Burlington and headed for the Notch, as some called it. But Papa was a cautious driver.

"Be careful now." Papa reflected her thoughts. "If you keep squirming, I'll wish we had stayed behind at the inn. After the ice last night, the roads are a little slick." Ice cracked underneath the horses' hooves, and water splashed on the sides of the coach as if to emphasize his point.

"Oh, Papa. It's a beautiful day." Sun glittered on the snow as it did after every storm, as if the world were once again created anew. "I even enjoy seeing snow again." She giggled. "I feel like I'm really and truly home."

At least Papa had allowed her to join him on the driver's seat. She twisted and turned, wishing she had a seat that could swivel and allow her to take in all directions at once. "Papa, you didn't tell me the trees had started to turn."

He scowled. "Did they ever grow leaves? We didn't even get our normal maple run this year. Business has been bad in every quarter."

Did he never think of anything besides business? "But look. We are traveling on streets of gold and red and orange. It's as if we're headed for the New Jerusalem." She stretched out her right hand and grabbed a single maple leaf. "I feel like I can reach out and touch heaven from here."

Papa looked at her sideways. "You truly prefer the countryside to being in the city?"

How should she answer such a question? Papa seemed genuinely interested, so she tried. "When I'm in Maple Notch, I feel as though God is within reach in everything I see and touch. When I'm shut up in buildings crowded together and the only grass I can see is in the park, He feels more distant." She coughed. "I know God is everywhere, in the city as well as in the country. But it's just easier for me out here." She lifted her face to feel the sun. "In New York, I can't even see the sky properly for all the rooftops and carriages passing by."

Papa sighed. "I only want things to be easier for you. Life in Maple Notch is harsh. This year is proof of that. Any one of those young men your grandmother Purcell introduced you to could have given you anything you wanted."

After that, they both fell quiet, and Beatrice heard water rippling and crashing over rocks. "We're almost home!" Her voice rose in pitch. The falls lay to the south and west of the Tuttle and Reid farms. Soon they would reach the farms. Would she see Calvin this morning?

Through the trees, she caught sight of the water and heard the roar. By this time of year, she didn't expect to hear the water running so high or so fierce. Another sign of this year of no summer.

Then the road turned away from the river, skirting the edge of Solomon Tuttle's farm and making its way through the fields. The cleared land lay fallow, the only possible harvest hay to feed the animals over the winter. Had Calvin's crop suffered a similar fate? She caught her breath and urged the horse forward with silent pleas.

A short distance farther on, they crossed the boundary to Calvin's farm. A smoky fog hung over the fields, unlike the clear skies they had encountered elsewhere on the day's journey. Through the haze, she saw stalks of corn and poles of beans sprouting from the earth.

"Look, Papa!" Like a little child, she couldn't contain her excitement. "Mr. Tuttle's field is growing!"

Papa grunted. "He's done well."

Better than his brother's field. Maybe other farmers had succeeded in growing a crop. *Lord, let it be so. Our people need it.* She squinted her eyes, seeking a glimpse of figures working among the rows. Here and there the smoke stretched thin to reveal crops growing and prospering as they should. But Calvin and Tobias were absent from the fields. Her heart sank quicker than the sun behind the mountains. She didn't realize she had so looked forward to seeing him today. If not today, she wouldn't see him until Sunday at the earliest, with all of Maple Notch watching.

Papa clicked his tongue, and the horses picked up speed in the direction of the river. Had he slowed down to indulge her fantasy? *No.* Papa had allowed her to return home, but marriage to a farmer just starting out was still out of the question—at least in his mind. No, he was interested in Calvin's farm for reasons of his own. The young man probably owed money on the land—was Papa calculating the return on his investment? She opened her mouth to ask, then chewed on her lip. A direct question would only get an evasive answer. "Leave business to the menfolk" or words to that effect. He had already given his comment on the state of the farm: well done.

As they drew close to the bridge leading on to Maple Notch, the sound of voices and ring of hammers filled the air. Papa checked the horses and slowed down as they approached. A gate stood across the bridge, barring their crossing, a man standing on either side—neither one of them Calvin. *Tobias,* and where Tobias was, Calvin was bound to be nearby. She looked and found him, waist deep in the roiling river water. She'd recognize that brown head of hair anywhere.

"We have company!" Tobias called out. He ran to the edge of the river bank and jumped over the barrier.

"Mr. Bailey!"

Calvin's head snapped up at the salutation. He caught sight of Beatrice looking at him; a lightning-fast glance passed between them before she looked away.

"And Miss Bailey. Thank the good Lord for your safe return."

"I should have made you travel in the coach." Papa spoke in a low voice to Beatrice. Raising his volume, he said, "Well met, friends! What has happened with the bridge?"

"The center planks cracked under the snow weight. Nothing we can't fix." Calvin's brother Solomon answered.

Calvin frowned a bit at that pronouncement. With his propensity for innovations, did he have something different in mind? She'd have to ask him the next time she caught him away from Papa. Maybe she'd misread his expression. She didn't want everyone to think she had been paying that close attention.

Papa was frowning. "At this time of year it's often possible to cross the river without the bridge." His statement of fact sounded like a challenge.

Mr. Reid came forward. "I wouldn't recommend that, sir. The water's high from so much snow melt this year. You want to protect your precious cargo." He smiled and bowed in Beatrice's direction. She felt heat burst into her cheeks and turned her face away.

"People count on this bridge to get into town. If they can't cross here, they have to go almost as far north as Franklin or down south of the falls. We need a reliable crossing to keep commerce flowing in and out of this neck of the woods."

"We're aware of that, sir. We should have the repairs completed and the bridge ready before the next Lord's Day." Solomon hesitated. "We are the ones most inconvenienced by the lack of a crossing. It cuts us off from town."

Would Maple Notch split into East and West, the way so many small communities did, all for lack of a bridge? Beatrice hoped not.

"I'll look for you on Sunday, then," Papa said.

Beatrice noticed the effort Papa took to control his features and smile at her. He thumped the top of the coach with his cane, and Mama poked her head out the window. "We must turn back to the Southbridge crossing to reach home. We'll arrive later than we had hoped." Under his breath he mumbled, "I knew we should have stayed in Burlington."

⁓

Beatrice was wondering if she would have an opportunity to speak with Calvin privately come Sunday, when she heard someone knocking at the front door. Her cat dashed to the door ahead of her, ready to greet their company. The parson's wife, Mrs. Cabot, stood on the doorstep.

"So glad to have you home. I was just informing your cook that the church ladies decided to hold a bake sale on Saturday. You know how they love to display their culinary skills," she said.

Preen their feathers. Beatrice didn't voice her thought. Instead she said, "We have many fine cooks in our community."

"Yes, we do." The smile Mrs. Cabot flashed at her let her know she guessed what she had been thinking. "And your cook has already committed to bring three pies. Now that you have returned, I wanted to clear it with you, and see if you wished to contribute something of your own."

Beatrice marveled at her skill in recruiting support. Mrs. Cabot could steal honey from a bear if she wanted to.

"And the purpose of the sale?" Mama had come up behind Beatrice.

"To raise money for the needy among us. So far, our income meets the demands, but we anticipate greater needs this winter." She coughed discreetly into her handkerchief. "Only a handful of farmers have succeeded in growing any kind of crop."

"Mr. Tuttle seems to have a fine crop." Beatrice feared she sounded boastful, but she had to express the admiration she felt at his accomplishment.

"True." Mrs. Cabot nodded. "Also, a few others have a number of plants that have survived the last two frosts that they hope will mature. But most have not. So—what would you like to contribute?"

Mama named a generous amount. Her parents had earned their reputation for contributing to worthy causes.

"I'll try my hand at making some lemon tarts," Beatrice offered.

Both women turned to look at her as if they had forgotten her presence. "But, Beatrice dear, Cook is already making pies. . . ."

"I'd like to do my part." Mama couldn't argue with that. That would give her an excuse to go with Cook to the sale. . .and see who came to bid and buy.

Mrs. Cabot beamed. "That is marvelous. I shall look forward to seeing you on Saturday. And perhaps you can remain after the auction to help us set up for school?"

School never started this early. "But it's only August."

Mrs. Cabot bent forward as if to impart a secret. "The school board thought it a good idea. The children aren't needed on the farms for harvest. In the spring, we can dismiss earlier so they can help with planting."

"Is my husband aware of this?" Mama's voice sounded high, the way it did when she struggled to keep a rein on her tongue.

"I'm not certain. The school board decided this past week."

Before Mama could interrupt again, Beatrice spoke. "We'll be happy to help. Does the school need any supplies?"

"Mr. Dixon has the list."

Beatrice made a mental note to check on a few families they often helped with what few school supplies were needed. A slate, chalk, some paper, and pencils. She thought of the books she had purchased while in New York. She would donate those as well, although perhaps she would read them first.

On Saturday morning Beatrice noticed people walking into town by midmorning, even though the bake sale wasn't scheduled to begin until eleven. The resident pair of geese honked to announce their arrival, chasing them away from their young—another thing she would miss in the city. She made herself stay in the kitchen, cleaning up from breakfast and shining the Franklin stove.

"That stove makes baking a lot easier than over the hearth, it does. No more scorchin' the puddings." Cook was kneading bread dough.

Beatrice nodded. "I never thought I'd finish the tarts so quickly. I should have volunteered twice as many." She laughed. "Or tried one of your recipes. I want to learn more."

"What for? You don't expect to fix the meals and turn me out of me home, do you?"

"I won't live in this house forever." *I hope.*

A smile chased around Cook's mouth. "Could that be why you're so anxious to get across the green?"

The geese honked again and dragged Beatrice's eyes to the window. She spotted Peggy. And where Peggy went. . .

"Go on with you. I'll get the maid to help me carry these things to the church."

"Thank you." Beatrice reached for the hat she had bought in Burlington. She was glad she had convinced the milliner to keep it simple. The plain lines of the empire dress and the mob cap matched and suited her coloring without looking out of place. Everyone said the pale rose color looked good on her. She hoped Calvin would agree. "Thank you for all your work. I know you didn't expect to be cooking our meals when you offered to bake for the sale."

"It's my pleasure. I'm only glad Mrs. Bailey didn't stop me when she came home." Cook downplayed her contribution, but her face beamed with pleasure. "Hurry on, now. Find us a good table to display our food."

Crossing the common, Beatrice lingered long enough to enjoy the sight of children darting around the grass. A good number had turned out for the bake sale.

"Miss Bailey!" Young Amy Tuttle—Calvin's niece?—skipped to her side. "We heard you came back. Just in time for the fun! Will you join our team for tug of war?"

"I don't know." Beatrice looked down at her dress. Perfect for a tea party. Not quite designed for holding on to a rope with all her might and sliding through mud.

"Please join us." A deep voice added his plea to young Amy's. Beatrice turned around to find Calvin only a few feet behind her. "The Reids have challenged the Tuttles to a match, and Tobias has joined their side. The traitor." His eyes twinkled, and he nodded in the direction where his friend stood talking with Peggy.

"Is Peggy pulling?" Beatrice was curious.

"She's one of their best pullers. So you'll join us, then?" Calvin took her question as assent.

Beatrice gave one last thought to her new outfit. It could be repaired or even replaced if necessary. But a chance for a day of fresh air and friendship couldn't be repeated. "I will."

"Good. With you on our team, we're sure to win." Calvin's gaze held hers longer than was necessary or even prudent, and Beatrice turned in the direction of the tables. "Are the games before or after the sale?" She saw round loaves of bread made with fine-quality wheat flour, truly a delicacy. Spice cakes and dried apple pies and. . . She wanted to sample them all.

"We talked about that. Some were for having the games first, fearful people will gobble down the baked goods so quickly that they would get sick. Others said the games could get, uh, messy. Like the times we played rounders at school."

She giggled at that. The one time she had returned from school with her skirt muddied and her arm bruised from running the bases, Mama had been scandalized. What would she say if the same thing happened today, now that Beatrice was a grown woman?

"So we're having the sale first."

Beatrice fingered her reticule. She didn't have as much as she would like to spend. . .she always loved to buy and then help distribute food to those whose mouths had watered but didn't bid. But she had already sent a good part of her free money to Mrs. Cabot when she was in Burlington. "Do people have coin for a sale this year?" She asked.

Calvin shrugged. "That's not the only thing that's being bartered this year. Take a look." He pointed to a sign propped behind the table.

"That looks like the one from Dixon's store."

"It may be the same one."

Goods and services had been added as alternative forms of barter, with a cash value listed next to each. Everything from darning socks to bringing in hay had a price attached, as well as goods from spun wool to seed corn.

Calvin said, "People who don't have money to spend can offer their services, so everyone can take part. And your father has agreed to match every gift of services or goods with actual cash money, fifty cents on the dollar."

Beatrice sucked in her breath. What did Papa expect in return? Or was this an expression of unusual generosity?

"His offer has encouraged more people to join in. It pleased me when I heard of it."

Beatrice caught sight of Mama marching across the green as if summoned by Calvin's comments.

The look on his face told Beatrice her mother could undo all the goodwill her father's gift had engendered, at least in Calvin's mind.

Chapter 8

Calvin noticed Mrs. Bailey's approach at the same time Beatrice did. She probably wanted to steer her daughter away from her husband's biggest debtor. At least, it felt that way.

In spite of the thunderous look on Mrs. Bailey's face, she spoke civilly enough. "Beatrice, Cook needs your help in setting up the baked goods." She turned to Calvin. "I'm sure you understand."

"Of course." Calvin smiled politely while Beatrice moved in the direction of the tables.

Behind her mother's back, Beatrice glanced back at Calvin and mouthed *later*.

Without anything more to do until the bidding began, Calvin sought out Tobias. "What did Peggy bring?"

"Something with cranberries. It smelled heavenly." He tucked his hands into his pockets. "It's a good thing they have the barter system going. I doubt I have enough spare money to buy a single cookie."

Calvin chuckled. "I'm in the same predicament." The two of them had already discussed what services they could offer and how much time they could take away from the farm. If only Mr. Bailey would let him pay the debt on the farm with the same method. No, nothing but cold hard cash would satisfy the banker.

"What did Miss Bailey bring?" Tobias asked, a knowing gleam in his eye.

Calvin felt foolish. "I didn't ask."

"Then what were the two of you talking about? You carried on quite a long conversation."

Calvin laughed. "I invited her to join the Tuttle team in the tug of war."

"Do you think you're in the schoolyard? That's no way to a lady's heart."

A slender thread of memory tugged at Calvin's consciousness. "Lemon tarts. That's what she'll bring. That's what she always brought to school affairs. As I remember, they tasted wonderful."

"And what did that lady who fed you at the picnic used to bring?"

"Miss Rusk? I don't remember."

"Uh-huh." Tobias winked.

People gathered in front of the tables. The parson, who would act as auctioneer, stood behind the first table. "The ladies of Maple Notch have outdone themselves in preparing for this effort to raise money for the needs in our community. We've all felt winter's sting in this year of no summer. Remember that the bank will pay fifty cents on the dollar for every service offered in bid, so bid high and often."

Scattered laughter broke out across the crowd.

The bake sale wasn't like a box social; bidding involved no commitment between the parties beyond raising money for the community. Still, the transactions often told a tale of romantic interest. Even though the cook's name wasn't announced with the baked goods, one could usually guess.

A crock of Indian pudding came up for bid, and Calvin's brother Solomon called out, "A day in the hay meadows for anyone who needs help." No one bid against him, and he won.

Calvin scratched his head and walked over to join his brother. "Isn't that Hilda's pot?"

"Of course." Solomon looked surprised. "She's my wife."

Only a handful of people bid actual cash. Calvin hoped Beatrice's father wouldn't regret—or even rescind—his offer to match a percentage of the money raised.

Everyone enjoyed the festivities in a year that had offered few such occasions. Next up came a cream pie—Miss Rusk's specialty. Calvin clamped his mouth shut and tucked his hands around his sides, not wanting any miscommunication to the young lady who seemed to have set her cap for him.

Tobias had no such compunction. The plum pudding Peggy and Aunt Hilda had brought came up early, and he shouted out, "A day's general labor, whatever needs doing."

"You should only get half-credit for that day." Uncle Stephen teased the young man after he won the bid.

"I'll have you know I'm quite proficient at"—Tobias waited until he was certain everyone was listening—"burning out stumps."

People clapped, Uncle Stephen along with them.

Dishes came and went, but Calvin didn't see anything that tempted him to spend his money. No lemon tarts had made an appearance. At length the fine flour bread—baked by the Baileys' cook, he had no doubt—was offered. A few people bid cash for the quality bread.

Next Pastor Cabot, who served as the auctioneer, displayed lemon tarts. Calvin noticed they featured the fluted edge that Beatrice preferred.

He knew exactly what to bid for the privilege of buying every last tart.

❧

"Don't fidget," Mama whispered to Beatrice when her tarts were brought forward.

Beatrice didn't think she had fidgeted, not unless turning her reticule over in her lap once counted. Why had she offered to bake? She remembered the ignominy of one occasion when no one bid on her basket except her father. Barely sixteen at the time, she had felt the sting of that rejection for months. Only with time did she consider that her position as the banker's daughter might have influenced the outcome as well. She closed her eyes and prayed it would be different this time.

Mr. Reid gestured first. "We offer a skein of fine woolen yarn."

The man was so kind. Perhaps Peggy had suggested it.

"Two bits." Mr. Dixon's voice rang out. Had Papa asked him to bid on her offering?

"I said you had no need to worry," Mama reminded.

But they were all married men, not that it should matter.

"A bushel of seed corn after harvest. For all the tarts." Another voice offered, and silence fell.

Calvin.

The resident geese chose that moment to honk, and Beatrice's heart celebrated along with them. A bushel of seed corn was worth more than twice what anyone else had offered for anything. This year it would be worth its weight in gold. A gentle heat leaped into her cheeks. Calvin would do that . . .for her?

Parson Cabot's eyebrows went up at the bid, but he continued as if nothing unusual had occurred. "It so happens seed corn is what we need most of all. Does anyone have another bid?" After a beat, he said, "Lemon tarts, sold to Mr. Calvin Tuttle."

Beatrice could have melted to the ground on the spot, so warm her heart felt.

In contrast, the look on Mama's face could have frozen the hot tea waiting by the tables, but Beatrice refused to let her mother's dour mood dampen her spirits. "The seed corn will be much needed next year. What a wonderful gift." She didn't speak to the special feeling that ran rampant through her heart from a purchase that ran tantamount to declaring Calvin's interest in her.

The auction ended a short while later, although Beatrice paid scant attention. She had eyes only for Calvin, as he bit down on a lemon tart and offered a taste to Tobias. He refused, his own mouth probably full of Peggy's cranberry bread. Sounds buzzed around her, but she paid little mind.

"Come, Beatrice," Mama's voice intruded. "The auction has ended, and it's time for us to head home."

"I'm staying for the games." Beatrice smiled at her mother. "A summer frolic for the young people. I've been looking forward to this since I missed the last party at Grandmother's house." Mama couldn't refuse that request. They had worried that she didn't spend enough time with people her own age.

Mama pursed her lips as if to object, but what could she say? Get home before dark? That posed no problem, since dark lingered past the dinner hour, even in these waning days of summer. We have no one to bring you home? With home across the green, she'd remain within sight of the house at all times. Be careful of strangers? Her parents knew everyone in Maple Notch. In the end, Mama nodded. "I trust you know what you're doing, dear."

"I do." Beatrice bent forward and bussed her mother on the cheek. "I shall have fun and see you later."

Beatrice fought to restrain herself from skipping across the grass like a young child chasing a hoop and walked with the measured gait expected of a lady. Soon enough, she could appease her high spirits when the tug of war started.

On the near side of the green, the Whitsons and Frisks clustered around one rope. Beyond them she saw the Reids and Tuttles. Calvin motioned for her to join them.

"Good to have you on our team." He smiled at her. "You're the winning member."

"I don't know." Beatrice pretended to study the Reid family gathered on the other side. "Your uncle's mighty strong, not to mention Tobias."

"But then there's Peggy."

"What are you saying about me?" Peggy came close and offered a neck-to-ankle-length apron to Beatrice. "That frock is too lovely to endanger in the mud." She winked at her cousin. "And we *will* drag you through the mud."

Altogether, ten people grabbed either end of the rope. The harsh fibers felt rough on Beatrice's hands. She hoped she wouldn't make a fool of herself. "Take your place in front of me. I'll protect you." Calvin stood in front of Solomon, the two of them anchoring the rope, and she decided she would let the ropes burn through her skin before letting go.

Before they could exchange another word, the parson called, "Start," and Calvin pulled hard, the rope slipping through Beatrice's hands as if it was smeared with butter. Then it slid back as the Reids answered the opening tug, and she grabbed hold. What strength she had, she would add to the fight. She dug her heels into the dirt, pulled with all her weight on the rope, and yanked.

Yelling, grunting, even the rasp of the rope fibers on her hands faded as she fell into the rhythm of stumbling forward and yanking back. Ahead of her, Solomon's children pulled and hollered. Strain creased Peggy's face, and Beatrice imagined she looked much the same, facial muscles taut. Then the rope eased and slid through her fingers, and the release of pressure sent her tripping backward.

Into Calvin's arms.

∽

Calvin saw the dismay looming on Tobias's face before he felt the rope give way. He staggered and righted himself in time to receive Bea's falling body. His arms slipped around her waist and kept her upright. She felt so right, so natural there.

Without a thought to the people milling around the green or the congratulations flowing around them, he twirled Bea so he could see her face. He leaned forward, looking for permission in her brown eyes as deep and dark as gingerbread. Her lips, bitten to a cherry red during the effort to hold on to the rope, floated before him, inviting his caress. He brushed them with his own.

"Calvin." Solomon's voice intruded on Calvin's thoughts and he came to his senses.

He broke the kiss and tipped Bea's chin toward him. "I shouldn't have done that," he whispered.

"I wanted you to," she said.

"Mr. Tuttle!"

Mr. Bailey.

Calvin's face tingled with embarrassment. He tightened his palms into fists, then relaxed them before turning to greet the speaker. "Good day, Mr. Bailey." At least his voice sounded somewhat normal.

"You." The man shook with such fury that Calvin feared he might strike him. He took one step closer, but Calvin didn't budge.

"Papa." Bea put a hand on her father's arm.

"Go home and change your clothes. We will talk later."

"But, Papa—"

"Now."

She looked at Calvin, who nodded. *I'll be all right.* A frightened look he longed to erase still in her eyes, she did as her father asked.

If Mr. Bailey had noticed the unspoken conversation between the two, he gave no indication. "Come by my office on Monday morning. We have business to discuss." He turned on his heel as smartly as any military officer and walked away.

Calvin would have preferred an all-out fight to the unspoken menace.

∽

After no sleep on Saturday night, Calvin didn't fare much better on Sunday. He had been awake since before first light Monday morning. Sleepless hours had passed as he lay on his tick through the dark hours of night, waiting for the rooster's crow as an excuse to start morning chores.

Tobias joined him in the barn a few minutes later, rubbing his eyes, and sat down atop a bale of hay. "I didn't know you were ready to announce your interest in Miss Bailey."

"Neither did I." Calvin tugged too hard on the cow's teat, and she lowed her complaint in a loud voice. He considered himself lucky that she didn't kick him in the head and knock over the milk bucket in the process.

Neither one of them said any more. They had said it all before, on the way home Saturday and into that night, exploring the possibilities from every angle. Calvin had endured the censured gaze of everyone in the congregation at the Sunday worship service. Only one thing remained clear: Hiram Bailey held the title to Calvin's farm.

Calvin took the warm milk to the cool spring and drew water for the cabin. If he must confront Bea's father, he wanted to look his best. Tobias hovered by his side, silently supporting him as he had all during the war. When at last Calvin left the farm, Tobias said, "My prayers go with you."

"Thanks. I need them." Calvin didn't know that even a prayer meeting with every member of his extended family in attendance would sway Hiram Bailey's mind. Only a genuine God-given miracle would save him from the wrath of the banker.

With the crack in the bridge repaired, Calvin made good time, planning to reach the bank before it opened. Every minute since Bailey's summons had lasted as long as a century. He wouldn't postpone the meeting any longer than necessary.

The air held a chill bite on this late August morning, and Calvin feared snow might fall yet again. He looked in the direction of the Bailey house on the opposite side of the green. This morning he yearned for some twitch of a curtain or other sign that Bea was watching and waiting with him. That way lay heartbreak, he knew. She might not even know about her father's demand, since she had left before he issued his challenge.

But Bea said she wanted to kiss me. Calvin tucked that memory into his heart. Determination to declare his intention surged through him. He straightened his shoulders and strode with firm steps to the bank, turning the handle. It didn't budge. Closed. He was debating what to do next when he spotted Paul Cabot, the parson's oldest son and the bank clerk, heading in his direction.

"Good morning, Mr. Tuttle." The young man had a good head for numbers and an inoffensive manner. "Mr. Bailey told me to expect you this morning." He turned the key in the lock and let them both into the dark recesses of the building.

Calvin had entered the bank only once before, when he finalized the loan for his land. Then as now, the cool shadows alternating with bars of sunlight from the windows attracted his attention. As striped as a jail cell, and as secure, only the items under lock and key were hidden in a vault built into the back wall. He'd heard that Mrs. Bailey kept her silver set in the bank except for special occasions. Imagine having something that you'd need to lock up for safekeeping. Almost everything he owned had been made at home and could be replaced with time and effort.

How could someone like Bea, used to fine silver and fancy dresses, ever be interested in him? But she said she was.

Young Cabot lit a fire in a small grate and placed a tea-kettle over it to boil. "Mr. Bailey likes his tea when he arrives."

Calvin wondered how long he would need to wait. To think he had expected the banker to be at work shortly after sunrise. Restless, Calvin wanted to pace back and forth. The bank building wasn't much larger than his own house; but aside from the counting desk, teller window, and a small partition for Mr. Bailey's office, the space was empty. Calvin made himself stay in the chair and kept his feet on the floor. He wouldn't betray his nervousness, not even to the clerk.

Cabot had time to open the cash drawer behind the counter and prepare the tea before Mr. Bailey arrived.

"Mr. Tuttle. You are here already. Good. Come this way."

"Shall I bring tea in, sir?" Cabot asked.

"Later." Bailey waved him away.

So this wasn't a social occasion, but Calvin already knew that. He followed Bailey into his office.

The man sat in his chair and steepled his fingers without speaking. He turned so that Calvin could see only his face in profile, and the likeness to Bea startled him, although her face was softer, rounder. They were father and daughter, after all, but. . . The silence lengthened and tested Calvin's resolve. He decided to make the first move.

"Mr. Bailey, you must know I hold Miss Beatrice in the highest regard."

Bailey swiveled his head in Calvin's direction. "Is that why you dragged her through the mud—literally—and kissed her for all to see like a common hussy?"

Heat invaded Calvin's cheeks, but he kept his voice even. "I regret the circumstances, sir, but I will not deny the feelings I have for Miss Bailey. I would consider it an honor if I had your permission to court her." There, he had said it. All the breath rushed out of his chest, and he couldn't have spoken again if a knife were held at his throat.

Bailey's eyebrows rose, and he studied Calvin with the brown eyes so like Bea's. Had the man considered forcing a wedding between the two? Some might feel it appropriate, even necessary, after the way they had embraced yesterday. The banker gave no clue to his feelings as he rose to his feet. At the window, he looked south, in the direction of the more settled communities in their new country. "I had hoped for better things for my daughter than to be stuck in the countryside. But she chose to return to Maple Notch."

So Bea had forced the return to Maple Notch. Some of the icicles of fear around Calvin's heart melted.

Bailey returned to his chair and looked Calvin straight in the eye. "But even here, I will not allow my daughter to marry any ordinary man who catches her attention. That includes you, Mr. Tuttle. You do not even own your own property free and clear."

Once again, Bailey steepled his fingers and tapped them together. "You are a man with innovative ideas. You alone have succeeded in protecting your entire crop for harvest. And I have heard rumors that you are considering a toll bridge, one covered overhead like a barn."

Calvin cleared his throat.

Bailey pointed his index finger at him. "Listen to me. I for one wish to see industry and innovation rewarded. When your harvest comes in, I would like to buy the bulk of your seed corn for five dollars a bushel. That kind of money will satisfy the lien on your property as well as provide some extra. A man with that kind of security might be worthy of my daughter." He leaned forward, brown eyes boring into Calvin. "What say you, Mr. Tuttle?"

Chapter 9

ive dollars a bushel. The words exploded inside Calvin's brain as he made his way home. No one ever paid that kind of money for seed corn.

No one ever needed to. Most years, corn was abundant. Often more grew than people could use for food or seed, and the extra went to fattening hogs.

Five dollars a bushel. The words kept repeating themselves in Calvin's mind, taunting him, tempting him.

The lien on his property, satisfied like that, with a snap of his fingers. More money available for other improvements. Calvin reached the bridge, repaired and sound enough for another winter, and thought about his desire to build a covered bridge. The money the banker offered would provide for that project, which would in turn bring in additional income in the future.

"A man with that kind of security might be worthy of my daughter." The words trotted through Calvin's heart as his feet plodded ahead.

Is this Your answer, Lord? Calvin threw the question to heaven, but he received no answer, not even a snowflake, in reply.

Tobias was hard at work in the field when Calvin rode in. Why did he feel so reluctant to share the good news with his friend? His success also meant success for Tobias. What was holding him back?

Tobias didn't wait but instead raced across the field to meet Calvin. "I expected you back some time ago. Tell me. Did he demand payment? What are you going to do?"

The quick questions reminded Calvin of their shared concerns and the prayers they had offered together during the night. He shook his head. "Not exactly." He drew a deep breath. "In fact, *he* offered to pay *me.*"

"What?" Tobias jerked upright.

"He wants to buy my seed corn."

"For some ridiculous price, I suppose? Take advantage of you?"

"Actually, no." Calvin heard the surprise in his voice. "He offered me five dollars a bushel."

Tobias whistled. "Even I know that's a lot."

Calvin's smile soured his stomach.

"What's wrong? That's good news, isn't it?"

"Better than demanding payment in full in cash." Calvin began the slow walk across the clearing. "You and I both know he's not doing it out of the goodness of his heart. He wants to make money."

"And—?"

"And that means he'll resell the corn to my friends and neighbors. Maybe even my family. For even more money, more than they can afford."

"Oh." Tobias slid down to the ground.

Calvin grabbed his hoe and began scratching at the ground. He didn't feel like working, but eating and talking appealed to him even less. Maybe physical labor would provide the clarity he needed.

∽

Contrary to Papa's threatening tone at the bake sale festivities, he hadn't done more than confine Beatrice to the house since Saturday. In other years, she might have chafed at being kept inside, away from her garden. But after the recurring freezes, she had given up hope for anything more than a potato or two. She wished she had tree stumps to smoke out.

Like Calvin. She looked out the window again. She had heard Papa's demand to meet with him this morning as she walked back to the house. What had transpired between her father and young Mr. Tuttle? Had Papa taken the anger that rightly fell on her shoulders out on Calvin? She swallowed past the lump in her throat. Patches, her cat, jumped onto her lap and pushed her head against Beatrice's hand.

A light knock sounded on her door.

"Come in."

Bessie, her maid, bringing the rose dress Beatrice had worn to the bake sale with her. She hung the dress in the armoire and stood back to study it. "It turned out right nicely, Miss Beatrice." Not a word of complaint for the additional work Beatrice had created in soiling the nearly new dress, only pride in a job well done.

"Thank you, Bessie. I'm sorry to have created so much additional work for you."

The maid started to leave, but Beatrice stopped her. In a fit of remorse, she went to her armoire and hunted for the lilac sprig frock that had pleased her so. It would look good on Bessie, with her coloring. "Take this. I shan't need it any more."

"But Mrs. Bailey. . ."

"Mama won't object. I'll explain."

After profuse expressions of gratitude, Bessie left. Beatrice sighed. Soon she must join Mama in the parlor, where another sewing lesson awaited her.

If only she could find a way to get rid of the ugly feelings inside, even as laundry was pounded against a rock, scrubbed, and ironed. Not that Beatrice had actually ever washed clothes—a skill she would have to acquire if she married anyone from Maple Notch. She didn't know how to be a proper farmer's wife. Perhaps she should marry one of the city men Papa had taken such pains to introduce her to. At least then she'd know what was required of her.

Stop thinking like that. She lifted her chin in the air. "I can learn." She spoke aloud to reassure herself. "I'll make my own clothes instead of stitching samplers. I can even learn how to spin and weave if I have to."

"What's that, dear?"

Beatrice twirled around. "I didn't know you were there, Mama."

Her mother came into the room, set down a tea tray, and fingered the dress Bessie had cleaned. "It turned out well." Like Papa, Mama hadn't spoken of the scene at the bake sale, as if their silence could make the memory disappear. Their kindness felt undeserved.

Remorse for disappointing her parents sent a pang through Beatrice. "I was preparing to come downstairs."

"Sit down, dear." Mama took one of the chairs by the window. "There's something your father wants me to talk with you about."

Uh-oh. Here it comes. Beatrice relaxed the fingers that had clenched her dress and sat down across from her mother, folding her hands in her lap. Avoiding looking at her mother, Beatrice gazed out the window. How could the sun shine so brightly when a chill had settled over her heart?

Mama didn't speak for a minute, instead busying herself with the niceties of pouring tea and stirring in a bit of cream. Memories of the childhood ritual lingered, occasions when Beatrice felt her heart would break and Mama offered comfort. Encouraged by the sign, Beatrice relaxed.

"Eat a bite of the shortbread, dear. We are concerned that you have lost weight recently."

Beatrice obediently bit into one of Cook's flaky delicacies, even though it tasted like ash in her mouth. She managed to eat two of the cookies, drinking two cups of tea. Mama was right. She *did* feel a little better after consuming some food.

Mama peered at her, as if assessing her state of mind. Apparently satisfied, she took her tea cup in her hand and held it to her lips, her little finger extended. "Your father has always hoped for you to have an easier life than we have here in Maple Notch. But when I told him of your obvious distress in New York. . ."

A sad smile flitted across Mama's face, and she set down her cup, staring resolutely at Beatrice. "Mr. Bailey met with Mr. Tuttle this morning."

Beatrice's heart tripped. "What happened at the sale...It wasn't his fault. It was mine. I shouldn't have agreed to the tug of war."

"That's as may be." Mama's gaze flicked to the repaired dress hanging in the armoire. "Mr. Tuttle might as well have written a message in the stars to do what he did. Everyone in Maple Notch will expect the two of you to begin courting seriously, perhaps even to read the banns."

Beatrice's heart skipped. Did her liking for Calvin extend to love? Was she ready to. . .marry? She thought she knew the answer. Heat flooded her cheeks and ran along her limbs to her fingers, where she touched the cup of hot tea.

"I would not speak so plainly if not for the outrageous behavior of the two of you. We felt we must act quickly. Mr. Bailey has come up with a plan that will ensure Mr. Tuttle's future without harming his pride."

When Mama didn't continue, Beatrice ventured a question. "What does he have in mind?"

A secret smile played around Mama's lips, satisfied that she had hooked her daughter's interest. "Mr. Bailey had already taken note of Mr. Tuttle's innovations. He would have offered him assistance sooner or later, only perhaps not so quickly."

Tell me.

"Your father is prepared to buy Mr. Tuttle's seed corn for a healthy amount. Providing he is able to harvest it, which it appears he will. One of the very few this year, as you know."

Pride flowed through Beatrice's heart. Calvin had succeeded. "But what will Papa do with corn?" Beatrice puzzled. He was a banker, not a merchant.

Mama shrugged. "Does it matter? After this year's poor harvest, he feels it is a wise investment. In return, he promises that Mr. Tuttle is welcome to court you once he satisfies the lien on his property." Mama's smile was genuine this time, a lip-stretching, teeth-showing grin. "You see, your father only wants to make you happy, after all."

A crumb of Cook's shortbread remained on Beatrice's plate, and its buttery richness appealed to her palate. She took another cookie and bit into it, savoring taste for the first time in several days. The sky looked bluer, and even the struggling grass managed to look green.

The world was made anew—for her and Calvin.

∽

The remainder of the week passed in agonizing slowness for Beatrice. She felt every second—eating enough to please even Cook, preparing seed to feed birds during the coming winter, watching the world outside her window. During her sewing sessions with her mother, she worked on a wedding gift for Peggy. The entire town expected an announcement at any moment.

In spite of all the activity, or perhaps because of it, the hours stretched from daylight to nightfall. She couldn't wait for Sunday, when she would have an opportunity to see Calvin.

"Am I allowed to speak with Calvin, then?" Beatrice asked during conversation with her mother.

Mama clucked. "It isn't seemly for you to chase him. Let him seek you out."

Monday went by. . . Tuesday. . . Wednesday. She'd hoped to receive word of some kind from Calvin, certain he would rejoice with her. Had he repented of the kiss they had exchanged after the tug of war? That thought sent a cold stab of fear through her heart.

Or maybe he's working all the harder on his farm. Now that Papa had agreed to their courtship in principle, perhaps Calvin had thrown himself into producing as much seed corn as possible. That thought offered a little reassurance.

Perhaps Calvin wouldn't speak with her until he had met Papa's conditions, once he had sold the corn and paid the bank. Never had the weeks until harvest stretched so far into the future.

On Thursday a light snow fell. Although not an unusual occurrence for early September, it signaled the beginning of the traditional snow season. To her relief, Indian summer returned the following day.

She decided to take advantage of the pleasant weather and approached her mother at breakfast. "I plan to go out today. To the store and to the parsonage."

Mama's eyebrows knit together then relaxed. "Be certain you wear your coat. The air may still hold a chill after yesterday's snow, and I hear some have taken sick."

"Of course." As long as Mama agreed to her going around the green unescorted, Beatrice would agree to anything, even wearing mourning. After so many days housebound, she longed to get outside and perhaps meet someone her own age. "Mr. Dixon expected new books in his next shipment." Hoping to forestall the complaint she saw forming on Mama's tongue, Beatrice hastened to add, "I also want to look at woolens. I'm thinking of making a cape for Papa for the winter."

Mama put a finger to her lips. "I won't say a word. Do you need Bessie to accompany you to help carry your purchases home?"

"No. If there is too much, I will arrange for Mr. Dixon to deliver it." While Beatrice enjoyed Bessie's company, she hoped for a few minutes of privacy. "If I meet a friend at the storekeeper, may I invite her home?"

"Of course." Mama smiled as if she had known Beatrice's true plans all along. "Today is market day, isn't it? I shall tell Cook to expect company for tea."

After a few minutes to gather her market basket, tie a bonnet under her chin, and don her cape, Beatrice headed out the door. Trading her slippers for boots proved a wise choice in light of the muck underfoot, still muddy after yesterday's snow. The green seemed barren without the family of geese. Since the young had matured, they'd disappeared the day before the snowfall, heading south to whatever warmer climes best suited their needs. She heard honking overhead and looked at a small group, perhaps only a single family, flying in the familiar V formation. Few flocks swarmed overhead this fall, translating into fewer geese to shoot and dress for hungry families.

Away from the shadow of the house and trees, the air felt remarkably warm, as pretty as a spring day, without the nuisance of the bugs that thrived in the early season. Unbuttoning all but the top button of her coat, Beatrice allowed the breeze to lift her skirts in a dance that matched her high spirits. She found a single red leaf by the side of the road and stopped to pick it up. With care, it might remain whole until she reached the house, where she could press it between the heavy volumes in their library. Dried leaves provided much opportunity for creativity during the winter months. She studied the ground for further material for floral arrangements. In her joy at being out of the house, she temporarily forgot her destination.

"Beatrice? Is that you?"

At the sound of Peggy's cheery voice, Beatrice looked in the direction of the river road. Calvin and Tobias accompanied Peggy. Not wanting to appear overeager, Beatrice retrieved a couple of pine cones before she straightened to her full height and walked toward them.

"Good afternoon, Mr. Heath, Mr. Tuttle." She was certain her face must be as red as a holly berry, but no one seemed to notice. Calvin appeared as discomfited as she felt, but she maintained her pretended indifference as she reached the trio.

Only Tobias seemed unaffected by the mood. "It's days like this that make fall my favorite season of the year." He peeked into her basket. "And you are gathering leaves."

"I use them to make floral arrangements during the winter months." Beatrice paused. How trivial that must sound.

"Yes. She makes marvelous things, doesn't she, Calvin?" Peggy's eyes danced with mischief. "We always save our corn silk and a few ears of Indian corn for her to use."

Calvin nodded in reply. So far he hadn't spoken. He had never seemed so reticent in her presence.

"Come, Mr. Heath," Peggy said. "It's time we played that game of check-ers you promised me."

"I did?" Tobias took a second look at Calvin and Beatrice. "Oh, yes, *that* game. Well, Calvin, you know where to find me." He tucked Peggy's arm into his elbow and walked to the store, her soft giggle trailing behind them.

"That was a tad heavy-handed." Beatrice felt compelled to speak when Calvin still did not speak.

At last, Calvin relaxed and chuckled. "Come, let's not waste this oppor-tunity they've provided us. We need to talk, you and I." He reached out his hand an inch before sticking it back in his pocket. "I would offer you my arm, but I'm afraid tongues will wag more than they already have—even if we are in full view of everyone in town today."

Beatrice relaxed enough to giggle herself. "We shall walk around the com-mon with a foot of space between us, then." They strolled at a pace more ap-propriate to baby's toddling steps than to adults. The point wasn't to arrive at a destination, but the time they spent together.

Beatrice waited eagerly to hear what Calvin had to say.

～

Calvin couldn't bring himself to meet Bea's eyes. Those dark-brown pools in-vited him to jump in and bask in their warmth. They reached the spot where they had won the tug of war, and he had taken advantage of the situation by kissing her. Resolutely, he stopped walking and turned toward her.

"I was wrong to take advantage of you at the bake sale. I have no excuse, except that you were in my arms, and. . ."

"And it seemed the most natural thing in the world. I know."

Her soft answer took Calvin by surprise. "You're not. . .offended?" He allowed himself to look at her.

This time, she was the one who dropped her eyes. A becoming pink colored her cheeks. "No."

That one word gave Calvin the courage he needed to speak further. "Your father spoke with me on Monday morning."

"Yes, I know." Further pink slammed into Bea's cheeks. "I noticed you walking into the bank."

"So that twitch of the curtain wasn't just my imagination?" Calvin al-lowed a teasing note to enter his voice.

"I was afraid of what Papa would do."

Concern raced through Calvin. "Was he harsh with you?"

"No." An unreadable expression crossed Bea's face. She bent to pick up a leaf. "Is it forward of me to ask what you discussed?" She bit her bottom lip, as if afraid of his answer.

Had Mr. Bailey said anything to his daughter? Did she know her father had opened the door wide for him to call on her? His mouth went dry. *Lord, help her understand.*

"He asked me about my crop, if I expected to have extra seed corn. I suppose he had heard my bid for those lemon tarts at the bake sale."

A smile played around Bea's mouth. *Good.* "Did you enjoy them?"

"They were as good as I remembered from school. I expect anything you make would be delicious." He smiled at her then, and she returned his smile. He could have drowned in the happiness he saw reflected in her eyes. He sighed. He had to tell her. "I told him, yes, I expected to have more corn than I can use myself. And so he offered to buy it."

He studied her face, looking for signs of surprise, and saw none. *She knows.* Was it even her idea? No. Mr. Bailey wouldn't make business decisions based on his daughter's recommendation.

She lowered her lashes. "What did you think of his offer?" Her voice sounded small but hopeful, as full of promise as one of the acorns she bent over to pick up from the ground.

"It was a very generous offer." That was true.

"So you'll accept?" Hope lit her face like a candle burning in a window on a dark night.

Lord, help me find a way to say the next, hard part. He glanced around the common, seeking a way to avoid the topic for a while longer. The church beckoned, but they couldn't go there as long as they were alone. The entrance to the emporium yawned open on this beautiful Indian summer day, but he didn't want to announce their business to the world.

No, this spot on the Maple Notch common would have to serve as the place where he opened his heart—and left himself vulnerable to her misunderstanding and rejection.

"I can't. I'm sorry, Bea, but I can't."

Chapter 10

Beatrice felt her mouth open in a silent scream. He *couldn't* accept Papa's offer? She backed away. "No, I'm the one who's sorry. I must have misunderstood. . . ." She turned in the direction of the store and took two hurried steps.

"Bea, wait."

How dare he use that nickname when he'd just broken her heart?

Calvin's hand landed on her arm, gentle and soft, not harsh like the pronouncement he'd made.

"It's not for the reason you think." His face had paled and hardened. The same expression she had seen on men's faces when they talked about being in the war. "I would do almost anything to win your hand." The words blurted out of his mouth, and he looked surprised that he had said them.

Heat crept up her neck and ears and into her face. She didn't know whether to feel angry or happy. "Almost anything?"

"Did you ask yourself what your father would do with all that corn? He doesn't need it. He's not a farmer."

"I suppose he would sell it. What does it matter? You'll have your money."

Calvin hung his head, staring at his boots, before he straightened his back and looked at her. "Come with me." He led her to the corner where they could see the paths leading out of town. "Over that way the Whitsons live." He pointed to the east. "And farther south on this side of the river, you'll come to the Frisks' farm." He went on to mention several families who lived in their community. "Who do you think will buy the corn?"

"Anyone who needs it. Mr. Dixon might act as the broker. What's the problem? Don't you want your neighbors to have your corn?" His obvious discomfort didn't make sense to her.

"He'll want to sell it for more money than he paid me."

"Of course." Beatrice nodded.

"But don't you see?" He sighed and moved his hands through the air like a teacher explaining something to a difficult pupil. "They won't be able to afford the prices he'll have to charge. They'll borrow money from his bank. It will be like what happened in Egypt during the famine. First the people sold their crops to Pharaoh, then their land, finally themselves. And I won't do that to my friends, neighbors...my own family. Putting everything people have made for themselves here in Maple Notch at risk." His gesture encompassed all the surrounding farms. "Not so I can make a small fortune." She saw tears in his eyes. "Even if it means losing my chance with you."

All breath drained from her body, and she willed herself to remain upright. She felt as though she had been led to a mountaintop, where she could gaze over all the wonders of the world—and then been pushed off.

"You're wrong." She forced the words through clenched teeth. "You *can* accept Papa's offer." She put up her hand when he started to object. "But you won't." She blinked back the tears that threatened to pour out of her eyes. "Maybe you are just a poor farmer with no more sense than God gave a rabbit, like Papa always thought." She grabbed her basket close to her chest and walked with quick, determined steps in the direction of her house. Her senses searched for some sound, some sign that Calvin had followed her.

All she heard was the wind whistling through the empty tree branches.

∽

The next day, Papa called Beatrice into his study before supper. She took a moment to compose her features before she entered. Even then, she stood at the door rather than sitting down in the Windsor chair.

"Sit down." The way he almost barked the request made her heart quake. Her legs shook as she settled into the chair and clutched the armrests.

Papa frowned at something going on behind them, perhaps Bessie cleaning in the hallway. After he closed the door, he took the seat next to Beatrice's instead of behind the desk. He took her hands in his, his dark eyes harboring a degree of kindness she rarely saw there. "Calvin Tuttle came to see me today."

Speechless, she swallowed, not sure if she wanted to hear what was coming.

"He refused my offer." Papa's voice sank deeper with every word, trailing off at the end. He studied their clasped hands as if searching for a reason why a man would do such a thing. When at last he raised his eyes to meet hers, she saw pain etched in lines around their corners.

But his mouth was set in familiar, angry lines. When he spoke again, his words came out clipped and hard. "He told me he discussed his reasons with you. I told him that any man with no more concern for his future than that had no business courting my daughter. He still refused my offer."

Beatrice flinched at the hot anger radiating from her father. Her own angry hurt rose in her throat.

"I did the best I could for you, my dear. You asked to return home. You expressed interest in this farmer—in a most brazen way. He has turned his back on both of us. Unless we suddenly discover a diamond in the rough among the other young lads of Maple Notch—something I sincerely doubt—you *will* return to New York. Your grandmother will see you properly wed."

"Yes, Papa." Beatrice held back her sobs until she reached the sanctuary of her room, where her tears scalded her cheeks at the thought of her father's heavy words.

~

Tobias put a hand on Calvin's shoulder as they approached the meetinghouse on Sunday. The Bailey family arrived at the same time, the two parents flanking Bea like prison guards. Even with his heavy heart, Calvin couldn't help noticing her glorious appearance. Golden ringlets framed her sweet face and drew attention to her doe-brown eyes. In spite of their painful parting, his heart still raced to meet her even while his feet slowed.

He knew the moment Bea saw him. Her chin came up, and she turned her face away. She had spurned him as thoroughly as though she had shouted aloud.

Calvin stopped moving, then forced himself to walk forward. *Pretend nothing is wrong.*

"I'll find a way to talk with her today, Calvin. She has no right to treat you this way," Peggy said, her face flushed from Tobias's gentle teasing.

Calvin shook his head. "Her father's even more set against me than he was before, and no one makes an enemy of Hiram Bailey without cost. And if Bea"—he swallowed past the break that his voice wanted to make—"if she agrees with him, then she's not the woman I thought she was." Once again his pace quickened, and he intercepted the family on the threshold of the meetinghouse.

"Good day, Mr. Bailey. Mrs. Bailey. Bea." Calvin greeted them as if they were no more than casual acquaintances. "This is the day the Lord hath made." He smiled, indicating all was well and inviting them to finish the verse.

Sparks flashed in Mr. Bailey's eyes. Bea's eyes focused on the ground. Only Mrs. Bailey showed any degree of compassion for the situation they found themselves in. "Go ahead in," the man told his family.

Beatrice followed her mother through the door without a backward glance.

Mr. Bailey leaned close to Calvin's ear and whispered, "Come near my daughter again, and you'll wish you had never been born. She's too good for the likes of you. She's leaving Maple Notch as soon as I can arrange transportation." He moved back to a more comfortable distance. "You're right, Mr. Tuttle. This *is* a beautiful day. I will rejoice and be glad in it. Good day to you." He doffed his hat and strode into the sanctuary.

Calvin remained so long in his spot that Tobias had to urge him inside. "Not yet," he said. "Do you remember when Jesus said to make things right with our brother before we bring an offering? Well, something tells me God wouldn't look too kindly on my heart right now."

Peggy hesitated on the front steps.

"You two go on in." Calvin took a step away from the door. "I'll join you later."

The strains of "The Sower" filtered out the door as Calvin turned in the direction of the common. He didn't intend to miss all the service, but for the moment, the anger in his heart kept him from worship. Only God's love could replace that hurt. That's what he could do. Think about good and lovely things—all the things that made God worthy of worship—and not about Mr. Bailey's unreasonable response. He could at least try. As he circled the green, ground he had walked hundreds if not thousands of times in his life, he sought those good and lovely things.

Overhead, a small V of geese honked, heading south toward warmer ground. The first good thing: God protected the geese and all other senseless animals. God would take care of people, too, if only they let Him instead of arguing with their Maker.

The geese came and went with the seasons—another one of God's gifts. This year, the seasons had been odd and off-kilter. Still, for the thousands of years since God gave the promise of the rainbow to Noah, spring had followed winter as surely as year followed year. He thought of the corn ready to harvest in his fields, and the family that would come and assist him in the morning. The stumps had burned to the ground, but smoke pouring out from under the ground assured him that the roots continued to burn. God had given him, Calvin Tuttle, a harvest when many others had none. That was indeed a good thing.

Calvin faced the church. His troubles with Hiram Bailey and his bewitching daughter were far from over, yet he felt at peace, reminded of God's goodness. He slipped into the pew beside Tobias and Peggy as the songmaster lined the next verse of the hymn. Tobias recognized the words from Psalm 23: "Surely goodness and mercy shall follow me all the days of my life: and I will dwell in the house of the Lord for ever."

Amen, Lord. Amen.

~

Beatrice was supposed to leave Maple Notch, perhaps forever, on Wednesday morning.

Snow started, single flakes falling like a lazy quilter, at dusk on Tuesday evening. Beatrice shrugged on her coat and dashed outside, sticking out her tongue to catch the flakes, letting them settle on her hand to study their intricate beauty before they melted from the heat of her skin. While she stood there, twirling and playing, the snow fell faster, first two flakes, then three, then so many that she could no longer distinguish the individual crystals.

This kind of snowfall usually heralded the beginning of winter in Maple Notch, although it was a few weeks earlier than normal. Of course, nothing about this year had been typical. Had winter ever ended in this Year of our Lord 1816, with freezing temperatures and snowfall at least once every month, including midsummer?

Even after the dreadful year they had experienced, she still loved the lazy, soft, first snowfall. Did it snow like this in New York City? Or did the crowded buildings and grimy streets hide the beauty of a world washed clean by new-fallen snow?

Beatrice told herself Calvin had made a mistake in judgment when he refused her father's offer, but her heart betrayed her. She still loved him. How could she leave Vermont for New York when that meant leaving a part of herself behind?

If it kept snowing like this. . .she might not have to.

∽

Calvin stood in his house, staring out at the snowfall. "Winter's here."

"Did it ever leave?" Tobias asked. In spite of his words of complaint, he was humming to himself. Ever since he had asked for permission to court Peggy, he often had a song on his lips.

At least one of them could hope to find true love.

"It's a good thing we got the corn in." Calvin didn't mention Tobias's cheery mood.

"What? Won't your wonderworking tree stumps clear the field?" Tobias looked up from where he bent over, polishing his boots.

Calvin shook his head in mock frustration. "Don't tell me Burlington's that different. Don't you recognize the first snow of the year when you see it?" Then he grew serious. "Besides, the last snow didn't completely clear. The fires have about burned themselves out, and the weather will stay too cold for the embers to keep the ground thawed." He shoved the bacon to one side of the frying pan and cracked in eggs. "It's a good thing we got all the animals snug in the barn, in case we're snowed in."

Tobias blew out his cheeks and huffed. "If it's that bad, no one will be traveling either."

The fork quivered in Calvin's hand, and he splashed hot grease on his hand. He stuck his hand in a bucket of water and counted to ten under his breath. "Doesn't matter to me."

"Uh-huh." Tobias picked up a piece of harness and began working it. "Tell that to the judge."

Calvin returned to the fry pan. This time he removed the bacon with care and spooned the whites over the tops of the eggs as they browned. "Mr. Bailey won't let me near Bea even if she stays in Maple Notch. It's time I face the truth. Whatever I imagined between us was just that—a figment of my imagination. If she thinks her father's business practices are always fair, then she's not the woman I thought she was."

"Could be she was disappointed when she saw your chance to get ahead fly out the window."

Calvin didn't know how to answer that. He had to focus on Bea's betrayal; otherwise he would hurt too much. In time, he would feel better. If God so willed, he'd find someone else. For now, he had to focus all of his energy on coming up with enough money to pay back Hiram Bailey's bank.

∽

A month later, Calvin's heartache hadn't lessened even one degree, although the temperatures plummeted to new lows. Come Sunday morning, upon arising, he slapped his hands together, seeking warmth. Giving up, he poked among the embers in the fireplace and held his hands over the flames. Good thing they had piled up firewood over the summer. This winter they seemed to use it by the forestfuls. One log would suffice for their morning preparations—no need to waste fuel when they'd be spending most of the forenoon at church.

Behind him, Tobias broke the ice in their water bucket. Next came the sound of a razor scraping against the skin. Calvin shivered. "I told you to let your beard grow out."

"Ah, but Peggy likes my clean-shaven good looks."

Calvin gritted his teeth. To his shame, a part of him begrudged his friend's happiness, but how he longed for his own. "Have you asked for her hand yet?" Not that he had any doubt as to what Peggy's answer would be.

"No." Tobias finished shaving and put away the razor. "There's the minor problem of how I am to support a wife." He grimaced. "And I doubt the local banker would look kindly on granting me a loan to buy land."

"Half of the profit from the crop is yours. It's only right." Calvin spoke from a sense of duty. If he split the profits, could he hope to repay the bank?

Tobias shook his head. "Only if there's anything left over after you pay the bank. That's what we agreed, and I'll hold you to it. Besides, even half the profits won't be enough for me to set up on my own. I'm thinking about returning to work with my father."

Tobias's mouth turned down in a rare frown, and Calvin pushed aside his own worries. Another thought surfaced. "Are you sure you've recovered from your fiancée's death?" Tobias had ended the war with a broken spirit and broken heart, after seeing his mother and sweetheart die.

His friend threw an astonished look at him. "I wouldn't be courting Peggy if my heart wasn't ready. You should know that, my friend."

"But how?" The words traveled from Calvin's heart straight to his mouth, bypassing his brain. Embarrassed, he busied himself pulling on his workday clothes. "I keep telling myself not to spend any more time thinking about what can't be. But my heart keeps drawing me back to Bea." He bent over to fasten his boots.

Tobias straddled the chair he had fashioned and faced Calvin. "I don't know. Give it time. It's only been a month." He ran his hand across the smooth wood of the armrests. "Besides, I have a feeling this isn't the end of things with Miss Bailey. She's still right here in Maple Notch. She hasn't gone anywhere. You still have a chance. . .you just have to decide what you want to do about it."

Calvin opened his mouth to protest, but Tobias spoke again before he could get a word out. "God knows her heart. Keep asking Him for wisdom. He won't lead you astray." He bent over to check the chair legs. "This one turned out well. I think I'll try my hand at making a rocker for Peggy. They say womenfolk like a good rocker."

Calvin accepted the change of topic. *Okay, God, I guess it's up to You. It always has been.* He looked out the window at the white landscape and wished waiting weren't so hard.

Or so uncertain.

Chapter 11

I still think you're making a mistake. No one is going out in this weather. Your father says no one has come into the bank all week." Mama fluttered in front of the door as if to bar Beatrice's exit.

"Mama, the church is only around the corner. I'll be fine." No matter how cold it was, Beatrice welcomed the chance to get out of the house. The ladies' mission meeting provided the excuse. "Perhaps next month it will be warmer, and you can come with me."

"Dress warm, then." Mama bundled Beatrice into her coat. Once she opened the door, she found herself grateful for the protection. Thick wool covered every inch of her except for a small space where her eyes peered out over the edge of the scarf. If she needed to dress in this many layers to walk the few feet from her house to the parsonage, would women from the outlying farms attend the meeting? She shivered inside the coat and hurried her steps. *God, please let spring—a real spring—come next year.*

She arrived at the Cabots' home first, and the parson's wife greeted her with a pleasant smile. "Welcome, my dear Miss Bailey." She took care of Beatrice's coat and accessories, then escorted her to a seat and thrust a cup of coffee into her hands. "Do you like sugar with your coffee?"

Nodding, Beatrice studied the familiar room. Sparse furniture crafted with love by members of the congregation dotted the room. Everywhere she looked, she saw signs of the gifts given by the people of the community to their first permanent minister. One simple child's sampler, with an outlined house and chimney and the words HOME SWEET HOME caught her attention. "I didn't know you still had that."

"Of course we do. I know how hard you labored over it and how proud you were to give us a gift you had made yourself. That was one of the most precious things we received that year." Mrs. Cabot hugged her. "We'll wait a few minutes, but I fear few will come in light of today's weather." She bustled over to the oven. Beatrice looked around the room again, this time noticing how empty the shelves seemed of food stuffs.

Mrs. Cabot removed a loaf of nut bread from the oven. "It finished just in time. I started on it late this morning, I'm afraid."

Where she had found the ingredients for a special bread, Beatrice couldn't guess. The shelves looked emptier than the fields after harvest. The sweet taste of the sugar in the coffee threatened to gag Beatrice with its wastefulness. She should have taken it black.

Mrs. Cabot cut them each a slice of the bread and served it on a plate. After she sat down, she said, "It appears we will be alone today, but we can still start planning for what the church will do for the needy in our community this Christmas."

"I have some ideas." Beatrice hesitated. Would Mrs. Cabot accept suggestions from someone with so little household management experience? "Since I have little experience stocking a kitchen myself, I asked Cook for her suggestions for staples and quantities and potential costs."

"Very forward thinking of you. You have inherited your father's business acumen."

Startled, Beatrice glanced at Mrs. Cabot but saw only the goodwill of a genuine compliment. The list lay tucked in her muffler. She pulled it out and unrolled the sheets. "Cook made two lists. The first she said included staples—the bare minimum to get by for a family for a month. The second she calls her 'luxury' list—her favorite foodstuffs for special occasions. I had hoped most people would have sufficient staples that we could include a good number of luxuries but"—her hand swept the room—"I would guess many people are living at the edge of starvation this year." Her gaze dropped to her lap, where she rolled up and then straightened out the thin sheets of parchment in her hands, aware that her words might be insulting.

"We have sufficient for our needs, dear Beatrice. God always provides. Let me see." Mrs. Cabot took the pages from her. "I would agree with your cook's assessment. Why don't we compare what we have on hand with her suggestions? I have set up a pantry in the back classroom at the church."

The two women donned their coats and mittens and crossed to the door that connected the house to the church. "Let's work quickly before our fingers are too cold to write," Mrs. Cabot said.

Beatrice stared at the sacks and boxes stacked high in the storage room. "I didn't expect so much."

"After you left, people took your suggestion to heart. Everyone contributed a portion of what they had on hand. God will bless this food, for much of it was truly the gift of the widow's mite."

The parson joined them to assist with moving the heavier items. At the end of an hour, they calculated the results.

"We have enough here for about a month and a half for every family in Maple Notch. We even have a few of Cook's 'luxury' items."

"People will make it last for at least two months." Parson Cabot spoke cheerfully. "Folks hereabouts can stretch a toothpick until it burns as long as a log. If we're done here, I'll go back to working on my sermon."

They agreed they were finished, and he returned to the church to study while the women returned to the parsonage. Mrs. Cabot poured them coffee, stronger now and even more in need of the sugar, which the parson's wife added without asking. Like the widow's supply of flour and oil, the size of the sugar cone didn't seem to lessen. Beatrice smiled at the fanciful thought.

"Enough for two months. More, since not everyone will need help. That's good, isn't it?"

Mrs. Cabot stirred some milk into her coffee. "There's fewer that will be asking than will be in need. We want to give a basket to every family in the church at Christmas so we don't hurt anyone's pride."

Every family. "Is it really that terrible?"

"It is." Mrs. Cabot nodded. "We'll keep some foodstuffs here, so that those in the most desperate circumstances can seek us out. But let me assure you, the supplies will be welcome in every household."

Enough for two months. January and February. "That still leaves half a year or more until the next harvest. If. . .if people run out, what will they do?"

"Eat what they can catch or kill. Survive, like the Pilgrims did that first winter at Plymouth. Mr. Dixon has agreed to carry accounts on credit if the need arises. And we'll all trust God for a better growing season in 1817."

The realities struck Beatrice as she walked home not much later. *"Dixon will have to charge more than they can afford. They'll need to borrow the money . . .from your father's bank."* Calvin's words haunted her. The people of Maple Notch couldn't afford to pay high prices for seed.

Not when they didn't even have the money to buy food.

⁓

Christmas Eve had arrived, providing a welcome break in the monotony of winter days. In a few minutes, Calvin and Tobias would make their way to Uncle Stephen's house for a celebration that would continue into tomorrow. Solomon and his family would join them. The two households had traded hosting holidays for as long as Calvin could remember. One day, he hoped he, too, could host their family gatherings.

"Not much chance of that." He looked around his tiny cabin. They didn't even have chairs enough for the adults to sit, nor space to place them if people brought their own. *I'll make it bigger next year.* Why did everything always have to be next year?

"What's that?" Tobias checked the presents they had bundled into a large bag.

"Talking to myself." Calvin grinned. "Too bad that rocking chair won't fit in the sack."

"It's in the barn. Mr. Reid is keeping it a secret until the big day."

"That's a serious present, you know. As good as—"

"I know. You don't have to tell me. I would. I will. . . ." The two men exchanged a look. "As soon as I can."

"If I know my cousin, she doesn't care about having a lot of things. She'll be happy most anywhere as long as she's with you."

"Tell that to her father." They grinned at each other. They both knew Stephen would agree to the wedding whenever Tobias asked.

"It's a good thing we have a sled to help us carry everything. We'd never make it on our own." In the spirit of the season, he began to sing "O Come, All Ye Faithful."

A knock sounded on the door.

"Company?" Tobias lifted his eyebrows as he headed for the door. "Parson! Mrs. Cabot, Miss Bailey. Come in."

Miss Bailey. Before the words could register on Calvin's consciousness, she had entered the room, her face full of beaming good will, her eyes pleading for—what? Understanding?

Belatedly, he remembered his manners and took off his hat. "Sit down and stay awhile. Would you like some tea?"

"Don't mind if I do." Parson Cabot settled on one of the sturdy Windsor chairs Tobias had made that fall. His hand brushed against the bag of gaily wrapped presents. "I see you were heading out for Christmas. We won't keep you long, but I'm glad we caught you." He handed a bundle of his own to Calvin.

Calvin unwound the string around the sack and peered inside. On top lay sacks of beans, flour, and a cone of sugar. "What's this for? We didn't ask. . ."

"No, but we are redistributing the food people brought to the church last summer. That was Miss Bailey's idea." He nodded at Bea, who turned red. "Everyone in the community will receive a part, even the ones who don't come to church except for marrying and burying."

"We can't take this. Save it for families. . . ." His voice trailed. He saw the steely look in Bea's eyes and the pastoral concern in the parson's.

"We only wish it were more." Beatrice's soft voice held undercurrents he couldn't decipher.

"Tobias, would you be so kind as to show me that rocking chair everyone's talking about? I've thought of asking you to make one for the wife." Mr. and Mrs. Cabot followed Tobias out the door, leaving Calvin alone with Bea.

"Was this your idea?" he asked in a strangled voice. "Just because I refused your father's offer doesn't make me a pauper in need of charity."

"The Cabots suggested giving food to every family in the community, although I wish I had thought of it."

A sheen of tears glimmered in her eyes, and he steeled himself against it. She walked around his house, her mittened hands touching his things, her gaze lingering on the shelf above the table where they kept basic supplies. The single room was functional but lacked those feminine touches that made a home. He wondered how it looked to her.

When at last she looked at him again, she had composed herself. "You are indeed well stocked compared to some homes we have visited. Some people have less than you do, for a family of six, seven, even more. I only wish we could do more."

What had happened to the woman with the let-them-eat-cake attitude? Voice husky, he said, "Then give them what you intended for us. We have enough to make do. The first settlers here survived on less."

She shook her head. "That would embarrass folks if they found out."

He thought on the problem. "But if we should bring a gift, privately, for the food pantry?"

A smile sneaked around her lips. "That might be acceptable. But please, keep this gift if you or any in your family can use it. Don't let your pride get in your way."

The teakettle whistled, and he realized she was still standing in her coat. He helped her out of it and led her to a chair. "Would you care for some tea?"

The small smile returned. "Didn't you say you were on your way to a Christmas celebration? And my parents are expecting me back soon." She pulled off her mittens and ran her finger along the smooth finish of the chair, but the expression on her face looked sad. "Please don't think less of me for wanting to respect their wishes." She glanced out the window. "Before the Cabots come back in, I want to say something." She spoke in a rush. "You were right. I see that now."

The door opened with her last word, cutting off any response he might have wished to make.

Their guests left a few minutes later, and the first stars were coming out as Calvin crossed the fields to Uncle Stephen's house with Tobias. They shone stark and bright against the darkening sky. He couldn't get Bea's last words, as she left with the Cabots, out of his mind.

"Let this be a season of peace and goodwill between us." She had said it so only he could hear, and pressed her hand against his sleeve. Now he touched the spot where her hand had rested, still feeling the burn through the layers to his skin.

A new season of goodwill. Was such a thing possible?
Had God answered his prayer at last?

∽

"The weather couldn't be any more perfect for a winter frolic!"

Papa had reluctantly agreed to let Peggy Reid spend the night with Beatrice in anticipation of the young people's party. The two young women looked out through the window at the clear blue sky, sparkling over a thick covering of snow on the ground.

"You'd think it was perfect weather even if the snow turned to slush and the sleds would bump down the hill over rocks," Beatrice said.

"Would not." But Peggy giggled.

"Why don't you admit it? You've been walking in the clouds ever since Tobias gave you that rocking chair for Christmas."

Peggy's giggle turned into outright laughter. "And yesterday was Valentine's Day."

"And a certain Tobias Heath just came back from Burlington. I know." The lighthearted banter fell flat on Beatrice's heart. If only she could be this excited about the day.

"Is your father still set against Calvin?" Peggy asked sympathetically, the giggle gone from her voice.

Beatrice nodded, glum. "I'm glad he's out of town this weekend, or else he might have changed his mind at the last minute and forbidden me to go to the frolic. He's convinced everyone wants to get me and Calvin together."

"Sh!" Peggy put her finger to her lips. "Don't tell anyone, but we do."

"Breakfast is ready," Cook called up the stairs.

The two women headed for the stairs. "I don't know if I'd ever get used to a house like this." Peggy lifted the hem of her skirt and descended a step. "Enough rooms to fill two stories plus an attic. Imagine."

"I'm sure there are plenty of houses like this in Burlington. They're just not as practical for a farmer." Beatrice tried to make light of the difference.

Peggy shrugged it off. "Something smells heavenly. I'd be as big as a moose if I ate here every day. How do you stay so slender?"

"It's easy when you don't have much of an appetite." Beatrice meant the statement as humorous repartee, but when Cook placed an egg cup in front of her, her stomach rebelled. Feeling the watchful gaze of three women—Mama, as well as Peggy and Cook—Beatrice made herself slice off the top of the egg and season the yolk and white left inside. Somehow she managed to get it down between bites of toast and generous helpings of tea. She made it last while Peggy went through bacon and oatmeal in addition to her eggs.

"Do you want to take a warming stone with you?" Cook fussed. " 'Twill be awful cold out there."

Beatrice imagined pushing a warming stone along with her skates, a small puddle trailing behind her on the ice. The image brought a smile to her lips. "We'll be too busy having fun to get cold. But thank you."

By midmorning when the worst of the nighttime chill had passed, they headed out the door for the church. Once the door closed behind them, Peggy said, "You might have fooled your mother, but you didn't fool me. You only picked at your breakfast." She clucked under her breath. "Someone has to get you and Calvin together before you waste away. And I have an idea."

"Miss Bailey!"

Beatrice's head whipped around at the sound of the familiar voice. Calvin. Even muffled as he was beneath scarf and rabbit-skin hat, his brown eyes gleamed with mischief and happiness. Or was she imagining he shared her happiness at being together again? Aside from quick, formal greetings at church, they hadn't spoken since their all-too-brief visit on Christmas Eve. Papa had made sure of that.

"Smile," Peggy whispered in her ear.

Beatrice did better than that. She slipped a mittened hand out of her muffler and waved. Calvin made as if to run to her across the common, but his legs sank to his knees in the snow. He shrugged, stood, and walked on the road around the corner. While she waited for him to draw close, several other young people arrived at the common. The air rang with the greetings and good humor of people released from their midwinter doldrums. When Calvin took her arm at the same time Tobias took Peggy's, it felt natural and right.

Tobias and Peggy fell back, allowing Calvin and Beatrice the illusion of privacy. Even with two dozen people milling around the church yard, Beatrice felt encapsulated in their own snowball, hidden from view to all but God.

"I feared I wouldn't see you today, that your father might forbid it." Calvin's voice sounded low, tender.

"He's out of town." She couldn't keep the smile away from her lips. "I told Mama I was coming, and she didn't speak against it."

Beside her, Calvin stiffened. What had she said to offend him now?

"I don't want to sneak behind his back." Calvin held himself rigid. "I'm still not good enough for him."

"Would you rather not see me at all?" What was wrong with the man? "The question isn't what my father thinks of you but what *I* think of you."

His hold on her arm tightened, then she felt it relax, one fingertip at a time. "Oh, Beatrice Alice Bailey, what I am to do with you? You keep bringing me back to what is important." His mouth opened in a crooked grin.

"Let's gather rosebuds while we may, for old time—and your father—will be a-flying."

"I didn't take you for the poetic type," Beatrice said.

"My mother's prized book of poetry." The scowl that had darkened his face cleared, and a genuine smile broke through, as warm as the sun high in the sky. "Let's go lace on our skates."

～

Parson Cabot had done a good job creating the skating pond, Calvin decided. Although numerous bodies of water across the Notch froze over during the winter, all of them posed difficulties. Often rocks and other debris frozen in the ice posed a threat. So when the church held a skating party, the pastor worked on creating an artificial pond behind the church. In the sunshine, it looked as clear as the floor of crystal in the New Jerusalem.

Last year Calvin had enjoyed the skating frolic, his first since he returned from the war. How much more he looked forward to this year, with Bea on his arm. He glanced down at her, her brown eyes alight with merriment, and the remainder of his hesitation about the day took flight.

He led her to a large boulder. "Let me help you fit your skates over your boots." Removing his mittens, he took the pair of metal blades made to fit her feet perfectly. They flashed with nearly new sparkle, finer than anything he had ever worn to skate. One Christmas, his parents had invested in metal blades when he had begged for them. He had swapped out the soles for larger ones as he outgrew the original pair, and he continued to use them, taking care that he didn't wobble and fall. With good maintenance, annual sharpening, and care wearing them, he expected them to last for his lifetime.

At least they were made of metal. Glancing around at the other young people confirmed several of them still used runners fashioned from animal bones.

He tightened the blades on Beatrice's small feet and checked them. "Is that comfortable?"

She stood. "Perfect." She glanced at the ice, longing in her eyes.

"Go on ahead. I'll join you on the ice in a minute." He didn't know that he wanted her to watch him attach his outgrown skates to his boots.

"Don't want me to see you trip over your own two feet?" Her smile let him know she was teasing. "I'm not going anywhere."

He looked at the blades in his hands. If they were to have a future together, she'd have to accept things as they were, the make-do reality of his life, not as they might wish them to be. Bending over, he pulled the loop tight against his right boot.

"These look like you've enjoyed many good times in them." He glanced up to see her turning the extra blade over in her hand. "I haven't had many opportunities to skate aside from parties held at church. Too dangerous, both Mama and Papa agreed." She looked longingly at the simple skate in her lap.

He finished with the fastenings and reached for the second blade. Their gazes caught, locked together.

"You may think my family is rich." She glanced away at the spot where Peggy headed onto the ice with Tobias. "But your family is rich in memories. I know which one I'd prefer."

Calvin's heart went to his head, leaving him senseless, and he couldn't have said whether he fastened the second skate on securely or not. The next thing he knew, he was on the ice with Beatrice. The two of them glided together as if they had done it all their lives, in perfect harmony—the way a couple should be. Had they skated together before? He searched for a memory.

"Do you remember the skating party we had, maybe a year or so before the war?"

Was she reading his mind? "Yes." He could picture her still: Peggy's constant companion, a shy young beauty even then, with glistening golden hair.

She giggled. "You were so grown up. I was longing to skate with you, but you didn't even know I existed except as Peggy's friend."

"And she asked me to skate with you." The memory cleared now. All he had wanted to do was to skate with Hannah White. Strange how all that had changed. At the time, he was certain his future lay with Hannah, but she had married while he was gone to war and had turned into a nagging housewife from what he had heard. God had spared him.

"And you graciously agreed to your pesky cousin's request and made me very happy indeed."

"I remember." He smiled at the memory. "You talked with me about how Parson Cabot enlarged the pond the summer before and what you had read in the almanac about the chances for the year's crops. You sounded like a right young farmer. At least until you quoted poetry at me." She had driven Hannah White out of his mind, at least temporarily.

Her cheeks brightened. "I was so thrilled that you were taking me seriously. I felt very grown up that day." Luminous brown eyes peeked out from beneath her bonnet. "You're doing it all over again."

The way she looked at him, adoration shining in her eyes, took all his willpower not to lean over and kiss the inviting lips. He wouldn't do that again, not here, not anywhere, until some things changed. He must speak his mind. He turned around, skating backward while holding on to her hands. "You know I care deeply for you."

"Yes?" She looked at him with such hope in her eyes that he hated what he must say next.

"And I believe you feel the same way about me." He held his breath. What if she said no?

She nodded, her cheeks blazing red.

"But your father has forbidden our courtship. Is it right for us to continue without his blessing?"

Her eyes widened at the sight of something behind him, out of his sight. Before he turned, he knew whom he would see.

Hiram Bailey.

Chapter 12

Parson Cabot skated to the couple with an agility surprising in a man of his age. "Calvin, Beatrice, I suggest you head to the parsonage. I will speak with Mr. Bailey."

Calvin tugged Beatrice's hand. "Can you walk in your blades?" She nodded, and they hobbled across the snow toward the back door of the parsonage.

"Good day, Mr. Bailey." Parson Cabot intercepted Papa in time to let them escape inside.

Beatrice collapsed on the closest chair, her whole body trembling. Her face felt frozen, as much from fear as from cold. "What are we to do?"

"How good to see you both today." Mrs. Cabot greeted them as if having people barge into her house with their skates on happened every day. "Would you like some tea?"

Shaking her head, Beatrice took off her coat and bent over to unfasten the blades. Calvin did the same.

"Don't worry, my dears. My husband will calm Mr. Bailey down before he brings him to the house." Mrs. Cabot handed a piece of still-steaming gingerbread into Calvin's hands. "It might be best if Calvin leaves now." Her suggestion was in reality a command, and they both knew it.

Calvin glanced at the door as if expecting it to burst open, then back at Beatrice, uncertainty written on his features.

"Go," Beatrice encouraged. "Let us pray as though our lives depended on it."

His shoulders stiffened, his manly pride fighting with his common sense.

"Sometimes it is better to retreat and fight your battle another day. My husband will speak with Mr. Bailey. Go in peace."

"Until we meet again." Calvin didn't waste more time arguing. He disappeared out the covered walkway that connected the parsonage with the church. Beatrice stared at the closed door, wondering if the impediments to a relationship between them would always remain so firmly in place.

"Do you wish me to speak for you, dear?" Mrs. Cabot's voice intruded on her thoughts. "Sometimes it is easier to ask someone outside the family to soothe troubled waters."

Beatrice could hear the nervousness in her laughter. "I feel like we're

Romeo and Juliet or Hero and Leander. I don't think there's anything you could say to Papa to change his mind about Calvin."

"But you love him, don't you?" The same sweet voice that had comforted Beatrice when she had fallen down during a race at the church picnic as a child invited confidences now.

"Oh yes, Mrs. Cabot. I do."

Boots stamped on the ground outside, heralding the arrival of the two men. "Then that's all I need to know." Mrs. Cabot opened the door. "Welcome, Mr. Bailey. Please do come in."

Beatrice brushed down her skirt. Not a single water stain smudged the perfect lay of her dress, as spotless as the day had been. She raised her chin. She had done nothing shameful.

"Beatrice." Papa's voice hung on a razor's edge between conciliation and anger.

"Papa. You must have had good success in Burlington to return so promptly."

His eyes flared, and she knew she had spoken amiss. "You weren't expecting me to return in time to see you skating with Mr. Tuttle."

She refused to let him shame her. "I told Mama about the skating frolic."

"But not about Mr. Tuttle." Papa refused to back down.

"We did not plan to meet, if that is what you are implying."

"Please, Mr. Bailey. Sit down. Have a cup of tea and some gingerbread." Mrs. Cabot shoved a cup in his hands before he could refuse it. He took the chair opposite Beatrice, his dark eyes matching hers stare for stare.

"I have told Mr. Bailey that both you and Calvin were in my sight the entire time and that nothing untoward happened. You appeared to be enjoying a few pleasant turns on the ice." In a burst of unwelcome honesty, the parson added, "And perhaps to discuss a few matters of concern to you both."

"I must accept the parson's word about what transpired between you." Papa spoke directly to Beatrice. "But I will not suffer that young farmer to speak against me. What did he say?"

"Surely that is a private matter between the two young people," Mrs. Cabot said.

"He said"—Beatrice raised her voice over Mrs. Cabot's objection—"that no matter what his feelings toward me may be, he refused to ask me to act against your wishes." Her voice came close to breaking into tears.

"That is well." Papa stared at the tea cup in his hand as if ready to throw it against the fireplace. "These are my wishes. I forbid you to speak to him or see him again. The man is not fit to be the husband of my daughter." He returned the cup to Mrs. Cabot. "I'm afraid I have no taste for tea this afternoon. Come, Beatrice, we are finished here."

"Do you object to my spending time with Mrs. Cabot?" Beatrice felt a temper equal to that of her father rising.

"What? You wish to stay?"

She nodded.

"Will you promise me that they won't use your home as a meeting place?" Papa turned to the parson. Beatrice shrank inside herself. No one should address their pastor in that tone of voice.

Mrs. Cabot nodded at the parson. "You have my promise." Although he said the words, he didn't appear happy.

"Very well. I will expect a man of the cloth to keep his word. And, Beatrice, I will know when the skating party has ended—I will expect you home right after." His back as rigid as Calvin's had been earlier, Papa marched through the door.

Once he had left, Mrs. Cabot walked across the room and opened the doorway to the church. Beatrice rose. Had Calvin been standing there the whole time? Would the Cabots allow them to meet in spite of the promise the parson had given?

Mrs. Cabot returned with Peggy, both of them wreathed in smiles. "I know you promised not to speak or meet with Calvin." Her friend's attempt to look serious failed, and she giggled.

"I fail to see anything funny about it." Beatrice accepted Mrs. Cabot's handkerchief and dabbed at the tears spilling from her eyes.

"Cheer up." Peggy handed a quill and paper to Beatrice. "You didn't promise not to *write* to him."

As Peggy explained their plan, even Beatrice's face lifted in a smile.

∽

"How much corn did Rusk say he wanted?" Tobias asked.

"What's that?" Calvin stared at Bea's latest letter, which Peggy had delivered that afternoon.

"Never mind." Tobias bent over the sheet of paper where they had recorded requests for seed corn. "You won't pay attention to me until you've read every word on that page at least a dozen times and committed them to memory."

Calvin grunted in agreement. His friend understood him well enough. Every day that passed without a letter felt like a year had passed. If he thought he loved Bea before, that love had flared into something rarer, finer, as he had seen deep into her soul through their correspondence. She detailed life as seen through her window, such as the fight of the tiny chickadees and the lowly sparrow to survive Vermont's harsh winter and the first signs that this year perhaps, indeed, spring would arrive.

They had agreed to read the same passages of the Bible every day—five Psalms and one chapter of Proverbs. So far they had read through both books twice. As they shared their thoughts, his love for the Lord grew in conjunction with his admiration for Bea. She was a woman whose value was above rubies, whose husband could trust in her.

"Have faith."

It took a moment for Calvin to realize Tobias had said the words, because he had read them so often in Bea's letters.

"I believe God will bring things together for all of us this spring. Peggy and I, you and Beatrice."

Calvin set down the paper. "From your lips to God's ears. I pray it is so." He found the place Tobias had marked on the ledger. "Whitson wants five bushels?"

"He's even offered us more money if we'll sell him extra."

Calvin shook his head. "One times one is still one. We can't make more than we have. I hope we have enough to sell everyone what they need, and if we're lucky, we'll have extra. Do we have a total yet?"

"We haven't heard from Frisk or the Johnsons, but of course they both salvaged some of their crops. They may not want to buy any from us." Tobias ticked the end of the pencil against his teeth.

Calvin ran his finger down the list. "Some have asked for more than they should need. Maybe they're afraid of another year like last year."

"Let's pray not." Tobias managed a lopsided grin. "You don't have any more stumps to burn out."

"If it happens again, I suspect the whole town will pack up and move south." Calvin looked at the numbers. "And some people have requested a bare minimum."

"Think it's a matter of how much money people can afford?"

Calvin shrugged. "I'm thinking about setting a limit. Two bushels of corn per farm if they're asking to buy. Including my own family. A dollar a bushel, the same price for everyone. That way everybody gets treated the same way. It hurts my head to think about who might need it more or less."

Tobias lifted his eyebrows at that. "You really don't want to make money on this, do you?"

"It feels wrong to profit from other people's tragedy." Calvin sucked in his lips and totaled the names on the page. "Twenty, twenty-three including our three family farms." He made a mark on the page. "And I might see about selling whatever is left to the mercantile over in St. Albans. They must be facing the same problems we are." He rolled his shoulders to ease out the kinks formed from huddling over the books for so long. "Come on, let's get outside. I'm going to see if Solomon will let me borrow his wagon."

"How about your uncle?" Tobias's grin gave away his thoughts.

"You just want to see Peggy," Calvin said.

"Anything wrong with that?"

Calvin's glance fell on the latest letter from Bea. Maybe they didn't need to leave right away. "Nothing. Nothing at all." He took a seat and pulled a fresh sheet of paper toward him. Dipping his quill in ink, he wrote *"Dearest Bea..."*

∽

"The plans I have set in motion for the sale of my seed corn will provide enough money to repay my debt to your father's bank." Once again, Beatrice moved her cat off the letter so she could read Calvin's message.

The door to Beatrice's room swung open, and she folded the page into the sleeve of her dressing gown. Bessie entered, bearing a ewer of warm water. She glanced at the sleeve of Beatrice's dress, where a white corner dangled.

"Did you hear from Mr. Tuttle again?" Bessie whispered as she poured water into the basin on the bed stand, where it steamed in the cool air.

Beatrice glanced at the door, fearful one of her parents might overhear.

"Mr. and Mrs. Bailey are in the drawing room downstairs. The mistress thought you might want to freshen up before the dinner party tonight."

Beatrice had enlisted her maid's help in corresponding with Calvin. So far, no one had guessed. Neither parent had forbidden it, but she had no doubt they would if they ever learned about it. She nodded. "I want to read the letter before I go downstairs."

"I'll tell your mother you need a few more minutes." Bessie winked at Beatrice. "Use the time any way you want to." She slipped out the door.

"If only I could avoid this dinner altogether." Papa seemed determined to introduce her to every eligible suitor within a fifty-mile radius. Tonight she was to entertain Reginald Perkins, the widowed owner of the emporium in nearby St. Albans. He was a man of at least thirty, with the appearance of a jolly peddler, if she remembered him correctly. She shuddered at the thought. A pleasant man, good with his customers, kind and a good friend—but would she want him as a husband? He held no interest for her.

Beatrice had already dressed as much as she intended to for the visit, donning one of the dresses they had had made during her stay in New York. Mama had asked her to wear the rose dress, but Beatrice couldn't bring herself to do that. Calvin favored her in pink, and she wore it to church if at all. There he could at least see her, even if they couldn't speak. The curls Bessie had helped style in her hair remained in place. With the extra few minutes the maid promised, Beatrice could cherish the rest of the letter.

Once I have satisfied the debt and we are on even terms, I will renew my request for permission to court you properly. Pray that your father receives me with kindness.

Oh, could it be? Beatrice hardened herself against the tears that wanted to flow. If she went down to dinner with red-rimmed eyes, Mama would ask questions. How she longed to sit down and dash off a reply, but Bessie couldn't buy that much time for her. Instead, she settled for a second reading of the letter, committing much of it to memory before she hid it in a box with pressed leaves and other childish mementoes she stored in her armoire.

After that, Beatrice put on her most important adornment—an interested smile—and went downstairs to greet Mr. Perkins.

The sight of the man waiting for her in the drawing room might have made her laugh in different circumstances. Mr. Perkins almost looked like a dandy. Had he ordered new clothing for tonight's dinner? If only she could feel any degree of interest in the man. In the flickering candlelight, set atop the table although twilight still shone through the windows, he looked eager, almost boyish, the lighting doing kind things to his eyes, erasing wrinkles, and revealing only his good humor.

"Miss Bailey. How lovely to see you again." He bowed in her direction. She offered her hand, and he kissed it. His voice was strong. She could imagine him calling orders across his store, or perhaps telling an engaging tale to his children.

He had a number of admirable qualities, but she felt nothing when she looked at him except possible friendship.

"It didn't matter where that mother cat took her kittens; Mandy always caught up with her. Eventually she gave up." Mr. Perkins finished a story about his youngest daughter.

Beatrice's guess had proved correct; he loved telling stories, especially about his three offspring. She could picture the three lonely children through his eyes: sweet, not perfect, but well behaved and healthy.

"Do you like children, Miss Bailey?" Mr. Perkins addressed the question to her.

Beatrice's heart sped at the personal question. How could she answer? If she said yes. . .but if she said no. . .

When she hesitated, Papa's lips tightened in the beginnings of a frown. "Of course she does." He wrapped his fingers around the coffee cup waiting by his plate. "How has business been? Has this year without a summer made it difficult?"

Once again, Beatrice squirmed. Between Mr. Perkins's question about children and Papa asking about business, she felt like she was sitting in on a bargaining session for her hand.

"Not too bad. A few people have purchased things on account, but I'm certain this year shall see improvement. By year's end, I expect to turn a tidy profit. Yes, indeed." He settled back against his chair and looked at Papa with the confidence of a successful man of business. "My family is well provided for." He looked meaningfully at Beatrice.

With the right man, I'd be happy with a sack of beans and a handful of corn-meal. But Beatrice knew better than to voice her thoughts aloud.

"In fact, a good piece of business has come my way recently." Mr. Perkins beamed, oblivious to Beatrice's indifference to his financial health. "I've found a source of seed corn to sell to our locals. Someone from your neck of the woods, in fact. You may know him—Calvin Tuttle?"

∼

"Looks like we have company," Tobias called out.

Calvin glanced up from where he plied his hoe to sift through the ashes from the tree roots. Here and there he found small chunks that needed to be dug out. By the time they finished, the amount of arable land would have nearly doubled.

His heart clenched when he saw their unexpected guest. *Hiram Bailey.* Calvin looked down at his stained breeches, his dirt-encrusted hands. *So be it. And God, give me the words to say.* The two men hadn't spoken since the day of the skating frolic, not even at Sunday services. Had he discovered the correspondence with Beatrice?

Bailey pulled up his horse. "Mr. Tuttle. May I have a word with you?"

In a low voice, Tobias said, "I'm praying." Calvin nodded and walked across the field toward his nemesis.

"Mr. Bailey. What brings you out here on this fine spring day?" Calvin matched the banker's even tones.

"I have a business matter I'd like to discuss with you. May we go to your cabin?" Bailey remained astride his horse. Calvin wondered if the height was meant to intimidate him. He refused to let that happen.

"I'm sorry, Mr. Bailey, but we are in the midst of spring planting, as you can see. I hope to come in to the bank later this month regarding the loan."

Bailey frowned, as if unsettled that Calvin controlled the timing of their discussion. "That's not what I came about. I heard you are selling your seed corn to the storekeeper in St. Albans." He waited, as if expecting an answer to an unasked question.

"That is correct."

Bailey pulled on his horse's reins but loosened them when the horse whinnied its protest. "If you have extra seed corn, I am still interested in buying it. For six dollars a bushel. Come now. You can't complain. You've made your point and played Joseph to the people of Maple Notch."

Calvin held his tongue.

"People elsewhere will buy the corn, no matter the price. Why not accept a transaction that benefits us both?" Bailey took off his riding gloves and slapped them against his bulging pocket.

The sweat on Calvin's back turned to ice water, chilling him to the bone. "My answer remains unchanged. No matter where they live, farmers are my neighbors just as the man on the Jericho Road was the Samaritan's neighbor. I can't accept such a high price." *Have I just said good-bye to this man's blessing on my courtship of his daughter. . .again?* "I will sell it to you for the same price I've charged everyone else. One dollar a bushel."

Bailey's face turned pale before it darkened into a deep red of rage. "Very well. I had hoped that you had gained some common sense over the winter, but I was wrong. I shall expect your payment in full in a week's time." He turned his horse around and galloped in the direction of the river.

"Why not take the man's money, if he's so anxious to give it away?" Tobias asked. "It's not like you have that much corn left over."

Calvin turned a murderous glare on him, and Tobias backed off. "Because it's wrong."

Calvin stopped paying attention. Bailey had run off, his horse at full gallop, and a sense of impending danger urged him to action. He stood debating the wisdom of going for his own mount when he heard a scream coming from the direction of the river.

Chapter 13

Get blankets and meet me at the bridge," Calvin hollered at Tobias as he sprinted in the direction of the scream.

Lord, let me get there in time. Calvin didn't know what to expect. A few feet shy of the bridge, he slowed down his pace to avoid the same fate he feared had befallen Bailey.

Calvin surveyed the scene in front of him with mounting panic. On the opposite side of the river, Bailey's horse stood some distance from the riverbank, its sides heaving and shuddering in near panic.

The middle of the bridge, where they had replaced planks last year, had broken, a gaping hole where solid wood should have been.

Of Hiram Bailey—no sign was visible.

Calvin dismounted and took a cautious step onto the bridge, then another. The wood at the near end of the bridge seemed solid enough for his weight.

"What are you doing?" Tobias spoke from the embankment.

"Looking for Mr. Bailey." He peered over the edge of the hole, fearful he might see a body impaled on one of the broken pilings, but he found no sign of him. "Mr. Bailey?" Calvin shielded his eyes from the sun glinting off the running water and looked downstream. If the river carried him. . . He shuddered to think about the rocks and other obstacles that lay along that route. If the man had worn a hunter's red jacket or even a mustard yellow, he would be easier to spot against the dark water and woods and rock.

"I see something."

Calvin turned in the direction Tobias pointed—a patch of blue wool had snagged on lichen-covered rock on the near side of the riverbank. They both crashed through the woods toward the rock. Faint moans reached them when they were a few yards away.

"He's alive!" Relief gave speed to Calvin's legs, and he smashed through branches to the side of the river. Bailey clung to a large boulder at the edge of the water, but his fingers looked blue and numb and ready to let go.

"We're coming, Mr. Bailey. Hold on."

"Give me the rope," Calvin called to Tobias as he pulled off his coat. Anything heavy or bulky would only hinder him. He moved cautiously, planting his feet on the slippery rock, finding a foothold and securing his weight before letting go of the tree leaning over the river.

Bailey's fingers loosened their grip on the lichen-covered rock. "Oh no you don't." Calvin grabbed the man by the elbows and pulled him onto the rock beside him. Bailey was saying something, but Calvin couldn't distinguish the words straining through his chattering teeth.

First problem solved. Now how did he get both of them back onto the bank where Tobias waited with the rope? "Throw one end to me."

Tobias did as he requested, and Calvin tied a knot around Bailey's waist. Maybe a foot, half a yard at most, separated the rock from the creek bank, but it might as well have been a mile with Bailey's inert weight. The man might not survive another plunge into the icy river water.

Tobias spotted the same problem. He found a stone wedged into the exposed riverbank and tested his weight on it. It held, and he climbed down to lean across the empty space. He had closed the distance by half. It would have to do.

Head or feet first? Feet, Calvin decided. If they did lose their hold and Bailey slipped into the water, better it be his feet.

Balancing himself on the edge of the large boulder, Calvin took Bailey in his arms and leaned toward where Tobias stood at the edge of the water. Slowly, slowly, he moved his arms up Bailey's torso, feeding his feet and legs toward Tobias.

"Got 'im!" Tobias called. He pulled Bailey's legs over his shoulder, until the banker looked like a fish ready to slide into the water. He gestured with his hand. *Keep him coming.*

Calvin watched Bailey's feet inch up the river bank until at last the man's head fell from his hands and almost threw him off balance. Tobias held Bailey in his arms.

"Wish I could paint a picture of this. If he survives." Calvin reached for the riverbank with one long leg and landed with a *whoosh* next to Tobias.

The two friends squatted beside the banker to make an assessment. At least he was out of the water. Before they did anything else, Calvin ran his hands up and down Bailey's arms and legs for broken bones. "I think his left leg is broken below the knee," he told Tobias. Rib cage next. Bailey moaned.

"Broken ribs, too?" Tobias asked.

"I'm no expert." Calvin probed Bailey's chest as gently as he could. "I don't think anything else is broken, but I'm sure he'll be bruised all over. We need to make a litter. The sooner we get him warm..."

They made quick work of constructing the litter out of two logs and a blanket, and trotted back to the cabin with their burden. "Go ahead to Uncle

Stephen's. Tell him what's happened, and ask him to come as soon as possible." Tobias left the yard, and Calvin picked Bailey up. He stretched the man out on his feather tick, removed his wet clothes, and covered him with a quilt.

Next, he built up the fire and set a kettle of water on to heat. The door behind him opened as he returned to examine Bailey's injuries.

"How bad is he?" Uncle Stephen joined him at the bedside and studied the prone figure. "All you can do is keep him quiet and warm, since there's no doctor nearby."

"That's what I thought." After his battle experience, Calvin knew the best course of action was to wait and see if infection set in. He would pray that didn't happen, because then amputation might be the only answer. "Do you mind staying here while I go to town and let his family know?"

"Of course." Uncle Stephen waved the question away. "Tobias will return in a few minutes with Hilda and Peggy. He'll have more attention than he may want."

"I don't know how long I'll be."

"Doesn't matter. Now go. They may already be worried about him at the bank."

Calvin climbed on his horse one more time and cantered past his fields, where the hoe lay abandoned in the soil. Tobias would take care of it. Funny how the importance of planting dimmed when a man's life lay in the balance. If Mr. Bailey usually returned home for his luncheon, Beatrice and her mother would expect him at any moment. Calvin had no time to lose.

Should he take the horse through the water or head north to the nearest bridge? Due to spring runoff, the water was running high, and the current was strong at the spot they had built the bridge. He wouldn't attempt the crossing there, but at the shallows about a mile upstream. The horse made his way across easily enough. Minutes later, they reached the road into town and raced onward.

Ahead of him, he saw the town common. The sun beat down on his neck, indicating high noon. He pulled up in front of the house, tied the horse to a maple tree, and ran to the door, pounding his fist against the solid oak.

Bea herself answered the door.

∽

"Calvin?" Beatrice blinked, not quite believing his presence on her doorstep. Had he spoken to her father already? Was the news good? A smile forced its way from her heart onto her face.

"Who is it, dear?" Mama's voice intruded.

"Please let me in." Whatever emotion Calvin's voice held, it didn't sound like happiness, and his clothes were damp. She opened the door wide enough for him to come in and called to her mother over her shoulder. "It's"—she stopped herself from saying "Calvin" in the nick of time—"Mr. Tuttle."

Footsteps hurried down the corridor, and Mama met them in the front hall, a faint frown on her face. She, too, saw something in Calvin's expression that made her pause. "I think you had best come in, Mr. Tuttle, and tell us your business."

Even as distraught as Calvin was, Beatrice drank in the sight, sound, smell of him. Fresh air and hard work, clothing stained. . .none of it mattered. He had taken off his hat and stood with his feet planted apart, a solid man from head to toe.

"It's Mr. Bailey. He came to see me this morning."

Beatrice let out an involuntary cry. Had Papa found out about their secret correspondence? Calvin caught her cry and shook his head.

"Did you argue?" Mama's lips returned to their straight, unhappy line.

"That's not why I'm here." He looked at the floor, then around the room, and finally returned his gaze to the two of them. "The truth is, the bridge gave way when he attempted the crossing, and he fell in."

Mama gasped, and she clutched Beatrice's arm. A lifetime of possibilities crossed her mind.

"We—Mr. Heath and I—fished him out of the water and took him to my house. My uncle is with him now."

"Is he—?" Beatrice hesitated to ask.

"His leg is broken, but nothing else appears to be broken. Tobias and I agreed the best thing for him is to stay put and rest."

"He needs a doctor." Mama fidgeted. "How can we get word to the doctor down in Burlington?"

"Take us to him." Beatrice trusted Calvin's judgment about the injury. "Did you come by the north bridge?"

Calvin shook his head. "My horse crossed the river. But with you ladies. . ."

"I can ride." Beatrice wanted to get to Papa's side as soon as possible.

Mama dithered in place, uncertain what to do. For a woman whose greatest concern usually involved the decision of when to change from winter wear to summer wear, she had never encountered such a challenge. "But Mama shouldn't ride."

"Perhaps we can tell Parson Cabot?" Calvin suggested.

"Excellent idea. He'll want to come, I'm sure."

"Mrs. Bailey, why don't you sit down?" Calvin led Mama to a chair as gently as if she were his own mother. "We'll take care of what needs to be done." He followed Beatrice into the front hall. "Perhaps I shouldn't have spoken so bluntly."

"You were good to come at all." Beatrice longed to put her hand to his rough cheek but refrained. "I'll gather a few things here while you go talk to the preacher. If Mama hasn't stirred, perhaps Mrs. Cabot can sit with her while we go and see Papa, you and I."

Cook bustled out of the kitchen as Calvin went out the door. "Mr. Bailey is late today. Do you want me to go ahead and serve lunch?"

At the everyday question, Mama began crying. Beatrice remained dry-eyed while she explained the situation. "Mr. Tuttle has gone to ask Mrs. Cabot to sit with my mother while I go to see Papa. We don't want to eat."

"I'll fix some tea." Cook headed back to the kitchen, but Beatrice stopped her.

"What can I bring that might help Papa?" Cook might know some folk remedies for treating injuries.

Cook clucked. "It sounds like Mr. Tuttle's got everything in hand. But if Mr. Bailey's leg is broke bad, he'll want the doctor to see to it. Otherwise, he won't walk right again. Don't you worry yourself with that. I'll get word to his clerk over at the bank, and he'll find someone to go for the doctor."

"Thank you. I'd appreciate that."

What must Papa be feeling now? Why had he sought Calvin out that morning? She wanted some answers on their way to the farm.

Beatrice explained Cook's plan when Calvin returned with the Cabots, and he nodded in acceptance. "We'd best leave the leg alone until the doctor can get here."

Mrs. Cabot fluttered around Mama. "You folks go on ahead. Stay overnight if you need to. Mrs. Bailey and I will be fine." She tucked a shawl around Mama's shoulders as if she were an invalid in need of care. With Papa injured and Mama distraught, Beatrice felt as though she had traveled from child to parent in the space of a day.

"I'll be praying for both of you as we ride," the parson promised.

Calvin took the lead on the road that led northwest out of town. "Are you going by way of the north bridge?" Beatrice asked sharply.

" 'Tis safest," Calvin said.

She turned her mare's head in the direction of the farm. "You said you found a spot to ford the river. I want to go by that route."

Calvin whipped his horse around. "I'll never forgive myself if harm comes to you while you are under my care."

"And I want to get to Papa's side as quickly as possible. Nothing will happen to me at the river." She urged her horse forward, not wanting to waste time in argument. The other horses fell in behind. A moment later, Parson

Cabot came alongside. "Miss Bailey, if I may make a suggestion."

"I'm not turning back."

"No, I'm not asking you to." He spoke in the mildest of voices. "But if I do not wish to chance the river when we see how deep it is running, will you allow Calvin to lead us by another way?"

Beatrice glanced at the parson. He visited his parishioners in all kinds of weather, fair and foul, be it day or night. She could trust him to not turn back for anything less than a truly dangerous passage. Reluctantly, she nodded.

At this point, the road widened enough for a wagon to pass into town—wide enough for the three of them to ride abreast. Beatrice wanted to ask Calvin what had prompted Papa's visit, but she hesitated to ask in front of the parson.

Parson Cabot rode with eyes that focused inward. Beatrice assumed he was praying until he said, "I can't help but wonder if God may use this difficult circumstance to resolve the dilemma the two of you have faced concerning Mr. Bailey's opposition. I have been praying for the Lord's healing, both of Mr. Bailey's body—and of the rift between you."

Calvin shook his head. "That would take a miracle. We had another argument this morning." He glanced at Beatrice, his face pale, solemn. "I fear his anger drove him to the reckless ride over the bridge."

"Did he. . .tell you not to write?" She had to ask.

"No." Calvin looked ahead to where the road wound around a corner on its way to the river. He nodded. "That's where we leave the road to get to the ford."

"So what did you argue about?" Beatrice refused to be sidetracked.

"He offered to buy my surplus seed corn for six times what I charged anyone else. I told him I would sell it to him for the same price I gave everyone else. He said I had no common sense." A wry smile twisted his mouth. "After that, I dared not speak to him of our situation. He was angered when he left, and then. . .I heard him scream." The smile disappeared, replaced by bitterness. "As if the Almighty was judging me for not accepting his help."

Or judging Papa?

"Perhaps the Almighty wanted to give both of you a second chance, without dollar signs and ears of corn coming between you," Parson Cabot said, pulling up his horse. "Isn't this where you said we leave the road?"

Once they were traveling through the trees, single file, conversation became impossible. *"That Calvin Tuttle."* Beatrice remembered how strange his name had sounded coming from Papa's lips. She couldn't help but overhear the conversation between her parents after the dinner with Mr. Perkins, since they had left the study door open.

"He knew I wanted to buy...going behind my back..." Mama's measured tones placated Papa, until Beatrice could no longer understand the words. He must have decided to go to Calvin one more time. The pair of them were too stubborn and proud for their own good. In that way the two men she loved were more alike than different. A branch smacked her in the face, and she batted another out of the way. She wouldn't tell Calvin, though. He would reject the very idea that he shared anything in common with her father.

They came upon the river suddenly. It looked quiet enough, but she had promised, so she waited for the parson to check it out.

"I believe it is safe enough to allow passage. However, Miss Bailey, your skirts. . . Mr. Tuttle, why don't you go ahead first? I will escort Miss Bailey safely across."

Calvin flushed, perhaps embarrassed by the thought of catching a glimpse of her lower limbs, but he agreed and crossed the river ahead of them. Once the trees hid him from view, Beatrice draped her skirts across her lap and the saddle horn. Her unmentionables might show beneath her petticoats, but God and people would forgive her. Her mare followed Parson Cabot into the water. The water eddied around the mare's legs as she plodded through to the other side with nary a tremor of alarm. Beatrice rearranged her skirts and smiled at the preacher.

He returned her smile. "We're ready, Mr. Tuttle."

Calvin reappeared, making sure he kept his gaze away from Beatrice's skirts. "It's this way."

They rode through fields, so empty-looking without the tree stumps. As soon as they came in sight of the cabin, Tobias crossed the field toward them.

"How fares my father?" Beatrice asked.

"Awake. Demanding to be taken home." Tobias scowled. "I'm glad you're here, Parson Cabot. Perhaps you can reason with him."

Beatrice surprised herself by laughing. "Then he must be doing fair." She caught Calvin grinning at her, and she knew that things would turn out as they should.

$\sim$

"I don't want to use the privy. Haven't you ever heard of a slop jar?"

Calvin gritted his teeth. He almost wished he had agreed to Hiram Bailey's demands and taken him home as soon as he regained strength from his accident.

"The doctor said you must exercise your leg for it to grow strong. That you need to walk." He quoted the doctor the Baileys had insisted on calling and hoped the recalcitrant patient would listen.

"I can walk around the cabin."

Calvin looked at Tobias, who shrugged. His look said, "What are you going to do about it?"

Calvin came to a decision. Plunking his hat on his head, he grabbed his hoe. "Mr. Bailey, I have offered to assist you to the privy, but you have refused my offer. We'll leave you to attend to your own needs. Tobias and I will be working in the fields until noon. We'll see you then. Good day." He slipped out the door.

Tobias followed. "Ah, sunshine and brown earth. A glorious day beckons." He eyed Calvin. "I expect any day away from the sickroom would feel glorious."

Calvin grunted. "I remind myself of what the Bible says about heaping coals of fire on his head. To do and do and do again."

"Even when he doesn't like it. I know." Tobias clapped Calvin on the shoulder. "Come, a morning's work outside will do us both good."

Calvin had to plant. If he didn't, he'd have no crop this year. They stopped by the barn, and he gestured to the barrels waiting by the feeding troughs. "Here's the final coal I'll heap on his head. I'll *give* him the extra corn. There's not much, five bushels, maybe. And he can sell it for whatever price he likes." He wanted the produce that had caused so much division and misery out of his life.

"Does your partner get a say?" Tobias teased, heaving a bag of bean seed over his shoulder. They had prepared rows for planting yesterday.

"Would you naysay me, brother?" Calvin rolled a barrel with their own corn seed toward the door.

"No, I think you're wise. Put this Year of No Summer behind us and move forward." He winked. "As long as we can do it in the company of certain ladies of our acquaintance."

Calvin bit his lip. His future with Beatrice was still far from certain, in spite of the parson's assurances that Calvin's "brave, valiant efforts to save Mr. Bailey's life"—the parson's words, not his—would not go unnoticed or unrewarded.

"We have another crop to harvest before you wed my cousin." The barrel reached the open doorway, and Calvin upended it into a wheelbarrow.

They planted their crops the way his father and grandfather had before him, corn and beans and squash growing together. The Indians had shown the first settlers the method, and so far no one had come up with a better system. Calvin had considered planting a grain like rye this year, but after the bridge's collapse, any extra money he had to invest would go into building another bridge. He had drawn up plans for a covered bridge, a toll bridge that would pay for the materials used in its construction within a year, two years at most. His arms swung in a steady rhythm while his mind raced with possibilities. Would his idea work?

"I'm going into town the day after tomorrow," Calvin told Tobias. "I have business to conduct."

At last he saw his way clear.

Chapter 14

Calvin whistled as he returned from town. The piece of paper crinkling in his pocket pleased his ears as much as bells on Christmas Day. The time neared when Mr. Bailey would leave the Tuttle farm, but before then, Calvin would have a serious discussion with Bea's father.

The sight of the finicky banker hobbling to the outhouse on crutches made Calvin want to chuckle, but he refrained. Instead, he held back his horse so that the man could return to the cabin in peace, unaware of an audience. Allow the man his pride. Today he would bow if need be to the one man who stood between him and Bea.

"Did you get it taken care of?" Tobias asked when he saw Calvin come out of the woods.

In answer, Calvin pulled the paper out of his vest and waved it around. "I've got it right here."

By the time they entered the cabin, Bailey had settled into a chair. He scowled at Calvin. "You chose a fine day to disappear. I told you I hoped to make it back home today."

"Yes, sir, you did. I've spoken with my uncle about that and arranged for a wagon to take you home this evening."

"About time." Bailey shifted in the chair with the grunting and mumbling that seemed a part of his every movement since the accident. He looked at Calvin, his face set in determined lines. "Not that I don't appreciate everything you've done for me. I am beholden to you." The words came out with obvious effort, against the grain of a man used to having others indebted to him and not the other way around.

Calvin took a seat opposite him and spread open the paper he had brought back from the bank. "I wished to speak with you, sir, regarding a matter of concern to us both."

"I suppose you mean my daughter. Beatrice Alice."

Calvin didn't answer directly. "Before I spoke with you, I wanted to come to you as a free man. That's why I was gone this morning. I went to the bank and paid off the lien on the property. You are not beholden to me, sir, but neither am I beholden to you. Not now."

Bailey studied the paper. "I suppose you had cash from the sale of your corn."

"And other things." He cleared his throat. "I know you are concerned that a farmer such as myself cannot provide for your daughter. So I've spent a good bit of time over the past weeks considering my financial situation." He sent up a short prayer. Would this idea work, his effort to reach out to Mr. Bailey in the language he understood best?

"This amount"—Calvin opened his book of accounts and pointed to the head of the first column of figures—"shows how much cash I have on hand after settling the debt with the bank." The second column read EXPENSES. "This is how much I expect to spend this year."

Bailey frowned. "That seems a trifle high."

"Not after I buy what I need to construct a covered bridge. I wanted to last year, and I'm sorry I didn't. I regret your accident and refuse to let it happen again to someone else."

Bailey harrumphed.

"But see here." The third column read INCOME. "By the fall, I will receive income from a small toll for crossing the bridge, as well as profit from this year's crop. If all goes as expected, my investment could double within twelve months."

Bailey leaned back, his face a mask, the one Calvin had seen when he had gone to him pleading for money to start up his farm. "This house is hardly more than a shack."

"But it won't always be that way. I'm sure you've heard the story about how my mother's family lived in a cave for part of the war, and now see their home. If your daughter marries me, sir, she may not always live in luxury— but she will never be in need. So help me God."

"And the extra seed corn you have on hand?" Bailey asked.

Would the man never let go of that corn? "I will give it to you, and you can do whatever you wish with it."

A small smile played around Bailey's lips. "I will pay you $1.50 a bushel. And I won't accept a penny less."

A dollar and a half? Could Calvin live with that? The seed wasn't worth that much, but. . . "I'll accept your terms."

"Very well." Bailey extended his hand. "You have treated me better than I deserve, Mr. Tuttle. And you appear to be a man of good business sense, as well as a man with the welfare of the community in his heart. If you choose to call on my daughter again, I will not stand in your way."

∽

The community of Maple Notch gathered to help Calvin with the bridge raising, and Beatrice couldn't wait to join the festivities. She put on his favorite pink dress. She had stitched a special sampler to present him on this auspicious occasion. SEEDTIME AND HARVEST HAVE NOT CEASED; A BRIDGE TO LOVE PROVIDES THE FEAST. The barn-like structure she had fashioned spanned a rippling brook, with lilac bushes growing on the banks, and was titled TUTTLE BRIDGE, 1817.

"Are you ready?" Papa came to the foot of the stairs. A slight limp was the only reminder of the awful accident that could have cost his life. Something had happened during his recovery; she couldn't believe the change in him.

"I've never seen you go to a barn raising before," she teased. Dressed as he was in Wellington boots and plain breeches, he didn't look like himself. She couldn't remember the last time she had seen him dressed in anything other than a waistcoat and trousers.

"We've never had a bridge raising in Maple Notch before. You look lovely, my dear." He offered her his arm. "I trust my appearance doesn't distress you."

"Not at all." She kissed his cheek. "I am proud of you."

The sun dappled the leaves of the trees, so very *green*, so right for the state of the *Verts Monts*—"Green Mountains." Beatrice inhaled the scent of bursting growth and fresh air, the feel of sunshine warming her skin, the sight of green deepening from the palest, almost white stems to the full-blown green of new grass. The Year of No Summer had passed, and 1817 promised to be a season of unparalleled growth.

But nothing mattered more to her than the man waiting at the bridge. As soon as they rounded the corner where they could see the river, Calvin stood out from all the others with his broad shoulders and his voice raised in instructions on the bridge building.

An invisible thread pulled his head in their direction as they approached. A smile as wide as the open sky bloomed on his face, and he ran toward the wagon. "Bea, Mr. Bailey. I've been waiting for you." He put his strong hands around Beatrice's waist and lifted her from the wagon. "With your permission, sir, there's something I want to show your daughter."

Papa nodded, and Calvin tugged her toward the stack of lumber waiting for the bridge raising. "There is something I must show you." He took her to the back of the pile, to a single log stretched between two tree stumps. What could he find so exciting about a piece of wood?

"You know the story of how my mother's family hid out in a cave during the Revolutionary War, and how Grandfather Tuttle was a Tory who didn't want his only surviving son to marry a patriot."

Beatrice nodded her head. Children from Maple Notch still camped out in the Reids' cave. But what did that have to do with the plank stretched out before them?

"And you probably know Pa helped them with their farm that summer."
Again Beatrice nodded.

"Pa told me about this once, but I had never seen it until I started cutting the timber we needed for the bridge. Look."

He pointed to the faded and scarred spot on the fresh-planed wood. Someone had carved something into the living wood years ago. Squinting, she managed to make out the letters. *JT* and *SR*. "Josiah Tuttle and Sally Reid."

"My parents. Their love crossed a chasm of divided loyalties and war and created a legacy that they passed on to me. I'm going to put this where everyone can see." He went down on one knee and took her hand in his. "Can we do the same, Miss Beatrice Alice Bailey? Can we build a bridge of love that will overcome the difficulties, whether natural or manmade, that come our way, with the help of the Lord?" He reached into his pocket and set a pocketknife on his palm.

Giddiness swept through her. She stilled her thoughts, her heart, her hands, and took the knife in her right hand. Bending over the board, she drove a straight line and added two loops. . .*B*. Again. *B*. A simple plus sign.

As her hand began the hard lines of the curve, she felt Calvin's hand settle over hers. He stood beside her, guiding her fingers as they carved a *C* and a *T*.

He studied her, his eyes dark with passion, and she felt breathless.

"My answer is. . ."

He took her hands in his.

"Yes."

LOVE'S RAID

Dedication

To my newest grandchild and only grandson, Isaiah Jaran. May you live up to your name, to proclaim the truth that the Lord is salvation.

Chapter 1

The grocer's wagon flew past Clara Farley as she walked down the road, the wheels spewing dirt and rocks that coated the skirt of the dress she had chosen for this special occasion.

The dust settled on Clara's glasses, and she dug blindly through her reticule, looking for the handkerchief she had tucked away earlier that morning. She rubbed the lenses while listening for approaching travelers. The road between Maple Notch and St. Albans carried a fair amount of traffic, but young Dixon had ridden as if the entire Confederate Cavalry chased him. Clara didn't intend to allow the next passerby to mow her down.

A glance back at the house she shared with her brother reminded Clara she had reached the midpoint to her destination. Either return home for a change of skirt and arrive late, or arrive on time with a dusty habit. She lifted her chin. She had never been late in her life, and she wouldn't start today—not with so much depending on the meeting at the bank. Picking up her skirts, she turned her face to the center of town.

By the time she reached the common ten minutes later, every man in the town center had gathered around the grocer's wagon. Among the mix stood one of the men she was supposed to meet at the bank in five minutes, the town constable, Daniel Tuttle. His brother Simeon, the banker, might be there as well, but Daniel stood head and shoulder taller than anyone else in town. She frowned. Had he forgotten their appointment?

Daniel looked straight at her and smiled, if that pained grimace could be called a smile, and touched the brim of his hat. So he hadn't forgotten their meeting, after all. She relaxed and waited to hear what news had the men so agitated.

Daniel's voice rose above the clamor. "If you'll all be quiet, Mr. Dixon will explain what happened this morning." He didn't speak louder. He didn't need to. He exuded the kind of confidence and control every successful schoolteacher mastered. If she could do half as well with her prospective students, she'd consider herself well ahead.

The men in the circle quieted down, and Dixon climbed back on the wagon.

"I had gone to St. Albans to make my usual deliveries like I do every Wednesday." Dixon allowed himself a self-satisfied smile at the mention of his marketing of Widow Lawson's fine, sharp cheese.

"T'weren't cheese that sent you back here quicker'n a jackrabbit," Brent Frisk joked. "'Sides, it looks like you still have the rounds of cheese there in the back of your wagon." He bent over and lifted one out of the bed as if to prove the truth of his statement. "So explain yourself."

Dixon's face blanched, and he looked at his feet. Clara inched forward, as eager as the gathered men to hear the news. Then his usual bonhomie reasserted itself, and he said in his best orator's voice, "Them Confederates have taken charge of St. Albans and robbed all their banks!"

Gasps echoed around the circle, obscuring anything else Dixon said.

"Them Rebs! All the way up here in Vermont?"

The question froze Clara to the core. Had the war, subject of many heated debates at Middlebury Female Seminary, arrived on her doorstep? It wasn't possible. She had spent hours tearing bandages, had read the accounts of Dorothea Dix and Clara Barton nursing on the battlefield, listened to her roommate Savannah's pining for her southern beau, mourned with pretty Miss Trudeau's grief when her fiancé had died at Gettysburg. But never, ever, had the war invaded Vermont until today. St. Albans was only a short ride away. She put her hand to her throat, checking that the top button was secure.

The men looked like they were ready to go to their homes, grab the nearest weapon, and race to St. Albans. These men, most of them unwilling or unable to go to a distant war, would fight like the old Green Mountain Boys militia when one of their own was threatened.

None of the men gathered had fought in this war and returned to tell about it—none except Daniel Tuttle, the newly appointed town constable. Her eyes sought him out. His right arm had clamped on to the stump of his left arm, as if by holding it tight he could hold in all the memories and feelings brought about by that war. His face darkened, but when he lifted his head moments later, his hazel eyes blazed. While the men continued throwing out suggestions, Daniel carried on a quiet conversation with Dixon. He nodded a couple of times before calling a halt to the hubbub around him.

"Looks like I'll have to earn my pay sooner than you expected." Daniel's lips lifted in a half smile. "Dixon thinks the folks of St. Albans fought back. I'm asking for a couple of deputies to ride with me and check out the situation."

Every man's hand shot into the air.

"I appreciate your willingness. Frisk, Gamble, you come with me. Dixon is in charge of gathering our local militia. Someone needs to stay close in case Johnny Reb decides to head our way next."

All around Clara, men straightened their shoulders.

"I'll send word once we've ascertained what's happened." Daniel jumped on the back of his horse faster than most men with the use of two arms, and the three men turned in Clara's direction. He paused in front of her. "I'm sorry to put off our business, Miss Farley."

Clara had almost forgotten her business with the Tuttles in the excitement of the announcement of battle at her doorstep. "Another time. Godspeed, Mr. Tuttle."

He touched the brim of his hat and kicked his horse into a gallop down the road past her farm.

∽

Men going into battle said they conjured up an image of the woman from back home whenever they wanted to remember there was life and beauty and reason after the ugliness of war.

Daniel Tuttle didn't have a sweetheart, but if he did, he'd bet she would have dark-auburn hair and ridiculous glasses that hid the beauty of eyes as gray as Clara Farley's. He knew the color, because he had spent enough time staring at her when they contested each other for every spelling bee at school. The change in her when he'd come home from the war had surprised him. But then, he had changed as well.

They had crossed the bridge heading into St. Albans when Daniel pulled up his horse. So far, no sign of any traffic ahead, nothing to mar this sunny autumn day with a hint of winter's chill in the air. "I'd better tell you what little I know. Dixon said there were two dozen of them rebels, more or less. One of them jumped on the steps of the hotel and shouted, 'This city is now in the possession of the Confederates States of America!' The soldiers herded everybody onto the town green. He said he was never so afraid in his life."

"So how'd he get away?"

"Dumb Rebs. They couldn't figure out if they were fighting a war or robbing a bank. As soon as they had their loot, they skedaddled out of there. Dixon headed back to Maple Notch to let us know."

Gamble scrunched up his face. "Do you think they'll take us for more of them Rebs?"

"Not likely." Daniel resisted the urge to scratch the stump, his constant reminder of the war. He grabbed his once-blue forage cap from his pocket and pulled it on his head. "We've all done business in St. Albans a time or two." He draped his rifle across his saddle horn and leaned forward. "Ready?"

Frisk and Gamble nodded, and the three of them took a slower pace as they approached town. They passed the still-smoldering remains of a burned-out woodshed. Daniel tightened his grip on his emotions. He didn't see any flames ahead, and no soot cloud darkened the sky. Perhaps this fire had no connection to the events of the day.

A group had gathered in front of one house, one that rivaled his grandparents' home for size and importance, and he recognized the home of Governor J. Gregory Smith. The governor was supposed to be in Montpelier this week, according to the paper. If he was at home. . .

Daniel sped up his horse.

"Halt!" A uniformed guard stopped him before he could approach the crowd. Daniel relaxed his face, making sure they could see the badge on his chest and the color of his cap.

"That's all right, Jones." A man dressed in the uniform of General Custer's cavalry strode up the path—the governor's brother, if Daniel remembered correctly. "Captain Tuttle, sir. Has the news of our little contretemps here this morning reached Maple Notch already?"

"Our grocer came to town making a delivery when the—incident—happened."

"Ah, yes. I remember seeing Dixon's wagon."

"We came to find out the true facts of the affair—and to learn if our militia could assist in hunting down the rebels."

Smith pushed his cap back on his head. "They've already hightailed back over the border to Canada, and we can't get to 'em there." He snorted in disgust. "They managed to make off with more than two hundred thousand dollars, and they killed a man and burnt down a woodshed, but that's all. Not much more than a skirmish."

Daniel doubted the folks of St. Albans would feel the same way, but after the battles the two soldiers had seen, he knew what Smith meant. "Send one of your men straightaway if they come back."

"The same to you." Smith turned his glare to the north, the direction where the rebels had fled. "I hope today isn't a portent of things to come—little bee stings up here in the north to distract the battles going on down south."

"Yes, sir." Daniel couldn't agree more. He had come home to escape the ravages of war, to heal, to recover his confidence, if he were honest with himself.

How could a man fight an enemy when he was missing half an arm?

～

After all the heated comments of the men gathered on the common, Daniel half expected to meet them racing down the road to St. Albans when he returned. But they stood in a straight line, Dixon inspecting their weapons and making notes on his grocers' pad. Every now and then, he motioned for his assistant to bring him something lacking in the man's kit. The group had doubled in size. Daniel spotted Clara's brother, Lewis, among the additions.

One of the Whitson twins noticed them first. He ran to his horse, his rump in the saddle before Daniel could open his mouth. "Where's the action?"

The gathering stilled with his shout.

Daniel waited until he reached the group on the common. "There isn't any."

"Are you saying they didn't rob the banks this morning?" Whitson demanded.

"I know what I saw." Dixon sounded tired, as if he had repeated his story countless times throughout the day.

"They escaped back to Canada, and we can't cross the border to chase them." Weariness washed over Daniel. This job was supposed to allow him time to recover, not demand he head back into battle. He longed to slip from his horse, eat a bite of supper, and relax, but the safety of Maple Notch came first.

What else? "They may come back and strike somewhere else next time. Be on the lookout for any strangers in town. We think the Rebs up in St. Albans came in two or three at a time. We'll post an extra guard by the bank, and we'll also patrol the roads leading into town." Roads left the town common in four directions: the one he had traveled that day, which meandered north to St. Albans; the one past his family's farm, going south to Burlington; the one heading east to Jeffersonville; and the one going west to Fairfax. He named the families and men responsible for patrolling each path.

The men scattered, talking amongst themselves. Only Frisk, Simeon, and a handful of others remained, the ones with homes and farms along the Old Bridge Road. They settled who would patrol the road that night, and the others left Simeon and Daniel alone.

"I'll look into hiring an extra guard for security at the bank." Simeon clutched the lapels of his coat close as the wind picked up and swirled leaves in their direction. "Although I've had trouble finding good men who aren't already working."

"I'll come by more often." Daniel swallowed a yawn.

Simeon peered into his brother's eyes. "Come home with me for a bite to eat. My Molly will have plenty fixed."

Daniel appreciated the offer and the good intentions he knew lay behind it. But he refused—not for the first time.

"Not this evening. I will come on Sunday, as usual. No, a simple dinner and a good night's rest are all I need." He managed a thin smile. "We can expect Miss Farley to present herself bright and early tomorrow."

Simeon's gaze wandered to the east side of the common, where their grandparents' house stood. "If she has her way, you will be our guest, like it or not, before too much longer."

Daniel shrugged. He'd seek a room in town if the house sold. How could he explain the desperate need for solitude that quieted his soul and restored his spirit, which needed healing as much as—nay, more than—his arm?

Which was why he'd just as soon Clara Farley did *not* get her wish to buy the Bailey Mansion.

But he didn't say any of that to his brother. Instead, he tipped his cap and said, "See you in the morning, then."

∽

Thursday, October 20, 1864

At least the day's delay had given Clara the opportunity to brush the mud splattered on her skirt. They were still in mourning. Papa's death only a few weeks after her graduation from the seminary still shocked her. God had blessed her with the will and training to be independent and strong. She needed it.

She paused in front of the door to Lewis's bedroom and lifted her hand to knock. No, she decided. He had been up late, patrolling the road to St. Albans, perhaps the most important route of all since it led straight through St. Albans and on into Canada. Even through the closed door, she could hear his loud snore. At least he had taken responsibility for the patrol.

Don't be so uncharitable, she scolded herself. A good four years younger than she was, he was hardly more than a boy pushed into the position of titular head of the family far too soon. In an unusual move, Papa had made her guardian of Lewis's portion of their inheritance until he reached his twenty-fifth birthday.

She descended the stairs and headed for the kitchen. After the delay in meeting with the Tuttle brothers yesterday, she had expected nerves to overtake her this morning, but she felt quite the opposite. Perhaps the trouble in St. Albans had put her dreams into perspective.

Or perhaps it was the memory of the solid confidence that oozed from Daniel Tuttle. He made her feel safe, and she was certain he would be fair. His brother Simeon, while a good man, was a banker and the grandson of a banker, and had about as much charm as most bankers she knew. In other words, like a caterpillar crawling across a leaf.

Wind rattled the windows, and she hoped Lewis would think to chop up some more firewood before cold weather settled in for the long haul. After she finished the dishes and set aside two muffins with jam on a plate for him when he awakened, she checked her appearance one last time in the hall mirror. The deprivations of war and her wire-framed glasses had done nothing to soften her pinched face. Her thick, not-quite-auburn hair was her one vanity, and she refused to feel bad about it. For this business occasion, she pulled it back in a bun and covered it with a dark-brown hairnet. She dressed simply. The craze for hoops puzzled her. What sensible woman would want her ease of movement restricted so by a contraption wider than most doors? She had bought one hooped dress for her graduation and didn't even wear it then, due to her father's ill health. Today she settled for a flowing skirt that would allow her to check out each and every room of the Bailey Mansion for its suitability as a girls' school.

At least she hoped she could check out the house that day. No one expected the eldest Tuttle brother, Hiram, to take a break from his farm as the harvest season drew to a close. Daniel might well be following up on yesterday's events. She sighed at the thought of facing Simeon alone, afraid his banker's face would put an end to all of her hopes and dreams.

She stopped by Lewis's room one last time on the way out. Groans issued from within, and she tapped on the door. "I've left you breakfast on the table." She took his mutterings as an acknowledgment and headed out.

At least today no one raced past her as she walked into town. She did run into Jericho Jones patrolling the road. He reined in his horse when he spotted her. "Where are you headed this fine morning, Miss Farley?"

"I have business in town."

Jericho frowned. "Can't it wait? We're encouraging people to stay close to home until we know those Rebels have disappeared for good."

Clara lifted her chin. "I'm not afraid. I have business in town that won't wait." She relaxed her posture. She knew she appeared haughty when she stiffened up like that. "Besides, I'm sure I'm perfectly safe with you and the other fine gentlemen of Maple Notch patrolling the roads."

He smiled his acknowledgment. "Nonetheless, I'll come back by, to check that no harm comes to you."

"Thank you, Mr. Jones." She didn't want to offend him. Enough talk circulated around town already about her progressive views. What had ever possessed her to ask at a ladies' meeting what was so terrible about women getting the vote, after all?

The crisp air encouraged a brisk walk, and she took quick, firm steps, noting spots where she would stop on the way home to look for leaves. Ever since childhood she had loved collecting leaves, but arriving at a business meeting with a bag of damp mulch wouldn't convey the impression she wished to create. If all proceeded as she hoped, she might indulge herself on the way home.

She only caught sight of Jericho Jones' figure one more time before she reached the town green. Somewhat relieved not to see the militia gathered in the center, she walked past the church building, down the west side of the square, to Bailey's Bank. Baruch Whitson stood straight and motionless as an iron post by the door. She looked up the long length of him and blinked. He reminded her a little of the guards she had heard about at the palace where the Queen of England lived.

"Mr. Whitson? Are you keeping all our valuables safe today?"

"As far as it's in my power, ma'am, yes." He winked at her, and she relaxed. His solemnity the moment before had frightened her. He opened the door, and she walked in, only to discover long lines of people had arrived before her.

Ahead of her, she saw a former schoolmate, Margaret Beacham, her reticule held tight in her hands. "Margaret? What's the cause for all the business this morning?"

Lines crawled over Margaret's forehead as she wrinkled her face. "Didn't you hear what happened yesterday, how those awful Rebels robbed the banks in St. Albans?"

Before Clara could answer, Margaret continued, "Of course you did. That's why you're here. To get your money before those Confederates rob us all blind. It's what any sensible person would do."

Clara froze. All her money, every penny left to her by her parents except for the house and its furnishings, lay in an account in this bank.

What would she do if it was robbed?

Chapter 2

C lara breathed in, counted to ten, then slowly released her breath. "That won't happen. Forewarned is forearmed, they say, and everyone is taking precautions against an attack here. Why, there's even an extra guard outside."

"What good is one armed guard against a platoon? They tried to burn down Governor Smith's home yesterday." If possible, Margaret's eyes widened even farther. "What if they try to burn down the bank, with us inside it?" She looked ready to bolt.

"If they do that, they can't get the money." Clara had seen this kind of hysteria before, when the prediction that "this war will be over by Christmas" had proved untrue. Once again, unnecessary fear stood ready to grab people by their throats, this time in her hometown.

"That's true." Margaret bobbed her head and inched forward in line.

Clara looked for Simeon Tuttle in his office but discovered him deep in conversation with the older Dixon, one of the wealthiest men in town. Given the crush of people at the bank today, she didn't expect he'd have time to see her. Her shoulders slumped. How long must her dream take second place behind more important matters?

A hand tapped her shoulder, and she jumped. She whirled around and found herself face-to-face with Daniel Tuttle.

"I'm sorry. I didn't mean to startle you."

Her hand flew to her mouth, and she pulled it away. "I was gathering wool, I'm afraid." She refused to look like a scatterbrained woman in front of this man. "I was hoping we could meet today to discuss our business, but your brother has his hands full this morning."

Daniel's eyes swept the crowd. Clara had the feeling he knew not only the names and ages of every person present but also the number, make, and model of every weapon brought into the bank. He brought his gaze back to Clara's face. "Give me half an hour. I'll meet you at the house. I would offer you a seat in our waiting room, but. . ."

"It's already occupied." Three more people had come in behind Clara while she was talking with Daniel. Pastor Beaton, who had come to the church after she left for the women's seminary, almost bumped into her. "Are you waiting in line, Miss Farley?" At her response in the negative, he swept forward to take her place behind Margaret.

Stymied by yet another delay to her business with the Tuttles, Clara considered stopping by the café for a cup of tea and a slice of toast while she waited. The establishment had closed for the day, as had Dixon's Mercantile and every other business in town except for the bank. The air was turning cold, so Clara went to the one place she was certain would have open doors—the church.

The building had changed some over the years. The elders had even considered enticing Richard Upjohn to design a new building. Clara was glad the congregation had decided against it. Comfortable pews had replaced backless benches, and an organ accompanied music once sung a cappella. A bell tower replaced the old steeple. Yet for all the changes, she felt a peace, knowing that people had come here to meet with God ever since the town was first established in 1763.

Her hand ran over the plates indicating who had donated money for which pew: IN LOVING MEMORY OF STEPHEN REID. . .HIRAM BAILEY. . . SOLOMON TUTTLE. . .JAMES DIXON. Founding fathers, all. The newest and shiniest one read IN LOVING MEMORY OF ALBERT L. FARLEY. Her eyes welled. "Oh, Papa, I miss you so!"

She sat down in the pew marked with her father's name and said a prayer that she had made the right decision regarding her inheritance. Lewis wasn't entirely convinced of the wisdom of her plan.

But every time she asked the Lord, she received the same answer—peace. Straightening her shoulders, she picked up her reticule and headed out the door.

∽

"Keep an eye out for trouble." Daniel spoke so only Whitson could hear. "I don't like the looks of that crowd."

"Yes, sir. Do you want me to stay inside the bank?"

Daniel considered the idea but shook his head. "Simeon will let you know if he wants you inside. Until then, I need you out here, keeping an eye on any trouble coming from the outside. At least no strangers have shown their faces in town today."

"Not that I've seen. You can count on me, Captain." Whitson's eyes gleamed, almost as if he wished some action would come his way.

"I'll be over at the Bailey House if you need to find me." Daniel shook off the feeling of unease that settled on him like a swarm of black flies in June and instead focused on his upcoming meeting with Clara Farley. "Go ahead and lease it. Sell it, if she'll take it." That had been Simeon's advice when

Daniel had sought him out a few minutes earlier. "With the run on the bank today, we could use the funds."

But Daniel didn't want to stay inside for any length of time, not until things returned to normal. A quick run through—that's all he would allow Miss Farley today.

As he thought of her, she stepped out of the shadow of the church and into the sunshine. The autumn light shown on her dark-chestnut hair and bounced off the sheen of her unrelieved black clothing. In spite of her severe hairstyle, modest style of dress, and those ridiculous spectacles, she couldn't hide her beauty. He kept his smile inside. She wouldn't want him saying so. From what he remembered of the dark-haired beauty, she'd keep discussion on a strictly business level. She would never use feminine wiles to gain an advantage. . .and was convinced she had no wiles to try in any case.

A fine mind and a sharp tongue, that described Clara Farley well enough. The day suddenly seemed more pleasing as he crossed the common, rubbing his hands in anticipation of the lively discussion he would have with the young miss. He lengthened his strides to make sure he arrived a few steps before she did.

"I hope I have not kept you waiting." Her soft voice didn't fool him, not when he knew her sharp eyes had marked his progress across the common.

"Not at all. I'm sorry I had to ask you to wait." He extracted a key from his pocket and opened the door. Grandfather Bailey was one of the few people in Maple Notch who bothered with locked doors. After the troubles yesterday, the precaution no longer seemed so strange.

How cold and quiet the house seemed, even though Daniel lived there now. The staircase gleamed as much as ever, and sun poured through the windows as it always had, but without the laughter of children, the smell of his grandfather's pipe, Cook's delicacies baking in the kitchen. . . what life was left in the house had died along with his mother.

If Clara noticed his hesitation, she didn't show it. "I've never been up-stairs." She set her right foot on the first step and paused to look up the wide sweep of the staircase.

"Grandfather liked to do everything on a grand scale." He smiled at her as he offered her his right arm.

She accepted without even glancing at the place where his left arm should be and ascended the stairs. "I was thinking the treads here are wide enough to allow numbers of people to move at a time. They're not narrow and restrictive, like some I've seen."

His hand tingled where their arms were linked. Upon reaching the second floor, she studied the stairs continuing on to the nurseries. "I'll check there later."

Clara went to the room at the front of the house. "This must have been your grandparents' bedroom."

He nodded. "Simeon removed a few pieces, but we will rent the rest furnished, if you like."

She scrunched her face and pulled a folding ruler from her pocket. "I think the space might be better used as a classroom. Do you mind?" She handed him the end of the ruler and gestured at the wall. Bemused, he watched her unfold it, then run it the length and breadth of the room, marking down numbers in a little notebook. She stuck the pencil behind her right ear and measured the windows next. She couldn't quite reach the top of the window pane, so he lifted his long arm and held the ruler for her. His eyes fell on the notebook, where he saw a rough sketch that approximated the layout of the room.

"I didn't realize you had studied architectural drawing."

She peered at him over the top of her glasses. "What, this? We studied room arrangement at the seminary, how to make the most of. . ." She paused in midsentence. "But you don't want to know all of that. Let me see the other bedrooms on this floor, please."

So there was a proper way to decorate a room? His lips curled at the thought. His mother had known how to make a house a home. Whether the small cabin she had lived in at the beginning of her marriage—now dubbed the newlyweds' cabin by the family—or the Bailey house, she had placed her own stamp on it. He reached down and lifted a pot with dried lilacs in it and felt her spirit in the empty spaces of the room.

Unlike Simeon's wife. Molly owned many beautiful things but could never make them coordinate. Clara could, he was certain of it. He'd have to find an excuse to visit the Farleys' home one day.

Clara made her way to his mother's room next. Daniel hesitated at the door. He knew that the writing desk still held the paper and quills she had used to write letters to his father during their secret courtship, when his Aunt Peggy had acted as a go-between. Once again, out came the folding ruler and notebook, neat figures and drawings added on its pages.

Did the woman intend to measure every room in the house? He thought about the old servants' quarters on the third floor. No one had been up there since he'd returned home, and cobwebs and who knew what else had collected over time. That decided him.

"I promised Simeon I would come back to the bank quickly. Things are too unsettled for me to spend much time on personal business." He stretched his lips in what his youngest sister insisted was a dazzling smile. "Perhaps we can arrange another time next week, when we are more certain if Maple

Notch will be affected?"

She opened her mouth and then closed it and smiled. . .her own version of a polite smile to match his. "I had my heart set on seeing the house this week. I will be here at ten o'clock tomorrow morning. Of course, if those Confederates do make another showing, I will reschedule."

He found himself agreeing to her suggestion. He escorted her outside to the corner where the road to her home ran, glad to see Jericho Jones patrolling the road. "Any sign of danger?"

"Not a thing. I've ridden down as far as the bridge to St. Albans, and you wouldn't know there'd been so much as a gun fired yesterday." He nodded at Clara.

"You should be safe heading home, Miss Farley."

She graced Jones with a genuine smile, not the polite version Daniel had seen earlier. "I'm certain of it, Mr. Jones. The Lord is paving my way with sunshine." She gestured to the sun directly overhead. "I intend to enjoy every minute of this beautiful weather for as long as it lasts." Picking up the edges of her skirt, she set off at a brisk pace.

She didn't look back to catch Daniel watching her when she stopped to examine scarlet maple leaves where they had fallen to the ground. When her posture relaxed, she looked beautiful—demure, even. A woman like that was open to life and love.

Daniel found himself glad that he had arranged another meeting with Miss Farley.

⁓

Clara had chosen a sensible violet gingham for today's meeting. After wearing the same outfit for two days, she decided she wanted a change of dress. A restless night had turned into a restless morning. So taken up was her mind with today's meeting with the Tuttles, she'd had trouble focusing during her quiet time. Prayers for a positive resolution to their business mixed together with an occasional guilty prayer for the people of St. Albans and others fighting far away.

Lewis was already in the kitchen when she came down. He looked her up and down, and she felt heat rushing into her cheeks. "What has you up so early?" she asked, more to divert his attention from her appearance than because she wanted to know.

"The lads and I want to check out a bit of business." He grinned his cocky smirk. "We could use some extra income if your plans go through." He looked at her again and smiled. "Looking as good as you do today, I'm sure you'll succeed." He poured himself a cup of coffee.

The strong scent of the hot beverage wafted across her nostrils. "I'll take a cup of that, if you please."

"It's strong." He poured her a cup.

"I know. The stuff you make always is. That's what I need this morning." She rubbed her eyes, yawned, and took a sip. No stronger than she expected, but still she frowned and shivered.

"Cream? sugar?" Lewis stirred some more into his cup.

"No. It doesn't make it any more. . .palatable." She slathered a slice of bread with honey butter. Sweets called for a strong beverage, like coffee. "Do you want a hot breakfast?"

"No." He grabbed an apple from the barrel. "Don't wait supper on me either. We may be gone overnight."

"What are you up to? Who are you going with?"

"Oh, the usual group. Bradford, Dupre, Ford."

He hadn't told her everything, but he was a man. She couldn't treat him like a child reporting to his parents. "Godspeed then, brother."

He leaned over and kissed her cheek. "I'll take that as good luck."

Lewis wasn't big on faith, one of her major prayer concerns alongside the war and her school. From the window, she watched him strap a satchel behind him on his favorite horse, Shadow. The dappled gray matched his impulsive temperament, while the silvery-white Misty suited her far better.

What business did he have in mind? In the wake of Wednesday's attack and yesterday's panic at the bank, she was glad someone had found reason for hope. *I'll take that as a sign of things to come.* She smiled at the thought. After she put away the breakfast things, she draped her coat about her and started down the road to town.

Cold snapped in the air, but the sky remained cloud-free. Before long, they would have the first snow of the season, but this was perfect weather for walking. Jones passed her on the way into town. His posture had relaxed since yesterday; he no longer peered into the trees, ready to jump at shadows.

Before she arrived at the town common, she saw Daniel riding in her direction. When he reached her, he dismounted. "Simeon wants to meet with us first to review your financial information."

Clara's heart skipped. That sounded promising. "Certainly. I have the information right here."

She expected Daniel to climb back on the horse, but instead he ambled beside her. They walked in silence for a short time. She was about to ask for news from St. Albans when he said, "I love walking through the woods in the autumn. 'Tis one of the things I missed."

Clara's travels were limited to a school trip to Seneca Falls to discuss the importance of the 1848 convention about women's rights. She would enjoy the opportunity to travel more. . .but not under the circumstances that had dragged Daniel away from home.

"Not that I missed our winters. They would have made camp life miserable." He chuckled.

"You can laugh about it?"

The amused sound stopped. "There was a camaraderie among the men, a sense of purpose, much as my grandfather must have felt when fighting for independence. That, and the music. There's nothing like music to ready men for battle."

"I am thankful for your service. Slavery has been a blight on this country ever since the beginning. If our Founding Fathers had taken a bolder stand then, there wouldn't have been a need for this war. For your sacrifice." She touched him on the shoulder above the arm that ended at the elbow. He jerked away.

"It is what it is."

They had reached the common. Daniel tethered his horse in front of the bank and led her inside. A few customers milled about doing business, but with none of the panic she had observed yesterday. Pastor Beaton stood at one of the windows, perhaps rethinking whatever business he had conducted yesterday. She hoped people would reopen their accounts for the Tuttles' sake. For the town's sake. A town needed a strong bank.

Daniel directed Clara to Simeon's office. As soon as he saw them, Simeon stood and bowed in Clara's direction. "Welcome, Miss Farley. Please take a seat. Would you like a cup of coffee? Tea?"

Clara cleared her throat. "Perhaps a glass of water?" Her throat might not manage the discussion otherwise.

Simeon motioned a clerk nearby and told him what was needed. Daniel settled in the other chair, drumming the fingers of his right hand on its arm. Clara felt his eyes studying her, a grin at his brother's antics lurking behind those light-brown eyes.

"Study your opponent for signs of their mood before speaking." Miss Featherton's words on conducting business came to Clara. *"Often you can gain more ground by taking a side path than by a direct approach."*

Daniel's posture told Clara this meeting was Simeon's show. Whatever reservations and opinions he might have about the lease didn't factor into Simeon's work with the numbers.

As for his brother? She couldn't read Simeon Tuttle as easily, aside from the treatment offered a favored customer. Perhaps he was glad that someone, anyone, wanted to do business in Maple Notch after yesterday's run on the bank. His eyes wandered to the cigar box on his desk. If she had been a man, he might have offered her one. Perhaps she could ask if she could take one home to Lewis; he would enjoy it. The thought brought a smile to her lips, but she refrained from making the request. She would best serve her interests with him by displaying her fine grasp of finances, as Miss Featherton had so often encouraged.

She dug her folder out of her carrying case and placed it on his desk. "I have brought an accounting of my finances, as well as my business plan, along with me today."

"How well prepared you are." A smile flitted across Simeon's face. "I have the record of your account at the bank in front of me." He laid the two documents side by side for comparison. Daniel slipped behind him and bent over his brother's back, a slim shadow of Simeon's more rotund figure. Clara expected Simeon to raise questions, but Daniel spoke first.

"I see there is a monthly stipend drawn on the account in your brother's name. A generous amount, by all accounts."

Clara felt a slight heat pulse in her cheeks. "My father began the practice, and I decided to continue it."

"But he is otherwise provided for? He has no claim on the estate?"

Anger raised the heat level on her face. "The disposition of my father's estate is none of your concern. I assure you that the money in the account under my name belongs to me."

"I didn't mean to imply otherwise."

Simeon looked up at the sharp tone in the exchange between the two of them. He smiled with his usual good humor. "We here at Bailey Bank have always appreciated the confidence your family has shown in our humble institution. I hope we can continue to do business together for years to come." A serious expression replaced his smile. "Please tell me more about your plans for a school. Is there truly enough demand that you believe a seminary here in Maple Notch will fare as well as the one you attended in Middlebury?"

Clara took a deep breath before answering. While the subject of education for women and the broader aspects of women's suffrage enflamed her heart, she didn't want to frighten the good men of Maple Notch with her progressive ideas. "I believe women need to prepare as fully for our place in society as men do. After primary school, our options are limited." She took a page from the folder and pushed it across the desk at him. "Here is my estimate of growth, starting with a small class in January. I expect full enrollment within ten years' time."

"Ten years?" Daniel's interruption ridiculed the idea. "In a decade, you will most likely be married, with a home and children to care for. What will happen to your school then?"

Clara counted under her breath before answering. "My business plan allows for additional personnel as the student body grows. Even if I am married with a dozen children, I expect to continue my involvement with the school." *Read my plan before you condemn me.*

Simeon looked up from the document. "She does appear to have laid a solid foundation for the school."

Daniel grasped the paper and ran his finger down the page without taking time to read it properly. "It still is a risk."

"All business contains an amount of risk," Simeon said.

Clara wondered if she should sequester herself from the brothers' quarrel or argue her point. She bit her lip. The words on paper expressed them as clearly as she could out loud. If she spoke, her emotions would carry her away...and she might lose her chance. She stared out the window, at the dust obscuring the common as surely as her doubts clouded her judgment.

Daniel saw the dust at the same time. "A posse of horses is headed straight this way!"

Gunfire cracked in the lobby.

Chapter 3

Daniel had his hand on the door leading to the lobby when it opened from the other side. A man much Daniel's size, but with a complete set of limbs and his face partially covered with a bandanna, grabbed Simeon by the arms. As he often did, Daniel reached with both arms, forgetting his left arm ended at the elbow, and the effort threw him off balance. When he stumbled, a second robber came up behind Daniel and removed the pistol from his holster, twisting his one good arm behind him before leading them out like condemned prisoners.

Gangly Pastor Beaton opened and shut his mouth. A third robber, an identical triplet to the other two in size and build, pointed to the bag in his hand. He went down the line, gesturing for each person to place their valuables inside.

"Are you Confederates?" Beaton asked. For answer, the robber pointed to his jacket. Daniel caught sight of a red rectangle; it looked like a Dixie flag, marked with a dark blue X and thirteen white stars. The jacket wasn't part of any official uniform, but Daniel had seen soldiers on both sides of the line with little by way of official regalia.

Watch, observe—find a way to chase these men down. Daniel's left arm ached with uselessness. If he had two good arms, why, he'd throw the man holding him onto the ground, grab his rifle, and change the situation in a heartbeat.

The man beside him prodded Simeon to his feet and pointed to the safe. Simeon looked at Daniel under his dark eyebrows, begging for—what? A miracle? A whole man for a brother instead of the weakling who had returned? Daniel twisted, but his captor tightened his grip.

While Simeon turned the lock on the safe, Daniel checked out the safety of everyone else in the lobby. A white-faced Clara stood beside the only other woman present in the bank at the hour, Myra Johnson, the bank's one female employee. A fourth robber crowded the male customers over beside the women. Although visibly shaken, no one appeared injured. So who had exchanged gunshots? Had anyone been wounded? Not one of the Confederates, unless he lay bleeding outside. Baruch Whitson?

A chill that had nothing to do with the October weather passed over

254

Daniel. He twisted again, harder this time, but his captor steadied the barrel of a Colt revolver, muzzle still hot and rich with gunpowder, against his temple. Daniel ceased his movement.

The first robber returned with Simeon, a bag heavy with cash and coins in his free hand. Simeon's face had taken on a pale shade of green. It would serve the robbers right if he vomited all over their shoes. Or it might stir their anger, and they might take it out on the nearest target. His brother. Daniel's stomach clenched at his helplessness. What he wouldn't give for two good arms.

The man holding Simeon took his keys and tossed them to a Confederate before tying him up. The other robber went into the office and found an extra set of keys. Meanwhile, Daniel's legs were being tied together by his captor so he couldn't run. Then the man secured Daniel's arms, as well. Satisfied at last, the robber joined the others, who left by the back door, one man keeping his weapon trained on their prisoners until they all exited. Before anyone moved, they heard the click of the key in the door and the pounding of hooves into the dirt.

To Daniel's surprise, Beaton moved first, coming to Daniel's side and untying the knots as simply as he would a pair of shoes. "Are you all right?" The preacher helped Daniel to his feet.

Daniel shrugged. "You take care of the others here. I have to go after them." He reached to his belt loop for a set of keys he kept hidden.

Whitson sat on the ground next to the door, hands, feet, and mouth bound, blood trickling from a wound to his shoulder. Daniel dropped down beside him. "No one was supposed to be hurt."

"No one told the robbers that." Whitson half smiled. "You go after them. It's a clean wound. I can wait."

Daniel hesitated. The robbers had taken his pistol with them, so he'd have to go to the jailhouse for a weapon. The mare that he had left tethered to the railing before his meeting with Simeon and Clara—that seemed so long ago—had disappeared. Sweeping his gaze around the square, he spotted no other horses. They must have been frightened or led away. A fifth member of the gang? He'd lose more time going to the livery after he had his weapon.

"I'll see about a horse. And then I'll take care of Mr. Whitson." Clara's quiet voice spoke from behind him. "You go on ahead."

⁓

Clara had followed Daniel outside. Had he realized one important clue the robbers had given away? He must have. She wouldn't waste his time now discussing it.

She had seen Daniel look around for his horse seconds after she had, and after speaking to him, she took off down the west road, where the livery sat a short distance from the common. Mack Jenson was forking fresh hay into the troughs for the animals when she reached the stables.

"Mr. Jenson. The constable has need of your three fastest horses."

"What's happened to his'n? Is she lame?" Jenson laid the hay fork down.

Clara didn't want to start the rumors flying, but it couldn't be helped. "No. A gang robbed the Bailey Bank just now. They took all the horses." When Jenson raised his eyebrow, she added, "I'm getting another mount for him and his deputies while he gets his guns. Hurry!"

"Too bad he can't have Lightning. Already rented him out last night to a customer intent on some serious revelry down in Burlington." Jenson blew out his cheeks and tapped a pair of tongs on each stall door as he passed. He paused in front of a stall that housed a palomino. "Spotty here's the next best." He continued down the line, picking out two more. "I'm surprised I didn't hear anything. I was shoeing horses a little earlier. Maybe it drowned out the noise." He wiped the back of his hand on his face, revealing a pale white patch. "Wait. Was that a gunshot I heard?"

"I'm sure they'll publish the details later." Clara didn't want to get caught up in a round of twenty questions with the livery owner. She hurried to get the saddle Jenson indicated for the last horse.

Halfway around the common, she met Daniel with Isaiah Dixon and the pastor by his side. "You got extra horses. Good." Daniel looked at the road beneath their feet. "Too much traffic passes this way for me to tell which direction they went."

"They didn't come by the store. I would have heard them," Dixon said.

"Mr. Jenson doesn't think they went by the livery," Clara said, "but he can't be sure."

"So they didn't go east or west, which leaves north and south." Daniel took one set of reins from her and swung onto Spotty's back, while the other two men mounted their horses. "We'll start with the north road and check for signs they've left the traveled path. They're not going to waltz into St. Albans."

"So you think they're the same men who robbed the banks in St. Albans?"

Daniel's face hardened. Clara almost bit her tongue. "Do you have another idea?"

She shook her head. "Just a possibility. We can talk about it later if you don't find them."

"I'll hold you to it. I don't want you going home until we've checked the north road." His fiery eyes held hers for a moment; then he dug his knees into the horse's side and they galloped away.

"He just told me to stay in town," Clara said under her breath. She blasted out her frustration between her teeth. "And I won't get to look at the Bailey Mansion today, either." She glanced at the sky. "If I believed more in signs, I would think You were telling me that the school was a bad idea."

So Daniel didn't want her going home along the road to St. Albans. His suggestion should rile her feathers, but instead, she felt warm and cozy, like a chick under its mother's wings. What should she do instead? She checked her reticule and found a few loose coins, enough for a bowl of soup and cornbread with a glass of milk at Fannie's Café. What would she do if Daniel hadn't returned by the evening? Her lips curved at the thought. She would have to head home before the sun deserted the sky, whether or not the constable had returned to town.

But as early as it was, Daniel still might find quick success, and she wouldn't need to spend her money on lunch, after all. A bird called from overhead and landed on the roof of the church. "That's a good place to wait." She walked through the always-open doors and took a seat beneath one of the windows.

I could have been killed! Fears she had been holding at bay rushed in, and she shivered inside her warm cloak. "Take ahold of yourself, Clara Farley." She forced herself to speak clearly, stopping the chattering of her teeth. "Nothing happened to you."

But it had. The consequences of the robbery crashed home.

The bank was robbed.

All my money was in the bank.

She stared at the empty cross high on the wall behind the pulpit. "Does that mean I've lost all my money? Everything Father left to provide for us?"

She sank to the kneeling rack in front of her. Somewhere a door opened, but she didn't stir. If she looked like a pious woman at prayer, no one would bother her. Only she and God knew the truth: She couldn't tear her thoughts away from the empty bank vault. The palette of her future, so recently as full of color as the forests in fall, was now as stark and relentless as bare trees in winter. She sniffled.

"Miss Farley? Is that you?"

Daniel Tuttle. She didn't want him to guess the cause of her dismay, not until she thought of a way out of her predicament. She sucked in her breath, dabbed a discreet handkerchief to her cheeks, and stood to her feet.

"Mr. Tuttle. Back so soon?"

"We followed the road into St. Albans and didn't catch sign the robbers passed that way. A winter storm met us on our way back." He pointed to the darkening windows. "Let me escort you home before the road becomes impassable."

She had gone about in bigger storms than this, but she nodded her acquiescence. "I'd best get home. Lewis will become worried about me if I am out in a storm."

"Do you wish to ride?" Daniel gestured to Spotty. Clara looked up at the horse's head, tall even for a horse, and full of spirit. "I'd rather walk, thank you."

Amusement lit his eyes, but he didn't say anything. "I'll lead him, then, and ride him back. Don't want to get caught in the storm myself."

Outside the church, the temperature had dropped, and wind howled through the trees on the common, stripping them of the few leaves left on the branches. She tugged the hood of her cape around her head and tightened the strings.

Daniel waited until she finished pulling on her gloves before he began walking to the northwest corner of the common, which headed toward St. Albans. "At least the wind is at our back. We won't be fighting it."

The wind did push her forward, speeding her steps. They walked in silence until they passed the building where the Widow Landry took in laundry, the last dwelling in the town proper. Snow sifted from the skies as they reached the open road. Daniel said, "I'd like to hear your theory about the robbers."

So he remembered. First she had a question to ask. "Did you hear them say anything?"

Individual snowflakes landed on his forehead as he scowled in concentration. After a long moment's thought, he said, "No."

"Neither did I."

"You think there was a reason for that? They didn't want to give away their status as Confederates by their accents?"

She shook her head and then realized he probably couldn't see her in the swirling snow. "I don't think that's it. From what I heard about St. Albans, they claimed the town for the Confederacy quite boldly."

He murmured his agreement.

"I'm afraid it's something else."

He paused midstride and turned her to him. "Go ahead. Spit it out."

"What if they didn't say anything because. . .we'd recognize their voices?"

Chapter 4

Clara waited for Daniel's answer, but he was already shaking off her suggestion. "We *saw* them. We'd have known them."

Her lips thinned into a straight line. "They all wore much the same clothes, and not more than two inches difference in height stood between them. With hats and bandannas hiding most of their faces, we couldn't see any facial features or hair. I don't think I'd recognize my own brother in that getup. Would you?"

He started walking again, and she hurried to catch up. When she opened her mouth to speak, he lifted a finger to his lips for silence, his brows creased in thought. Maybe he was like Papa that way; he would consider facts presented to him before making a decision. They strode along for several yards, the horse following docilely behind them.

At last Daniel broke the silence. "That makes my job easier. . .and harder."

The faraway look in his eyes didn't invite confidences, so she didn't comment. The brisk pace he set generated warmth as they plodded ahead through snow that began to stick to patches of ground away from the road. She hoped Lewis had decided to come home early after all, not staying out late as he'd expected. A light in the window and warmth in the house would be most welcome.

When they climbed the last rise before her farm and she saw that the house remained unlit and unwelcoming, Clara suppressed a sigh.

"No one's home?"

She shook her head, and he frowned.

"I hate to think of you out here alone with those robbers about."

"No one will hurt me." She had learned how to present a brave front from her days as an assistant teacher with Miss Featherton at Middlebury.

Daniel insisted on seeing her to the front door.

"Do you want to come in for a quick cup of hot tea?"

"I've got a long ways to go before I sleep." Daniel tipped his hat, and she could see that the storm had done nothing to dim the fire in his eyes. "Thank you for the offer."

She shut the door behind her and shivered, whether from the banked fire or from the absence of both Daniel and Lewis, she couldn't tell.

∾

Daniel climbed onto Spotty's back and spared a moment to stare at the dark, lonely cottage. He wished he could whisk Clara away to a cozy fireside with the blink of an eye, some place where she could be waited on and warmed instead of having to do the work of two people. That brother of hers never had been much good. Off gallivanting today, no doubt. *I hope he's stuck somewhere cold and unpleasant.* Daniel shook the thought off as soon as it occurred to him. Lewis might be no good, but he was all Clara had since her father's death. Imagine his life without his brothers Hiram or Simeon.

He clucked, and the horse started moving, head bowed into the wind. Daniel debated walking instead—it would keep him warmer—but decided against it. Better to cover the distance in less time.

Thinking of Hiram, Daniel remembered that his brother had invited him to the family farm today, with news of the progress regarding their grandparents' house. Snow stuck to the brim of Daniel's hat. Hiram wouldn't be surprised if he didn't come in this weather. Daniel had asked his nearest neighbor to deliver the news about the bank robbery. With dark falling fast, Daniel would spend the night at the Bailey house in solitude, the way he liked it.

The way he had always liked it. So why did the image of a certain auburn beauty measuring the parlor now intrude on his thoughts? Two lonely hearts—that was all. Snowy winter nights called for cozy couples in front of warm fires. He straightened his shoulders and encouraged Spotty to move faster.

He might paint a pretty picture, but such was not for him. Would never be for him.

No one would want a one-armed man who couldn't even defend his own bank.

∾

Daniel didn't make it to see Hiram on Saturday either. In the morning, he opened shutters to a world bristling with ice, although the remains of last year's grass showed where a dog's footprint had padded down the snow. A bright sun shone overhead, but that didn't guarantee warming weather. He cranked the window open and stuck his head out—cold enough to burn his tongue.

Shutting the window, Daniel felt his heart pounding, readying his body and spirit for the coming hunt. Times like this he could almost *feel* the blood flowing down his left arm into the fingers of his left hand. How could his body deceive him so? He growled at the stump as if it held the answers.

As his usual penance, he shaved his chin with cold water, as if he could force his body to accept the truth by shocking it into reality. Sometimes he added a cold breakfast to his punishment, but not today. Common sense said to warm the body and carry as much warmth as possible with him into the biting cold.

A few minutes later, he had coffee going in a pot—black mud, Simeon called it, but that was the way he'd drunk it in the army, and that was the only way he knew how to make it. Next he started oatmeal cooking, adding a dash of maple syrup into the mix. Sugar heated up a body almost better than any warm drink. He'd learned those lessons the hard way, around low campfires while wearing the thinnest of uniforms.

He slipped biscuits into the oven. Bacon? Yes. He fried up enough for breakfast and lunch and then forced himself to sit still long enough to eat between big gulps of coffee. Only after he emptied the pan of oatmeal and prepared bacon biscuits for lunch did he head to the closet where he stored his winter gear. He fingered the warm wool of his greatcoat. It would hang loose on him now, but worse than that, the left arm dangled where a hand was expected to appear at the cuff. He might let it go except wind would whistle up the emptiness like a chimney vent, freezing his chest along the way. He dug a jar of safety pins from the desk in the study and did his usual awkward job of pinning with one hand.

At last he could leave. Maybe he could borrow one of Hiram's horses, as soon as he could head out in that direction, and return Spotty to the livery. He kept hoping the robbers would release their horses and that his mare would return home.

Dixon had arrived at the jail ahead of him. "Figured you'd need me today. I doubt many people will make it to the store. My wife gave me a proper scolding for going out."

Daniel smiled. Dixon's wife was one of the sweetest souls in Maple Notch. If anybody wanted to feel better, they just went to the mercantile and sat down with a cup of tea and conversation with Mrs. Dixon.

Unlike the opinionated, vocal, *particular* Miss Farley. The reminder of her theory stirred uneasily within him.

"I heard an interesting idea about the robbery last night."

"From Miss Farley, I suppose."

Daniel cocked an eyebrow.

"Don't look so surprised. I know you took her home last night, and she has an opinion on everything." Dixon sounded like he didn't often agree with Clara's ideas.

"Is there something wrong with that?" Daniel took out his Remington, checking the cylinder and the action.

"Well, Captain, I mean no offense. It's just that she has opinions about things best left to the menfolk." Dixon ran his finger along his mustache. "I guess that's what comes from growing up in an all-male household. Mr. Farley treated the girl as if she were his oldest son."

"Anybody can tell God gave her a sharp brain. I'm sure He intends for her to use it." Daniel put the pistol down with more force than he intended. "This latest notion of hers does make sense. Those men yesterday didn't look like any rebels I ever encountered."

"Of course not. They wanted to blend in."

"Then why sew a Dixie flag on your jacket? Clara—Miss Farley—thinks they could be locals. And I'm thinking she's right."

"Impossible!" Dixon's eyes grew as wide as the penny candy he sold at his store.

"Hear me out." Daniel laid out Clara's reasons for thinking the criminals were local.

"I suppose she handed you the names of the suspects while she was at it?"

Daniel acknowledged the jab with a half smile. "No, she was as blinded as the rest of us because these may be people we know. They could even be people we like. People we've gone to church with."

Dixon slumped back in the chair. "There was a time around these parts that if you were looking for trouble, you'd head over to Whitson's farm straightaway."

Daniel waved that away. "I've heard the stories, too, but that's all in the past. Young Baruch is as sound a man as there is. He even got injured defending the bank."

"He's got four brothers."

Daniel glared at Dixon, who lifted his hands in defense. "I'm not pointing fingers. I'm just saying Baruch is the best of the bunch. Not going to be your family—you'd be shooting yourselves in the foot to do that." He grimaced. "Sorry."

Daniel waved it away. "Let's not worry about motive. Pretty soon we'd eliminate everyone in the county because we know them. Let's think about what we observed about them."

"I didn't see them, remember? I can't help."

Someone nudged the door open. "Is this a private meeting, or may I join you?" Pastor Beaton's thin face appeared at the door, and Daniel remembered he had been part of the cavalry before becoming a pastor.

"Come on in. I'm glad you could join us. You were there and might help me remember something I missed."

Beaton took the only remaining chair in the jail and pulled up next to Dixon. "Have you considered the possibility that locals committed the robbery?"

Daniel shot an amused glance at Dixon. "Actually, I have." Honesty compelled him to add, "Miss Farley suggested the idea. What did you notice about the men who were there yesterday? How many of them?"

"Four, maybe more."

Daniel nodded. "All men?"

Dixon raised his eyebrows again, so high that Daniel was afraid they'd creep into his hairline and disappear.

"We don't want to assume anything. If one of them was a woman, that would be another reason not to open their mouths."

Beaton drummed his fingers on the arm of his chair. "I suppose it's possible, but I doubt it. They were too tall." His lips twitched. "Besides, they didn't look like any women I've ever met."

"My thinking, too." Daniel closed his eyes, picturing them in his mind. "They were all right around five-nine, on the tall side for a woman."

"Any chance it could be a family? Them Whitsons have more sons than you can shake a stick at." Dixon addressed his question to Beaton.

Daniel's lips quirked. "And they're tall. That's why we asked Baruch to guard the bank. Figured he'd frighten robbers away."

Beaton shook his head. "They wouldn't shoot their brother."

Daniel wasn't sure about that. Not after fighting in a war that divided families in half as surely as the Revolutionary War had divided Patriots and Tories back in his grandparents' time. "Right now I'm not putting names to paper. I want the best description we can get."

"I can't say who was tallest. They never stood together."

"The one who held me was the biggest." Or did Daniel want to think so, a small ointment to sooth his injured self-esteem? "But not by much."

"Clothes? Of course, they could have changed," Dixon said.

"I didn't take notice," Beaton admitted. "I took my lesson to look beyond the outside all too literally. I saw inside their black souls." Bitterness edged his voice. "God forgive me and help me to forgive them."

"They were dressed like most people around here, farm folk." Daniel's laughter rang hollow. "Between the wide brims of their hats and those bandannas pulled up to the top of their noses, I couldn't see their eyes or their hair."

"That probably means their hair was cut short." Dixon smiled at their surprised expression. "As a haberdasher, I notice where a man's hairline falls below his hat." He held his hand up before them. "Your descriptions could fit half the men of Maple Notch. So they look pretty average." He turned down one finger. "We don't know what their voices sound like, because they didn't speak." He turned down a second finger. "And we certainly don't want to know what they taste like." His middle finger joined the others flat against his palm.

Daniel smothered a laugh. "That leaves smell and touch. The guy who grabbed me had gloves on." He made himself remember the sensation of the leather touching his skin. "Roughened. They've been used a lot. From cowhide, I'd guess." The smell of pungent manure and clean dirt filled his nostrils, and he almost gagged.

"What is it?"

"Cow manure. He hadn't bothered to clean up."

"Did you notice any other odors, any resembling a shaving cream?" Dixon prodded.

Daniel shook his head. "They smelled like they hadn't had their weekly bath for a month."

"That's not entirely true." Eyes closed, Beaton rocked back and forth on his chair. His nostrils twitched as if trying to track down an odor to its source. "Spicy. It reminded me a bit of church, and of a home kitchen at the same time." He opened his eyes. "I smelled an unusual scent, some kind of hair tonic or possibly cologne. It could have been one of the customers, of course. But I smelled it most strongly when the man passed in front of me to take my valuables."

"He didn't come near me. That might explain why I didn't notice it." Daniel worked his tongue over his teeth before turning to Dixon. "Do you sell anything that might smell like that?"

Dixon frowned. "Spices, church, and a kitchen? Are you sure you don't mean one of Mrs. Beaton's Sunday dinners?" At Daniel's glare, he said, "Of course not. But what kind of spices? Shall we repair to the store to smell all the spices I have in stock?"

"So we're looking for a farmer who uses fancy cologne. Great." Daniel snorted. "We might try your test tonight, but let's make use of the sunshine and cover the roads we didn't check out yesterday, starting with the one going east."

∽

"The snow's not so bad," Clara informed Pooches, who gamboled at her feet. "We should have come out long ago."

He barked as if to say, "It's wonderful!" He fell on his back and rolled, matting his golden fur with mud and slush. If the snow were deeper, she might have joined him and made snow angels. But this snowfall was so shallow a blade of grass could still stick through.

Lewis might not have stacked wood by the fireplace before he left, but he had prepared a cord of wood and left it in the woodshed. More remained to finish. Perhaps she could work on it later today. Maybe the exercise would work its wonder on her mind and keep her from worrying about Lewis.

Where was her brother, anyhow? Had he found a warm and dry place to stay when the weather hit? If he didn't come home tonight, she might ask the constable to keep an eye out for him.

After getting wood stacked in the kitchen, Clara went back outdoors to split more firewood. Miss Featherton had believed in exercise for her girls and wanted them to be independent. More than once, Clara had found herself grateful for the practical instruction her professor had included in her preparation for life in the year of our Lord eighteen hundred and sixty-odd.

She grabbed a pair of gloves and settled her feet about a shoulder's breadth apart. She checked the first log for knots. Not finding any, she aimed for a spot slightly off perpendicular. Sliding her hands down the axe, she swung it down with a satisfying *thud*. A chunk fell on the ground, and the scent of wood chips exploded in the air. A few chops later, she was done with that log. The second log went just as quickly. The sun was shining, and her heart singing as it often did when she spent time out of doors. She tied a bandanna around her head to keep hair and sweat out of her eyes. If she kept moving this fast, she wouldn't have to trouble Lewis for some time yet.

What will I do if I've lost all my money? The question refused to leave her alone. She and Lewis already lived simply. They never wanted for anything; they could change their menu to go without meat one day a week and make their clothes last another year. Since her return from seminary, they had taken care of all repairs themselves, although she had hoped to hire help once she started the school. If they didn't have the money for that, she'd find another way. She jutted her chin out. She'd work longer hours—or find a better solution—and Lewis could pitch in more as well. He knew how important the school was to her, to them.

Does he?

Clara chose to ignore the doubts that wanted to creep into her mind. She set the next log on the stump and brought down the ax.

If Lewis doesn't understand, Daniel does.

The thought halted Clara's momentum. Why did she think that? Daniel seemed to be dragging his feet about selling the house, although he did have a lot of other things going on. She had seen the amused look on his face as she measured the rooms the other day.

Come Monday, she would see the Bailey Mansion, or know the reason why not.

The longer she worked, the slower she moved, and she had to push to finish the last few logs. The ax shuddered against the wood, and she had to swing it an extra time or two to get it to split right. Clouds filled the sky, and she shivered inside her sweat-soaked chemise. A cool breeze blew through the blowsy sleeves of her dress. She hurried to put the ax in its proper place, to stack the wood for easy retrieval before loading the carrier to bring back inside. Only then did she head inside for comfort. She fumbled with starting a fire in the stove and heated water for tea.

∽

Lewis didn't come home Saturday night, but Clara didn't much care. Sunday morning she woke up with a fever and cough and made the rare decision not to go to church that day.

Monday morning dawned, the sun clear and bright. Clara's bout with illness had disappeared except for a minor sniffle. Lewis's continued absence bothered her more. She settled her cape over her shoulders and considered whether to walk or ride into town. As soon as she stuck her nose out the door, she sneezed and decided she should take Misty—or stay home, which she refused to do. *What will Daniel think if he encounters me on horseback?* The question made her smile. The guards remained on patrol, for all the good they had done last Friday. Then again, the robbers might have been apprehended by now, and she hadn't heard the news.

That was the most likely story. Every person in Vermont looked for the Confederates who had stormed into St. Albans last week. By now, everyone must have heard about the Maple Notch robbery as well, whether or not the same gang pulled both jobs. No one could escape detection that long, could they?

Clara had traveled halfway to town when a familiar figure on a familiar horse approached her. Lewis, coming home at last. She nudged her mare into a trot and came alongside him.

He stared at her through bloodshot eyes, and her heart sank. *Oh, Lewis. Not again.* He had taken off like this after Papa's death, but he had promised never to do it again. The greeting on her lips faltered, and she sat in the saddle without saying a word.

"Go ahead. Tell me how despicable I am and how disappointed you are. The trees are ready to hear all about it." His arms swept in a wide arc, and he swayed before wincing with pain. "Why does the sun have to be so bright today?"

The scolding fled from her tongue. She turned her mare to their farm, and Lewis's horse followed. At least Shadow looked well. Wherever Lewis had been, his animal had received proper care.

How Lewis could be drunk on a Monday morning perplexed Clara, since taverns closed on Sundays. Perhaps he had stayed in a private residence that kept spirits on hand. Once at the house, she helped him from the horse. The muscles in her shoulders, still sore from overuse on Saturday, protested, but she could do most anything when she set her mind to it. Once Lewis landed on the ground, he could walk on his own two feet by leaning on her.

Pooches raced to greet Lewis and stood on his hind feet, planting two big paws on his chest. Lewis swayed, and Clara stumbled a bit under the weight. "Down, boy."

Not receiving the enthusiastic greeting he had hoped for, the dog satisfied himself with running around the pair in circles until they hopped into the house. "You stay out, now. That's a good dog." Clara closed the door in his face.

Lewis collapsed into the chair closest to the fireplace and hung his head in his hands. Clara didn't know where to start. Clean clothes? Fresh coffee? Bed?

Coffee, she decided. He couldn't do anything for himself until he sobered some. At school she had heard tales about pouring cold water on someone in an inebriated condition. If the coffee didn't work, she'd try that next.

After she started the coffee, she went out to take care of their horses. The beasts shouldn't suffer because of Lewis's bad choices. Even so, she rushed her normal routine a bit. The coffee had finished brewing when she returned, a good, strong drink like he preferred. She poured a mug half full and brought the coffeepot out to the parlor with her.

Lewis's head had dropped back against the chair cushion, and snores and moans alternately emanated from his mouth. Should she let him sleep?

Exhaustion from everything she had done over the past few days swept over her. No! Why should he get to sleep? She shook him, hard, and he blinked at her. "What's up?"

She thrust the coffee cup into his hands. "Here. Drink this."

He took a sip and gagged. "This is stronger than tar. Stronger even than the way I make it."

She glared at him. "It takes strong coffee to combat strong drink."

A tiny grin tugged at his lips, and he drank it down. "Satisfied?" He leaned back in the chair.

"Not so fast. There's plenty more where that came from." She poured him a second cup. "Do you think you can eat anything?"

The green face he turned in her direction gave her the answer she expected. When he finished the second cup, he didn't ask. He held a trembling hand out to Clara, and she filled it again.

He drank it down in one long swallow—maybe the only way he could stomach the taste—and set the mug on a side table. "I refuse to drink another drop. I don't want to have an accident in addition to all the other problems I have. And now"—he stood, locking his knees together—"I will head to my bed."

Clara opened her mouth to speak. Before the words came out, someone knocked at the door.

Daniel.

Chapter 5

Daniel saw the movement behind the curtains and waited before knocking a second time. When Clara answered the door, she came out on the stoop with him and shut the door behind her. She looked mussed, as if she hadn't bothered to fix her hair that morning, and her cheeks pinked in the sun.

"May I help you with something?"

Her question made him realize he hadn't yet said a word, let alone explained his visit. She looked at him as if she expected him to set a bag of goods for sale on the ground and start hawking his wares. The day-old beard on his chin probably didn't help matters any.

"When you weren't at church yesterday, I was worried." There, he'd said the bald truth. "With all the ruffians running through Vermont these days, I was afraid harm might have come to you."

"As you can see, I'm doing fine." Her face softened. "You've had no luck in finding the miscreants?"

He shook his head. "I've talked with most folks from town, but I haven't caught up with Lewis yet. Is he here?"

Clara's face went still, and her mouth writhed with unspoken words. "He's. . .indisposed at the moment."

A dozen possibilities flew through Daniel's mind, but soon he identified the most likely possibility. "He's drunk."

"No." She dragged the word out. "Not exactly."

Daniel considered his options. "If he's sober, he should be able to answer some questions. And I wanted to speak with you about our business matter as well." He waited for her answer.

"Very well." She opened the door, and he followed her inside the vacant room. "He mentioned going upstairs to rest. I will ask him to come down." She grabbed a shirt lying on the floor and headed upstairs.

Daniel hadn't visited the Farley home before. Old Mr. Farley must have mounted the rack of 10-point antlers, fashioned into a hat rack. The rather yellowed antimacassars protecting the chair backs might have been made by Mrs. Farley, long deceased. A dozen things pointed to Lewis's presence in the home. A pipe rack, the muddied floor where his feet had rested, a faint odor of spirits. For signs of Clara, he had to look to the bookshelf, where a Bible rested with a ribbon marking her place, and stationery tucked away for her next letter.

All in all, it was a comfortable, lived-in room, but not a room decorated with the intention of receiving company. What would she do if given free rein in the Bailey house? Would she allow it to run into this state of comfortable disarray, or would she keep it spotless for her students?

He decided he wouldn't mention the subject to Simeon. His wife kept their house like a museum. Of the two, he preferred Clara's approach. He shook his head. He was thinking as if the house already had passed into her hands. That was the problem. He wanted her to have the house so he could see her frequently.

The real reason behind his trip today had little to do with Lewis and more to do with seeking out the contrary Miss Farley. Back at the jail, Dixon had drafted a chart for the men of the town, tracking what they knew about their movements on the morning of the robbery. Lewis's was one of several blanks left, and Daniel had decided to start the day with him. He hoped Lewis could make a good accounting of his day, for Clara's sake, if nothing else.

Clara returned to the parlor. "He'll be down presently. Would you like something to drink? Coffee? Tea?"

He spotted the coffeepot on the side table. "I'll take a cup of that, if there's any left. I can get it myself." He grabbed a mug from its rack over the table and lifted the pot.

"Oh, but it's terrible coffee. Thicker than March mud." The panic on her face made him want to laugh.

"That's just the way I like it. How did you know?" He lifted the cup to his lips. "Perfect. It takes considerable talent to make coffee like this." The chuckle that escaped her warmed him deep inside.

"At least let me get you a piece of lemon cake, lest you think coffee sludge is the extent of my culinary talents." She didn't wait for an answer but went into the kitchen and returned with a three-inch slab that made his mouth water to look at it.

The cake melted on his tongue, its tangy sweetness the perfect complement to the harsh coffee. He forced himself to pause after two bites. "You missed an important announcement at church yesterday."

"I'm sure I missed more than that." She sneezed. "I hate being away from the Lord's house."

"I know you are a customer of the bank. And I also know you didn't join the general panic and remove your funds on Thursday."

She stilled her hands, their hold tighter than a dead man's grip.

"The robbers cleaned out the money stored in the bank."

"I guessed as much."

The fearful acceptance in her voice tugged at his heart.

"Cheer up." He took another bite of cake and moaned with pleasure. "A bank's assets don't consist simply of cash on hand. Simeon has invested the money wisely and expects a good return for years to come. In other words, he has personally guaranteed the funds of everyone's deposit. It may take a day or two longer than before to access ready cash, but your funds are safe."

She turned her head away and reached into her reticule for a dab of white lace to blot her tears. "Thank you for telling me."

He leaned forward. "Your welfare matters to me." The way she looked at him with those dove-gray eyes, he'd have promised to grow wings like a bird and fly to the moon if she asked him to. Another gulp of harsh coffee brought him to reality, and he settled in his chair. "When do you want to reschedule your tour of the house?"

"And the appointment with Simeon. Provided no one else decides to rob the banks of Lamoille County." The twitching of her lips suggested she held back a laugh. "Actually, I was going to go into town today, but. . .something else came up."

"I have a few more people I need to see today. Let's plan on early tomorrow morning, after school starts."

"I'll be there."

He had time to finish the cake and imagine what else she could cook if she set her mind to it by the time Lewis came downstairs. He had taken time with his appearance, shaving his chin close, brushing his hair back, donning a clean white shirt. He had prepared to conduct business, but so had Daniel. He was a soldier pursuing the enemy—if he could only identify him.

"Well, Captain Tuttle, Clara said you wanted to see me." Lewis took the biggest chair in the room, the one designed to accommodate Mr. Farley's girth, and crossed his arms across his chest.

He must know about the robbery by now. Clara was a witness, after all. But Daniel knew better than to tell a witness something he might not know. "You had a rough weekend." He made it a statement.

"I confess, I did." Red shot through the eyes that so resembled Clara's in color. "To think those rebels could make it all the way up here. I was shocked, and even a little scared." He spread his hands as if in apology. "Perhaps I'm a coward."

Any man who sees the world through the bottom of a bottle is a coward. But Daniel didn't voice the maxim. He had seen too many men seek courage from any source, including liquor, to chastise Lewis. Neither would he let it interrupt his interrogation.

"When did the binge start, Lewis? How long were you drinking?"

The man blinked as if surprised at such a crass question. "Some friends and I went to the tavern on Friday night. We had heard about the robbery, and we didn't want to go back in case the robbers were still around."

"Which friends?"

"The usual."

Daniel wondered if he would have to drag the names out when Lewis continued. "Bob and Rod Whitson. Ned Whimsey. They were with me the whole time."

Daniel thought about Dixon's distrust of the Whitsons. The twins Lewis mentioned had earned a reputation notorious even for their family.

"There were others? Part of the time?"

"I believe there were," Clara said. "He also mentioned Dupre, Ford, and Bradford. Didn't you, Lewis?"

"I don't remember exactly." Lewis waved his hand in front of his face. "Things got blurry after a while."

A small groan directed Daniel's attention to Clara. The details must be difficult for her to hear.

"So when did you get to the tavern? And when did you leave?"

The tale Daniel pulled out of Lewis included a few times and places and names to check, a sordid tale of nearly three days of a drunken spree. Daniel forced himself not to lecture the young man.

"I'll verify the information you've given me. If you think of anything, anything at all, that might lead us to the criminals, please let me know." He couldn't keep quiet, not entirely. "This kind of behavior does no good for anyone involved—least of all yourself." He left before his temper led him astray. No one should treat Clara the way Lewis did.

∽

Clara's conscience pricked her. Lewis might have started drinking on Friday afternoon, as he said. But neither one of them had told Daniel he'd left home before breakfast. He could have done everything exactly as he said—after he had gone with the others to rob the bank.

Foolishness. Lewis wouldn't have robbed the bank, robbing himself in the process. He was often lazy and even thoughtless, but he wouldn't bring terror to innocent people.

With Daniel's departure, all the starch fled from Lewis, and he sprawled in Pa's old chair. "If you sit like that, you'll ruin that beautiful shirt before you've worn it for an hour," Clara said.

"Then I'll have to take it off." Suiting action to word, he started unbuttoning the cuffs.

"Lewis, you can't stay down here *naked*." As a matter of fact, Lewis had often pulled the stunt as a young boy. But he was a man grown, even if his behavior over the weekend called that into question.

"Then I'll go upstairs." He was about halfway down the front of the shirt now. "I want to rest awhile before tonight."

"Tonight?" Visions of Lewis rejoining the lads for another round plagued her.

"Don't worry. I shall be here for supper and in my own bed at a respectable hour." He threw his arms around her in a brotherly hug and kissed her on the cheek. "I know there must be a God, because I don't deserve a sister like you."

With comments like that, how could Clara stay upset with him, even if his theology was wrong? "Chicken and dumplings?" she asked after his departing back.

"My favorite."

Clara's hopes of a brief afternoon nap faded as every step of making the dumplings took longer than usual—starting with chasing the chicken all over the yard. She tasted the broth. It was a tad too salty, but Lewis wouldn't notice. He poured salt onto everything he ate before taking a bite, enough to burn away his taste buds.

When at last the dumplings were bubbling on the stove and applesauce heating in a pan, she settled down in the closest chair and laid her head on the table.

She hadn't counted more than ten sheep before she heard the tread of Lewis's footstep, but by the clock, fifteen minutes had passed. She grabbed crockery from the shelf, set it out, and retrieved a pitcher of milk from the cold cellar.

"Milk?" Lewis sounded as unbelieving as a heathen at a church service. "I'm not six years old, Clara."

She leveled a look at him, and he put his hands in the air in mock surrender. "Very well, I'll drink it. Tonight."

After ladling out the dumplings, she sat down to enjoy the meal with her brother. She didn't say a word about his activities over the weekend. Instead, she asked, "Do you think George McClellan has any chance of being elected president?"

The way Lewis looked at her reminded her that he had few political interests. "I'll make sure I get to the polls and vote. My first time, you know." He flashed a saucy grin in her direction.

She bit her lip at that statement. Would *she* have the right to vote, a right her brother took for granted, anytime within her lifetime? How old would she be? Women in Vermont, herself among them, fought for that privilege even now. But she kept those opinions to herself. She wanted to get Lewis in a good mood.

They bypassed the emancipation amendment—that seemed obvious to both of them—and instead discussed whether Governor Smith's lieutenant, Paul Dillingham, was the best choice to succeed him.

She had intended to make apple brown betty, Lewis's favorite fall treat, but settled for warm applesauce with a cinnamon stick in it when she ran out of time. If it stayed chilly today, she might heat some apple cider for a going-to-bed drink. Apples were good whatever form she ate them in.

She added gingersnaps to the warm applesauce. Lewis leaned back in his chair. "That was a delicious supper. Just what I needed." His eyes had brightened, only a few red lines sneaking through the corners to indicate the abuse he had put himself through over the weekend. With a clean shirt, shave, and the tired bags under his eyes smoothed out, he looked young, healthy, and whole.

After setting out fresh coffee for them in the parlor, she took a seat opposite Lewis. The time had come to speak her mind.

"I expect you heard that Baruch Whitson was injured during the bank holdup the other day."

His expression darkened. "Do we have to talk about it? I got enough of a grilling from your Captain Tuttle."

Clara bit back the retort that rose in her throat—Daniel wasn't her anything—and shook her head in a gentle denial. "Nothing like that. I just wondered if Mr. Simeon Tuttle would want to hire another guard until Mr. Whitson has recovered. He might hire more guards because of the current situation. I would."

"And you want me to apply?" Lewis scratched his chin.

"You're a good shot. And strong. You'd do a good job." *And maybe a steady job will encourage you to stay away from taverns.*

Light danced in Lewis's eyes, and she could see the idea take hold. "You say he might be looking for more than one guard?"

"Bound to, don't you think?"

"I think I'll check it out." He bounced out of his chair and came over to kiss her on the cheek. The affectionate look he sent her way warmed her straight to the toes. This was the kid brother she knew and loved.

"I'll put in a good word for you with Mr. Tuttle when I meet with him again."

The spark in Lewis's eyes flickered, but he patted her on the shoulder. "A quiet night at home is just what the doctor ordered for tonight, don't you think?" His grin wobbled. "Maybe you can read me some of that Thoreau that you're so fond of."

"A visit to Walden Pond. That sounds delightful." She'd love to lose herself in the simplicity of Walden Pond and not deal with the shenanigans of humankind, which weren't nearly so predictable. Next to the eternal truths revealed in the Bible, Thoreau enthralled her the most.

She dug in the bookshelf for Papa's copy of the original edition and sat down. Pooches draped himself across her feet as she settled down on the horsehair sofa her mother had loved. She felt Mama's presence most powerfully when she sat there, wrapped up in a coverlet Mama had quilted with her own hands. As always, Clara smiled when she read the title page. " 'I do not propose to write an ode to dejection, but to brag as lustily as chanticleer in the morning, standing on his roost, if only to wake my neighbors up.' " A cheerful shout as lusty as a rooster's crow in the morning—that would chase away the problems of the past few days. "We shall have to visit Concord some day."

"You always say that when you start in on Walden." Lewis laughed at her.

She lifted her chin. "I shall go there with my students, at the very least." She turned the page to the first chapter and began reading. " 'When I wrote the following pages, or rather the bulk of them, I lived alone, in the woods, a mile from any neighbor, in a house which I had built myself, on the shore of Walden Pond, in Concord, Massachusetts, and earned my living by the labor of my hands only.' " She spared a glance at Lewis, wondering if this was the best choice of reading material when encouraging her brother to seek steady employment, but she shrugged and lost herself in the beauty of the woods.

The flames burned low while she read. Her voice cracked as she sneezed and coughed, and at last she gave up. Lewis stirred and put fresh logs in the fireplace. "I'll finish up down here."

Times like this, Lewis was so sweet, she could almost forget the worry he had caused her over the weekend.

Almost.

∽

" 'Only that day dawns to which we are awake. There is more day to dawn. The sun is but a morning star.' " Daniel closed *Walden* and put it back in its space on Grandpa's shelf. Thoreau alternately enlightened and confused, expanded and enraged. The mental exercises had proved most helpful while Daniel was in the army, helping to keep long hours of boredom at bay. He wondered what Miss Schoolmarm Farley would say if she knew he had carried a slim copy of the book with him in his knapsack, next to his Bible. When a rainstorm had washed away his tent and the two books with it, he wasn't sure which he missed more.

He shook his head. He knew better. Thoreau was only a man, with man's words. He doubted people would be reading them two, three, or however many thousands of years from now, the way they did the Word of God as given in the Bible. No man's words could change a life the way God-breathed scripture could and did.

He walked around the house, as he did each night before bed. Should he go down to the jail to see if any news had come in about the robbers? He shook himself. No need. If something happened, Dixon would alert him straightaway. He needed sleep, but as he had been so many nights before battle, he was too restless to do more than doze. Unlike the battlefield, where he could stare at the enemy's campfires, here he battled an invisible and unknown enemy.

As in the war, his enemy was someone close to him, a fight between brothers and neighbors, the bitterest fight of all. He frowned. At least he had proved his two brothers innocent of the crime. Hiram stayed busy night and day at the farm, and besides, he was well short of five-nine. Simeon had been at his side when the robbers came.

Not that Daniel seriously suspected either one of them. But he had vowed to consider every man in the vicinity, be they friend, family, or foe. As constable, he had to act fairly, but his heart heaved a sigh of relief when he could eliminate his cousins and nephews from the suspect list.

About two dozen possibilities remained, three if you counted men a little too old or who didn't quite fit the physical description they had of the robbers. Tomorrow, he would check the alibis they had provided.

Perhaps he should have gone out tonight. He could have spoken with the barkeep who had served Lewis Farley and his cronies. No, best he wait until morning, when the man might be sober, if cross.

Daniel strayed up to the top floor of the house. Opening the door to the nursery, he could almost see shadows of his former self kneeling in front of the toy chest. He'd had enough toy soldiers for a battalion, and they marched into battle time and again. He recreated the two battles of Fort Ticonderoga. When he could convince Simeon to join him, they took the parts of their father and his friend Tobias, lurking around Burlington during the second war with Britain. As a boy, Daniel had dreamed of the day he would become a soldier like his father and grandfather. He cupped his left elbow with his right hand. Others before him had died. He shouldn't complain about the loss of a limb.

Although, God forgive him, at times he thought he'd be better off dead. God had protected him from himself, and he had survived healthy of body and of mind. But the sooner he got out of this house, designed for family and children, the better off he'd be. He shut bedroom doors to the taunting echoes of childhood laughter before retiring downstairs.

Hiram counseled him to hold on to the house until the day he had a family of his own to fill the rooms. But Daniel knew better. He would never have a family of his own.

Chapter 6

Early the following morning, Daniel heard someone pounding on the door. Frantic that he had missed a new development regarding the bank robbery, he jumped into his breeches and fumbled into his shirt while racing down the stairs.

Clara Farley waited at the door. One look at his disheveled state, and she glanced overhead, her nose wrinkling up into her glasses. "I'm sorry. I didn't realize it was so early. You did say to come by this morning and. . ."

He became aware of the empty sleeve dangling below his elbow. He hadn't taken the time to pin it up as he usually did. His shirttails dangled below his waist. Stubble covered his cheeks, which was a good thing, because he could feel heat rushing into them. Since she had a brother, she must have seen men before their morning ablutions, but he was nonetheless embarrassed.

Propriety might dictate she remain outside while he dressed more thoroughly, but the gusty wind stirring her hair convinced him otherwise.

"Come in and wait in the parlor while I make myself presentable." Without further pleasantries, he escaped to his bedroom and dressed himself properly. This morning no comb could tame his hair, so he settled for a splash of tonic. That reminded him of the description of the odor Beaton had detected during the robbery. He didn't feel comfortable asking men what kind of hair tonic or cologne they used; he had peeked around their homes when he could and let his nose do the investigating the rest of the time. Nothing had come to light so far.

He returned downstairs to a deserted parlor. From the back of the house, the odor of sizzling bacon grease and stout coffee teased him. As he made his way down the hall, he heard sounds stirring in the kitchen. Clara had unearthed one of Grandmother's aprons, a yellowed pinafore, and was stirring enough scrambled eggs to feed Hiram's family. Bacon nestled on a stack of toast in the center of the table.

"You're fixing breakfast." *Brilliant conversation.*

She turned around so fast that she almost spilled the eggs from the cast-iron skillet. "It was the least I could do, since I arrived at such a terrible hour." Wrapping her hand with the pinafore the way he had seen his mother do hundreds of times, Clara used it as protection against the heat of the coffeepot as she poured him a mug. "I made it extra strong. I believe you said you liked it that way." She wrinkled up her nose in that endearing way of hers, as if she couldn't believe it.

"I do." He blew on it to cool it a tad and then took a deep drink. "Ah. Just right." He gestured at the eggs she spooned into a bowl. "I hope you're planning on eating something with me."

"Don't worry about me. I had breakfast before I left home." She poured tea from a teapot she had steeping and sat down across from him.

She was so thin, it wouldn't hurt her to eat a little more. She needed someone to take care of her. "I insist. I can't eat all this by myself. You must have developed some appetite on your walk into town." Without waiting for her answer, he grabbed a plate from the cupboard and added bacon and buttered toast to a mound of eggs.

She smiled and nibbled on a slice of toast the way he had seen his sisters do when they wanted to be polite. He pretended not to notice, and soon she tucked into the food with a genuine appetite.

As soon as she cleared her plate, she reached for the now-empty bowl and stood to her feet.

"Sit down." Daniel was surprised how much he enjoyed bossing her around. "Keep me company while I finish eating these delicious eggs. I'll clean up later." He smiled at her, and she eased back into the chair.

He couldn't remember the last time he had eaten such a pleasant breakfast. The only thing missing was hot buttered biscuits.

"I didn't even think of biscuits." Clara looked ready to jump from her chair again, and Daniel realized he had spoken aloud. Now he felt heat rushing into his cheeks. Maybe she would blame the color on razor burn.

Daniel swallowed every bite while drinking three cups of coffee and could have eaten the food Clara had consumed if she hadn't already finished it.

She looked so right, so comfortable, in that kitchen, which had intimidated even his mother. The room had been the cook's domain, and few people challenged it. He could get used to sharing breakfast with a woman like this every day. *Stop it*, he reminded himself. No woman would want him, certainly not a woman as fine as Clara. He took care of the dirty dishes and stilled his racing feelings before returning to the business at hand.

"Thank you for that delicious meal." He rubbed his midsection in appreciation. "Where do you want to look first?"

"I'd like to start with the attic rooms." Her fingers fumbled with the apron ties.

"Let me help you." As soon as he reached for the bow, he could have cursed himself. Her two hands were better than his single hand. He stood behind her, breathing in her fresh scent, like gardenias. She seemed to sense his hesitation and leaned back into him, making it easy for him to hold the strings in place with his stump while his right hand picked the knot apart. He managed to untangle the threads, and she lifted the loop over her neck before replacing it on the hook. He looked at her, their eyes only inches apart. "You said you want to see the attic first?" His voice came out like a schoolboy's.

She nodded.

He smiled, hoping to put them both at ease, and moved to the stairway. He'd never seen her in a hoop dress that he could remember. He didn't know how women managed with those things, although Dixon said they sold almost faster than he could get them in. She didn't lack the funds, so maybe she found the style silly?

They reached the staircase, and he decided she avoided them because of their impracticality. Hoop skirts called for sweeping staircases, even wider than the ones in this house. He enjoyed watching the sway of her hips as she ascended the steps without the assistance of the rail, not pausing even at the second-floor landing. On the third floor, she peeked into the two smaller side rooms, where the staff had slept, without taking measurements.

A pleasant sigh escaped her lips when she walked into the nursery. "What a lovely room. You must have many happy memories of this place." She walked straight across the room to the window looking out the back. "From the looks of it, there was once a lovely garden back here."

"My mother's pride and joy. Her interest in growing things is what drew her to my father, back in that horrible Year of No Summer when frost killed the crops."

"I don't know how my parents met. Mama never told me before she died, and then Papa was too sad."

How unfortunate. Daniel knew the history of his family back to the days his great-grandfathers had helped settle Maple Notch at the end of the French and Indian War. "I was sorry to learn of your father's passing. I didn't know him well, but from what I could tell, he was a fine man."

"He was." She bent down to examine the books on a low shelf, and a nostalgic look crossed her face. "I see some old favorites here." A smile erased the earlier pain. She pulled out a book with a cracked leather binding. "Your Bible. Of course." She leafed through it, smiling here and there. "I can tell this has been well used."

"A chapter every morning and night from the time I could read. Grandfather wouldn't let me read anything else until I heard from God."

Continuing her perusal, she giggled. "Weems' *Life of Washington* I might have expected, or Webster's spelling book, but *Love Triumphant* by Abner Reed?"

"I do have two sisters." He managed to keep a straight face. He would never admit to reading the book to discover how to get a girl interested in him. His attempts had failed, in any case. No sweetheart stayed behind when he went off to war.

She lifted a stack of magazines with pages half torn out. "Oh, I read so many of these. They look like they'll fall apart if I handle them, though." She settled them back into their place on the shelf and stood. "This room would make a marvelous studio." She took out the same notebook he had seen before and made notations.

A pang struck Daniel's heart at the thought of dismantling the room that held so many childhood memories, but he chided himself. "Will you want to make changes to the structure?"

She finished making a note before she looked up. "If I buy the house, I might."

"And you plan to turn it into a school? For women?"

She looked at him as if he was slow. They had discussed all this before. "Yes."

His heart beat rapidly. He hated to think of this place that had once been both home and retreat turned into an institution. *Where's your sense of family, of the legacy you've been handed?*

Simeon's voice played in his head. *It's too much house for you by yourself. And the truth is, it's too valuable an asset to let it sit unoccupied and unused.*

If they were in a different part of the country, the house would make an excellent place for recuperating wounded. A lot of houses had been pressed into service that way. But praise God, the only action Maple Notch had seen was the robbery last Friday, and only Whitson had sustained any injury.

Be a good steward. Pass it on to someone who can make use of it. Simeon's advice came back to mind. Ever the businessman, he was also a faithful Christian. Trust him to make a spiritual application out of a business decision.

But Daniel wasn't ready to let go, of either the house or its history. He would also miss the excuse to meet with the opinionated Miss Farley. His desire not to see the house changed warred with his curiosity about what she would do with it.

Clara snapped her notebook shut and turned to him. "I'm ready to see the first floor."

∽

Clara took in every detail of the solid carpentry of the house, the smooth finish of the floor, the quality of wood in the stair rail. Hiram Bailey had prepared a fine home for his bride, built with pride and quality, and had kept it equipped with the latest of conveniences. It offered plenteous space and a pleasant learning environment—both important qualities in any institution of learning.

She had peeked into the front rooms on her way to the kitchen that morning. An occasional guest in the Bailey home, she had seen the front parlor on numerous occasions. The only room she had never visited on the first floor was the study. Rumor said Hiram Bailey kept a fine library, and she wanted to see for herself.

One glance at the walls of the room confirmed the rumor. She had only seen so many books in one place at the seminary's library. "May I?" When he nodded approval, she took down a title at random—a bound copy of Thomas Paine's *Common Sense*. The pages showed signs of multiple readings. She put it back on the shelf and ran her fingers along the row until she came to a Bible.

"Be careful," Daniel said.

A chunk from the middle of the Bible fell into her hands. Pencil and pen marks covered the pages. "You should keep this somewhere safe." She put it together again and laid it carefully on the edge of the desk, not attempting to stack it back on the shelf.

"I probably should put it away somewhere, but I enjoy reading my grandfather's thoughts. I still read a chapter morning and evening, like he said. Besides, not many people come in here."

Clara continued skimming the titles, row after row of neatly aligned books alphabetized by the author's last name. At last she came to a shelf with an empty spot among the books, suggesting a volume had been removed. She had reached the place where Thoreau's books would be. She found *Civil Disobedience* and *Slavery in Massachusetts*, but *Walden* was missing.

"I'm reading *Walden* at the moment. You won't find it there."

She felt his hazel eyes burning into the back of her neck.

"I made it my goal to read every one of Grandfather's books." He came alongside her. "Then I might start adding to his collection."

She covered her laugh with a hiccup, but Daniel glanced at her.

"Do you find the thought amusing?"

Her hiccup hadn't convinced him. "Oh, no, not at all. I was just reading *Walden* myself last night. I find parts of his work—unsettling. Thought provoking." Clara's hand dropped from the spine of the book she was touching. "I was smiling at the thought of a verse from Ecclesiastes that my schoolmistress used to quote."

" 'Of making many books there is no end; and much study is a weariness of the flesh.' Ecclesiastes 12:12. It was my favorite verse when I wanted to get out of schoolwork." Daniel smiled as he quoted the verse, peeling years away from his face. "Now I find reading very restful."

"I envy you. Access to all these wonderful books." A quick estimate suggested more than a thousand books lined the shelves, and she hungered to read them all. She turned to face Daniel. "I want to buy the books with the house."

Daniel didn't answer, but rather circled around behind his grandfather's desk and took a seat. From there he exuded power and authority, but she refused to let him intimidate her. She took the seat facing him, inching forward, holding her back ramrod straight.

He placed his right hand on the desk, and Clara caught herself looking for the other one. He didn't appear to notice her rudeness. "So you are interested in purchasing the house." He said it as if engaged in a game of chess, plotting his next move. His normally expressive eyes had darkened, blank as wood.

She wondered what he had in mind. She could only play the game piece she had planned to start with. "Yes. I have an appointment to discuss terms with Mr. Simeon Tuttle when we finish here. I am certain we can reach an equitable arrangement."

A faint smile tugged at his mouth. "What if I said the house is no longer for sale?"

Chapter 7

After all the meetings, all Clara's hopes and dreams, did Captain Daniel Tuttle intend to crush her like a bothersome black fly? Good humor fled, replaced by a black veil even darker than her skirt. The *nerve* of the man.

"You should have informed me that the place was not for sale before our business together commenced." She could hear her own voice, stilted, high pitched—vinegar and not honey. She swallowed once, then again. Her mouth felt dryer than the mill pond during a drought. "I have no wish to waste your time any further." She stood and tucked her reticule under her arm, seeking escape before she fell into a thousand pieces.

"Miss Farley—Clara—please sit back down." He came around the desk before she could blink. "I'm sorry I startled you. Let me get you a drink."

He stayed gone long enough for Clara to breathe deeply and regain some degree of composure. Perhaps he was still willing to sell the house. After all, he had only asked "what if?"

He returned with a pitcher of water and two glasses. He poured them each a glass and gestured for her to imbibe while he polished off his own with a long swallow. She surreptitiously swished the first few sips around her mouth, moistening the parched places.

"Let me explain myself better. After further thought, I'm not ready to let my grandparents' home pass out of the Tuttle family."

She took another sip of water, determined not to let her agitation show.

"But I do agree with Simeon that the house needs to be used for something more than a bachelor's residence. So, what would you think of leasing the property instead?"

Leasing. Her mind raced with the idea. "We would need to agree upon the length of the lease. I won't set up school and then have you change your mind two months later."

"Of course. I don't anticipate needing it...any time soon." An indefinable something crossed his face.

"I planned to make changes so that it would be more suitable as a school."

He leaned back. "I want to approve any changes."

Did he plan on watching over her shoulder, ready to take over the reins at the smallest sign of weakness? She looked deep into his eyes and decided no, he didn't. Something else was at work here.

Daniel found himself wishing Clara needed a hundred changes made. Then he would have almost endless excuses for spending time with her. But he sensed she might resent his interference. "I'll ask Simeon to draw up the terms of the lease."

Clara frowned.

"Is that a problem?"

She straightened her back further, if that were possible. "An independent party should draw up the contract. I know of a lawyer in St. Albans. We can consult him. I will need to discuss financial details as well. Will you handle that, or will your brother?"

I will. The words tripped on the tip of Daniel's tongue, but he knew he shouldn't do it alone. "I'll tell Simeon what I've decided, and we'll plan on meeting with him in two days' time."

"Good. I will bring some preliminary requests for changes to the house at that time." She cast her glance at Grandfather's desk, and Daniel wondered if she imagined herself in the massive chair, dealing with recalcitrant students.

No, he doubted she would spend much time confined behind a desk. She would be among her students, encouraging, instructing, ordering when the need arose. He found himself smiling. "I look forward to seeing what you have in mind."

"I mustn't take any more of your time." She stood. "Are you making any progress is finding the robbers? Is there any chance they are those Confederates who robbed the bank at St. Albans?"

Considering the fact she was the one who had first raised the possibility of local involvement, her question surprised him. "From all accounts, no. Those gentlemen hightailed it back to Canada, and the authorities up there won't turn them over. You'd think we were still at war with Britain." He shook himself. "Unfortunately, no one is acting suspiciously."

"Suddenly rich? Spending money like there is no tomorrow?"

They arrived at the front door, and he trapped one side of her cloak between his elbow and chest while helping her drape the other side over her shoulder. Awkward. He couldn't even help a lady into her coat without twice as many steps as a normal man. "I'm a little surprised. It suggests a degree of self-control I wouldn't have expected of these ruffians."

"Consider this." She swirled, her cloak settling in soft folds around her feminine form. "The raid on St. Albans presented the opportunity. But they might have been planning the robbery for a long time."

For a moment, Daniel lost himself in the depths of her charcoal-rimmed, gray eyes. He saw intelligence and humor and a liveliness she kept far too hidden. He was drawn to her, as helpless against the tug as metal drawn to a magnet, and he wanted to see more and more of her. "You have made some excellent observations about the robbery."

A pleased surprise lit her face, and he continued. "I would appreciate hearing your insight into this crime. Your feminine intellect"—her eyes flared at his turn of phrase—"approaches the problem from a different angle."

The glare softened.

He plunged ahead. "Are you willing to meet with me from time to time to discuss my progress in the investigation?"

She studied him, one gloved finger on her pursed lips, as if judging the genuineness of his request. The hand lowered and covered her heart. "I believe you mean it, Captain Tuttle."

He held back a smile and nodded.

She shook her head. "Few men of my acquaintance would ask a woman for advice on a criminal matter." She held out her hand. "It would be my honor, sir."

Honor. The word rang hollow in a heart wanting. . .what, he couldn't bring himself to put into words. He took her hand. "To our joint endeavor. May we find quick success."

∽

Clara wanted to skip around the town green as she left the Bailey Mansion. Daniel's decision to lease the house and not sell it surprised her, but the advantages revealed themselves after a little thought. A lease involved no permanent commitment for either party. She would give her all into setting up the finest girls' school Vermont had ever seen. If it succeeded, she would press the Tuttles for a sale later. If it failed, she would determine what steps to take if and when that happened. Miss Featherton had told her she would always have a spot on the faculty at Middlebury, but Clara desired to stay in Maple Notch. At least until Lewis was settled.

If he is ever settled, a rebellious voice in her head insisted.

But no thoughts of schoolrooms made her legs want to break their steady gait. Daniel Tuttle wanted her help in hunting down the robbers. He valued her intelligence. He said so. And in a society that placed more importance on a woman's looks and command of the wifely arts than on the quality of her mind, she found his invitation refreshing—compelling, even.

Clara couldn't face going straight home to household chores. The coins in her purse would pay for a cup of coffee and one of Fannie's famous cinnamon rolls while Clara sketched changes she'd like made to the Bailey

Mansion. Passing the school where she had spent many happy hours as a child, she decided to take another detour. What alterations had been made since her student days? Maybe she could pick up some ideas for the renovation of Bailey Mansion.

She opened the door to a loud clamor. Two boys—adolescents—threw spit wads at each other. About halfway down the aisle, a gaggle of girls giggled over the desks. At the front, the youngest children sat in a semicircle. One of them leaned back in his chair and looked straight at her.

"That old spinster lady is here!" He shouted at the top of his lungs, and the room quieted in an instant. All eyes turned on her, including those of the pastor's wife, Mrs. Beaton. Clara wanted to leave and slam the memories behind her, but a good school mistress always kept her chin up and moved forward.

"Nicholas Whitson!" The usually serene Mrs. Beaton sounded a cat's whisker away from chasing the boy out of the schoolroom with a broom. "Go stand in the corner."

Then she glanced at the clock, and her shoulders sagged. "Children, go ahead and take your lunch break."

Pandemonium broke out again as they all scrambled for their lunch buckets and dashed out the door. Mrs. Beaton rubbed the back of her neck as she walked down the center aisle toward Clara.

"Where is Miss Stone?" Clara asked. The same teacher who had shepherded her through her last few years in Maple Notch still taught the local school, becoming the town's institutional old maid. *Apparently I've been elected to join their ranks.* The blush she had suppressed earlier spread across her cheeks at the thought. At least Daniel saw something of worth in her. She raised her chin.

"She suffered a terrible cough in the night. The Sexton children arrived with the news this morning and begged me to take over school for the day. But as you can see. . ." Mrs. Beaton sighed. "My calling is not to the classroom."

"Let me teach this afternoon, then. Tomorrow, too, if Miss Stone is still sick." Clara's heart pounded. She was still sniffling, but she felt well enough for school. Teaching usually increased her energy.

"Oh, would you?"

Clara put a hand to her mouth to cover the laugh that bubbled up at the relieved expression on Mrs. Beaton's face. "I'd love to."

"But—" Mrs. Beaton glanced at the corner where Nicholas had his nose plastered against the wall, his fingers tracing patterns on the planks. In a lowered voice, she said, "I'm mortified by what that young scamp said."

Clara waved it away. "I've dealt with worse. Go ahead and leave. I'll take over. And I'll plan on coming back in the morning."

"If you insist." Mrs. Beaton grabbed her satchel like a drowning man finding a piece of floating wood. "I'll bring you a sandwich, so you have some lunch." She scurried out the door.

Clara spared a thought for Lewis as she took a step in Nicholas's direction. Her brother could fix his own lunch if he came home, she decided. She stopped a foot away from the boy. He squirmed and sneaked a glance over his shoulder, dread masking his face.

"Do you have something you wish to say?" She spoke to his back.

"I'm sorry for calling you a spinster, Miss Farley."

"Apology accepted." She didn't blame him for repeating something he heard at home. "I will expect you to treat me with respect this afternoon. Can you do that?"

Back still to her, he nodded.

"Then go outside with the others to eat your lunch. Play in the sunshine. I'll give you some extra time."

He dashed for the door, then paused, smiling at her with a grin missing two front teeth. "Thank you, Miss Farley!" When Mrs. Beaton returned with a sandwich, Clara asked about the morning's lessons. As she suspected, they hadn't accomplished much. After a brief discussion to establish each group's assignments, Mrs. Beaton fled in the direction of the church.

Clara perused the history book the older students had been assigned to read. It could have been the same volume she used as a student, every bit as boring: a list of battles and dates and names of people now dead instead of the living, breathing story of people like the children, who had once laughed and loved. All, or almost all, children in the school had at least one ancestor who had fought in one of America's wars.

She knew at least one family that sent soldiers to every war back to the French and Indian War before Maple Notch was founded. The Tuttles. An idea formed in her mind. This afternoon, after she left the classroom, she would stop by the jail. Daniel Tuttle was the perfect person to teach in her classroom.

∽

Daniel's weary horse needed no encouragement to head home as dark descended. Another fruitless day spent establishing alibis. All the wives said their husbands had gone out to the fields, but would they know if the men had sneaked away for an hour or two? They might not know, but he doubted the married would run the risk.

Stopping by the jail, he was surprised to find Clara Farley waiting for him. A frisson of pleasure removed the weariness that had settled on his shoulders.

"Constable! I'm so glad to see you." Clara looked up from the note she was writing.

"Miss Farley." He nodded at her and removed his hat. "How may I help you this evening? Have you uncovered the culprits on your own today?"

A confused look sped across her face. "I'm afraid not. I'm here about another matter." She gestured with the paper in her hands. "I'm filling in for Miss Stone at the school, and I'd like your help."

School? The change of subject threw him off balance. "I'm at your service."

"The Tuttle family is one of the founding families of Maple Notch. You told me about your grandparents the other day. Who better to tell the pupils about the history of the United States than someone whose family has seen it from the beginning?"

He still didn't follow. "I don't understand. What do you want me to do?"

She blinked. "Why, tell your family's story, of course. Especially about the wars. I believe a personal touch would bring our history alive to the children."

His insides clenched. He didn't want to talk about his war, ever, and certainly not to children.

She swept on, heedless of his reaction. "Textbooks are full of dates and names and statistics. I want the children to know why we're fighting. And you can do that better than most. I've also asked young Nicholas Whitson to bring in his father."

Daniel snorted. "Whitson?"

"A peace offering of sorts." Her cheeks glowed, but not from cold. The possibility enthused her, transforming her into as lively a lass as any in Maple Notch.

He could no more say no than a fly could escape a spider's web. "When do you need me there?"

"When is it convenient for you?" she countered. "I thought we might breakfast together at Fannie's Café." Her cheeks glowed brighter than before. "To discuss my ideas about the investigations, and a few changes I would like to have made to the house." She spoke so fast her words blurred together. "That way, you could come straight to the school and still be on your way early."

"Is seven too early?" he asked.

∽

The sky had darkened to a deep purple before Clara made it home that evening. She found Lewis in the kitchen, holding canned green beans in one hand and a jar of applesauce in the other. Egg whites coated the counter, and she could smell burnt food from the door.

"Where have you been?" he growled.

"I'll tell you over supper. Go sit down. I'll fix something for us to eat."

Since she still had chicken stock left from Monday's dinner, she could fix a quick vegetable soup and cornbread.

She set the stock to simmering on the stove and added a variety of vegetables as well as a dash of salt and pepper and parsley. After she whipped up the cornbread, she cleaned the counter and scraped the eggs Lewis had burned into the slop bucket. She went to the pantry for a few chunks of ham to drop into the soup. Lewis hadn't taken anything for his lunch. Where had he eaten, then? It didn't matter. He was home tonight, not out drinking again.

Within an hour, she brought food to the table, but Lewis didn't come when called. When she sought him in the parlor, he had closed his eyes and splayed his limbs across the overstuffed chair. She knocked on the door, and he awoke, a startled doe expression in his eyes. Then he sniffed appreciatively. "Smells good."

"Wash your hands before you come sit down." She knew he hated the reminder, but like most men, he was no better than a little boy when it came to table manners. He joined her at the dining table a few minutes later, dressed in his Sunday-go-to-meeting clothes, spiffy, if a bit wrinkled.

"Do you want to return thanks this evening?" She always asked. He always deferred to her.

"I believe I will."

He bowed his head and began so quickly that he had said "Lord God Almighty" before she had closed her mouth.

"I thank Thee for Thy bounteous blessings to us who are so unworthy. For this food, and for the hands that prepared it. And I thank Thee for providing a job. Amen."

Before Clara could process or transition, Lewis said, "I'm famished. Let me have some of that soup."

She brought the tureen to him and ladled out a full bowl. "You have a job?" She kept her hand steady against the expectation of surprise.

"Guess who's the new bank guard?" He pointed to his chest. "Me!" He struck a somber pose but couldn't keep it, his mouth twitching with a smile. "They had me start right away, and they want me back tomorrow."

"Permanent?" Clara's breath caught in her throat. She took the tureen to her own bowl and ladled out a smaller amount.

"At least until Whitson is better." Lewis shrugged. "If I do a good job, Mr. Tuttle said he'll find another job for me at the bank. Maybe as a teller."

Clara blinked at that. "That's wonderful."

"This is delicious!" Lewis almost slurped the soup down in his excitement. She hugged his enthusiasm close to her heart. He hadn't acted this happy since Christmas when he was five years old. The last year their mother was alive. Soon his spoon hit the bottom of the bowl.

"Have some more." She had hardly started hers, but she pushed the tureen in his direction. "Take as much as you like."

First he cleaned the bowl with a chunk of cornbread, and then he ladled more soup to the rim. "So, did you settle your plans with Mr. Daniel today?"

Lewis never asked about her day. If landing a job changed him this much, she wished he had found one sooner.

"He offered to lease me the house."

"I thought you wanted to buy it."

"I did. But this may work just as well."

Lewis took his time with his second bowl of soup. Before his next spoonful, he asked, "You're excited about this. Tell me about it."

Once the floodgates opened, she talked without touching her soup. Lewis not only listened, but he also asked intelligent questions. When she slowed down enough to finish her bowl, she scooted her chair to the corner of the table near his chair and laid the notebook with her rough plans for the school—classrooms, dormers, library, the works. She sighed. "I don't know how many changes to ask for. If I ask too much, he might decide not to let me lease the house at all."

Lewis pushed the bowl away from him and leaned back, an amused gleam in his eye. "I doubt that. If you ask me, Mr. Daniel is interested in you."

Heat she couldn't blame on the now-cooling stove flooded her cheeks. "That's ridiculous."

"I agree. Why should you settle for half a man? Why, even at your age, with your inheritance, you should be able to attract the finest that Vermont has to offer."

"Why, you. . ." Anger pounded into her temples. "I do not intend on 'settling' for any man. And if I was interested, Daniel Tuttle is more of a man than I could ever hope to attract if I was eighteen and beautiful and not. . ." Anger fled her, tears taking its place.

"Oh, sis." Lewis put his arms around her in an awkward hug. "I spoke without thinking. I didn't mean to make you feel bad." He patted her shoulder. "You'll find somebody. I know you will."

Clara sniffled, but she blamed it on the lingering cold. "That's all right. I have every intention of becoming Maple Notch's resident spinster, famous countrywide for her school. That's all I've ever wanted."

Liar, her traitorous heart whispered.

Chapter 8

Clara took extra time with her toilette in the morning. She decided to break from wearing mourning, for the sake of the children. That's what she told herself. Nothing spelled gloom quite so loudly as funeral attire, and she wanted her pupils to enjoy their day at school. Lewis's words about Daniel last night had nothing to do with it. Nothing at all.

She chose a spruce green and beige gingham that she'd been told highlighted her eyes, with only a black armband to indicate her continued mourning. But the children didn't explain why she fiddled with her hair. She even pinned hair rats, made from strands she pulled from her brush, under the hair on either side of her head, to give her face a softer, rounder shape. If only she didn't need glasses to see. The thin frames emphasized her straight, pointed nose and hid the depths of her eyes. She slipped a reddish brown hairnet into her satchel, in case her hair fell down, alongside sheet music of her favorite songs. Music and story were her preferred methods to teach America's history, not dull dates and names. She'd let Miss Stone drill that information into them when she returned, if she felt it was important.

She left biscuits and bacon in the warmer oven for Lewis when he woke up. When she had informed him of her morning appointment—with enough blushes to paint the sky pink with sunrise—he pretended not to notice and only said he didn't need to report to work until nine.

She took Misty. Lewis had insisted on it, expressing concern for her safety while traveling in the dark. Had the robbery brought them to this, fearful of their neighbors and jumping at every shadow in the trees? She hoped the hysteria would soon pass.

Violence of any kind made a community uneasy. Maybe that's why she didn't enjoy studying the minutiae of war. Even so, she agreed that freedom— from Britain's tyranny and for the slaves—was something worth fighting for.

What stories would Daniel tell? Would he mention realities best left unshared with children? The older boys, who hoped the current conflict wouldn't end before they could enlist, needed to hear the truth. But not in the schoolroom. Daniel had an ear for a good story. He might stretch the truth upon occasion, but his audience would remember the story all the better for it.

She knew she'd remember every detail. His eyes burned with truth and passion, burrowing his way into her heart, no matter how much she denied it to Lewis.

Even though she arrived at the café early, Daniel was already there to help her down from the saddle. After she tethered the horse to the hitching rail, he turned so she could tuck her left arm in the crook of his right elbow, and they entered the establishment like any couple might. She turned her face aside so that he wouldn't see her telltale blush, but she sneaked glances to take in his appearance. He, too, had taken pains with dressing. His white shirt had been pressed, the left sleeve neatly pinned under his elbow; his breeches looked clean; and his hair, combed and slicked back. He looked better than fine—he almost looked like a man come courting. She shooed that thought away.

"How lovely to see you here today, Captain Tuttle! And Miss Farley, it's been far too long." Fannie, the hostess, seated them near the window, where all comers could see her prize patrons. "How may I serve you today?"

Daniel smiled at being given the place of honor. "I'll have your Lumberjack's Special."

"Two of everything, and I'll heat the syrup for you." Fannie turned to Clara as she poured coffee for Daniel—*not* the dark sludge he made for himself, she noted. "And for you?"

Clara had avoided breakfast at home so she would have an appetite, but the butterflies in her stomach wouldn't welcome greasy fare. "A bowl of oatmeal, with some tea, please." The ham sandwich and apple she had packed for lunch would have to hold her over until supper.

"That's not a very big breakfast." Daniel smiled at her and sipped the coffee. Sighing, he pushed it away. "That wouldn't keep a mosquito awake long enough to suck my blood."

Clara pushed the creamer and sugar at him. "Try these. They cover a multitude of sins, Papa used to say."

"If you call café au lait coffee." But he smiled and stirred in a little of both. "It does improve the taste, even if it doesn't keep me awake." He studied her over the cup, which looked as delicate as a chickadee in his hand. "You look nice today, Miss Farley." The hesitation in his voice belied the warmth in his eyes, as if he couldn't help saying the words.

The compliment left her so flustered she said the first thought that came into her mind. "I thought you might wear your uniform."

What warmth she had spied in his eyes fled, replaced by granite. "The last uniform I was wearing wasn't fit to come home in."

She blanched. His last uniform was the one he wore when a cannonball shattered his arm. In a small voice, she said, "I'm sorry."

"Don't be. I survived. Many less fortunate didn't. I tell myself at least I still have both my legs."

The arrival of their food saved them any further discussion on the subject. He had withdrawn into some angry, lonely place. How could she cheer him? Talk about the robbery, since that was one reason for meeting that day? No, she decided. Not yet. In his present mood, he might take it as an accusation for his lack of progress in the investigation. Nothing she could think of would bring back that spark.

A thought occurred to her and made her smile. If she couldn't cheer him up, she'd give him a different target for his anger. "What do you think would happen if I showed up at the town hall on election day to cast my vote?"

He laid down the fork he was bringing to his mouth. "What did you say?"

"I asked what you would do if I came to the town hall to vote on election day. The election *is* only two weeks away, after all." She looked down at her plate, but she had finished the oatmeal, and her appetite had returned. She gestured Fannie over and asked for more tea and a soft-boiled egg.

When she met Daniel's eyes, she didn't encounter anger, but rather, amusement.

"I do believe you're serious." He smiled.

She tossed her head and felt some of the pins she had used to tuck her hair into place fall out. "If I teach the class tomorrow, I plan on holding a mock election—and let the girls cast their votes as well as the boys."

His mouth opened and shut again, without a single word passing his lips.

She dabbed at her mouth with her napkin to hide her amusement. "The day will come when women will vote, you know. I hope it's in my lifetime. If not, certainly in my daughter's." She realized she had spoken of a daughter she had no prospect of bearing. Clara could see the girl, a lovely, auburn-haired beauty with fiery hazel eyes that lit up like the sun. Heat scorched her cheeks.

∽

Fannie returned with the requested food, and Daniel took advantage of the time Clara spent cutting the top of her egg off to drink his coffee.

Within seconds, Fannie arrived to refill his cup then went off to serve other patrons. He frowned at the pale-brown surface. Too much coffee in the cup to make café au lait. Instead, he drank from his glass of water. "I suppose you plan on teaching these radical ideas in that school of yours." His smile stretched wider.

Clara look so stricken, so worried, that he hastened to put her mind at rest. "Don't worry. I won't hold it against you. In fact, people might pay good money to see you give a speech on the subject."

"It's not a laughing matter." She lifted her chin in that way that said she wouldn't listen to any arguments.

"Who's laughing? I think I'm on to something here. Make Maple Notch the greatest learning center in all of Vermont. All of New England, for that matter. Why limit our horizons to those young ladies you hope to bring here? Why not enlighten young men as well?"

When he saw the thoughtful look cross Clara's face, he regretted the words he'd uttered in jest. She sat straight in her chair, spoon poised over her eggcup, eyes alight with some inner thought process. When she came to life again, she shook her head and took a bite. "What you propose is an intriguing idea. Someday, perhaps, but for now, I am happy to further educational opportunities for young ladies." She put down her spoon and looked at him. "I apologize for my earlier question about your uniform."

He stiffened, and she must have noticed. She hastened to add, "I was thoughtlessly thinking of the classroom like a stage, and what props an actor might bring. That's not quite what I mean. I hope you understand." She dropped her gaze again.

He took her hand in his. "Look at me." In the depths of her eyes, he saw a mirror of the anguish he allowed himself to feel on his worst days. "I know you didn't mean to offend."

She sipped her water then moistened her lips with her tongue. "You don't have to discuss your own experiences in the war unless you want to. I have no desire to bring back unpleasant memories."

He rubbed the back of her hand with his thumb. "Don't worry. There are some good memories. I can mention friends and training and campfires and belief in God." He could fill hours in the classroom without mentioning the smells of decay, the frigid cold and the stifling heat, the metallic taste of blood in his mouth, the horror of the surgeon's knife. . . . He trembled.

Now she held *his* hand. "It might be best not to mention your part in the current conflict at all. Some of the students are. . .overeager, shall we say. I'm afraid they would pester you with questions."

He regained his equanimity. "Then all the more reason I should tell them something. They all know I fought in the war, and if I don't mention it, they may ask me questions I don't care to answer."

He had been there from the beginning with the Army of the Potomac, from its first skirmish during the Peninsula campaign back in '62 through the horror that was Gettysburg, when General Sedgwick issued his famous order, "Put the Vermonters ahead and keep the column well closed up." When they covered the draft riots in New York, Daniel began to think he might survive the war unscathed. Then his regiment joined in General Grant's overland campaign, and half their number died or were wounded. Only five months had passed since then. As soon as the surgeons determined Daniel would survive the infection that set in after they amputated his arm, they sent him home. The town rewarded its hero with the position as constable. His mouth twisted. No one had foreseen bank robbery or the Confederate invasion of Vermont.

Clara's hand, a lifeline that kept him from sinking beneath the morass of his memories, withdrew from his grasp, and she reached for her reticule. Then he felt a sheet of paper slip beneath his fingers. He looked down and saw a sketch of the second floor of the Bailey Mansion.

Her lips straightened, eyes bright behind her glasses, she had moved on from discussion of the war. Her businesslike demeanor reminded him of how wrong he was to think of Miss Farley in any terms except that of friendship.

"The second floor would be our dormer floor. I would like to divide the master bedroom into two separate compartments."

Divide up his grandparents' bedroom? *I promised I would consider the changes she wanted.* Maybe he expected suggestions along the lines of extra shelves or furnishings, not structural adaptations. He studied the drawing, but it made about as much sense to him as the maps their captains used to draw up before a battle. He saw things better in person than on paper. "I'll study it and get back to you."

"Very well." If she was disappointed, she hid it well. "It's time for me to get to class. I'll expect you in about half an hour, then, after I've called roll?"

Overriding his protests, she paid her bill and left, taking all the morning brightness with her. He shivered in her absence and set about making his plans for the rest of the day. After he finished at the school, he would go to Stowe to see if any of their stores sold a hair tonic like the one the robbers used. So far, Dixon hadn't been able to identify it.

As much as he might like to spend the day with Miss Farley, he had work to do.

⁓

Clara looked at the second hand creeping around the clock. She had never called a class to order so quickly. Five minutes remained until she had asked Daniel to arrive. Nicholas Whitson's father had declined the invitation. What could they do to fill in the time? They had already read scripture and recited the Lord's Prayer.

An idea jumped to her mind. "While we are waiting for our special guest, I'm going to give you a quote. Raise your hand if you think you know who said it."

What had she done? Did she know them well enough herself? Of course she did. She had excelled in oratory at school and loved stirring patriotic speeches the best of all. Marshalling her thoughts, she pronounced, " 'We hold these truths to be self-evident, that all men are created equal, that they are endowed by their Creator with certain unalienable Rights, that among these are Life, Liberty and the pursuit of Happiness.' "

Little Libby Whitson raised her hand first. "It's from—"

"Wait until I call on you, Libby." Clara hated to douse her enthusiasm, but rules had to be followed for the contest to be fair. "You raised your hand first, Libby. You may answer. But if you are incorrect, I will ask someone else for the answer." She nodded for Libby to speak.

"That's from the Declaration of Independence. By Thomas Jefferson."

That girl deserved a gold star. "That's right, Libby. How about, 'I regret that I have but one life to give for my country'?" Clara was pleased to see that young Phineas Tuttle—Daniel's nephew—raised his hand a fraction of a second before Libby.

"Yes, Phineas?"

"Nathan Hale, ma'am, when them Brits were about to execute him."

"Exactly right. Well done." She beamed. She heard a creak at the back of the room and saw Daniel slip in. He motioned for her to continue.

"How about, 'We the People of the United States, in Order to form a more perfect Union, establish Justice, insure domestic Tranquility, provide for the common defense, promote the general Welfare, and secure the Blessings of Liberty to ourselves and our Posterity, do ordain and establish this Constitution for the United States of America.' "

"That's easy." Libby frowned. "That's from the—"

"Libby—" Clara warned her.

"The preamble to the Constitution!" Phineas finished.

Would those two young ones compete with each other all the way through school the way she and Daniel had? She wanted her seminary because of girls like Libby with bright, inquiring minds, who deserved a broader education than the public school provided. "You are correct. Remember to raise your hands. Who wrote the preamble?"

Libby's hand shot up first, and Clara nodded for her to speak. "It was written by Gouverneur Morris"

"And the year?" Clara noticed Phineas squirming in his seat.

Libby frowned. "17. . .uh. . .98?" A note of uncertainty crept into her voice. Clara had noticed she sometimes reversed her letters.

Phineas shot to his feet. "It was 1789, Miss Farley."

"You're both right. I have one last quote for you. Every one of you should know this one. Who said, 'In the name of the Great Jehovah and the Continental Congress!'"

No one raised their hands for a moment. Phineas's hand started to go up, but he pulled it down.

"I know the answer to that one." Daniel moved forward from the back door, where he had waited. "Ethan Allen, leader of our own Green Mountain Boys during our War for Independence, right before he captured Fort Ticonderoga."

The class groaned.

"With Miss Farley's permission, I'd like to give you one last quote."

She nodded.

He stood with his feet shoulder-width apart. " 'Four score and seven years ago our fathers brought forth, upon this continent, a new nation, conceived in liberty, and dedicated to the proposition that "all men are created equal."'"

Clara knew, but no one in the class raised their hands. "Let's think about it, class. A score means the same thing as twenty. If we make it into a math problem"—she took chalk in her hand and went to the blackboard—"we'd have to say—"

Young Tommy Tooms's hand went up. "Four twenties. Eighty."

"Plus?"

"Seven," Daniel prompted.

"Eighty-seven," Tommy said. "And he said eighty-seven years ago, so we'd have to subtract the number, right?"

"Very good, Tommy!" Clara wrote 1864 at the top of the board and the minus sign with 87 below it. "What's the answer?"

Tommy's hand went up again, but Clara nodded to Anna Preston this time. "One thousand seven hundred seventy-seven."

Clara covered her smile. "Or as we call the year, 1777. What was happening back in 1777?"

"He was talking about the War for Independence." Daniel smiled. "He mentioned a new nation, liberty, and equality."

Phineas's hand went up next. "How do we know he said it in 1864?"

"Excellent question, Phineas." Clara was pleased Daniel's nephew thought to ask.

"He actually spoke the words last November, in 1863. Any guesses?" Daniel looked up and down the rows of students.

Daniel's choice of quotation surprised Clara. She'd thought he planned to avoid discussing the battles of the recent war, but she played up to his game. "I believe I know the answer. President Lincoln spoke those words at

Gettysburg, where one of the worst battles in the war took place. They dedicated a national cemetery there. He said, 'The brave men, living and dead, who struggled here, have consecrated it.' He wanted to honor the people who gave their lives." She paused, realizing she was speaking in place of Daniel.

Tommy turned his attention to Daniel. "Is that where you lost your arm?"

Chapter 9

The eye of every student in the small schoolroom fastened on his stump. Daniel cleared his throat. "No, I lost my arm in a later battle."

Clara poured a glass of water and brought it to him, apology weeping from her eyes. "I'm all right," he whispered.

She clasped her hands together and faced her students. "Class, please give a warm welcome to our guest today, Captain Daniel Tuttle."

"Are you going to tell us about that battle?" Tommy persisted.

"No." That boy must be one of the ones Clara had warned him about. "I only wanted to remind us all that men—and women"—he glanced at Clara, who gave him a small smile—"came to the New World seeking freedom. They were prepared to fight, and die if need be, to defend it."

He studied the assembly. Young Libby had the beak nose of the Whitsons. Others, all freckles and smiles, hailed from the Frisk family. A few of his younger relatives were in attendance, as well. Others he didn't recognize.

"When did your families come to Maple Notch?"

Dates ranged from 1763—when the town was first settled, at the end of the French and Indian War—to as recently as 1862, when the Beatons had taken over the pastorate of the church.

"If you count the French and Indian War, which ended just before my great-grandparents came here, the men of Maple Notch have been involved in five wars." He lifted up one finger. "My great-grandfathers fought in that first war and earned the land they built their farms on. They won the land from the French and made Vermont an English colony.

" 'Tweren't but a dozen years later that we were fighting again." He lifted his second finger. "My great-uncle died at the second battle of Fort Ticonderoga, fighting so we could be a free country."

He saw several children, especially among the lads, squirming in the seats, bursting to speak. He recognized a hawk-nosed lad. "I'd guess you're a Whitson." Something triggered in his mind, and he set it aside for later.

"Yes, sir, Nicholas Whitson. My great-granddaddy fought in the Revolutionary War."

Cries of "mine, too!" rang across the room, and he nodded. "And that's why we're here today, and we have a flag with thirty-five stars—including the thirteen states who claimed to have left our country." He lifted his third finger. "Britain didn't want to let us go. So we ended up fighting them again in 1812. My father fought in that war."

He looked at the flag, the same patriotic fervor swelling in his breast that had led him to enlist when they still thought the war would be over by Christmas. If he had to do it all over again, he would. "And now here we are, fighting another battle to prove *all* men are created equal. Even if their skin is a different color. I went off to fight. A lot of men from Vermont did. Yes, I lost my arm, but I consider myself fortunate. Other men, men I considered my friends, lost their *lives*."

He walked behind a diorama a previous class had erected to illustrate the crossing of the Delaware River by George Washington. "All those battles you study about? People like me, your fathers, uncles, and grandfathers fought in them. We fought because we believed freedom was worth dying for. And some of you may well do the same."

As fast as the words had come to him, they left, and he stopped. "And I guess that's all I have to say."

He looked at Clara, who returned his gaze with an amazement that made her eyes even larger than her glasses normally did.

The children stood and clapped while Clara stayed rooted to her spot. When at last they stopped and the silence grew uncomfortable, she joined him in front of the class. "Thank you for reminding us of the price that has been paid so that we may remain free. You have given us a lot to think about. And now, class, we must say good-bye."

She began clapping again, and the children joined in, quieter this time. Her eyes strayed to the back door. He had been so focused on her face, on the lights dancing across the planes of her cheeks below the rims of her glasses, that he hadn't noticed the door opening. Dixon stood there, gesturing for his attention.

Daniel headed for the back, shaking hands as he walked down the aisle. Dixon leaned close to his ear and lowered his voice. "They've hit the bank again."

∾

Clara had followed Daniel to offer him her thanks, so she heard Dixon's announcement. She hoped the clapping kept the news from the children. She bent forward. "My prayers go with you," she whispered.

"Your brother is safe," Dixon assured her before he left.

She took a deep breath and turned around. "And now, class, here is what I want you to do." The wind blew at her back as Daniel departed with Dixon, leaving her cold and alone and a little afraid.

The Lord is with you, she reminded herself. *Don't be afraid.* The children depended on her. Even young Tommy Tooms, who towered at least half a foot taller than she did and hadn't finished growing.

"I have an assignment for you to complete by tomorrow."

Groans erupted around the classroom.

"I think you'll like this one. I want you to talk with your fathers—"

Anna Preston's face fell, and Clara remembered her father had died before she was born.

"Or uncles or grandfathers about your family's history with the army and navy. Your mothers may know the stories, too. Like Captain Tuttle's family, most of your families have sacrificed to make us free. I'll leave a note for Miss Stone, so she will know what we have been doing." If Clara taught tomorrow, she'd write up the stories in a blank book.

Time for morning recess had come, but Clara hesitated to let the children outside with the commotion of more bank robbers on the loose. If only she could go and find out what had happened herself. The hours until the end of school would drag by. Perhaps Mrs. Beaton could spell her at lunch, and she could take a break.

The children glanced to the windows, expecting their recess.

"Before we take recess this morning, I want to start our lessons." She assigned some of the students the math examples on the board; the oldest she gave the task of using their spelling words in a sentence. "Remember you will be judged for penmanship as well as spelling." She brought the youngest ones forward with her.

Later, while the children donned their cloaks, Clara checked outside the building. Discovering all was quiet, she led the children down a short trail to a dell she remembered from childhood. They had behaved so well during the extended session, she allowed them a few extra minutes to run out their energy.

Poor Daniel. He had spoken so bravely about the war, and now, once again, he faced an enemy. She filled the minutes with prayers for him, for his safety, for the apprehension of the men responsible for the robbery.

The children returned to the schoolhouse in good spirits, and she rotated the assignments. Before they started, she said, "I have another special treat in store for you today. If you finish your work in time, I'm going to read one of my very favorite stories at the end of school."

She took the middle group through the McGuffy Readers while the little ones practiced spelling words. She challenged them to think of as many words that had a long *O* as they could. "The one who spells the most correctly will get a special prize." She smiled at them. They nudged each other and set to work. The oldest ones outlined the second chapter of their history book and discussed a group project to teach it to the rest of the school.

At last, lunchtime came, and Mrs. Beaton arrived so that Clara could have a break. She grabbed her lunch sack and headed outside. Ordinary quiet sounds greeted her, as if nothing evil could assault her town. But it had. She cut across the common at her fastest pace, eager to see Lewis. Dixon had said he wasn't hurt, but he could be suffering even if he didn't receive a scratch.

Why had the robbers struck a second time? At least the St. Albans' raid made some kind of twisted sense. To Clara's way of thinking, this second robbery confirmed Confederates didn't rob the Bailey Bank, but rather locals intent on mischief.

Finding the bank door locked, Clara knocked at the entrance. Mr. Simeon himself came to the door. "Miss Farley, please come in. We've been expecting you, although I wasn't sure when you'd be able to get away."

"Thank you. I can't stay very long." She slipped past him into the obscurity of the cavernous room. A light gleamed beneath a door at the far side of the building.

"This way." Simeon led her around the obstacles in the way and opened the door. Lewis, a little pale, waved when he saw her. She rushed to his side and hugged him.

"I'm fine, Clara." He managed a weak smile.

She sensed his embarrassment and let him go. "What happened?"

"I. . .had to answer a call of nature." His face reddened deeper than a ripe tomato.

"Don't let him say that. He was our hero." Simeon took his seat behind his desk. "When he saw the horses outside, he came in the back way to warn us. They grabbed him and held the pistol to his temple." The banker sounded as proud as if he were boasting about his own son. "Not that we needed any encouragement. No man's life is worth any amount of money." He lowered his voice, although who he thought would hear him in the enclosed room, she couldn't guess. "We transferred money from one of our other accounts to help cover the losses. Now. . .now." He shook his head.

"He thinks one of us must have tipped off the robbers, since no one but bank employees knew about the transfer." Lewis shrugged his shoulders. "If you think I did it, just look at my sister's face. She didn't expect this. I didn't even tell her about your plans."

"It's *awful*." Miss Simington, an older woman who had worked at the bank for as long as Clara could remember, twisted her handkerchief in her hands. "We're questioning each other when we need to stand together."

"Now, Eunice, I think you at least should stay home until this—

danger—has passed." Simeon patted her hand like an affectionate older brother.

"But I've opened the bank every Thursday morning for the past twenty years, while you have your breakfast meeting with your directors. It's my job." She sniffed back tears. "Will we open for business tomorrow?"

From the glances over the poor woman's head, Clara guessed the question had been asked and answered before. "You have a lot to discuss, and I need to get back to the school." She wished she could have seen Daniel as well, but he must have left to chase the robbers. "I am praying for all of you."

Lewis escorted her through the dark lobby to the front door. In privacy, he hugged her to the bone. "I was scared I would never see you again." He grasped her hands. "Wait for me before you go home. I don't want you wandering the roads alone."

"That does seem the wisest course." Leaving, she waved to him as she walked across the common as she had thousands of times before. She wished Daniel could escort her home. *Shame on you, Clara Farley.* So what if he had expressed extra interest in her over the past few days? The responsibility for the safety of all of Maple Notch weighed on his shoulders.

⁓

Daniel and Dixon stopped at the bridge that crossed the river to his family's farm before continuing on the road down to Burlington. "You go on ahead to the other side." He motioned for his companion to continue.

The signs outside the bank had suggested the robbers split up when they left the bank. Daniel and Dixon had followed the clearest trail, headed west. His other deputies went after the other trails.

The robbers started on the main road, but soon their horses' hoofprints became obscured in the heavy traffic that passed along the road. He and Dixon scoured the sides of the road for any signs that the robbers might have headed into the woods. All that effort only resulted in lost time. People had crossed and crisscrossed this part of town so often over the past hundred years that it would take a mind reader to interpret the signs.

The people of Maple Notch might have named an ex-soldier as their constable, but he was no expert in detection. Give Daniel a target, and he could shoot with deadly aim. He used to be real handy in a fistfight, too, but he had yet to figure out how to make up for his missing arm. He couldn't think of a solid reason they had hired him. As soon as he had finished the six months they had offered him, he'd have to figure out what to do with the rest of his life. He wasn't cut out to be a policeman.

Below him, water rippled over rocks, a gentle October flow. The river could cover a multitude of sins when it came to escape. He nosed around the bushes that hid the bank, checking for any broken stems or torn leaves that might suggest horses had left the road to cross the riverbed.

He heard the *clip-clop* of hooves on the bridge and Dixon emerged. Daniel looked at him, but Dixon shook his head. "No luck."

The wind stirred, and Daniel heard an unexpected sound that made him think of another possibility. "Hold on a minute while I check something." He approached the bank and crouched down to peer under the bridge, but it was too dark to make out anything. He'd have to get underneath and check it out.

"Let me." Dixon came alongside, but Daniel shook his head. A stubborn streak a mile wide wouldn't let him admit he couldn't still do the things he had done before the war. He might not have two hands to grab on to outcroppings anymore, but he was taller now than he had been as a boy. He sat down and wiggled forward as far as possible before he jumped. His left arm flailed helplessly at the bank during the short drop. He couldn't seem to stop those involuntary reflexes.

"Are you all right?" Dixon's voice trailed after Daniel, but he didn't answer. He dropped to his belly and crawled forward, keeping out of sight of the dark underbelly of the bridge. With about two yards to go, he stopped moving, listening for movement. This close, the water sounded louder, a small whirlpool circling where it pushed past the pylons. A lone woodpecker knocked against a nearby tree.

Wood creaked overhead. Daniel tensed, watching for movement. None came, and he decided it must have been the wind whistling through cracks in the floor of the bridge. The next time he went to the farm, he'd tell Hiram the bridge needed some repair.

Daniel crept closer, coming up on his knees and grabbing his pistol as he prepared to expose himself to anyone who might be lurking. Silently he counted *three, two, one* and plunged ahead, weapon pointed straight ahead. A raccoon ran past him, chattering about the disruption, dropping his prize on his way past. No other life forms greeted him.

The small round object the raccoon had dropped gleamed like a drop of sunlight on the ground, and Daniel's heart beat faster. Raccoons liked to collect shiny things. Taking a stick, he cleared the space around the object until its outlines became clear: one bright gold coin.

He let out a low whistle. He couldn't prove this coin belonged to the bank batch, of course. But he'd guess he could search every person in town that day and not a one of them would have gold on his person. Once he pocketed the gold piece, he studied the area underneath the bridge for other signs of the robbers' passage. The bridge had become a favorite spot for people for all kinds of reasons. Town frolics found their way there year round.

As a boy, he had hidden under the bridge, waiting for courting couples to pass by. People called it the "kissing bridge," claiming if a man took his time crossing it, he could steal two kisses from his gal. Deep gray eyes hidden behind thin glass frames swam into Daniel's mind, and he imagined her lips soft beneath his.

He chased the thought away. He didn't discover anything else, but he'd bet his bottom dollar that the robbers had passed overhead. He crawled from beneath the bridge and stared up the bank.

Dixon stood there, rope ready in his hands. "Thought you could use this to help you get up." That was Dixon, helping Daniel without making him feel helpless. He grabbed the rope with his good arm, found his footing, and managed to scramble up the bank.

As soon as Daniel crowned the top, a wide grin broke out on his face. "Look what the raccoon found for us," he said as he took the hankie out of his pocket and unwrapped the coin.

Dixon held the coin up to the light and pinged it with his finger. "That's the real thing, all right."

In the bright noon sunshine, Daniel saw fluff caught in the ridges of the coin. "Be careful with that. It's probably just the sack the robber carried it in, but I'll check it out. Maybe we'll get lucky." He pocketed the coin again. "Come on. They went over the bridge."

In the half light of the bridge, Daniel couldn't see any details. "I'll have to come back with a light. I'll borrow a lantern from Hiram when we come back." He rubbed his hand across his forehead. "If we had come straight ahead instead of stopping for every bent twig, we might have caught them here."

"You did what you thought was best," Dixon said. "Don't beat yourself up over it."

Daniel's attention snagged on a much-marked spot on the wall: the courting plank. Nearly every couple in Maple Notch carved their initials there, ever since his parents had started the tradition when his father had built the bridge. His grandparents were there, too, carved when the plank was still a tree growing in the woods. He came from a proud lineage, but what would they think if they could see the mess he had made of the robbery?

Clara would say they wouldn't have done any better. They were ordinary people, not ancient Greek gods. He smiled to himself at the thought. Forget mythology. Neither did they have the wisdom of Solomon nor the strength of Samson.

Maybe lunch at his brother Hiram's house would help him figure out the next step.

∽

" 'He loved his country as no other man has loved her; but no man deserved less at her hands.'" Clara closed the pages of the magazine. Young Libby had tears in her eyes, and no one spoke a word.

The children had held Clara to her promise. When they finished early, she pulled out the December issue of the *Atlantic Monthly* to the opening pages. The anonymous story "The Man without a Country" affected her class the same way it had touched her when she read it for the first time. Philip Nolan, the man condemned to live with his outburst that "I wish I may never hear of the United States again," became both the most pitiable and noblest of patriots before his death.

"One more thing."

Around the classroom, groans erupted.

"I am going to ask Miss Stone to give you extra credit if you bring back an essay about all the reasons why you love the United States." She smiled. "You are dismissed."

The children piled out of the classroom quickly, all except one. Libby crept close to her. "Can I find that story in a book? 'Cause I know I can't borrow your magazine."

Clara shook her head. "As far as I know, it's only been published in this magazine." She looked at the pages she held in her hand and debated. Did she dare let go of them long enough for Libby to copy the story? She knew from sad experience that lending a book often meant she would never see it again.

She looked into the girl's bright eyes and burned with purpose to see *this* girl expand her knowledge. "I must hold on to this copy for future classes, but I will write out the story and give it to you." She tapped the magazine against her chin. "I may even be able to get a copy from one of my friends."

"You would do that for me?" Libby's feet danced with excitement.

"I would." Clara thought of Daniel's practice of reading from the Bible morning and evening before he would read anything else. "But I want you to promise me something."

"What is it?" Libby looked like she would run to St. Albans and back.

"Promise me you'll read your Bible every day. We both love a good story, but only God's words will last forever."

"I will do that. Thank you, Miss Farley!" Libby made it as far as the door before she turned around again. "I like Miss Stone, but I wish you were our teacher."

Clara hoped she would teach Libby again someday, at her own school. From the door, she watched her students scatter to the four winds. Should she have dismissed them with robbers about? Surely the criminals wouldn't harm innocent children.

The bank hours usually ended half an hour after school let out, but Clara didn't know about today, with the robbery. She would copy the story for Libby while she waited after she walked around the town green. At her school, she would move as many classes into outdoor learning experiences as she could.

She had circled the green once when Lewis headed in her direction from the road leading to their house. She moved to meet him. "Did they let you leave early?"

Lewis nodded. "Mr. Tuttle said there wasn't anything left worth guarding, so I might as well go home. He looked pretty discouraged."

A stone settled in Clara's heart. Did this latest development mean he had lost his depositors' money?

"You didn't have to come back for me. You could have sent a message, and I would have found another way home."

"No." He smiled at her. "I am taking you out to dinner tonight. You've put in a hard day with those young critters and deserve to relax."

"Where did you get the money to pay for a meal?"

"I'm a working man now." He cocked his thumbs on his shoulders.

"You should keep that money."

"Clara." He sounded exasperated. "You take care of me all the time. Let me do something for you for once." In that moment, he looked just like Papa, and her heart melted.

"Very well. This one time." She accepted his arm and walked with him to the café.

Chapter 10

Late-afternoon sunshine poured through the windows, giving the interior of the café a warm, friendly feeling. At midafternoon, Clara and Lewis were the only customers.

The bell on the door rang as they entered the room. "Just a minute," Fannie called from the kitchen.

Lewis took advantage of the delay to walk down the counter. "Look at that pie. Mmhmm." He grinned at Clara.

"I don't want dessert."

"Of course you do. This is my treat, remember?" He grinned again. "Pumpkin pie or spice cake. A hard choice."

"Eat your meal first." She used her best schoolmarm voice. "You shouldn't eat dessert unless you clean your plate."

He arched an eyebrow. "Yes, ma'am!"

Fannie came from the kitchen. "Miss Farley!" She blinked twice. "I don't often have the pleasure of your company twice on the same day."

Would the overly talkative waitress tell the world Clara Farley was a spendthrift, not to mention too lazy to cook a meal?

"And Mr. Farley." Fannie relaxed her face into her best simper. "I heard about your bravery at the bank today. Were you hurt?"

"I didn't do anything special." He bowed in her direction. "Thank you for your concern."

Fannie led them to the front table and rattled off their choices. "If you care to wait until after four, you may choose from our dinner menu."

"What say you?" Lewis asked.

"That's only half an hour from now. It will be getting dark before we head home. . . ." Clara chewed her lip. "But why not? My brother doesn't take me out to dinner all that often." For tonight, she would relax and pretend Fannie believed she had a dozen lads chasing her. Even if one was her brother.

"Then we will each have a bowl of soup for now, and we'll be your first dinner customers." Lewis turned on a smile full of sunshine and charm, one Clara recognized from long experience.

In spite of Lewis's good humor, Clara wished a man of more serious demeanor could join her for dinner this evening. Daniel had no one to fix him a hot meal, to take care of him after his hard day. She suppressed the desire to jump up from the table and take a hot plate over to the Bailey house.

The town constable occupied altogether too much of her thoughts recently.

∽

Lunch with Hiram provided no answers to Daniel's questions, but at least he left with a full stomach and a pan full of leftovers.

"You're too thin. You need to marry some nice young woman and let her take care of you." Hettie piled enough food for a week on his plate.

"Hush, woman." Hiram chuckled. "Don't take any mind of Hettie's fussing. She just wants the best for you."

Later, after they finished eating, Hiram followed Daniel out to the barn, where he fed the horse a handful of oats. "I know you think no one will have you. But I bet Hettie could find half a dozen women between now and Sunday dinner who would be more than willing to take a chance on you."

Daniel felt like jumping on the horse's back and dashing down the road as fast as the gelding could gallop. But he wouldn't treat his brother that way. "Don't even suggest that."

"There's someone." Amusement laced Hiram's voice. "Someone has finally caught your eye."

"It's nothing." Daniel fiddled with the saddle straps.

"There *is* someone." Hiram tapped his chin. "But who? You've talked with nearly every female in Maple Notch since the robberies began." His eyes, as dark a brown as their father's had been, searched Daniel's for clues. "But it's none of them." He snapped his fingers. "I know. You have been doing business with Miss Farley."

A muscle in Daniel's cheek quivered at the mention of her name, and heat scampered up his neck and into his cheeks.

"Miss Clara Farley." Hiram shook his head. "She's a bit thin and spinsterish for my taste, but—"

"She's no spinster." When Daniel saw the mirth in his brother's eyes, he knew he had revealed more than he intended. "I saw her at the school today. Miss Stone is sick." He looked sideways at his brother. "Now, that one *is* a spinster."

Hiram snickered.

"Phineas performed well. You should be proud." By the time Daniel finished detailing his nephew's accomplishments, he had derailed Hiram's interest in Clara. Or so he hoped.

"Hettie will see Clara at the ladies' meeting next week." Hiram clapped Daniel on the back as they headed out of the barn. "I'll ask her to do some sleuthing of her own."

Of all the... Daniel wished the subject had never come up with Hiram. But with his father gone, his oldest brother tried to take his place. Daniel shouldn't resent his...concern. But no one in the Tuttle family had ever needed a marriage broker, and they wouldn't start with him. Not if he could help it.

Then you need to speak to Clara of your interest before someone else spills the beans.

That thought scared Daniel more than all the enemies he had faced in battle.

∽

Daniel put his brother's interference out of his mind to consider how best to pursue the robbers. Had they headed south, down toward Lake Champlain and New York? Headed up river and crossed back at the next bridge?

The circle of suspects had tightened, limited to the people aware of the gold shipment. That included a handful of people on the Burlington end and a slightly larger number at this end, as well as anyone they might have told. He'd have to ask Simeon for a complete list. A conversation with his brother was his best choice, since trailing the robbers had proved useless. By now, they could have circled back and arrived home as if they had never left. His shoulders slumped. He was useless as a lawman.

Once he arrived in town, he headed straight for Simeon's house, a few blocks away from the bank. His brother opened the door before he knocked. "I've been expecting you." Simeon looked resigned when Daniel reported his lack of progress. He provided Daniel with a list of all his employees, which exceeded two dozen people in all. Another two hours passed while they sifted through who knew about the shipment, who had been at work, and who had the day off, but at last Daniel had as much information as Simeon could provide.

"If you had to guess?" Daniel prodded.

"Believe me, I've thought of very little else." Simeon shrugged. "I don't want to think any of them are guilty, but someone must be. Let me sleep on it overnight. There's something niggling at my mind, but I can't quite place it."

The following morning, Daniel stopped by the café for his usual breakfast. "Will Miss Farley be joining you this morning?" Fannie asked as she ushered him to a small table toward the back corner. He smiled to himself. Alone, he didn't get the same special treatment he had received yesterday. Bright curiosity rimmed her eyes. Had the community started linking his name with Clara's on the basis of a single meal?

"No."

"She's been coming in real regular. She was here last night with that handsome brother of hers." Fannie's smile said she had succumbed to Lewis's charms. With his charm, he might marry before his sister did. Some men had all the luck.

Or all the trouble. He smiled at the memory of his father's cheerful warning against marrying in haste and repenting at leisure. Marriage to a woman like Clara wouldn't be easy, but he would never get bored, either.

Daniel's stomach clutched. He wanted to see Clara again, but not here, where all the ears of Maple Notch could hear their private business. Perhaps he should go to her home, since he needed to speak with Lewis about his whereabouts over the past two days.

When Fannie poured his coffee, she took something out of her pocket and rubbed it with her apron. "Will you take a look at this?" She handed him a gold coin, as shiny as the day it had left the mint.

She dropped the coin in Daniel's palm, where it burned like it had just left the refiner's fire.

∽

When Clara awoke in the morning, the sun had already risen. Surprised Lewis hadn't invited her to join him for breakfast, she threw on a dressing gown and checked his room. He lay motionless in his bed.

"Lewis! Get up!"

He opened one eye. "Oh, it's you." He closed it again.

"Your job!" She sat next to him on the bed and nudged him in the side.

"The bank won't be open today. Mr. Tuttle told me he'd send word when he needs me again."

She threw her hands in the air. "I wish you had told me last night." If the bank closed for several days, when would she have a chance to speak with Mr. Simeon about leasing the house? With days sliding toward November and winter weather, she might not be able to open the school in the spring as she had hoped.

"Sorry."

Clara sniffed. A faint odor of liquor wafted through the air, and she got down on her knees. A partially empty whiskey bottle sat under his bed, right next to a coin purse, much fuller than it should be from two days' work at the bank. She felt its weight in her hand, drawing it out from beneath the bed.

"Wait, Clara, I can explain."

"Later." Grabbing the bottle, she marched out the door, down the stairs, and threw it as far as she could. It smashed with a satisfying thud against a nearby maple tree. She slid down on the front steps and wrapped her arms around her waist. Tears she had held back when her father had died, when her hopes for the school had been delayed and delayed again, when every possible suitor had turned and run, all surfaced at this final indignity.

Lewis came behind her. "Clara, it's not what you think."

"It's exactly what I think. I've blinded myself to your wrongdoings all along. Go. Get out of here. And don't come home until you're ready to make things right."

Lewis put a hand on her shoulder, but she shook it off. He plodded toward the barn, each step hitting her heart hard. The barn door banged, and horse hooves clattered down the lane. Lewis had taken her at her word, and she couldn't call him back.

Clara knew all this without watching, even though she curled herself into a ball, trying not to see or hear or feel. No feelings at all would be better than the despair that overwhelmed her.

"Clara!" A different voice, a beloved voice promised comfort and succor. *Daniel.* "What happened to you?"

A small part of her came alive at the sound of his voice, the part that wanted to enjoy sunshine and sing for joy. She opened her eyes and unwound her arms from around her middle. She looked into eyes fiery with compassion and worry—for her. He took her fingers in his right hand. Shivering, she glanced at the place where their arms touched. . .and saw the ribbons dangling from the end of her dressing gown. Her hand shot to her mouth. "I'm not dressed."

He chuckled. "I noticed. Do you feel well enough to get into some clothes?"

"I have to." She dashed inside and up the stairs, passing a full length mirror as she did so. Rather than horror, the figure that she saw bespoke of feminine allure. Oh, not her curves. Her nightdress, while not appropriate attire, was modest enough. But color flushed her cheeks and her hair framed her naked face, her gray eyes sparkling with the wash of her recent tears. She looked almost. . .pretty. In light of the heartrending start to her morning, the sight mocked her.

She poured water into a basin and scrubbed her face until it gleamed from the effort, tear stains banished. A quick brush of her hair sufficed before putting it in a bun. Last of all she slipped into her blackest outfit, as befitting her mood.

When she went downstairs, she hoped Daniel hadn't left. She found him in the kitchen.

"I made you some coffee." He grinned as if it was an old joke. "Café au lait style, or at least my attempt at it."

She smiled, her fakest smile yet, and settled into a chair. "Thank you."

"Have you eaten breakfast?"

"That's none of your concern."

He took one step toward her, smoke gathering in his eyes, and ran his knuckle along her cheekbone. "I'd like to make it my concern, Miss Clara Farley. Anything that troubles you troubles me." Then he smiled again, as if he hadn't just turned her world on its head, and grabbed a handful of eggs from the egg basket. "I'll fry us up some eggs."

Clara put one hand to her cheek, once again hot to touch, her heart seared with the briefest flicker of kindness. She wanted to run and shout to the skies. She wanted to slide through a crack in the floor. What she had to do was decide whether to tell the lawman her suspicions about her brother.

No, she decided. Not unless he asked. She wouldn't lie, but neither would she offer suspicions without proof.

She took a loaf from the breadbox and turned to the knife drawer. Daniel placed his hand over hers. "Breakfast is my treat this morning. You go sit down." Slicing the bread, he held it over a flame as if he had done it forever.

Clara wished he would let her do something so she could calm the riot in her mind. Did he think he could announce "anything that troubles you troubles me" and expect her to be unmoved? To cover her confusion, she sipped the coffee, a perfect dark roast lightened with milk, which warmed her to her toes.

He must have noticed when she finished the cup, because he appeared at her elbow with the coffeepot. "Do you want some more?"

"Yes. It's delicious."

He poured a bit of coffee in the cup and then added milk warmed in a pan before stirring them together. "I understand heating the milk is the secret to a good cup. I'll let you add whatever sugar you want."

After he set breakfast on the table, he carried on light banter while they ate. With each bite, she regained a portion of her equanimity. When she had finished, she felt less frightened of speaking with him, even if not quite ready.

Daniel cleared the table and fixed them both another cup of coffee. "Shall we move to the parlor?" His gentle smile encouraged her to move.

Daniel took the overstuffed chair that was Lewis's favorite seat, and Clara's worries returned. She set down her coffee cup.

He leaned forward. "I am willing to listen to whatever upset you so this morning."

No. I can't. I won't.

He paused, and when she didn't answer, he spoke again. "But I suspect you're a lot like me. You don't want to talk about it." He raised an eyebrow, and she nodded.

"That's what I thought. So, I'll tell you why I came here instead. I need to talk to Lewis, is all. We're concentrating on—"

"Bank employees. Of course." She couldn't put off the decision any longer. Should she say something or not? "I'm afraid he's not here."

"I noticed his horse was gone when I put my horse in the barn." Daniel sipped his coffee. "When do you expect him home?"

"He doesn't tell me his plans." *I made him leave.* "He may not come back for a few days, since the bank is closed."

"And do you know where he went?"

She shook her head, and he sighed. "Please tell me as much as you know about his movements this week."

"I suggested he apply for the job. Which he did." The fact that it had brought her so much joy at the time now hung heavy in her heart. "He spent the last two days at the bank, and last night he took me out to dinner."

"Dinner at the café. Fannie mentioned that to me this morning." Daniel looked to the window and then back at her. "She said he paid her with this." He reached into his pocket and pulled out a gold coin.

～

The color that had brightened and softened Clara's face fled in an instant, and Daniel's heart sank. *No, please, no.* He didn't want his suspicions confirmed any more than Clara would want to believe it.

"He said Simeon paid him yesterday." She glanced away.

Daniel turned the coin over in his palm. "Do you know if he has more coins like this?"

She hesitated. "Not for certain."

He waited her out. He didn't want to put words into her mouth, but silence often provoked further conversation.

"I found a coin purse in his room, but I didn't look in it. For all I know, it's filled with pennies."

"Let's go see, then, shall we?" Without giving her time to protest, he set down his cup and headed for the stairs. He heard her soft tread behind him and paused. "It's that way." He didn't need her to point the way since a faint but perceptible odor of liquor was evident.

Clara followed him as far as the doorway. "The coin purse was underneath the bed." Misery dripped from her voice.

Daniel's hand scooted around the cavity but encountered nothing but a few dust balls. "It's not there. Does he have any other hiding places?"

She hesitated, perhaps unwilling to intrude on her adult brother's privacy. Her mouth thinning in a straight line, she went to the bureau and opened the second drawer, where she pulled out a cigar box from the far corner.

"As a boy, he put his most prized treasures in here." Clara ran her hands over the top. "A never-fail fishing lure. The ribbons he won at school. Any rock that he found especially interesting. That kind of thing." She lifted it to her ear and shook it, as if guessing the contents. "It's too light for anything heavy."

"Let's open it and see, shall we?"

Clara gave it to Daniel, her teeth biting into her bottom lip, and retreated to the door.

The box that had seemed enormous to him as a boy now fit in one hand. He hefted it and looked at the clasp. "Doesn't look like it's been opened for a while." He smiled at her, and the worry on her face lessened by a fraction.

He lifted the cover and breathed a sigh of relief. Nothing there but the mementos of a man's boyhood, darkened by grime deposited over the years. To make certain, he lifted out the items one at a time, checking for anything hidden at the bottom of the box. A sheet of paper, folded in half, detailed a map with X marking the spot of some buried treasure. The crude writing and crayon pronounced the work of a child, not a grown man. Not that he expected Lewis to leave a map to his treasure, in any case.

The thought wouldn't leave him alone, though. What had worked well before might serve the same purpose a second time. He and Clara needed to go on a treasure hunt.

Chapter 11

D o you know anything about this?" Daniel handed Clara the map. He headed out the bedroom door and back down the stairs. He heard a slight giggle and relaxed.

"Lewis was fascinated by the stories of the famous pirate LaFitte." Her face softened, and he saw traces of the young girl she had been. "Papa told him no pirates ever came to Vermont, that we don't even have an ocean here, but Lewis loved to pretend. He spent an entire summer searching for buried treasure. Whenever I needed to find him, I'd have to follow his latest treasure map."

"Did he bury treasure of his own?" Daniel wiggled his eyebrows.

"Of course!" She covered her mouth with her hand. "Oh."

Daniel took a deep breath. He wished he didn't have to ask the next question. "Can you find the spot marked on this map?"

"But he was just a child. . . ." Her voice trailed away. "I know exactly where it is. Come with me."

She could have avoided the question, but Clara wasn't that kind of woman. Tension screamed from her shoulders, as rigid as a plumb line, but she led him outside. "The big red box is the barn, of course." She pointed to an overgrown field to the west. "And the round green circle is the field Papa let lie fallow. Behind that are the trees. The black circle is the well, or rather, where the well used to be." She studied the map again, a crude *X* covering a field of purple and blue. "He dug his hole in a patch of wildflowers. He made me mad when he destroyed all that beauty for pretend treasure. It's this way." Without warning, she took off across the yard, and he let her take the lead. Right now, she'd welcome his company about as much as a polecat.

She led him about a five-minute walk into the woods, far enough to feel like an adventure to a small boy. The place where she stopped looked a lot like the woods around them.

"I believe this is the place, although it's hard to tell." She gazed into the tree branches. "The tree has grown since then, but I see the crook where I used to climb." Her face colored. "I spent a summer climbing trees before I decided no girl should do such a thing." She shook her head. "Whatever he buried is in this spot. There's only one problem." She gestured. "Neither one of us brought a digging tool."

"That's all right." Daniel bent down to examine the spot. "No one has dug here for years. We'd know if there had been any recent activity."

The last of the worry lines disappeared from Clara's face. "Then he hasn't been here." She acted like it proved Lewis's innocence, but then her shoulders slumped. "Not that that means anything."

Daniel put his good arm around her shoulders. "Let's head back. Things will sort themselves out." She allowed his embrace, leaning into him, and his heart sang.

⁓

Clara welcomed Daniel's strength of mind, of character, of body. How tired she was of doing things on her own, taking care of a brother like a parent instead of being his older sister and friend. She made no move to put space between her and Daniel, lost in their own private Camelot. She could rest there forever. All too soon they reached the fields and then the yard. He let go of her shoulder and opened the door to the barn.

She lit a lamp to chase the shadows. If only she could find a lantern of truth to light the way through the mess with Lewis. She looked out the open door, willing him to return with an innocent explanation. In her heart, she knew that wouldn't happen.

"Even if he is involved, he didn't act alone." Daniel shuffled his feet.

She turned a snort into a hiccup. "Does that make it any better?"

"Maybe not in the eyes of the law, but it matters to me. Sometimes a group of men will do things they would never do as individuals." His eyes grew dark, and she wondered if some dark memory haunted him.

He shook himself and walked to the back wall. "Are these yours?" He pointed to a pair of heavy saddlebags.

She shook her head. "They belong to Lewis."

"Do you mind?" Assuming her assent, he lifted the bags from the peg and brought them to her. As soon as he opened the bag, odors assaulted her. The condensed aroma of tobacco and whiskey cleared her breathing, and spices reminiscent of church and kitchen tickled her memory—Lewis's cologne.

"I'll have to take this with me." Daniel didn't move, his forage cap in his hand. "I won't tax your conscience and make you promise to tell me when you see Lewis again. I will leave that between the two of you and God." He looked at her then, and the sad smile on his face made her tingle all over.

She wanted to throw herself into his arms, to promise him the moon, but she couldn't. "I appreciate that."

He handed her the map, letting his hand linger a moment longer than necessary before he grabbed the reins of his horse. The horse moseyed toward the barn door, keeping pace with her steps. After mounting the horse, Daniel paused. "I meant what I said earlier. Every word." He bent over and kissed the top of her head. Then with a kick into the sides of the horse, he burst into the sunshine and headed away from Clara.

She wandered into the house, dazzled and dazed. She looked in the same mirror that had reflected her in her dressing gown earlier. The same rosy cheeks and bright eyes stared back at her. She patted the top of her head, where she could feel the imprint of his kiss. Before she could change her mind at such a foolish act, she grabbed a pair of scissors and cut a small swatch of hair from the crown of her head and slipped it into a locket. Not until she finished cleaning up the breakfast dishes did she realize they hadn't once discussed her plans for the school. Where had her brain disappeared when it mattered? Hiding in the shadow of her heart, apparently. If she couldn't get Daniel Tuttle out of both heart and head, she might have to find another place to start her school.

From then on, the day worsened. The promising sunshine of early morning clouded over by midafternoon and settled into a perpetual twilight indicative of snow. Where had Lewis gone? She regretted her threat. The last place he needed to go was among people who would encourage further wrongdoing. "Lord, You know where he is. And he is Yours." At least she thought Lewis was a Christian. As a boy, he had gone forward at a revival meeting and been baptized. For a time, he hungered for spiritual things as much as she did. What had happened to him?

The hours stretched out like the expanse of the ocean the one time she had seen it. Even *Walden* couldn't hold her attention today. Turning mattresses and adding quilts burned some of her energy before she extracted the *Atlantic Monthly* to copy the story for Libby.

By day's end, snow fell like a fine mist, covering the ground with a crazy quilt design. She went to the barn for the evening chores. The unique aroma of Lewis's cologne seemed to hang in the air, taunting her. How hadn't she recognized it before? Maybe she could blame it on her sniffles.

The door swung open, light outlining a shadowy figure on horseback. Afraid as never before, Clara backed into the far corner, where she hoped the darkness would hide her. But then she recognized the profile and knew her brother had returned.

Lewis whistled, a march that rang in her ears, and she slid down the wall. He had no right to be so happy, not when he had brought such misery on the town.

The time had come for Lewis to take accountability for his actions. She would go to Daniel in the morning and tell him she would help him in any way she could.

∽

"Are you certain about this?"

Clara's determination almost faltered under the kindness of Daniel's gaze, but she held on. "Yes. If he's innocent, I want it proven. And if he's guilty, then. . .I do him no favors by protecting him from the consequences of his actions."

The weight on Clara's heart had lightened when she found Daniel at the jail, since she didn't leave home until after Lewis had left. What if he asked questions about her destination? *Oh, I'm just going into town to talk with Captain Tuttle about catching you and the other bank robbers.*

"Very well." Daniel drummed his fingers on the desk. "Your timing is perfect. Simeon is joining me in a few minutes to discuss our plans." He stood and retrieved a coffeepot from the stove. "Want a cup? I'll warn you: It's my usual mud. Maybe I should serve it to you in a bowl with a spoon."

She giggled. Trust Daniel to find a way to bring humor to the sad situation. "I'll pass, thank you."

He poured himself a cup and put the pot back on the stove. "I'm surprised you came into town, with the snow last night."

"That dusting wouldn't keep a bear in his den unless he had already settled in for his winter's nap." She didn't know if she was pleased or offended that Daniel saw her as a fragile flower ready to wither at the first sign of bad weather.

He saluted her with the cup.

Silence stretched. "Did you ask about the saddlebags?" She had to know the answer.

Daniel's smile faded. "Beaton recognized the scent. It was the same one he smelled on the day of the robbery."

A sliver of hope disappeared with the answer. Clara glanced at the clock. As the minute hand inched toward the top of the hour, the front door opened, and Simeon Tuttle poked his head in.

"Daniel, I didn't know you had an appointment. I'll come back."

"No, come on in. Miss Farley is going to take part in our discussions."

The banker hid well any surprise he felt. That inexpressive face probably served him well in business. Not Daniel. His eyes ranged between surprise and delight and anger with very little attempt to hide his emotions.

Simeon dragged the only other chair in the room to the front of Daniel's desk and cocked his head in Clara's direction. "How can we help you? We're not ready to finalize the arrangements about the house with the recent problems at the bank."

She shook her head. "That's not why I'm here." A glance at Daniel told her he left the explanation up to her. Tugging her bottom lip between her teeth, she said, "I want to get to the truth about Lewis. If he is involved, and even—Lord be thanked—if he is not. And to identify who else might be responsible."

"Ah." Simeon settled back in his chair and rubbed his chin with his hand. "I appreciate that."

"Daniel—Captain Tuttle—said you had a plan?"

"We worked it out yesterday." Simeon glanced at Daniel, who nodded. "We need to replenish cash in the bank, since they wiped us out."

"Of course."

"Don't look so worried." Daniel smiled at her. "We have a plan."

So you say. "And that is?"

"A decoy." Daniel gestured for his brother to explain.

"I will let it slip that we are expecting a lockbox by carriage tomorrow— on Saturday, when the bank is ordinarily closed. The carriage will stop at the bridge, where the money will be transferred to a single rider."

"Me." Daniel grinned. "As well as a posse of men prepared to take action, but they will be well hidden."

Clara's heart shuddered. The proposal exposed everyone involved to danger.

"We're going to be sure they know exactly where the exchange will take place. When I examined the old bridge yesterday, I noticed a lot of good hiding places. An excellent place for an ambush."

"If robbery is attempted, we'll catch them red-handed." Excitement stripped years from Simeon's countenance.

Clara caught sight of the handcuffs dangling from the wall behind Daniel's desk, ready for the bank robbers. A vision of Lewis dragged off to jail like a common criminal swam before her eyes, but she hardened her heart. He would only be arrested if he was involved. "How can I help?"

Simeon held his hands in front of him, and she noticed how white and clean they were, indicative of someone who worked with his brain and not with his hands. Unlike Daniel's strong, brown hand, which promised single-handed rescue if the need arose. "Please tell Lewis that we need the bank employees back in the morning. I'll send a messenger as well, but I want to reinforce the request."

Daniel blew air from his cheeks and slapped his hand against the heavy desk. "And if you should happen to mention the gold shipment. . ." His eyes grabbed hers, daring her to say no.

The windowless building crowded in on Clara, stealing her breath with its stale odor of past sins and justice applied. "I'll do it." With those words, she stood. "Now, if you'll excuse me." If she didn't leave soon, she'd faint on the spot.

Once outside, deep breaths of the cold autumn air shocked her into alertness. She considered going to Dixon's to check for new books. Before she had decided her next move, Daniel and Simeon left the jailhouse.

As Simeon headed for the bank, Daniel approached her. "I've thought about your requested changes to the house."

Thoughts swirled in Clara's head for a moment before the change of subject registered. "Good. I've wondered what the status was." She forced a chuckle. "When I wasn't worrying about Lewis."

"Shall we discuss the changes over one of Fannie's fine breakfasts?" He gestured in the direction of the café, a smile warming his face, as if the fact she had agreed to betray her brother didn't matter.

"I already had breakfast, but a cup of coffee would be nice." She laughed. "Real coffee. No offense meant."

"And none taken." He offered her his arm, as if they did this kind of thing every day, and she accepted it.

If they walked arm in arm in plain sight around the common many more times, the town would buzz with gossip of their courtship. Clara allowed herself to look up at his face, his strong chin, matching her strides to his purposeful movements, and she forgot anyone who might be watching.

Good cheer fell like mist when they entered the café; the red-and-white checkered curtains and the white linen tablecloths made even a lowly breakfast meal feel special. Fannie greeted them at the front. "I'm glad to see you again. We have two cinnamon rolls left. I'll ask Cook to set them aside for you."

Daniel's murmur of approval overrode Clara's protest. Fannie poured coffee without asking while she took his order, the Lumberjack's Special, and then disappeared into the kitchen. He noticed Clara's astonished look. "I may not get any lunch. This'll have to do me."

"You don't need to apologize. Lewis rarely eats breakfast."

At the mention of her brother's name, Daniel's cheeks darkened, and Clara regretted her comment. She didn't want anything to mar their pleasant exchange. "I'm sorry. I shouldn't have mentioned him."

"Of course you should. He's your brother." Daniel poured cream and sugar into his coffee but paused before stirring it. "Don't make the mistake of thinking all men are like him."

His gaze seared her from the top of her head down to her toes, and she drank from her glass of water to cool off. "I don't." Her voice sounded small, even to herself. She forced her lips into a smile and looked up. "You said you've considered the changes I requested?"

He took a handful of papers from his pocket and unfolded them, evening out the creases as he placed them on the table. "I agree with most of them, but I have alternate suggestions for a couple of your ideas. . . ."

∽

Daniel could have stayed at the café all day. As it was, he put his hand over the top of his coffee cup when Fannie tried to refill it for the fourth time. A few people had already started to wander in for their luncheon.

Discussing the school—both the physical space and Clara's rather radical ideas—brought her to life. Daniel loved watching this Clara. She argued her ideas as skillfully as Lincoln and Douglas in their famous debates, and her voice rose in pitch as she hurled words at Daniel. With every cup of coffee, her speech sped up, and her cheeks blazed with more color until the red and white patches on her face could have provided the inspiration for the checkered pattern of the curtains. Her hands flew in a dozen directions as she explored and explained what she needed for the school. Through her eyes, he could see her vision.

With his refusal of that final cup of coffee, the time had come to go. "So if we are agreed, I'll order supplies from Dixon and arrange for the work to start." A part of him wanted to deny her the school, to instead offer a future with gray-eyed children who would bring his grandparents' house to life again. But no. The man who won Clara's heart must understand the passion that drove her. Daniel would no more snatch that away from her than. . .he would have given his arm if he had had a choice.

But someday, maybe. . .

A man could dream.

Maybe the time for dreaming was over. Maybe it was time for this man to act.

Chapter 12

Daniel rode down the road that connected the Tuttle farm with Maple Notch. Land west of the river that separated them from town had once been mostly wilderness. His great-grandfathers had worked their entire lives to carve holdings out of the forest.

In time, the Tuttle and Reid families multiplied. Now a patchwork of small farms belonging mostly to members of Daniel's family spread west from the river toward Burlington. Hiram lived on his father's land. The family would make room for him if he chose to lay down his badge once his term of office was over.

Daniel knew he could succeed in farming, even if his arm would make adjustments necessary. After all, he had grown up with the rhythms of the seasons, of planting and waiting and harvesting. But his heart didn't lie with the land, nor with the bank, the way Simeon's did. He had come to enjoy his job as constable, even the testing that the robberies brought.

Before he lost his arm, he had considered joining the cavalry to protect the expanding western frontier. But continued military service was no longer an option. Not to mention the reasons he had discovered to stay—especially one gray-eyed beauty.

He paused by the original Reid homestead. Its current resident, one of his cousins, worked in the field, harvesting the last of the pumpkins and winter squash. Would Clara like to be a farmer's wife? Like him, she had grown up on a farm. But her eyes were on a bigger prize—training young women for the future. They both longed for new horizons.

He clucked to his horse and urged him forward. If he didn't live in the Bailey house, and if he didn't want to farm, where would he choose to live? Except for an occasional stand of trees, the wilderness on this side of the river had been transformed to cultivated land. He couldn't hide in a hermit's cabin and live off the land, not here, not like Thoreau talked about in *Walden*.

He reached the bridge. At some point, his father had stopped charging tolls. Simeon reinstituted the practice, stating they needed money to maintain the bridge. Some day the town might take over management of the bridge, but for now, the Tuttle Bridge remained the possession of the family that built it.

His horse pounded onto the bridge, the sound of hooves echoing in the empty space. Not too long from now, Hiram would need to keep the floor snow-packed, so that sleighs could run across the boards unharmed. The wood had dulled to a weathered gray, a sturdy testament to its workmanship.

In the silence, Daniel could sense fiddle music and the shrieks of children. The cold air cleared the scents of horse and food and dirt ground into the boards. If the wood could talk, it would tell the tale of Maple Notch's history. Tomorrow would add another chapter to the ongoing story.

Horse hooves struck the boards and stopped. Sunshine outlined a feminine figure on horseback at the other end of the bridge.

∽

Clara didn't have a good excuse for coming to the bridge. She only knew that when she didn't find Daniel at the jail, she felt compelled to keep riding west in the direction of the Tuttle farm.

The cold of approaching winter hardened the mud underfoot and made a smooth ride. With no one to report to and no duties for the morning, she indulged in a brisk ride. Miss Featherton would approve of the exercise.

Clara gave Misty her head and let her race, spirit free, just shy of dangerous abandon. Wind whipped her hair and beat her skin, ridding her of any doubts and imperfections. When they reached the rise before the bridge, she pulled Misty up and started again at a slower pace.

"What a glorious day!" As she shook her head, her hair tumbled to her shoulders, and she laughed. When she spotted the Frisk farm, she realized her clothing had gone awry. She tugged her skirts farther down her legs and swept her hair into the hairnet. A few stray hairpins allowed her to pin wisps of curl into place. Horse and rider proceeded at an orderly pace to the bridge. Clara peeked over the edge of the bank, where the river gurgled over a few rocks in its path.

She paused at the entrance to the bridge to allow her eyes to adjust to the light. In here the river sounded louder, almost ready to explode from its banks and run across the fields. She dismounted and took a few steps forward.

"Hello, Clara." A voice spoke out of the semi-darkness.

She jumped back. "Daniel? Is that you?"

"Nobody else here except us mice." Daniel stepped out of the gloom a few yards away from her.

"Mice?" The word came out as a squeak.

"Are you afraid of a few little mice?" He tilted his head, waiting for her answer.

"Let's just say I don't care to run across one unexpected." She moved forward, eyes scanning the walls for any sign of vermin. A mouse skittered by her feet, and she shivered. Approaching, Daniel hung his coat around her shoulders. The warm wool, saturated with his masculine scent, chased away her nervousness.

"Where were you headed? I don't often see you out this way."

Clara didn't want to admit the truth—that part of her hoped to run into him. "I used to ride all over town when I was a girl. Misty could take me home even if I didn't touch the reins, couldn't you, girl?" She leaned over and ran her hand down the mare's neck, and Misty nickered in response. "You've discovered another one of my unwomanly vices. When I was younger, I pulled on Lewis's britches to make riding easier. I've grown up some." She sighed. "But I still love a good ride. We won't have many more beautiful days like today this year, so I indulged myself."

Daniel chuckled. "I doubt you could hide your gender if you chopped your hair as short as a man's and swore like a sailor." His hand swept up and down. "From the pretty curls on top of your head to your tiny feet, you're all woman."

This time heat started from the roots of her hair and traveled to her shoulders and below. She could only hope the dim light hid her high color. Averting her face from him, her gaze wandered the walls of the bridge. A spit of light shone through the cracks, highlighting spider webs overhead.

Daniel took his place beside her and stared in the same patch of wall. A half smile formed on his face. "I was looking at that just the other day." He tugged her hand in the direction of a scarred plank of wood. Its significance didn't register for a handful of seconds.

"That's—"

"The reason it's called the Courting Bridge. New initials have been added since I left for the war." He peered at some of the newer etchings in the wood. "ID and DR—Isaiah Dixon and Deborah Robson, 1862, unless I miss my guess."

Clara had seen the spot before, of course. Whenever the school picnicked near the bridge, the girls would giggle about who might carve *their* initials on the bridge someday. For someone who knew the parties involved, the couples' plank was better than the church registry as a record of love and marriage in Maple Notch.

Daniel leaned in before shifting a few inches to the side. He ran his fingers along the older marking on the wood, then stopped, his fingernail tipped into a groove. "There it is." He beckoned her closer.

The letters had worn over time. "I'm sorry, is that a *T*?"

"JT and SR. My grandparents, Josiah Tuttle and Sally Reid." His hand dropped by a couple of inches. "And here are my parents—CT and BB."

"Calvin Tuttle and Beatrice Bailey."

He smiled an acknowledgment. "My father discovered the tree when they felled lumber to build the bridge. He added his initials later." He stood back. "Hiram and Simeon are here, too, somewhere." His voice sounded wistful, as if uncertain if he would ever get to add "DT" to the family tree.

And whose initials did he dream of coupling with his on the plank? She could see them, bold, decisive strokes—DT and CF. Tears stung her eyes. In spite of his seeming admiration for her, how could the town constable have any interest in the sister of a common thief?

∽

Daniel felt Clara pulling away from him, when he wanted to hold her close and safe from harm. He had bared his heart; she must know of his interest in her. Unless she was rejecting him. He went cold at the thought.

Somehow in this moment on the bridge, where they seemed as alone in the world as Adam and Eve in the garden, he had hoped for a kiss. For some sign that at least she returned his affection. But when he glanced at her face, her eyes glittered with some dark emotion that left no room for romantic fiddle faddle. She turned in the direction of her horse.

After she climbed onto her horse's back, she faced him. "I'm glad I ran into you. I wanted tell you that Lewis knows the shipment will be coming early tomorrow morning."

Lewis. Daniel wished his name had some Bs and Ts, sounds he could spit out of his mouth. The name Lewis sounded weak, like the man. How could he ever hope for a future with Clara as long as her brother stood between them?

"I want to be here when you spring the trap."

An objection rose in Daniel's throat, but he swallowed it down. She didn't like setting her brother up, and who could blame her? She had a right to see how everything turned out. Besides, if he didn't plan for her presence, she'd still come, putting herself and the whole operation in danger. "Very well. I'll show you where to wait."

She opened her mouth to protest but had the good sense not to speak. If he thought she would put herself in danger, he might lock her in a cell for the night. "Where?"

His mind raced. The convoy would approach the bridge from Burlington to the south. The robbers might hole up on either side of the bridge, or even underneath. He led her to the far end. "The best place is going to be that stand of trees." He nodded toward a spot at the corner of his cousin's property.

She nudged her horse forward, and he followed until they were both beneath the evergreen boughs. Swinging the mare around, she peered through the dense branches. "I can't see anything from here." She trotted the horse forward until only the tail ends of the branches stood between her and the clearing. "I can see a little bit from here, but not much."

The problem was that they could see her as well. Once again he wished he could lock her in a jail cell until the excitement was over.

She sat back in the saddle and looked at him over her shoulder. "Your men won't be waiting here. It's too far away to help if something goes wrong."

Even before she opened her mouth, he knew what she would say. "I want to be with them." She must have seen the hesitation in his face. "I insist. I have a right. If I'm. . .betraying—" At the word, her voice broke, but her back remained ramrod straight. "If Lewis is involved, I want to see it for myself."

Daniel's admiration for Clara grew in proportion to his frustration. This maddening woman refused to stay behind the sidelines. She didn't close her eyes to what was wrong with the world, but rather sought to change it. He couldn't change her mind any more than he could change himself. He didn't know that he wanted to.

"A sentinel will be up there." He pointed to a small hilltop a short distance away, almost indistinguishable from the forest around it. "He can see the road as well as much of the surrounding countryside. He'll know when someone approaches the bridge."

"What if they come early?"

"He'll be in place before dawn. In fact, he's spending the night up there." He smiled grimly. "It's my brother Hiram. There's no one better than he at this kind of thing. He climbs up there when he's hunting for deer and always comes home with meat."

"And the others?"

"The men driving the wagon—young Dixon and a few men from Burlington—will circle back after they hand the money bags over to me."

"Money bags? Surely you're not carrying actual currency." Her gray eyes had retreated behind her glasses and the hood of her cloak, to where all he could see was a dark gleam.

"No, but the bags will look full. They have to believe we have money." He and Simeon had spent a couple of hours weighing out stones equivalent to a shipment of gold coin.

"Will you have someone waiting at the bridge?" She broke the edge of the trees and returned to the open, her eyes scanning the empty farm fields. A lone eagle hovered overhead.

Daniel stared at her a long moment. "You're not going to give up, are you?"

She shook her head and urged her horse to move ahead. "I don't much know about such things, but I haven't seen anything that would provide good cover."

"How much do you know of the Tuttle family history?" He came beside her.

"Enough. You told us a lot on Thursday."

"I didn't mention this part. Come this way." He left the road and guided them through a narrow stand of trees. "They'll be waiting here. At the Reids' cave." He brought the horses to a halt in front of an opening low enough that both of them would have to stoop to enter.

∽

"Of course." Memories washed over Clara, tales so tall she never quite knew if she believed them, stories of the Reid family living in a cave during the War for Independence.

"Yes, it's all true. At least most of it is." Daniel smiled and offered her his hand. "I was about to say the bank is too steep, but if my great-grandmother managed it when she was in a family way, I'm sure you'll be fine. Just watch your footing."

Clara bent over and peered into the dark recess. "I can't see anything."

"Let me." He took her place at the opening and felt around inside, coming up with a candle. He lit it and, bending down, entered the cave. She followed behind.

The cave smelled dank and musty, as if no air blew through to an exit on the other side. Stones marked an old fire pit in the center. A mouse whisked away in the shadows, hiding in the spout of an old coffeepot. For some reason, she didn't mind his presence here. Mice belonged in underground places. She only hoped she would never have to share their living quarters.

"Look out the entrance." Daniel interrupted her inspection.

She stuck her head out the opening and let the fresh air caress her face. He stooped down beside her. "There's the bridge." He pointed up and to the left. "We can see people entering the bridge from either end or even someone hiding underneath."

Clara could almost imagine shadows dancing on the rocks beneath the bridge, and she fought a temptation to pull back. She had nothing to fear on a sunny afternoon. "Can you see the cave from the bridge?"

She felt more than saw him shake his head. "Not unless you know where to look. Or unless someone lights the candle." She heard his hiss of breath, and the candle sputtered out. "Which they won't tomorrow."

A man on horseback approached the bridge from the side heading into town. Pastor Beaton carried a rifle swung over his back and a pack on the horse, probably filled with his Bible and other things that would bring solace to the more far-flung families of his parish. He had been an army chaplain in his earlier life, spending ten years in the military, including service in Mexico, before he became their pastor.

The horse's hooves alerted them to his passage across the bridge. He paused on their side of the bridge, only a few feet away from their hiding place, and dropped the toll in the waiting box. They could see the underbelly of the horse, the slightly worn leather of the girth that needed to be replaced, but the pastor appeared to have no knowledge of their presence. Clara followed his passage until he disappeared a few yards past the bridge.

"Satisfied?" Daniel grinned.

"When do I need to be here?"

Chapter 13

Lewis dashed Clara's last hopes of escaping oncoming events when he left home before dinner on Friday night, telling her not to wait for him. When she arose early in the morning—so early some might call it a late night instead—he hadn't returned to his room. He had taken the bait.

During the few minutes it took her to assemble food for breakfast and lunch, she hoped Lewis would breeze in, even if he stank like a drunk skunk. If he came back, she might tell him the gold shipment was a trap, that he should stay as far away from the bridge as possible.

She shivered, the kitchen cold without the heat of the stove, and wondered if she could keep up the pretense.

In the end, her hesitation hadn't mattered. Lewis hadn't come home. She dressed in breeches—not wanting to give any passersby reason to wonder why a woman would wander alone outside at that time of night—tucked a pistol into the waistband, and left the house as the moon started to set.

Daniel hadn't wanted her to walk so far, but what choice did she have? If Lewis spotted Misty at the bridge, he would suspect trouble. Even if she left the mare in town, Lewis might still be suspicious. No, she would do better to arrive on foot and leave Misty at home. She had plenty of time. In the cool reaches of the night, she practiced the swagger that men seemed to use when walking. What had Daniel said once? "You're all woman, from the pretty curls on top of your head to your tiny feet." Her face burned with the memory, and she felt under the brim of her cap for her curls. None had escaped, at least not yet, and no one could see the size of her feet in the dark. So perhaps she could pass for a male.

The sky had changed to a shade lighter than black by the time she reached town. A dark figure approached her out of the shadows, and she jumped.

"It's me." A deep voice she recognized as Daniel's reassured her. He drew near and pulled back his cap, revealing the banked embers of his eyes in the pale light of his face. He fell into step beside her. "I would tuck my arm beneath yours, but people might wonder why I was walking arm in arm with another man." She felt a ripple of silent laughter pass down his side. "You didn't fool me, though."

"You knew I was headed this way."

"True. Do you want some coffee? I have some on the stove in the jail. Fresh made, so it's not undrinkable yet."

She glanced at the still, dark sky and gauged she had some time to spare. But staying in the light and warmth of the jail only delayed the inevitable. "My nerves are already frayed. I don't need something else to make it worse. Another time." *When I'm visiting my brother in jail.* "Have any plans changed since yesterday?"

"Nothing you need to know about." He stopped beneath a tree at the southwest corner of the common. "Go as far as the bridge. Brent Frisk will meet you there." He gripped her left arm with his right. "Do you want to call the whole plan off? We can, even now." Shoulders rigid with tension, he looked as though he might crack apart into a dozen separate pieces, and his fingers bit into her skin.

Tears sprang to her eyes, but not from the pain. "No. Lewis must accept responsibility for his actions."

"I wish. . ." He cleared his throat. "I wish things didn't have to be this way."

He released her, and she caught hold of him instead. "I do as well. I wish you didn't have to put yourself in harm's way because of my brother's actions."

She stared into his eyes, and in an instant they blazed from banked coals to a raging fire. He pulled her to himself in a tight embrace, kissed her briefly on the lips, and released her. "Go."

The cry rent her heart.

∽

Daniel waited beneath the tree until even the smudge of Clara's shadow disappeared in the distance. He wanted to run after her. To at least sit with her in the dark cave, to keep her company and comfort her as she waited for the inevitable. But he had a different role to play in the day's events.

I wish you didn't have to put yourself in harm's way. Oh, Clara, if she only knew. He would stand between her and death and pour out his lifeblood, if need be. Due to a last-minute change of plans, however, he didn't anticipate any true danger today.

At length he shook himself out of his reverie. If anyone caught sight of him lingering at the corner of the green, staring down the road when the moon had fallen and no light existed to see by, they would wonder about the object of his thoughts. Across the common, footsteps scurried down the street, probably Fannie on her way to the café to begin the day's baking. In another hour, he might be able to convince her to serve him a cup of her ridiculous coffee and a hot-from-the-oven cinnamon bun before riding out to keep his appointment with doom at the bridge.

Daniel hadn't done more than doze last night, so he should have felt exhausted, but his eyes stayed open as they had before many a battle. No amount of counting sheep jumping over fences had put him to sleep. A short nap might refresh him, if he could manage it. He unlocked one of the cells and stretched out on the thin mattress. In the corner, he heard a scuffling and half expected a mouse to crawl up his leg. A smile lifted his lips at the memory of Clara's fear of the mouse on the bridge. Not long ago, Hiram's cat had had a litter of kittens. He'd grab one of them as a mouser.

Something creaked, and he bolted upright, staring into the inky blackness of the office. "Who's there?" Grabbing his revolver, he ran to his office, only to feel a breeze pushing past cracks in the door.

He went back to the cell but gave up on sleep. Bending over, he found the tiny hole where the mouse had disappeared at the approach of the big human ogre. Could anything fill up the hole so a small creature couldn't crawl through? The floor could use a thorough sweeping. Lye soap and bleach might be needed to soak the smells out of the walls.

At last he judged enough time had passed that he could pretend it was the start of an ordinary day. First off, he'd make a quick stop at the house to shave the whiskers from his cheeks and change clothes into something unremarkable.

Half an hour later, when the grandfather clock in the parlor announced five o'clock of the morning, he left the house as refreshed as clean clothes and cold water could make him. By this hour, he could squeak into the café. He needed to be around people before he set out on his quest for his imagined opponent, a dark, evil shadow who wanted to haunt his dreams at night. Something of even less substance than the mouse and her babies.

A single lamp on the front table in the café provided all the light for the dining room that morning. Light gleamed from the kitchen. "Fannie?"

She came out, still wearing an apron dotted with flour. Not everyone knew that Fannie baked all the pastries for the café herself, although she depended on a cook for meals. "You're early." She wiped her hands on the apron before removing it and hanging it on a peg. "Let me light more lamps."

"I'll just take a cup of coffee and a cinnamon roll. I've got to get going." He settled down by the front table, where the one lamp provided sufficient light. Fannie poured him a cup of coffee and bustled into the kitchen. She returned a few minutes later with the requested roll and a slice of ham, quickly browned. "It isn't much, but a man needs more than a sweet roll to keep him going."

Daniel let the roll melt in his mouth and chewed down the ham between swallows of the coffee. From his seat, he saw Simeon passing by and longed to call him in. Daniel could imagine Fannie's reaction if that happened.

Mr. Tuttle! I suppose you want to join your brother? And what brings the two of you out so early this morning? Knowing Fannie, she would pass on the news to all of her customers.

No, that wouldn't do at all. In a few hours' time, the whole town might buzz with the coming affair at the bridge, but until then, Daniel needed to stick as closely as possible to his usual schedule. He finished the meal a tad more quickly than usual and left money on the table. "Keep the change." He headed out the door.

The sky had moved from pale gray to pale blue shot with brilliant pinks and yellows in the east. He returned to the jail. One last time, he checked that his pistol was loaded and ready for action. His saddle was fixed to receive the money bags. He climbed onto his horse. The gelding sensed his direction, for before Daniel even flicked his reins, he'd turned his nose in the direction of the bridge. When Daniel's shift of the rein confirmed the direction, he set off at a trot. The temperature this morning was about ten degrees higher than yesterday morning; no frost hardened the ground, and the ride went as quietly as it could with four hooves hitting the ground at regular intervals.

Daniel's nerves itched to give Spotty his head and let him gallop, but the horse might need his wind later. Besides, if he hurried, he might arrive at the bridge too early. At most, he wanted to arrive half an hour before the carriage from Burlington. They had planned to leave before daylight to make the rendezvous.

When Daniel reached the bridge, he dismounted, casually scanning the area for signs of another presence. He led Spotty to the side of the road and tethered him to a tree. Daylight caught him pacing back and forth like an army sentry in front of the east entrance to the bridge. From there, the men waiting in the cave could see him, as well as anyone in or under the bridge. The last rays of the rising sun might distort their vision for a few vital seconds, long enough to give him an advantage.

Fifteen minutes remained, twenty at most. Every drop of coffee he'd drunk over the past twenty-four hours stretched his eyesight. He felt like he could see to the depths of the earth and all the way to California, but in reality he couldn't even see the cave on the far side of the river.

He hoped that didn't prove a fatal error.

∽

Clara counted Daniel's steps as he paced back and forth. Forward march, ten steps. About face. Ten steps return. Each step as carefully measured as if his feet knew the width of the bridge and could pace it blindfolded. Something about his determined pace troubled her.

"Miss Farley." Frisk, one of Daniel's deputies, tapped her on the shoulder. "I need to change places with you."

She stepped back. How foolish of her, staring like a spectator when the men in the cave with her needed to watch for Daniel's safety.

Daniel's safety. "He's setting himself up as a target." She wanted to scream, to run out of the cave and tell him to go away.

"Stay still, ma'am. We won't let anything happen to the captain."

The ground overhead trembled, suggesting the approach of the carriage. Several stones tumbled down the slope and crashed into the water, and Clara leaned past Frisk far enough to see half a dozen men crawl from beneath the bridge.

Rifle shots rang out. When the smoke cleared, Daniel had disappeared from view.

Chapter 14

Clara jolted to her feet, poised to dash out the entrance.

The carriage, with Dixon and two other men she didn't recognize, continued full speed onto the bridge.

The men from the cave raced to join them. Only Frisk paused long enough to yell. "Stay in the cave! Captain's orders."

I won't stay behind. I'm not defenseless. She grabbed the pistol she had tucked in the waistband of her breeches. Her racing heart jumped ahead of her onto the road, but she forced herself to check her surroundings. All the action remained at the far side of the bridge, and she dashed forward.

She took a second at the entrance to the bridge to let her eyes adjust to the semi-darkness of the interior. The reverberating echoes sounded like she imagined an earthquake would, the monstrous noise threatening to tear down the bridge and everyone on it. Horses' hooves pounded on the planks like sledgehammers. A dozen men's voices snarled together, a black cloud of incomprehensible noise. Her mind catalogued the sounds. She heard more pounding of fists and shouts than gunfire and took small comfort in that. After her eyes had adjusted, she crept forward. "That does it!"

Daniel had his good arm around the neck of one of the assailants, dressed in the same hat and bandanna she had seen at the bank.

"You think you have it easy because you're dealing with a crippled man?" Clara hardly recognized the raspy voice as Daniel's.

"You think you can have your way in *my* town!" He yanked his arm so hard that the man flailed for breath.

The handkerchief slid down from his nose under the pressure of Daniel's arm, and Clara recognized the face of one of the Whitson twins—Rod, she believed. Where Whitson was, Lewis would not be far behind, but none of the figures in front of her reminded her of her brother.

"I've got him." Dixon appeared at Daniel's side and tied Whitson's hands together. Daniel gave his neck a final tug before he let him go.

They tied each man's hands together and then tied the robbers to each other. Daniel walked by and whisked the hats off their heads. "The Whitson twins. Whimsey, Bradford, Dupre, Ford." He spit out each name. "Not a one of you is missing."

No one except, that is, for—Lewis.

"Surprised?" A low voice spoke in her ear, and she screamed. All the men froze in place for so long that the robbers could have escaped if they weren't already bound.

"Clara!" Daniel's voice, half exultant, half exasperated, boomed and echoed through the bridge chamber. "I thought I told you to stay in the cave."

"You were in danger." Her voice quavered. "The shots. . ." She realized how silly she sounded, as if she, a lone woman, could protect him if all his accomplices had failed.

"I was never in any danger." Daniel's eyes blazed in the dark, and he crossed the space between them in a few easy strides. "Not with Lewis on my side." He draped his arm over Lewis's shoulders.

"I have a lot to tell you." Lewis said, low enough so that only she and Daniel could hear.

"What happened?" She stared at the two men, one of whom she had loved since childhood, the other who had become dear to her over the past few weeks. She wanted to bang their heads together for letting her worry so, about *both* of them.

∽

Daniel shut the door on his protesting prisoners and turned the key until the lock clicked into place. "Fannie will bring you supper. It's too late for lunch." She would have brought food—if only to hear the news firsthand—but he wanted them to squirm a little bit. He turned to his deputy. "You sure you don't mind staying?"

Dixon sat behind the desk, feet planted on the ground. Daniel felt sure that his face mirrored the foolish grin on his friend's. The accused robbers would stay in the Maple Notch jail until they were taken to the county seat for trial. Until that day came, Daniel and Dixon would take turns guarding them. "Go on with you. Get down to that girl of yours before she decides you're not coming."

Daniel laughed as he hadn't in years. On his way out the door, he reached for his forage cap where it hung on its peg, then dropped his hand. The time had come to put Captain Tuttle behind him. Daniel was more than ready to be a civilian lawman. He had grown into the name of Constable Tuttle.

He found Lewis and Clara in the café. They must have gone home, because Clara had exchanged her breeches for a lavender gingham dress. Her face shone with greater color than usual, her excitement at the morning's events evident in her features. He joined them at the table.

"I ordered for all of us. I hope you don't mind."

"Good idea. So, Lewis, have you told Clara our plans for this afternoon?"

He shook his head. "I was waiting for you."

Clara punched her brother in the arm. "He hasn't told me *anything*, only that I would have to wait for you." The smile on her face faded. "Lewis, you knew I suspected you."

"And you were right." Lewis screwed his face into tight lines. "I did take part in the first robbery, helped them gain entrance for the second, and gave them information about today's shipment."

The look Clara threw Daniel's way let him know she wondered if her brother should be confessing all of this in front of the constable. She didn't know he had already heard the whole story.

Fannie arrived with the sandwiches—thick slices of roast beef with mustard on fine wheat bread, with a side dish of potato salad. Daniel knew she wanted to learn the news. "Give us a few minutes, Fannie. I'll tell you all about it later."

A mutinous look on her face let him know *later* wouldn't be as satisfying as *now*, but she nodded. "I'll bring you out a pitcher so you can refill your own glasses, and then I'll leave you alone."

The lunch hour had passed, and with Fannie's departure, they had privacy. Daniel decided to put Clara's worries to rest. "Lewis came to me late last night. Told me about their plan to rob the shipment today at the bridge and offered to help me stop them."

"Wasn't I surprised when he told me they *wanted* us to make the attempt, but I could help." Lewis's part involved making sure the guns had no ammunition or would misfire. He also promised to warn Daniel of their approach.

"The rocks hitting the water," she remembered.

"We wanted to catch them red-handed, you see."

The shots Clara had heard had come from Daniel, fired as a warning. Unbeknownst to her, Daniel had additional men waiting on the town side of the bridge, ready to come to his rescue.

"So between the men in the cave and the men on the carriage and the men with me, we outnumbered them two to one. It wasn't even a fair battle." Daniel grinned. "I like those kinds of odds."

"And this afternoon?" Clara took a bite of pumpkin pie, and a bit of whipped cream landed at the side of her lip. She licked it off, and Daniel's tongue thickened too much for him to speak.

"I'm going to show you where we hid the money." Lewis picked at his pie. "What's left of it, that is." His shoulders collapsed in on themselves, like a piece of paper folded in half.

Act like a man, Daniel chided him silently.

Lewis unfolded his shoulders and put his hands palms down on the table, his eyes fixing Daniel to his seat. "I will make what restitution I can. I'll work for the rest. If anyone will hire me, that is, after what I've done."

Daniel looked to Clara. Would she offer to make up the difference? Tears glinted behind her glasses, but she didn't speak.

"I'm sure the judge will take your cooperation into consideration when it comes to sentencing."

A single tear escaped Clara's left eye and slid down her cheek. He longed to reach out with his hand and brush it away, but he held himself back.

"Sentencing?" Confusion clouded Clara's face. "But you didn't arrest him."

Daniel looked around, not wanting the slightest whisper of this conversation to reach Fannie's ears. But before he spoke, Lewis answered. "He told me I was under arrest when I went to him this morning. I don't have to stay in jail, however, as long as I show up at court on time."

Clara turned her mourning dove eyes on Daniel. "You took a big risk."

Uncomfortable with her appreciation, he shrugged. "I figured it was worth taking a chance on someone who came forward like that." He took the last bite of pie. "Are we ready to go?"

∽

The horses worked their way through dense trees to a spot far southeast of town, not far from Whitson's farm. Branches tore at Clara's face and dress, making her wish she still wore the britches. She only hoped all the rents could be repaired.

Whatever tears the brambles created in her clothing could be more easily repaired than the rents to her heart. Her worst fears about Lewis's involvement had been confirmed, yet transformed somehow by his offer to help Daniel. Why hadn't either one of them told her?

"It's there." Lewis pointed to a gigantic oak that must have been standing before Columbus discovered America. As they approached, she could see the tree was dying from rot from the inside out, dry limbs caught in the lace of the upper branches, the roots pulling loose from the earth.

Daniel dismounted and helped her down before grabbing the shovel from the back of his horse. He handed the tool to Lewis. "Dig."

Instead, Lewis dropped to the ground and pushed aside a pile of damp leaves sitting between two of the biggest roots. The ground he exposed had been recently disturbed. With a few shovelfuls of dirt, the edge of a burlap sack emerged. She held her breath.

He tugged out two bags and set them on the ground before digging deeper with the shovel. This time he exposed a canvas sack almost sunshine bright in its newness. He dug all the dirt around it and then used both arms to lift it out. Clara guessed that bag held the gold coins.

After he placed all three sacks at Daniel's feet like a penitent's offering, Lewis took a step back and crossed his arms behind him. Trying to present an unthreatening appearance, she supposed.

"Is that it?" Daniel asked.

Lewis nodded. "We spent a chunk of the bills on that weekend drunk. When we grabbed the gold coins, we realized we couldn't spend it without drawing attention to ourselves, so we decided to each take a little but to leave most of it here and decide how to divide it later." A pale pink dusted his cheeks.

Daniel muttered something that sounded like "honor among thieves."

"I can't be sure, but I don't think anyone has disturbed it since we buried it."

When Daniel opened the burlap sacks, paper money and coins spilled out. Neat stacks of ones and fives, tens and twenties were banded together. He thumbed through them, counting swiftly. "Missing about fifty dollars from what Simeon told me."

"That sounds about right." Lewis pointed to his feet, encased in a new pair of Congress boots. "Want my boots? I bought them with some of that money."

Daniel growled, and Clara moved to her brother's side. She put her hand on his shoulder, a small, comforting gesture like their mother used to offer. "And the gold coins?"

"The bag is plenty heavy. But I'll have to wait until we get back to town to count it out and verify the amounts." Daniel let a few coins slip through his fingers. "Recovering this means a lot. I'm pretty sure Simeon will speak on your behalf to the judge."

"Restitution. It's the right thing to do, and doesn't the Bible say something about paying back more than what you took?" Lewis grimaced. "I guess the court will determine how much."

Daniel hefted the three bags with his single arm as if they weighed no more than a straw tick and secured them in his saddlebags. "Let's go, then." Instead of returning the way they had come, he moved forward. "I'm pretty sure we're close to Whitson's farm from here. I want to check on how Baruch is faring." He paused. "And make sure Mr. Whitson has heard about the twins."

Clara doubted their welcome, but she mounted her horse. After a moment's hesitation, Lewis joined them. They let the silence of the forest envelop them.

"The house is just through those trees." Lewis nodded and trotted his horse straight ahead.

A shot rang out, and Lewis screamed.

∽

Daniel burst through the trees in two seconds. Lewis lay on the ground, blood streaming from his shoulder.

"Stay away from me and mine." Old Whitson waited on the porch, his feet spread far apart, rifle held against his shoulder.

"Mr. Whitson, it's me, Daniel Tuttle, the constable." His hand wanted to reach for the comfort of his pistol, but he resisted. He took a step forward.

"Don't move." Whitson shook his rifle. "You Tuttles have always been trouble. Now you've got my boys in jail."

Daniel didn't think Whitson would appreciate a reminder that his sons had robbed the bank and brought it on themselves. He stayed still. "I'm right sorry about that."

Whitson snorted.

Daniel moved a step closer. He caught a glimpse of something out of the corner of his eyes. "How is Baruch faring?" He dipped his chin, and Baruch moved into place behind his father.

With a single movement, Baruch removed the rifle from his father's grasp. "I'm doing much better, thanks for asking." His expression didn't offer much more welcome than his father's had, but he took in the heavy saddle bags on the back of Daniel's horse. "So it's true. My brothers robbed the bank."

Daniel felt movement behind him. Lewis had pulled himself to his feet and took his place at his side. "They did, with some help. Including mine."

"So you caught the shot." Whitson glared at Lewis. "Too bad I just winged you."

"I'll be all right."

The four men faced off, none of them willing to move, claims and counterclaims roiling through the air. Again Daniel sensed movement, and Clara slipped past him to stand between the opposing sides.

"Mr. Whitson." Looking as harmless as a dove on her nest, Clara smiled as if this was an ordinary social call. "I wanted to tell you how much I enjoyed having Libby in my class this week. She told such wonderful stories of how your family fought in the War for Independence." She waved her hands as if indicating the strands of the story and moved forward. "And now your son Baruch has proved just as brave. Something more to add to the lore of Maple Notch."

Some of the vinegar went out of Whitson's face. "That's true. She's a real cracker. And I've always been proud of Baruch."

Clara had defused a sour situation by the simple expedient of reminding Whitson of two children who gave him cause for pride. She'd make a fine teacher—no doubt about it—or even a politician. Daniel's lips curled at the thought. She'd argue that women should be able to hold public office, if they wanted to.

"I reckon I'd like Libby to go to that fancy school of yours, if you ever get it started."

"And I'd be honored to have her." Clara closed the distance between them and shook his hand, as grimy and smelly as he must be.

With a sister like that, Lewis was bound to turn things around. She wouldn't give him any choice.

When Clara cocked her head in his direction, Daniel felt the full force of her smile. Now that he had nabbed the robbers, he would let her know she had no choice, none at all, when it came to a husband.

Epilogue

After Christmas, when winter held Maple Notch in its grasp, most people stayed at home if they had a choice, but not Clara. Too much had happened since the raid on St. Albans for her to take the time off.

The robbers had been taken to Hyde Park to await trial. Lewis remained free, although he would stand trial with the others. His lawyer held hopes that he would receive a reduced sentence for his role in capturing the gang and returning the money. Lewis wasn't asking for any special treatment. He said he had disobeyed the law of God and the law of the land and deserved punishment. Those words alone made Clara want to weep. Aside from those tears, she was happier than she had been for a long time.

Between Lewis's problems and Christmas festivities, Clara had to rush to prepare the Bailey Mansion for the first class of the Maple Notch Seminary for Females. Two of the older girls from the local school would join two boarders sent her way by her mentor, Miss Featherton, on the first of February. Daniel had proved easy to work with. His suggestions for her plans proved sensible in most cases; she'd had to argue her point on a few others.

Daniel. He was the main reason she couldn't stop smiling and didn't feel the cold, even when snow fell like it did today. Since the confrontation at Whitson's farm, he had spent every spare minute with her. She told herself it was only because they had to conclude the business about the house, nothing more.

Her traitorous heart didn't always agree, however, reminding her of the time he had kissed the top of her head, or the tender way he looked at her when he thought she wouldn't notice as they explored his grandparents' house.

"You're looking fine."

At the sound of Lewis's deep voice, Clara whirled around, causing her skirt to swish in a wide circle. She had fashioned two new dresses with wider skirts, still avoiding the ridiculous hoops. They swirled in unexpected directions when she turned abruptly, but oh, they made her feel so feminine.

"Don't forget these." He reached for the ermine muff he had given her for Christmas. "They're perfect with your coat." He removed the red cloak from the coat tree and draped it over her shoulders. "Have fun today."

Someone knocked, and Lewis opened the door to Daniel. Fashionable ladies might make him wait, but not Clara. She saw the sleigh on the road in front of her house, and she giggled like a schoolgirl. What could be better than a sleigh ride in the twilight of a winter snowfall with a man—especially this man?

"I take it you are ready." Daniel bowed deeply. The dark-blue overcoat looked magnificent on his manly figure. He went bareheaded, and his ears looked red.

"Your head," Clara said. "You'll catch cold."

"I have a hat on the sleigh. But I don't care for knitted caps." He shook his head, and some of his hair fell over his ears. "That's why God gave us hair, after all."

They said good-bye to Lewis. Clara slipped as she minced her way across the icy expanse of her yard, but Daniel held her tight, a solid, sturdy man. No one he cared for would ever come to harm.

He helped her into her seat and tucked a blanket around her. "And here's a warming brick for your feet." He put something warm underneath her boots. A moment later, he joined her on the sleigh.

A matched pair of white horses, almost as white as the falling snow, pulled the sleigh, and the bells on their harness jingled as they trotted down the road. The runners glided over the icy surface that had proved so hazardous to her feet. They skimmed down the road as easily as a duck swimming in water. The snow lent an air of newness to everything around them.

They reached the town green in a matter of minutes. Pastor Beaton came out of the church. "Beautiful day for a sleigh ride, isn't it?"

Daniel saluted him without answering. His ears had turned so red Clara feared they might suffer frostbite. She wiggled her left hand out of her muff and reached for the nearest ear, rubbing it between thumb and forefinger.

Daniel jerked. "Watch out! That tickles!"

She laughed. "Then wear your hat." Without waiting for his answer, she took the knitted cap she found on the seat and pulled it over the crown of his head until it covered his ears.

He took them around the common twice, each turn of the sleigh causing her to slide a little closer to him. The third time around, he headed the horses down Bridge Road. "I helped Hiram roll snow across the bridge yesterday." He wiggled his eyebrows, which snow crystals had turned to a hoary white. "I'm warning you, I'll take off my hat as soon as we stop."

She laughed. "Why are we stopping on the bridge?" *It is called The Courting Bridge.* Did she dare hope?

He turned his gaze on her, something unreadable in his eyes. "You'll see."

345

A few minutes later, the bridge came into view. The falling snow had turned it into a winter fairytale, a place wondrous enough for the Eskimos she'd read about in faraway Alaska. She wished she could capture the bright red walls, the white snow mounded on the roof like a European castle, in paint.

Daniel slowed the horses, and they plodded onto the bridge. *They call them kissing bridges, because if you drive the team slow enough, a fellow can kiss a girl twice before you get across.* That bit of folklore jumped into Clara's mind, and she felt her cheeks heat, probably turning as red as Daniel's ears.

But Daniel made no move to kiss her and, in fact, let the horses come to a complete standstill in the middle of the bridge. "Remember where we are?" White teeth showed between his dark mustache and beard, grown over the winter months. He tugged the hat off his head.

She resisted the obvious—Tuttle Bridge—and looked around her. To her left, a few feet from where Daniel held the reins to the horses, she saw a scarred wooden plank. Her heartbeat sped.

He seemed to sense the moment she recognized the spot, jumping down before helping her out of the sleigh. He clasped one of her hands in his and walked with her to the plank. Once there, he let go of her hand to pull a knife from his pocket. "I think it's time we add our own bit to Maple Notch history." He nodded at the plank. "If you're willing?"

One look in his eyes told her that her traitorous heart had guessed right, after all. "As long as we do it together."

"I wouldn't dream of doing it any other way. How about—right there?" He found a blank spot to the right of his parents' initials.

She placed her right hand over his larger one and felt him draw the knife down in a solid stroke, the left side of the *D*. A *T* soon followed, then the plus sign. He lifted his hand away and placed the knife in her palm. "Do you want to finish?"

Now his hand covered hers as her fingers drew the uncertain curve of the *C* and then an *F* into the wood. She closed the knife but didn't move. Instead she leaned back into the breadth of Daniel's chest.

"Clara." His voice caressed her name. "After the war, I never thought God would have a woman for me."

She shifted, wanting to turn, to look him in the face, but he held her firmly in place.

"But then I met you again. I ran into you everywhere I turned, it seemed. It didn't take long for this stubborn fool to realize I loved you more than anything in life, except for my Lord and Savior." His shoulders shook, but his voice held firm. "I'm not much of a catch. I'm missing half an arm, and I don't know if I want to be constable of Maple Notch for all my life or where else God might lead me. But there is no one who will love you more. Tell me, Clara, are you willing to join your life with mine as we have joined our initials?"

This time when she turned in his arms, he didn't stop her. She brought her hand to where it rested on the stump of Daniel's left elbow. "This"—she increased the pressure ever so slightly—"makes no difference to me. You are more of a man than anyone else I know. As long as you don't mind an old maid who wears glasses."

"I hope her students—and her daughters—grow up to be just like her." He touched her cheek with the back of his hand. "Is that a yes?"

She looked into his hazel eyes, fiery now with need and desire. Daniel freed her hair from its hairnet, running his fingers through the long tresses. "I love you, Clara Farley." He shouted it at the top of his lungs.

"Oh, Daniel." She traced her finger over his beard. "I love you, too."

Their lips joined in a kiss sweet enough to last a lifetime.

A Letter to Our Readers

Dear Readers:

In order that we might better contribute to your reading enjoyment, we would appreciate you taking a few minutes to respond to the following questions. When completed, please return to the following: Fiction Editor, Barbour Publishing, Inc., P.O. Box 719, Uhrichsville, OH 44683.

1. Did you enjoy reading *Maple Notch Brides* by Darlene Franklin?
   ❑ Very much. I would like to see more books like this.
   ❑ Moderately—I would have enjoyed it more if _____
   _____

   _____

2. What influenced your decision to purchase this book?
   (Check those that apply.)
   ❑ Cover   ❑ Back cover copy   ❑ Title   ❑ Price
   ❑ Friends   ❑ Publicity   ❑ Other

3. Which story was your favorite?
   ❑ *The Prodigal Patriot*   ❑ *Love's Raid*
   ❑ *Bridge to Love*

4. Please check your age range:
   ❑ Under 18   ❑ 18–24   ❑ 25–34
   ❑ 35–45   ❑ 46–55   ❑ Over 55

5. How many hours per week do you read? _____

Name _____

Occupation _____

Address _____

City_____ State_____ Zip_____

E-mail _____

APPALACHIAN WEDDINGS

THREE-IN-ONE COLLECTION

BY

DEBBY MAYNE

The West Virginia mountains offer a beautiful backdrop for three inspirational stories of love as Emily, Kim and Mandy navigate the treacherous trail of romance.

Contemporary, paperback, 384 pages, 5.1875" x 8"